THE STONE MAGE
& THE SEA

FIRST BOOK OF
THE CHANGE

Book 2
  The Sky Wardens and the Sun

Book 3
  The Storm Weaver and the Sand

E-Rights/E-Reads, Ltd. Publishers
171 East 74th Street, New York, NY 10021

www.ereads.com

The lines quoted in Chapter 11 are taken from the poem
"A Dream Within A Dream" by Edgar Allan Poe.

THE STONE MAGE & THE SEA

FIRST BOOK OF THE CHANGE

BY SEAN WILLIAMS

E-Reads®

For Ryan

CONTENTS

Part One:

Seeking

CHAPTER 1

LIGHT ON THE SAND

FATHER and son were on the run when they came to Fundelry, a small, coastal village on the stretch of the Strand known by its ancient name of Gooron. The sun was low in the sky, shining wanly through a spattering of wispy clouds. Kneeling on the front passenger seat, Sal clutched the roll bar with one hand to keep his balance as the buggy bounced along a winding path through the dunes. Its engine grumbled when his father tapped the accelerator; prickly grass and scrub crunched loudly under its wheels. He couldn't hear the sea over the racket as he supposed he should by now.

His father didn't like being this close to the sea and, although Sal didn't know why that was so, some of that nervousness rubbed off on him, too. It was impossible to avoid. Tension showed in the way his father drove. His knuckles were white around the wheel, his movements quick, almost curt: accelerating sharply when a wheel lost traction, then braking just as quickly when a slope turned out to be steeper than expected. His gaze flicked restlessly to the fuel gauge, to the gear lever, to his son, to the scrub whipping by, and to the way ahead, as though he were uncertain about which way he was going.

Why he had brought them so, deep into Sky Warden territory, Sal had no idea.

"How much longer?" Sal asked. The dunes around them were too high to see over, even standing on the seat. If Sal had ever been so close to the sea before, he couldn't remember it.

"I'm not sure. Have you been counting the milestones?"

"Yes. One hundred and thirteen."

"The man in Gliem said less than a hundred. He must've been wrong." Sal's father shrugged. "Still, we should be there by sunset. If it's light, we can have a look around and see what's on offer. Maybe grab something to eat. And then..."

His voice trailed off. Sal knew what usually would have followed: find a room for the night, or for a few nights perhaps; the next day, find a job to help replenish the buggy's alcohol reserves; locate another destination--the next town along the Strand, or even the next region--then move on. The most important thing of all was to stay hidden from the Sky Wardens.

And that was how it normally went as they traveled across the Strand together: they arrived, they stayed briefly and unremarkably, then they left. Only this time, Sal was coming to suspect, was different from the others.

The sandy road doglegged sharply, took them back almost the way they had come. Through a gap between two particularly large dunes, Sal saw the sky as it would appear closer to the horizon, a markedly lighter blue than it was overhead. Gray specks wheeled over something in that new distance. He thought he could hear the harsh cries of birds he had read about but never seen before.

Gulls.

* * *

The path joined a worn but sealed road before entering town. Its waysigns were faded; clearly, the road saw few travelers. Fundelry promised similar facilities to the thousands of other towns along the Strand, and these included a hostel, a bath house, a school, a fishery, a grain silo and an ironmonger who doubled as a mechanic. No surprises there, apart from the last: engineers of any sort were rare this far from the Interior, where metalworking was common. But that knowledge was welcome; the buggy had clocked its odometer limit many times over and could always use a proper service. The last had been four months and a thousand kilometers away, in Nuud.

They followed the sealed road southward at speed, relishing the relative smoothness of the ancient tarmacadam and the wind sweeping through their hair. Sal whooped, forgetting his uncertainty in the joy of the moment, and his father smiled at the sound. Few ancient roads had survived the ravages of time, and they rarely saw any other motorised transport so close to the coast. Sal and his father were alone on the entire length of this road; it was theirs to enjoy, for the moment.

Then they hit the edge of town and they were forced to slow down, because the road disintegrated immediately, as though an ages-lost machine had run out of tar at that point and never returned to finish the job. With sand once again under their wheels, and acutely conscious of the sound of the motor breaking the sleepy silence, they trundled slowly into town.

The ironmonger-cum-mechanic wasn't far beyond the municipal border. At the familiar sign of crossed spanners, they drew off the road and under the shelter of a low, rusted verandah. With a crunch of gears, the buggy jerked to a halt. Sal's father climbed out and removed his hat in order to wipe the sweat from his forehead.

A dark-skinned man in heavily patched overalls stepped from the shadows under the verandah. Young but careworn, as though he had always endured life rather than reveled in it, he wore a charm of polished brown stones threaded on a thong tied around his neck.

"That's either a Comet or a fair copy," he said, indicating the buggy.

"A copy," Sal's father replied, "but it serves us well enough."

"That's all that matters. You've obviously looked after it." The mechanic strode forward, holding out his hand. "Josip."

"Gershom," said Sal's father, his voice economical, wasting no energy. They shook hands firmly. "This is Sal. Short for Salomon."

"But getting taller by the day, eh? How old are you, boy?"

"Twelve."

"A good age."

Sal nodded politely, fascinated more by the mechanic's charm necklace than by anything he had to say. Like the man's trade, it was an oddity along the Strand, where people used Sky Warden charms made of crystals and feathers instead of stone. Even odder was the fact that Josip didn't have the fair skin of someone from the Interior, as Sal did, to explain the charm's origins. Sal couldn't imagine how Stone Mage lore could have made it so far south.

"Are there rooms near here?" his father asked. "We'll be staying the night."

"See Von. She runs the hostel on the main square. It's not much, but she's reasonable and you look like you could use that."

"Work?"

"Harvest is over, but..." Josip the mechanic thought for a moment. "Come back tomorrow. I'll see what I can rustle up."

Sal's father nodded his thanks and put an arm around Sal and together they headed back to the buggy.

The mechanic's call followed them: "You can leave that in here, if you want." He was pointing at an open shed full of boxes and tools next to the verandah. "I can make space, and you'll keep the keys, of course. It'll be less obvious than parking in the open."

Sal's father hesitated for a second, automatically reluctant to trust a stranger too far. But...

"True," he said. "Thank you."

The mechanic smiled as though they'd bestowed an honor on him, and moved off to find room for the buggy.

Sal studied the town as they walked along the main road, still heading south. It felt the same as all the places he had visited over the years; in some ways, though, it was very different. There was sand everywhere he looked: underfoot, piled in drifts against buildings, filling up corners where it hadn't been swept away. The air smelled strongly of salt. As well as crumbling stone structures rarely more than a single story high, they passed shanties leaning in hollows by the road, as though made of driftwood deposited by a freak storm that might return at any moment to sweep them away again.

Having spent his entire life on the move, Sal quite liked Fundelry's air of impermanence. It made sense to him. Its proximity to the sea, though, was another thing entirely.

Few people came out to watch them pass. He supposed the others were working: fishing, or repairing nets, or teaching children, or doing whatever else the villagers here did this late in the day. The ones he did see were darker in color than his father, whose skin was light brown rather than black, and they were much darker than Sal. The villagers stared openly at them as they passed, making him feel uncomfortable. They stood out as strangers in every place they went, but they rarely encountered such open curiosity.

When they reached the local census building, they stopped to check in. The Strand administrators were as strict about procedure as they were about democracy, and the Sky Wardens imposed stiff penalties on those who failed to declare their movements. The forms Sal's father completed were yellow with age, giving the impression that such formalities were rarely needed here.

"You just passing through?" asked the young woman behind the counter with an air of distrust.

"Maybe." Sal's father's false signature entwined around itself like a snake. "Is there much to see or do around here?"

"No."

"It's lovely weather, anyway."

"It can change overnight."

Sal's father smiled, but said nothing.

"Do you know where you'll be staying?"

"We're looking for a hostel run by someone called 'Von'."

This only seemed to confirm the woman's poor impression of them. "Up the road, on the far side of the main square."

"Thanks." Sal's father made to leave, then stopped as though a thought had just occurred to him. "I don't suppose you know a man named Payat Misseri?"

"Should I?"

"He was an old friend. I heard he passed through here at some time or another."

"If he's not from here, I don't see how you can expect me to have heard of him."

"I thought it was your job to know these things."

She sniffed. "I'm only filling in for Bela. She's gone home."

"Well, maybe we'll come back in the morning."

"We're closed tomorrow."

His smile didn't falter. "Another day, then. Goodbye."

When they emerged from the office, the sun was setting. For the first time, Sal consciously noted the sound of the sea. He recognized it instantly, even though he had never heard it before. It hissed like an asthmatic giant trying to sneak up on them.

His father stood on the steps of the office for a moment, looking around. "Now where? Bed or browse?"

Sal shrugged, tired from the long drive but too nervous to sleep. He didn't think a third option--to leave--was open to him, even though their reception so far had been far from welcoming.

"It'll be dark soon," his father said, answering his own question. "We should at least find a room before they close their doors."

Sal shifted his pack into a more comfortable position as they walked along the street. Everything they owned, apart from the buggy, rested on his and his father's backs. It would make a pleasant change to sleep indoors, if they could find somewhere to take them. Part of him hoped they wouldn't.

As they headed deeper into town, the buildings became more solid, as though the outer fringes were an afterthought, and a temporary one at that. Nothing appeared to be open. The main square was instantly recognizable, even though it wasn't a square at all. It was a large, circular space of densely packed sand surrounded by shop fronts and storehouses. A water pump at its center marked the focus, several low benches gave it character, and eight metal poles taller than a person and topped with glass globes delineated its edge. Well-worn lanes issued in every direction from the square.

One of these lanes led south to the sea. The end of the road, Sal thought. Through the growing gloom he could see a gray mass of water heaving and shifting barely a hundred yards away, with little but a stretch of low dunes to keep it at bay. It looked dangerous. The sight--or perhaps just a sudden chill in the air--made him shiver.

There was only one hostel facing the square: a squat, two-story building that might have been the oldest in town. Its windows were shuttered. Sal's father strode up to the verandah and knocked once on the door.

It opened immediately. Light spilled out into the square, silhouetting a tall woman with wild, orange hair. The light behind her cast her face in shadow, giving her a threatening air.

"What do you want?" she asked with a voice like two rocks scraping together.

"A room."

"Can you pay?" Sal noticed that her hand was firmly on the door, ready to slam it in their faces.

"With coin."

"That'd make a nice change." The woman's eyes seemed to glint although no light shone on them. "Show me."

Sal turned around. His father reached into his pack and produced a small number of toughened glass disks. Sal heard them sliding over each other in his father's palm; he could almost identify them by sound alone, they were so few in number.

They seemed to satisfy the woman. "Come in, then." She turned to let them into a low-roofed reception hall lit by gas lanterns and smelling of stale bread.

Pulling a thick book out of a drawer in a desk along one wall, she noisily cleared her throat and wrote down the answers to her questions.

"It'll be fifteen per room. One or two? It's not as if I have a shortage this time of year."

"Just one. Two beds."

"How long for?"

"As long as we need."

"No questions, huh?" She grunted. "I'm Von. Breakfast is included. You pay me one night in advance every morning and I'll let you stay."

The book slammed shut. Carrying a lamp, she showed them up a flight of stairs. Noticeable for the first time was a slight limp in her left leg. Sal wondered how she had come by the injury, and whether it had anything to do with the roughness of her voice.

At the top of the stairs were several guest rooms. Von led them to one in a corner of the building. Inside were two single beds, a chest of drawers, and a door leading to the floor's common bathroom. The air smelled of dust and starch. Through the sole window, Sal could see the sky turning from red to gray with the last rays of the sun. The sea was black, invisible, a hole in the world.

Something flew past the window with a glint of eye and feathers, and he jumped, startled.

His father touched his arm. "What?"

Sal shook his head quickly, feeling stupid. "Just a gull."

"I probably don't need to tell you to keep it down," Von said, less gruffly than before. "Just be aware that I do have another guest at the moment, and he likes his privacy. If you need anything in the night, use this," she said, showing them a bell-pull by the door. "Otherwise, I'll see you in the morning."

Sal's father nodded. "Thank you."

With a last, long look at them, the woman put the lamp down on the chest of drawers, closed the door and left them alone.

Sal picked the bed furthest from the window and hefted his pack onto it. His father sat down heavily on the other bed and removed his boots.

"It's not so bad," his father said, testing the mattress springs. "Better than the ground, anyway. See if you can get a breeze in here."

Sal nervously went back to the window, and confronted

his own reflection: black hair vanishing into the darkness of the falling night; light skin standing out like parchment on a puddle of ink. Glinting on the left side of his face was the silver ear-ring he had worn longer than he could remember, its three tiny holes looking like flecks of dust.

The window had been painted shut around the edges. No gulls surprised him this time. Without turning, he asked, "Dad?"

"Yes, Sal?"

"What are we doing here?"

"What do you mean?"

"Are you really looking for that man--the one you asked about at the office?" Although his father had described him as an old friend, Sal had never heard the name. "Is that why we've come here?"

"Misseri? Maybe." His father smiled. "If I say 'yes', you'll only ask me why I'm looking for him and I'll be no better off."

Sal was about to press his father for more information, when light flickering in the square below caught his eye. A lantern of some kind--although he could see no telltale flicker of flame--burned on one of the poles like a miniature yellow star. An oval-shaped pool glowed on the ground below it.

Another light flared to life, an eighth-turn around the square. This time Sal saw a dark figure stepping away into the shadows.

"There are some things you can't run from, Sal," his father went on. "It's time I faced them head-on. They would've caught up with us in the end, anyway, here or elsewhere …"

"What sort of things?"

In a darkened corner of the window, Sal's father's reflection shook its head. Where Sal was all lightness and dark, his father was the pale tan of kangaroo leather. Hair and skin and eyes were the same color, making it hard to tell his age. His father said Sal had inherited his looks from his mother--most especially his eyes, which were many shades of blue mottled with white flecks. But Sal's father rarely spoke about her. He rarely spoke about anything important, these days.

Sal wondered if he was referring to the Sky Wardens. The men and women who controlled the Strand seemed as unreal to him as demons or ghosts, and he had had as much actual experience of them. The ones who chose not to live in the Haunted City were always on the move and usually easy to avoid. But unlike demons and ghosts, he knew that Sky Wardens were real. He had seen pictures of them and heard the stories. There had been a couple of close calls. He imagined them to be giants, with robes the same deadly blue as a desert sky. The crystal torcs they wore around their necks flashed like lightning in his mind, and their eyes saw into everything.

Sal didn't know that they were, in fact, what his father was talking about, this time. Ever since Gliem, his father had been distracted and concerned, and Sal had worried that he might have done something wrong. But his father wasn't angry with him; he just seemed worried. The fact that he wouldn't talk about it only made Sal worry too.

Another light flickered into life below, and another, and the reflection of his father vanished, replaced by faint hints of movement through the glowing pools. Sal tried to follow them, but could not. He couldn't even be sure they were there at all.

Eight lights now burned on the square, and he noticed a handful more scattered through the town. They didn't banish the night, but they at least pushed it back a few meters. The town felt slightly friendlier for it.

But there was still the sea, churning away at the edge of his hearing--and a nagging feeling that he was being watched.

He stepped away from the window, and realized only then that his father had failed to respond to his last comment. Sal turned and saw that the man who called himself Gershom--which meant "exile" in a very ancient tongue--had fallen asleep fully clothed. Clearly no questions would be answered that night. Again.

Sal turned down the lamp and wished he could silence his own doubts so easily.

CHAPTER 2

THE ART IN HER EYES

THE next morning, after a simple but filling breakfast of salty porridge and bread, Sal's father returned to the mechanic's, hoping for work. No mention was made of their conversation of the previous night. Sal did, however, get permission to go exploring.

"Just be careful," his father said in the hostel's hallway.

"I know, Dad. If there are any Sky Wardens here, I'll keep well away from them."

"Good." He looked as though he was about to say more, but changed his mind and went out the front door. Sal wasn't far behind.

The town was much livelier by mid-morning, with people of all ages out and about to beat the afternoon heat. He could hear them before he even left the hostel: children shouting and laughing; a dog barking a staccato counterpoint in the middle distance, excited by the ruckus; adults talking too quickly for him to follow. Stepping outside was like diving into a completely different world. He was grateful for the shadowy verandah to hide in.

The square was full of children of all ages; maybe forty in all. Some were playing, while others sat on benches reading from books or talking among themselves. A couple of adults sat to one side, watching as the children went about their activities. Occasionally they intervened, but more often they seemed content merely to observe.

This was the local version of School, he realized. During break; or maybe School was conducted in the square all the time. As long as the standard syllabus was dealt with, the Sky Wardens didn't care how each town went about it. Sal had seen Schools with very rigid codes of conduct and classrooms that looked more like prisons; he had seen ones where the teachers and students conversed as equals. He preferred to be taught by his father, who filled in as best he could when they were on the road.

Watching from the shadows, he knew he should join the students of Fundelry, and could do so at any time he wanted. But his father had given him the day off to settle in; that only happened in towns where they intended to stay longer than a week or two, and was more evidence that this wasn't an ordinary stop. He didn't want to waste his chance to find out why they had come to this place.

Sal turned away and walked along the verandah.

"Hey!"

He glanced back over his shoulder. A shock of white caught his eye: a solidly built teenager with white hair and pink skin. An albino. The albino was standing next to a small boy whose nose and ears would have looked more at home on a bilby. The second boy was younger than Sal, and looked nervously at the albino's hand on his shoulder.

"Hey, you!"

The albino waved his free hand, but instead of replying Sal headed quickly down the side of the hostel, pretending he hadn't seen.

Putting the incident behind him, he headed west, parallel to where he knew the beach to be, although it was hidden by dunes on that side; he wasn't yet ready to face the sea, either. The sun was clear and the air smelled of fish. Gulls whirled above him, lazing on updraughts or swooping for scraps. Their cries competed strongly with the School behind him, producing an odd aural mix of people and birds.

The sound of human voices grew louder again as he walked. A couple of blocks on he discovered the reason why. There, a long, narrow road served as the town's market. Stalls and sellers were packed together in rough lines like too many plants crowding for a glimpse of sunlight. Vendors called out and buyers haggled over a constant background noise of clucking chickens and mewing alpacas, while idle browsers picked through the merchandise looking for bargains.

Sal kept an eye out for the sky-blue clothing worn by the

Wardens, but saw none in evidence. Still, he was nervous as he walked through the crowd, admiring wooden carvings, dried fish, different types of grain, herbs and other produce. He didn't know whether the market was an everyday occurrence or whether he and his father had happened to arrive when it was active. Clearly, though, more than one town was involved. Fundelry possibly served as a gathering place for merchants and customers from neighboring communities as well as locals, with profits from the market supporting several cottage industries apart from fishing.

But the goods were irrelevant to him. He was more interested in the people. Not only was their skin universally darker than his, but they also had accents different from the ones he was used to inland. That made their cries more difficult to understand. Sometimes he felt they were calling in a completely different language or singing in an ancient tongue--the latter idea supported by the odd snippets of music he heard as he strolled cautiously through the crowd.

"Jewellry worn by the ancient Sun Line! Drum chili all the way from Yunda! Nets charmed here at half the going rate!"

The sound of a guitar and small flute playing a duet caught his ear and drew him in search of its source. Music was a novelty in his life. His father owned no instruments and had never encouraged him to learn, but he sought it out when he had the chance. Minstrels sometimes paid for tunes he had memorized from listening to songs in other towns. His memory for melody was good and he could sing well enough to get the idea across.

He followed the sound to a stall selling tools imported from the Interior. He studied a knife, shining in the center of the display, as he passed. The pommel was crudely fashioned, probably cobbled together from a broken blade and resold as new. Inland, such a poor job would never sell, but finely crafted metal was a novelty along the Strand. A good-looking fake might garner a high price among those who knew no better.

The music came from behind the stall. Before he could

slip between the stall and the tent next door, the occupant of the tent reached out a clawed hand to grab his sleeve.

"Fortune, son? You look like you could use a good telling."

He found himself eye to eye with an ugly old woman. Her hair was bone-white in shocking contrast to her dark skin. Shaking his head, he tried to pull away, but her grip was every bit as strong as her gaze was piercing and her spiel relentless.

"I have sand, glass, dice and cards. I can do palms and irises as well, and will even look at the bumps on your head if that's what you want. They're all the same; it don't matter which tool I use. When the Change is strong in someone, y'see, it comes out whether you ask it to or not. I'll lend you some of mine, for a price. Just say the word, and the future will be yours."

The stench billowing out of her tent made him gag.

"What?" she asked, drawing away. "Shark got your tongue?" She cackled. "You're a quiet one, right enough, and I'd wager you don't have any money, either. Why am I wasting my time with you? You should be in School, anyway."

He thought desperately of his father's warning not to attract any attention. "I--I'm sorry. I'll go now, if you let me."

The old woman's fingers didn't ease their grip. If anything, they tightened, and the hair on Sal's arms tingled. He felt as though she was looking right into him, under his skin.

"Yes. You go on your way. I have things to do. And so do you, I wager." Then she let go of him and pushed him backward. "Aunty Merinda will give you one piece of advice for free: don't eat Sancho's pies. Unless you like dune rabbit, of course--which means cat round here."

She cackled again and the meat vendor across the street cast her a dirty look.

Sal backed down the length of the market, away from the old woman's stall. The music had gone. All he could hear now were the gulls again, squawking over the cries of the humans below, and he felt, for the second time, as though he was being watched.

He didn't feel safe at the market after that. He explored the
northwest side of town until midday, finding little else of
note, until thirst forced him back to the hostel. His father
still hadn't returned--or, if he had, hadn't left a note with
Von. The proprietor of the hostel had a look in her eye that
told him he wasn't welcome to hang around, so he went
back out into the streets, this time taking a bottle of water
with him.

He had noticed on his return to the hostel that the square
had emptied of older children, and now even the younger
ones had disappeared. The earlier ruckus must have been
a break, after all. He could hear toddlers laughing, not far
away, and he was tempted to join the older kids' classroom
to get out of the heat. When he couldn't find the class,
though, a small part of him was relieved. He had been saved
the embarrassment of walking unannounced into a roomful
of strangers--a chore he had performed many times before,
but never learned to like. The students must have taken the
afternoon off, so joining them could wait another day. He
wasn't lonely on his own: he had had years to get used to it.

He headed east, away from the market this time, along
a nondescript road that followed the line of the shore for a
while then curved away north, inland. The sea was hidden
by a series of high dunes sporting large tufts of grass and
bushes. Grains of sand stung him every time the wind blew.
The sky above was very blue, with only a few scattered
clouds moving quickly from west to east. The scrub-lined
road looped around a dozen or so empty-looking houses
then joined the main road that led southward into town.
He passed several small gardens along the way; the flowers
were all either yellow or orange, and there were few trees
larger than two or three meters high. A barren graveyard
huddled in the lee of a low hill; most of the headstones were
weathered or broken and the names were all unfamiliar:
Vermeulen, Trowse, Kyriakidis, Bax ...

His puzzlement grew. Nothing he saw marked Fundelry
as special; just another Strand town, no different from
others he had visited, except that it was as close as he could

get to the sea without standing in it. Left with the mystery of why they had come there, he found himself missing the things he was most familiar with: the sound of emptiness and the wind skimming the road; endless plains and the horizon unfolding around him; time spent alone with his father, thinking or telling stories; the earth rolling endlessly beneath him, one way or another.

Sal decided to turn right at the main road and head north, thinking he might find Josip the mechanic and see what his father was up to. Just before he reached the main road, a head ducked out of sight behind a wall. He half-saw it out of the corner of his eye. Startled, he looked to confirm the impression. There was nothing there, and he almost managed to convince himself that it hadn't been there at all. A glimpse of brown hair and a dark face--it could have been his eyes playing tricks on him.

But why, he asked himself, would they do that? They would see a flash of blue, or the glinting of a crystal torc, if he really wanted to scare himself. Still, he had an odd feeling that someone was nearby. It unsettled him, made him nervous. He wasn't the sort to imagine things.

As he turned to walk up the hill to Josip's along the road he and his father had walked the night before, he heard a faint noise very much like a footstep from the way he had just come. It certainly wasn't his water bottle sloshing. He told himself to keep walking up the hill without looking back. If someone *was* there, he didn't want to look guilty or afraid. He just wanted to get away.

At the census building where his father had filled out the forms, the sound came again. This time he did look back, and someone was definitely there. Too slow for him to miss, they ducked out of sight behind a fence. He walked faster. The hair had been a different color--black, rather than brown as before--but that didn't matter. *Be careful*, his father had warned him, and he intended to stay out of whatever trouble he might find himself in.

The footsteps started up again after the briefest of pauses. He broke into a trot, and the sound of pursuit intensified.

He was being chased, and by more than one person. Instead of turning to confront them, he sped up. Within moments he was running with his head down, heartily glad he'd left his pack at the hostel. Even without it he was soon panting for breath and boiling hot from the inside out. Above his gasping, the footsteps chasing him sounded very loud.

Then, without warning, the footsteps ceased. He looked over his shoulder to see what had happened.

He ran headlong into something and rebounded as though off a wall. Someone had stepped out in front of him. Big hands pushed him the rest of the way to the ground. He glimpsed white hair before falling on his back. Someone laughed as he scrambled to his knees, spitting sand.

"Hey there, stone-boy." The albino loomed over him, an unusual and threatening figure dressed in cut-off shorts and gray cotton smock. He was missing a tooth, the gap visible inside his mouth as he leered down at Sal. "Where are you going in such a hurry?"

"My father--" Sal gasped.

"What about him?"

"I was just--"

"Running to him like a baby?"

"No, I--"

"So what's the problem?"

The albino picked him up by the shirt-front, then threw him down again. Sal's bottle of water spilled open, staining the sand gray. Behind him, someone laughed. Great, Sal thought. An audience was all he needed. But there always was one. People like the albino thrived on them.

"Where you from, stone-boy? This must seem pretty dull compared with your big cities. Maybe we should liven things up for you. Eh? Would you like that?"

Sal never knew whether to stay quiet or talk. Pleading to be left alone only confirmed that the bullies had the upper hand.

Halfway to his feet again, he tried to be amiable. "I like it enough as it is, thanks."

The albino leaned into his face. "You like it here? Really?"

"Yes." Sal was standing now, and dusting himself down without taking his eyes off his opponent.

"Then why wouldn't you talk to me before? Aren't I posh enough for you? Is that it?"

"No, of course not--"

"Good, because we don't like strangers coming here and telling us they're better than we are. That makes us annoyed."

The albino nodded to someone over Sal's shoulder, who tripped Sal from behind.

"*Really* annoyed."

More laughter from the albino's cronies, one of them a girl. Sal clenched his fists and closed his eyes. A single deep breath, then he would spring to his feet and retaliate as best he could. He'd be pounded into the sand for sure, but at least he would go down fighting.

"Haven't you lot got anything better to do?"

The voice took everyone by surprise. Sal froze on the verge of moving.

"This is none of your business, old man," said the albino to someone Sal couldn't see.

"I think that's for me to decide."

"I think you should keep moving and let us get on with what we're doing."

"Do you think *he* agrees?"

Sal didn't dare look up but knew the man was talking about him.

The albino's voice was thick with venom. "I think *he* knows when to keep quiet."

"I see. Well, perhaps we should ask the Selector, see what *she* thinks. I bet she won't take kindly to reports of bullying, or dodging chores."

"You wouldn't dare--"

"Bet your life on it?"

It was the albino's turn to back down, and Sal could tell he hated it from the snarl in his voice.

"Fine. Stick up for your own kind."

"How ironic coming from you. Your skin is paler than his."

The albino drew breath sharply. "I'm warning you, old man--"

"You don't frighten me, boy. And your dad doesn't frighten me either. Do send my regards next time you see him, won't you?"

The albino spat into the ground by Sal's hand, then moved away. Sal watched his big feet recede with intense relief; he'd been expecting a parting kick for sure.

"That's better." The man's voice came closer.

Sal checked that the albino had definitely left. He saw three boys and one girl, all, except the albino, with black hair and deep-dark skin, strolling away down the road-- determinedly nonchalant, as though nothing had happened. None of them was the bilby-faced boy, the only other person Sal would have recognised.

Then a hand was thrust at him from above, and he found himself staring into the strangest face he had ever seen.

The old man had skin that had been weathered dark brown. Strands of straggly gray hair poked out the back of a very old cap. Pale gold ear-rings hung from the high points of both ears, which stuck out firmly as though on constant alert. His eyes were slate-gray. The man's oddest features were his tattoos: tight-wound spirals on his temples; circles on either side of his nose, like an extra set of eyes; and an up-pointed triangle on his chin. All had been executed in black ink on his dark skin, and were very fine work, probably the finest Sal had seen in all his travels.

Tattoos were mainly an Interior thing, like pale skin. They were as uncommon on the Strand as willy-willies. The only other person he knew who had one nearly as good, if not as intricate, was his father. It was much smaller, a green cross on the back of his father's left hand.

"Are you still with us, boy?" the man asked, his voice amused and light.

"I--I'm sorry," Sal stammered. Thinking, *so much for staying out of trouble*, he raised a hand and let himself be helped up.

The old man indicated the four teenagers receding into

the distance. "They're not bad kids, really," the old man said. "Just bored. Every year I pray the Selector will take the bright ones away before bad apples like Kemp can spoil them forever. If there is a Goddess, I hope she's listening."

Sal suddenly found those gray eyes back on him.

"Eh? Are *you* listening?"

"Oh, um. Thank you." Sal still didn't know what to say beyond that. His benefactor wore a rough sackcloth vest and cotton pants, with leather sandals on his feet. He stood an inch or two higher than Sal, looked at least five times Sal's age, and radiated an indefinable energy. Sal had never met anyone quite like him.

"You don't talk much," said the man, nodding. "You're too busy observing. That's good. Still, come say hello to Shilly. She's my apprentice, just over here."

The old man's hand descended on one shoulder and gripped it tight. Sal couldn't have pulled free if he'd wanted to.

Shilly was a girl smaller than him, although he could tell she was slightly older, crouched by the side of the road and doodling in the sand with a twig. She didn't seem to have noticed the incident, or was prepared to ignore it. Sal was intensely grateful for that.

"Shilly, this is--what's your name, boy?"

The girl looked up expectantly. Her face was small and heart-shaped with high cheeks. Her muddy brown hair, bleached at the tips by the sun and held back in a ponytail by a thick brass band, looked like it hadn't been washed for weeks. She wore a simple blue dress that was slightly tattered around the hem. Her feet were bare.

Her eyes were the most intense green he had ever seen.

"Sal," he managed.

"Hello, Sal." Her voice was firm, almost challenging. Her dark toes dug into the sand beneath her, and she stood. "*Are you from the dry lands?*"

"Of course he isn't," said the man, waving dismissively. "You're no stone-boy, are you, Sal? Even though you have your family's eyes."

"I do?"

"Of course. As clear as glass. Only fools like Kemp--
and the Goddess knows there are too many of them in this
world--will not see what *their* eyes show them. You take
after your mother, I'll wager."

Something in Sal fluttered. "What do you know about
my mother?"

"I didn't say I knew anything." The old man sighed
and touched a pendant around his neck. "There's a storm
coming."

Sal glanced up at the blue sky, thrown off by the sudden
change in subject. An unruly flock of seagulls tumbled in
the air above them. "Doesn't look like it to me."

Still fingering the pendant, the old man said, "Tash says
so, and Tash is never wrong. You have somewhere to stay?"

Sal nodded.

"Good. You'll need it. The weather here can be fierce
when it wants, like the locals. You need to be careful." He
raised an arm and gestured for the girl to join him. "Come
along, Shilly."

"You're going? But--"

"We have work to do down at the market. Shilly and I
were on our way there when we noticed you needed help,
and we were already late."

"Bye." The girl smiled at him over her shoulder, the light
tips of her hair dancing on her shoulders. "Watch out for
the scabs!"

Sal didn't know what she meant, but knew he owed the
old man for helping him. "Thank you!" he called again as
they walked away.

The girl winked, then turned to watch where she was
going. The old man said nothing.

Left feeling scattered by both encounters, Sal stood
in the middle of the road for a long moment. Something
about the old man and his apprentice made him curious;
the hints about his mother and Shilly's knowing smile in
particular. He considered following them to see what they
did at the market, or maybe asking Josip about them. But

following them could get him in more trouble, while asking the mechanic would mean explaining what had happened with Kemp. He would be embarrassed if his father found out from the mechanic rather than from himself. Besides, asking questions would be difficult when he hadn't been told the old man's name.

He turned to continue north up the hill to the mechanic's workshop. He hadn't gone far when markings in the sand where the girl had been squatting caught his eye. She had been doodling, he remembered. Stepping across the road to take a closer look, he found himself staring at himself--a sketch that managed in only a few lines to sum him up perfectly. It was uncanny; she had captured him after only a minute or two's study.

The portrait was winking at him. Underneath, in simple block characters she'd written:

MIDNIGHT

Only then did he realize that Shilly's hair color matched that of the first person he had glimpsed hiding behind the wall back on the other road. She and the old man had been following him before Kemp and his darker-skinned friends had attacked. The two of them hadn't stumbled upon him by chance at all.

Fundelry was getting weirder by the second.

Footsteps behind him made him jump. He turned, thinking that Kemp and the others had come back.

But when he turned all he saw was his father walking back into town with a broad smile on his tan-skinned face.

"Hey, Sal. I've been working!"

Sal felt a shiver of relief that he wouldn't have to fight anyone. "That's fantastic, Dad."

"It's certainly welcome. What are you doing here? Still exploring?"

"Kind of."

"Find anything interesting?"

Sal opened his mouth, then shut it. He had fully intended to explain what had happened to him, but a fear of getting into trouble stopped him now the chance had arrived. His actions might not have brought a platoon of Sky Wardens down upon them, but they had certainly attracted a degree of unwanted attention. He was uncertain enough of his footing in Fundelry without getting his father offside as well.

"Not really," he said, erasing both the portrait and the message from the sand with a slight movement of one foot, wishing the entire incident could be as easily erased.

"Good," his father said, putting an arm around his shoulders and pulling him close. "Let's go back to Von's and get a proper meal in our bellies. My shout, eh."

"Sounds great," Sal said, letting himself be tugged along. It would be a definite relief to escape Fundelry for a while.

CHAPTER 3

A LIFE AMONG THE STONES

NONE of his encounters with the locals left Sal's mind as easily as he would have liked. He lay awake for hours that night, trying to sleep but reliving instead his humiliation at the hands of Kemp, the bizarre old lady in the market and everything the old man and Shilly had said.

After meeting him on the road to Josip's, his father had been as good as his word. They had gone straight back to the hostel and bought a home-cooked dinner--their first for a very long while, and tasting of salt, like their breakfast. Von watched them eat it with an amused expression. She didn't seem so hostile, given the extra money in her hand. Sal's father explained that Josip would find him odd jobs around the town as they arose, an arrangement that suited him, since he would have no single employer to whom he would owe notice if he decided to leave. The rate of pay was low but enough to keep them, with a small amount left over for repairs to the buggy and fuel.

After the meal, Sal's father went to talk to the local School, teachers about enrolment. While his father was gone, Sal helped Von clear the dishes and wash them in startlingly hot water.

"Do you know a man with lots of tattoos?" he asked, drawing imaginary lines on his cheeks, forehead and chin. "Like this? And ear-rings?"

Von pondered his description. "Can't say I do, and I know most people around here." Her gaze sharpened. "Why? You get into trouble today?"

"No, nothing like that. I met his apprentice. Shilly."

"Oh, I know *her*," she nodded. "You don't mean old Lodo, do you?"

He shrugged. "Do I?"

"You must do, since she's 'prenticed to him. Can't say I've noticed any tattoos, though."

Sal frowned. Maybe he'd imagined them, or they were easier to miss than he recalled. "What does he do?"

"Nothing but cause trouble, if you ask some people. Alder Sproule's been trying to run him out of town for years now, but Iphigenia--she's the Mayor--she lets him stay. And I'm for that. Lodo does nobody harm and a whole lot of good--in little ways, if you know what I mean. This heated water, for starters. And that knife--it broke a year ago, but you'd never know it now."

Von clattered noisily at the sink as though there was more she could say but wouldn't, while Sal tried to guess where the dry dishes went. Her hair was flame-red in the light of the sunset shining through the kitchen window. Dyed, he thought, although he couldn't see any roots coming through. The color was too vivid to be real.

MIDNIGHT, Shilly had written. What she meant by that, he wasn't sure, but he was curious to find out. At the very least, he could ask her what she had meant that afternoon when she had told him to watch out for the "scabs". If he saw her again. There was no guarantee that he would.

"What are you looking at?" Von asked, her voice sounding like a chair leg scraping across slate tiles.

He realized that he'd been staring vacantly at her, and stammered an apology. Before he could work up the courage to ask about Kemp, his father returned.

They retired early and his father fell immediately asleep, as he had the previous night. After watching the lights in the square come on--and this time sensing an unexpected familiarity in the shadowy figure moving from each one as it flared into life--Sal sat up reading some old books he had found under Von's stairs. Their quality was crude, and the subjects not what he would've chosen, but he so rarely had a choice that their novelty alone kept him up late, squinting in the wan lamplight. He wasn't conscious of falling asleep, but the monotonously turning wheel of his thoughts finally did the job.

There was Kemp, large and threatening, and the old man, powerless in the dream to stop the albino's attack. School loomed like an ancient black keep, smelling of stone and weight, and all the charms and tattoos in the world couldn't keep it away. Von burned in a fire while his father looked on, saying nothing. Shilly drew a picture of herself that came to life and dragged her away. A faceless woman in the misty distance looked lost and sorrowful, surrounded by looming pale blue giants with ice for eyes--and only as a single chime hauled him out of sleep did Sal realize that she was his mother ...

He sat bolt upright in bed, his heart pounding. The echoes of the bell--the simple tolling of the village clock marking the beginning of night proper--still rang in the air.

Barely half-awake, he leaned forward. A bright moon stared back at him from the night sky outside. He shivered.

MIDNIGHT.

Climbing quietly out from under the covers, he tiptoed to the window, half expecting to see nothing. Below, standing in the center of the square, her face clearly visible in the town's ghostly lights, was Shilly. She was looking up at his window.

He stood frozen for a moment, wondering if he should wave to get her attention or go back to bed, and knowing he should do the latter. It was what his father would expect him to do. But he was torn. He had a hunch that she could help him. She might be his only chance to find out what was going on--why she and Lodo had been following him, and maybe why his father had brought him to Fundelry in the first place. They weren't necessarily connected, but the fact that they *might* be made the risk worth considering.

Shilly lowered her eyes and turned to walk away. That decided him. Hunch or not, he didn't want her to think he was ignoring her, or that he'd been too stupid to work out her message.

Grabbing his pants and coat, he tiptoed out of the room. Loud snoring came from one of the other rooms nearby, and Sal was careful not to make any sound as he ran down the hall and stairs. He winced when a step creaked underfoot, sure that Von would pounce on him. But she didn't. He made it to the front door undiscovered.

It was unlocked. He slipped outside and stood on the verandah, still holding his clothes. The noise of the sea was very loud in the cold night air. Waves boomed like falling mountains, sounding so close he almost expected one to crash down on him.

The square was empty, but she was nearby. He could feel her, like something he had lost that needed to be found.

"Psst," said a voice from his left. He turned, and there she was, peering around the corner of the hostel.

"Are you going to stand there half-naked all night, or are you at least going to put your britches on?"

He looked down at his legs; they were very pale in the moonlight, almost luminous. His face was red, though, as he tugged his pants on and shrugged into the coat. He realized only then that he'd forgotten to grab something to put on his feet.

"That's better." Shilly smiled at his discomfort. "Now you're decent, we can get going."

"Where to?"

"The old boy wants to talk to you."

"Why doesn't he come here, then?"

"Too open, I guess. He keeps his reasons to himself. All I know is, the sooner you get it over with the sooner I can go back to bed. That's reason enough for me."

Maybe, he thought, but it hardly satisfied him. He would be gone longer than he had thought. What if his father woke up and noticed he wasn't there? What if something happened to him? Alone in a strange town in the middle of the night with people he hardly knew, anything could go wrong.

But somehow the words just didn't come.

"If you're done arguing," she said, "let's get moving, eh?"

He followed her down the side of the hostel and into the shadows. They didn't go near any of the lights, but he was glad they were there. No matter where he went, he would know that the hostel was near the ring around the square, the brightest place for kilometers.

He was very conscious of the patch of light in the sky behind him as she took him northwest out of the town and over a series of steep dunes rather than along a road.

"Where are we going?"

"Shh. I'm concentrating."

With no conversation and little light, he focused on the smooth sand beneath his feet and how it contrasted with patches of sharp grass. There was a gusty, fitful wind. On it he could smell the sea and Shilly, the latter a spicy tang like rosemary with overtones of something sweet. His mouth tasted like sleep and he hoped his breath wasn't bad.

She stopped without warning and he bumped into the surprising boniness of her shoulder.

"Somewhere here..." She rummaged through a dense clump of bushes. "I'm still not used to doing this at night, which is probably why he sent me. He's always trying to--ah!"

A shower of sand caught Sal unawares. He spluttered back a step and coughed, blinking furiously.

"Oops, sorry," she said, sounding genuinely contrite. "Look. We're here."

He blinked through the sand in his eyes. Where a moment ago there had been nothing but the backside of a dune, there was now an open oval doorway taller than a person. Golden light glowed from inside, pale but seeming very bright to his dark-accustomed eyes. Warm air rushed over him.

Shilly took one step across the threshold and waited for him to follow. When he didn't, she grabbed his hand and tugged him inside.

"You really need to be more assertive," she said. "Otherwise people will never even know you're there."

That's the idea, he thought, but didn't say it aloud. Instead he looked around the room as she closed the door behind them.

They were standing in a small antechamber, roughly spherical in shape, which appeared to have been dug out of a hillside. The walls were reddish-brown too, more like soil than sand, and sealed with a clear glaze. Golden veins snaked through the glaze. Light flowed over the walls like honey.

A tunnel led from the antechamber deeper into the ground. When the door had closed, Shilly dusted her hands and indicated for him to follow her.

The tunnel was only a handful of meters long, but it felt as if it took him to a great depth beneath the surface of the earth. At the bottom, the old man was waiting for them. There, in a room furnished with cushions and low tables, surrounded by tongues of fire frozen in cages of glass and rocks that glowed every color of the rainbow, Sal made a small connection.

"It was *you* ..."

"I?" The old man rose from a cushion by a low table. His tattoos glistened darkly.

"...who lit the lights in the square!"

"Really? What makes you say that?"

Sal wasn't sure exactly. The way the shadowy figure had moved was part of it, and so were the contents of the room. The rest was pure instinct. "It *is* you, isn't it?"

"Yes," said the old man. "I make and repair the globes."

"Chalk one up for the newcomer," Shilly said. Pouring from a large clay jug, she handed Sal a drink of water. "Any other insights you'd like to share with us?"

He ignored her. "How do they work?"

"They trap light during the day," the old man said patiently, "which I call forth every evening. It's a small skill, really--most of the art lies in making the globes. Still, every town should have a glass-blower. I've found it a civilizing thing. You wouldn't believe the problems I had when I first came here..." He shook his head in amused reflection, then suddenly extended his hand. "A pleasure to meet you under better circumstances, my boy. This is my workshop. You can call me Lodo, if you like."

That was the name Von had suggested. Sal took the hand and shook as firmly as he could.

"When we met today ..."

"Yes?"

He wanted to ask about Shilly's picture, why the old man had helped him with Kemp, why the two of them had been following him before then, and why Von had never noticed Lodo's tattoos even though they stood out like tribal scarring to Sal's eyes--but what came out was: "You said there was going to be a storm."

"Hasn't it hit yet?" Lodo looked at Shilly, who shook her head. "Well, it's coming, trust me. Tash says so. See." The old man produced the pendant hanging around his neck from beneath a stained work-shirt. From a distance it had looked like a thumb-sized lump of polished gray stone. Close up, Sal could see that it was carved in a rough likeness of a person, with the blunt, exaggerated features of a fetus.

"Yadeh-tash is a charm," Lodo said. "It feels storms passing over the feet of mountains before they reach here. But it can't tell me precisely when they'll arrive--which doesn't make it much use as a predictive tool. Still, I have an affection for it. I've worn it a long time."

Sal would have liked to look more closely at the charm, but Lodo put it back under his shirt.

"Are you interested in these things?" the old man asked.

"I guess."

"So is Shilly, here. Aren't you?"

"He's my teacher," the girl said proudly. "He's training me in the Change."

"As much as I can." Lodo moved around the room as he talked, picking things up and putting them back down again, sometimes exactly where they had been before. "She has no innate ability, no spark--but there is much more to the Change than that. A Change-worker's job, on the mundane level, is often done by the talent many ordinary people have in tiny, tiny amounts, plus that which can be found in natural features. For centuries, cabals and congregations have been using this accumulated background potential without knowing it. Given the right skill, any source can be exploited. Here." He held out a hand, and Shilly gripped it with a delighted smile. "I would be grateful for some heat, my dear. My old bones grow tired of the chill."

Sal didn't know what he was talking about. He had heard of the Change--everyone had--but the room was already stifling. That thought fled as Shilly bowed her head and concentrated for a second. A large black stone in the center of the room issued a loud crack, as though it had split in two, and a flickering blue ring appeared around it, much like a gas flame but with no visible source. Even from his position a couple of meters away, Sal could feel the heat radiating from it.

He stared in wonder, and was chilled despite the heat. He had seen something like this before, although he wasn't sure where. In a dream perhaps, or a long, long time ago.

There was a buzzing noise in his head, like a swarm of bees looking for somewhere to land.

Lodo sighed and released the girl's hand. She looked up, pleased.

"Much better--much better, indeed." The old man warmed his hands on the strange fire and gestured that Sal should take a seat on a cushion near it. He did so, ignoring both the heat and the odd sensations in his head; perhaps they were related. Shilly likewise sat on the other side of the stone.

"Theory accounts for a lot when given the right resources, you see," Lodo said, pacing restlessly. "Talent is like iron ore: useless until you know how to refine and work it. That's why the Selectors look for the brightest students, as well as those born gifted with natural talent. Shilly's growing knowledge will guarantee her a place in any community she wishes to join, when I and my small talent are gone."

"Will she be Selected?" Sal asked.

"Not if she can help it." The old man chuckled, leaning his wiry frame against a bench crowded with crystals. "Our ways are different from those of the Sky Wardens. That's why I'm living here in a hole in the ground, playing teacher and keeping the local streets safe at night. It's not much, but it keeps me out of trouble, and sets me apart from those with whom I'd rather not be associated."

Sal studied the old man with a new respect and interest. The Sky Wardens governed the coastal regions of the Strand by virtue of their innate abilities, not because they happened to be born into the right family. He knew that much. Although some Lines did produce an unrepresentative number of children gifted in the Change, it was well known that any child anywhere could be born with the talent. Each year the Selectors--mobile Sky Wardens with individual territories--scoured the Strand town by town, partly to oversee local elections and perform other official duties, and partly to look for children who might become Wardens. Many hopeful teenagers spent long nights wishing to be spotted.

The Strand was huge, however, and there were numerous isolated communities. That brief annual contact with a Selector was all many places received. As a result, some children slipped through the Sky Wardens' net. These lost talents usually became weather-workers or fortune-tellers or other lesser Change-workers; Aunty Merinda, the old woman who had grabbed him in the market, was probably such a one. Perhaps Lodo, too, although he seemed to have the Change in a way different from the Sky Wardens. Where their charms influenced air and water, his seemed to involve stone and fire--giving him more in common with the Stone Mages of the Interior. Sal wondered how he had come by the knowledge. Perhaps he had stumbled upon it, or had been taught by a gifted ancestor just as he was now teaching Shilly. The Stone Mages themselves never came so close to the coast.

Such speculation quickly exhausted Sal's knowledge. His father avoided any mention or manifestation of the Change, just as he avoided music and the Sky Wardens. He didn't trust the change: he said it was dangerous. To be so close to it now made the hair on the back of Sal's neck stand on end--and made him wish that he had paid more attention to the tales told by fellow travelers around highway campfires.

"How does it work?" he asked.

At that Lodo laughed. "One thing at a time, my boy. It

has taken Shilly eight years to progress this far. You want me to enlighten you in one night?"

"So why *did* you bring me here?"

"To find out what you are," Lodo said, matter-of-factly.

Sal looked away. He found himself staring at Shilly, who winked.

"The mosquitoes are bad tonight," she said. "Did you notice them on the dunes? I was eaten alive."

He shook his head. "They don't bother me."

"Oh?" said the old man, who had moved around behind him. "Some people are lucky that way, I hear."

"I guess."

"Or it might have something to do with this."

Sal felt a hand at his ear. "Hey!" He jerked away, too late.

"I thought so." Lodo was holding his ear-ring and studying it closely.

"Give that back!" He jumped up, but the old man dodged his grasping hand with surprising agility. Light glinted through the ring's three tiny holes like stars through clouds.

"Do you know where this came from?"

"I don't care. Just--"

"Not so fast, my boy." Lodo avoided another grab. "If I'm right, this is very old and very rare. I spotted it the moment I saw you, but couldn't make the connection. What's it doing on you, here, now?"

"I've always worn it." The frustration of having lost something so close to him nearly made him choke.

"I'm sure you have. Do you know where your father found it?"

He shook his head.

"Was it your mother's?"

"I don't remember my mother." This blurted out before he could stop it.

"Really? How interesting."

Sal opened his mouth, then shut it. The pressure of the old man's gaze was making him feel very uncomfortable. He was suddenly very conscious of the fact that he was an unknown distance underground with two people he hardly knew and only one door leading to freedom.

Lodo offered him the ear-ring. He snatched it out of the old man's hands and returned it to its proper place, fuming.

"I'm sorry," Lodo said. "That wasn't very fair of me. Would you like me to tell you what it is?"

Sal managed a surly nod.

"It's a ward. A charm of protection, if you prefer. It keeps harm away from its wearer, where that harm comes from dumb or inanimate things. Like mosquitoes, for instance, which you say you aren't bothered by--along with colds, I'd wager, or broken bones. The ward helps you avoid them, without you even knowing." Lodo smiled. "When I say 'dumb', of course, I'm not talking about boys like Kemp. Only you can fight those battles."

Sal nodded again. He was indeed immune to many of the small maladies the people around him occasionally endured. And he hadn't ever broken a bone. But that didn't necessarily prove anything. As far as he knew, his ear-ring was just that: a sliver of pierced silver with a gap barely large enough for his lobe to fit through, so he could slip it in and out of the hole it occupied in his ear.

"Do you know why you are here, Sal?" Lodo asked. "In Fundelry, I mean."

His defensiveness was automatic: "Why should I tell you?"

"Why *shouldn't* you tell me?" the old man shot back. "That's more the point. Why the secrecy? What are you afraid of? What are you running from? Can you tell me that, Sal?"

The sudden barrage of questions took him off-guard. They were the same ones he had been asking himself in recent weeks. "I--I don't know."

"Well, I don't know either, but I do think your father is looking for something. No one comes here without a reason, even at the best of times, and I can tell that you two aren't exactly perched on the summit of life. Do you have any idea what that reason might be, what the thing is that he's looking for?"

Sal warred with himself for a second. Just like Lodo, he wanted to know what his father was up to, but talking about it with strangers wasn't the right way to go about finding out. He knew that--and he also knew that he hadn't had any luck on his own. Although he didn't have much to bargain with, giving away some of it might be the only way of getting more in return.

"My father's looking for some*one*," he said slowly, "not some*thing*."

"Really?"

"An old friend, or so I heard him tell someone."

"Do you know this friend's name?"

Sal thought hard. What had it been? Mystery? Misery? "Misseri, I think. Payat Misseri."

The old man's eyebrows went up. "How interesting."

"You know him?"

"Well, yes, I do."

Interest quickened in him. If he could give his father the whereabouts of this man, maybe he could justify the entire midnight excursion. "Can you tell me where he is?"

"That's not so easy to answer. It's clear *you* don't know him, so your father's obviously not as good a friend as he might like to pretend."

Sal frowned.

"Don't be dense," said Shilly. "It's him--Lodo. *He's* this Misseri character your dad is looking for."

It was Sal's turn to look surprised. "Really?"

"I'm saying nothing of the sort," said Lodo, scowling at his apprentice. "Shilly is faster than a startled sandpiper at times, but not nearly cunning enough for my liking. You've given me no good reason to admit to anything, young man, whether I am Misseri or not. Until you do give me a reason, I will not tell you anything about him."

"But--" Sal stared at both of them in turn, slightly stunned by the unexpected turn of events. "But how do I know you wouldn't be lying, anyway? I told you the name first. You could just be *saying* you recognize it."

"That's true," Lodo agreed, while Shilly rolled her eyes.

"And it's very sensible of you to question me. But you must see my side of this too. It would be very sensible of me to lie. Just because you seem harmless enough, that's no reason to throw all caution to the wind. Your father could mean this Misseri fellow ill, or could be working for those who do." Lodo tapped the triangular tattoo on his chin with one long forefinger. "So we have attained something of an impasse. Quite unexpected."

Sal didn't know what to say. Here he was, most likely sitting in the company of the man his father had come all the way to Fundelry to find, and that man was refusing to do anything about it!

"Very strange," Lodo mused, running a hand across his lined face. "'Payat' was an old use-name. *Very* old. I'd thought it quite forgotten by now ..."

There was a jewel embedded in the old man's little finger that Sal hadn't noticed before. It looked like a ruby--blood-red and brooding--and it made him think. Use-names were mainly a Stone Mage custom, like nick-names, although Sal and his father both had one. Their real or "heart" names were a secret known only to each other, as Lodo's probably was by his family, whoever or wherever they were. Sal assumed that he and his father had been granted theirs during their travels in the borderlands, where Stone Mage customs were stronger and the two of them were well-known. Sal's heart-name was Sayed, and his father's Dafis.

The fact that Lodo had a use-name--combined with his talent with rock and heat--struck Sal as highly odd. Perhaps Stone Mages *did* come this far into the Strand, after all. One at least, anyway ...

He surprised himself by yawning. Tiredness, heat and confusion were taking their toll. He needed sleep more than he needed mysterious encounters in the middle of the night with people he still didn't know were trustworthy, for all that they had helped him with Kemp.

"I should go," he said. In the morning he would confront his father with what he had seen and learned. Maybe then, finally, Sal would find out what he was doing here, and what he should do next.

Neither Lodo nor Shilly moved, though. Shilly remained sitting on her cushion, legs folded beneath her, watching him solemnly.

"I know what you're thinking," said the old man. "It's too risky to trust us. Your father has warned you to be careful who you talk to and you're afraid that you've done the wrong thing."

Sal jumped. Was the old man reading his mind, now? "I--well, that is--"

Lodo held up a hand and smiled. "That's okay, my boy. Only a fool is offended by the truth. You have no reason to trust me, or any other stranger. To do so in your position would be foolish--especially when you don't actually know what your 'position' really is. Is that more or less what you would like to say?"

Sal nodded. The old man was about as far distant from his image of the Sky Wardens as it was possible to get, but that still didn't make him trustworthy.

"Yet you came here with Shilly," Lodo said. "You trusted her that far. How do you justify that?"

"I--can't," he said, remembering the hunch that had come to him when looking down at her in the square. It had just felt right, apart from any other justification he might have had.

"I thought so," mused the old man. "Light is a by-product of heat just as heat is a by-product of light. Separating the two is very difficult. It's the same with knowledge and talent. So rarely does one come across two such divergent poles, with essences so pure and uncorrupted. And as they say, opposites attract."

Sal wasn't sure what Lodo was talking about. Was the old man trying to suggest that he had some sort of calling to the Change? Or something else entirely? Either way, he felt himself beginning to flush--and that was worse than any embarrassment the old man could have inflicted upon him.

"I *really* must--" he began.

"Yes, yes." The old man shook his head as though waking from a dream. "I'm sorry. You're right. Shilly, would you--?"

"I can find my own way."

Lodo smiled. "At least let her open the door for you. That's something you can't do on your own, yet."

Sal nodded, feeling his flush deepen. He hoped that in the reddish light of the room it would be mistaken for shadow.

"Sleep well, Sal," the old man said with a faint smile.

Shilly showed him the way up the tunnel and back to the round antechamber. There she touched something on the wall and stepped back as it dissolved in a shower of sand to reveal the night outside.

"Are you sure you'll make it back okay?" she asked.

"Positive." He found it hard to meet her eye.

"Good, because there's a chance I might decide to follow you in a minute to make sure. And if I find you stumbling around in the dark, as lost as a blind rabbit, I'm really not going to be very impressed."

He stared at her, then, for a long, shocked moment.

"I'm joking, you fool," she said, clapping him on the shoulder. "Get out of here before the old man starts charging you rent."

He stepped out of the hole and into the night, relieved to be out of the heat--and alone at last.

When the door shut behind him, he felt as though he had been dunked in a bucket of tar. It was very dark, much darker than it had been before. There was no moon, no stars, no light at all. His eyes took forever to adjust. It was cold, and the wind seemed to have picked up dramatically.

He had only a few seconds to realize why before the storm hit.

CHAPTER 4

THE EYE OF THE STORM

THE rain struck him like an avalanche of water. He was nearly deafened by an enormous crack of thunder from directly overhead. The storm filled the night, leaving no room for him. He dropped into the lee of a dune for shelter, but it was no use. He was instantly soaked.

There was no way, though, that he was going to ask Shilly for help getting back to the hostel if she came looking for him. He would manage it on his own. This was something he *could* do himself.

He forced himself to stand up and set off through the storm, searching with every flash of lightning for visible landmarks and hoping his sense of direction remained true. He was certain the town lay to the left of the entrance to Lodo's underground workshop. No lights were visible over the dunes, but that wasn't surprising. He had only ever seen so much rain during the monsoons that swept through the borderlands from the north--and if this *had* been a monsoon that had caught him and his father on the road, they would have taken shelter beneath the buggy, well away from any obvious flood paths. Here, he was brutally exposed. There was nothing between him and the naked ferocity of the storm--which was getting more powerful, not less.

And it was *cold*. He was shivering in minutes. It felt as though the rain had come directly from the great icy wastes that lay far to the south, over the ocean. Not even in the dead of desert's night had he ever been so frozen.

He pressed on, slipping and staggering up one side of a dune then tumbling and splashing down the other. Time passed in a blur. He didn't seem to be getting anywhere, but he didn't have any choice other than to keep going; even had he wanted to go back to ask Shilly's help, he could never have found the entrance to Lodo's workshop again.

Soon he was covered in scratches caused by the plants he stumbled across, invisible in the utter darkness. He felt like he'd been flayed, and imagined his blood running freely and washing away in the water running off his skin--as though he was dissolving in the rain, losing his identity. He wondered what would happen if he fell over and couldn't get up; perhaps the wet sand would absorb him like salt, and take him away forever.

It was then, after he had been stumbling blind for half an hour without finding any sign of the town, that he felt, again, as though he was being watched. Or if not actually watched this time, then passing under the gaze of a huge and distant eye, peering over the horizon at the storm and its work. The eye of a giant, or a god. It didn't frighten him, but it did make him feel very small. A giant might reach down and crush him, or a god simply snuff him out of existence.

He offered a half-hearted prayer that neither would happen. He didn't believe in the deities whose worshippers he occasionally encountered in his travels, like Lodo and his Goddess--but something in that distant stare left him in no doubt of *its* existence. Whatever it was, it was real. And if it could spare a moment to think about him, going around in circles in a storm, kilometers from the nearest fire, he would be grateful ...

Clang!

He stopped in his tracks, refusing to believe his ears. He couldn't credit that he had just heard the chiming of a bell from somewhere in the dunes. *That's it*, he told himself, hugging his arms around his chest for warmth, the chattering of his teeth almost drowning out the thunder, his muscles aflame. *Might as well lie down here and give up.* It would be a relief...

Clang!

The sound came again, cutting through the downpour from somewhere to his left--faint but clear, no hallucination.

He turned to face the sound, then forced himself to climb

to the top of a dune that lay between him and its source. Wiping the water from his eyes, he saw a light.

He still almost didn't dare believe it. It was a long way off and barely visible through the rain. Not one of Lodo's globes, but a real lantern, flickering and sputtering. Probably not Fundelry, then, but he wasn't about to turn away from the only hopeful sign he'd seen so far.

A flash of lightning revealed a shadowy figure standing next to the lantern, on the top of a distant dune, waving something in one hand.

Clang-a-lang-a-lang!

The boom of thunder following on the heels of the lightning almost drowned out the bell, but there was no disbelieving it now. Sal slipped down the dune in an ungainly rush and hurried up the next. The light was still there when he reached the top. Two dunes later, the lantern had gone out, smothered by water no doubt, but the bell remained to orient him. He followed it as best he could, and when he became confused, he waited until lightning struck to find the person who wielded it. The bell-ringer looked familiar, but not until Sal was only a dozen or so meters away, limping along a dune valley with water up to his ankles, did he recognize him.

It was the small boy he had seen at School that day, with Kemp--the one who looked like a bilby. He hadn't seen Sal, that much was clear; his eyes were narrowed against the rain, searching the dunes, looking determinedly over Sal's head. He was dressed in a raincoat that was probably as useless against the rain as Sal's clothes. The lantern lay at his feet, given up as a lost cause.

For a moment, Sal wondered if the boy had been sent to look for him. Why else would he be out walking on the dunes, trying to attract attention? But no one knew Sal had gone; even if they had found him to be missing, they couldn't have known where he had headed. The boy had to be hoping to catch someone else's eye.

Behind the boy, when darkness had returned and thunder

seemed to split the sky in two, Sal saw the lights of Fundelry shining against the sky.

He almost sobbed with relief. The town lay in a completely different direction from the one he had been following before he had heard the bell. Offering silent thanks to the boy who had unintentionally guided him to safety, he followed the dune valley as far as he could, then began the up-and-over trek back into town.

It would have been easy to believe, the next day, that the whole night had been a dream. A nightmare. Some events stood out, but his memories of them were faint and confusing: Shilly and Lodo, the storm, the god-like eye in the sky, the bilby-faced boy and the bell. He could hardly credit that they had happened in just one night.

His legs were covered with scratches and bruises, his legs and back were stiff and sore, and his clothes were damp. He vaguely remembered staggering up to the hostel foyer, bitterly cold, and undressing before going inside to avoid leaving splash marks on the stairs. How late it had been when he'd climbed shivering into bed he didn't know, but dawn had come all too quickly. His father's hand shaking him awake, telling him not to be a lazybones, had come as a shock. He had rolled over and gone back to sleep with a surly grunt.

When he did get up, the storm had wound down to a light drizzle and his father had gone. He cursed his tiredness: the morning would have been a perfect time to see if Lodo was the man his father was looking for. Now he would have to wait until later, when his father finished work, to ask him.

Von had some cereal left over for him in the kitchen. When she asked about the wet clothes hung to dry in his room, he explained that he had washed them in the night's rain while his father slept.

"Why not wash all your clothes?" she asked, looking at him strangely.

"I had to have something to wear today."

"What about your father's?"

"Half he was wearing, and I didn't know what he wanted done with the rest." Sal could feel himself reddening under her penetrating stare. "Is rain like that normal around here?"

Von shifted her gaze out the window, to where gray clouds covered the sky. "This time of year, anything's possible." She scowled back at Sal. "Foolish to get your clothes wet when you don't need to."

"There'll be work for dad, after the storm," he said, trying again to change the subject. "I can see damage from here."

"He said he'd be looking," she said. "If you want to find him, try Josip, the mechanic. He'll know where to go. Otherwise, you go to School."

Sal groaned. He'd forgotten about that.

"Mrs Milka came by earlier." Von looked as though she was enjoying Sal's discomfort. "She supervises the senior class and is looking forward to having you for the next week or two. It's not often we see people from the Interior down here. There's bound to be a lot you can tell the class about it."

Sal opened his mouth to protest that he wasn't from the Interior, but shut it before a word came out. This far south, pale skin and the dry lands invariably went together in people's minds, even though there was a large degree of mixing in the zones where Interior and Strand met. If Von and the teacher thought he was from the Interior, that could only have been because his father hadn't corrected their misconception.

"There's no reason to be nervous, Sal," said Von, although her wide smile said she hoped it was otherwise. "And the school's in the round building. You can't miss it. Look for the weathervane on top of it."

Sal thanked her, even though he had no intention of going. He had more important things to do.

When he reached Josip's, he was surprised to see the buggy out in the open and his father leaning into the bonnet.

"I thought you were working," Sal said.

"I thought I would be too." His father's head and upper body appeared. "And I thought you'd be at School."

Sal shrugged. The thought of facing Kemp on so little sleep made all his aches and pains double in intensity. The only reason he'd consider attending School that day was to ask Shilly what "scabs" were, as he'd forgotten to do so the previous night. Finding out what he was doing in Fundelry had been the greater priority.

"I want to ask you something."

"Go ahead. While you're at it, hand me that number eight spanner."

Sal walked over to the toolbox and found the spanner. On the way back, he saw Josip watching from the shadows of his verandah with a lazy grin on his face.

"Hi, Sal," the man called.

"Hi," Sal said back, annoyed that he and his father weren't alone.

He turned to hand his father the spanner and banged his head hard on the upraised bonnet.

"Ouch!"

"Are you all right?" His father looked up at him.

Sal rubbed at the sore spot, more irritated than hurt. The ward supposedly protecting him from bumps and scrapes didn't seem to be working this morning. "I'll get over it."

His father studied him with mild concern. "Didn't you sleep well last night?"

"Guess not."

"You can blame the sea air for that. It's meant to be good for you, but I've never believed so. Can't stand the smell of fish, personally."

"Is that why we've never come to the sea before?"

"No," said his father, wrinkling his nose. "But it's good enough for starters. Now, what did you want to ask me?"

"It can wait."

Sal rubbed at his scalp, and bent into the bonnet to see if there was anything he could do to help his father. A chance to fully service the buggy's engine came rarely and had to be taken advantage of. The noisy gearbox his father had been complaining about for weeks lay partly dismantled on a tarpaulin by the buggy. In stages, over the coming days, each piece would be cleaned and greased and put back in its place. Sal took it on faith that the buggy would work as good as new afterwards.

He didn't like working under the bonnet much, despite knowing how useful such skills would be one day. The buggy was an important part of their lives. It carried them from place to place; it was shelter when they had nowhere else to stay; it even earned them money at times, ferrying goods or people from here to there, the machine being much faster than camels or horses on proper roads. His father had never told him where it had come from, and rarely talked about the future, but Sal assumed that it would one day be his. He needed to know how it worked for those times when it didn't.

Josip didn't move to offer them a hand. Sal revised his estimate of the age of the mechanic. Instead of an old-looking young man, he now thought Josip might be a well-preserved man in his late thirties.

"I heard a story once," the mechanic said, "about a Sky Warden who ate a fish and turned into a dolphin."

"I know the one," said Sal's father. "That was Velzeboer, a third-century Syndic. He'd been drifting to water and a dish of raw fish tipped the balance. He turned before the eyes of his dinner guests, who carried him out to sea before he drowned in the air. He slipped out of their grasp and was never seen again." Sal's father looked up from the engine. "All these years later, his Line still carries the dolphin on its herald."

Josip put down his empty glass and applauded lightly. "You know more about our history than I do. Unusual for sand folk, I would've thought."

"We're not from the Interior," his father explained for- -Sal thought--the millionth time. Yet his tone was patient, accepting the confusion. "Neither quite in the Strand nor quite out of it. We hear a lot of stories from both sides that way, sometimes lots of different versions of the same story. It helps to know the facts behind them."

"Have you any more you'd care to share?"

Sal's father looked embarrassed, then: "I'm sorry. I really should concentrate."

Josip's smile broadened. "Of course. Another time, perhaps." The mechanic stood and went back into his workshop.

Sal took his chance now they were finally alone. "Dad," he whispered, "that man you're looking for. Have you had any luck finding him?"

"I haven't had time yet."

"What does he look like?"

His father shifted nervously under the bonnet. "Well, it's been a long time, and he'd be quite old now. But he has rank markings on his face, like tattoos. They wouldn't have changed, so he'd certainly stand out around here. I'll find him soon enough, if he's here."

Sal kept any feelings of satisfaction to himself. "Why don't you just ask someone?"

Again his father seemed nervous. "I'd rather people didn't know I was looking."

"Why not?"

Sal's father glanced at him. "Why are you so curious?"

"Because I think I've seen him."

"Really?" It was Sal's father's turn to bang his head. "Ow! Where?"

Sal had considered how to answer this question. He wasn't sure he'd done the right thing going to Lodo's workshop the previous night, especially if Lodo *wasn't* the man his father was looking for, so he wasn't going to admit to it. It would be better, he'd decided, to get the two men together. If Lodo did turn out to be Misseri, then Sal could tell the truth in a much better light.

"At the market, yesterday," he said, following Lodo's own lead. That's where the old man had said he was heading, the previous day.

"Did it look like he'd be back there again today?"

"Maybe. I'm not sure."

"Well," his father said, "it's worth taking a look. Help me get this manifold out, then we'll clean up."

Sal tried to concentrate on the engine, but he couldn't keep his mind from wandering. Something in his words had triggered a shift in his father's mood, a subtle restlessness that was as infectious as a cold.

"Dad?"

"What now, Sal?"

"Were you ever a Change-worker?"

His father looked at him in surprise. "What makes you ask that?"

"Just wondering." He tried to sound idly curious, although in his mind's eye he saw the weird fire Shilly had lit in Lodo's workshop.

"I wasn't a Change-worker, no." His father's eyes narrowed. "I don't have a drop of talent in me, and that's the truth."

Talent wasn't essential in order to use the Change, judging by the way Shilly had used the old man's strength to light the fire. But Sal didn't argue. "What happens if the Sky Wardens find someone using the Change in ways they don't like?"

"That depends," Sal's father said cautiously. "Most people fake the Change in order to rob you. But there have been rogue sorcerers and necromancers--mad Change-workers using their talents for evil rather than good. When they're caught, they're tried and dealt with. Some are executed. Some are imprisoned in places where they can't harm anyone else again--places that suck the Change out of them like a desert sucks water."

"What about the ones who don't want to join the Sky Wardens--or the Stone Mages? People who aren't evil, just different. What happens to them?"

"Well, that depends."

"On what?"

"On whether they're caught," said Sal's father.

Sal was about to ask why they had to hide from the Sky Wardens all the time when the workshop door slammed shut with a loud bang. Josip had returned with another drink. Sal's father's face closed up.

"Did I interrupt anything?" asked the mechanic cheerily.

"No, no." Sal's father returned to his work. "I was just telling Sal to make himself useful and hand me the screwdriver."

Sal reached for the tool and slapped it into his father's outstretched hand. He didn't know why his father was so unwilling to talk about the Sky Wardens and the Change, unless the answer took the form of a folktale, like that of the Syndic Velzeboer who had turned into a dolphin. Once he might have given it up as too hard to pursue, but the fire had been lit in his memory and wasn't going out.

The morning passed before his father decided to call a halt. By then, the last remnants of the storm had been burned away by the sun, leaving the air humid and suffocating. Sal was sweating heavily as they made their way to the other side of Fundelry, to the market.

The double line of stalls was even more crowded than it had been the day before. More traders must have arrived from neighboring towns, Sal assumed, bringing their children with them. There was a clown, a couple of jugglers, even a small brass band. Incense lay heavily in the air. A podium had been erected at one end of the market thoroughfare and people milled around it as though waiting for something to happen. Most seemed relaxed and cheerful enough, although Sal saw tension in a few of the uniformly brown faces. Maybe the day's business hadn't gone as well for some as they had hoped.

Cautious and watchful, his father led them along the stalls, looking at the local produce and studying the people they passed. His father bought them meat and vegetable pies from the seller the old woman had accused of padding out his prime cuts with cat meat. It tasted good enough to Sal as he picked through the steaming filling. Aunty Merinda had apparently gone for the day; her tent sat empty apart from a pyramidal arrangement of twigs, string and feathers in its center. A charm to keep it safe until she returned, Sal assumed.

They stopped to examine swatches of brightly colored cloth at a stall run by a large woman, clearly dressed in her own wares. "My weavers were all trained in Bellizzi," she boasted. "And my dyes come exclusively from the Desert Port region--as you, sir, can probably tell."

"I wouldn't know," admitted Sal's father, sniffing the cloth. "The color is pretty, though."

She looked down her nose at them. "'Pretty'?"

"Beautiful. Bright. I'm sorry. I don't know the right words."

"And you probably don't have the money, either." She smiled broadly, then, and winked. "At my prices, few people here have. Do me a favor and pass on the word, should you come across anyone with an eye for finery. Otherwise I'll move on next week."

"We'll tell them," Sal's father promised. He nodded good day, and she pounced on the next customer who looked vaguely interested.

Sal noticed that, on a number of similar occasions, the vendors left him and his father alone. They weren't pressured to sample goods or to haggle over a bargain. They were allowed to browse unchallenged, or were spoken to as equals. He wondered if they really looked that poor, or if there was something else at work.

When he asked his father, he was told: "They can tell by our skin that we're travelers. Even if we had the money, we don't have a need for the sorts of things these people are selling. They can afford to be friendly. If we met them out on the road, though, and asked for food or lodging, it'd be a different story."

They were studying jewelry in a stand near the far end of the market. Sal's father picked up a tiny charm bracelet and held it to the light while a brawny guard watched him closely.

"This is from Millingen," he said to the narrow-faced man running the stand.

"Well spotted, sir. You've been there?"

"A couple of times, when the boy here was young. I worked in one of their sweatshops for a few months. That's how I recognize the welds on these links. They haven't got any better, have they?"

The man behind the counter stared stonily at him for a moment. "As you say, sir."

Sal's father put the bracelet back on the counter, and winked at Sal. Then they left to do another circuit of the stalls.

Thus far, Lodo had been noticeable only by his absence. Sal had hoped they'd bump into him at one of the stands, but there had been no sign of either him or his apprentice. When they reached the end of the market and his father said they should head back to the hostel, Sal despaired of ever getting the two together.

"It's bigger here than I thought it would be," his father mused as they were jostled by a portly food seller.

"What do you mean?"

"I mean, I imagined it would be smaller." Sal's father glanced at him, then seemed to realize that his answer hadn't explained anything. "Less crowded. Less like a city. Look at this." He waved at the crowd. "We might as well be back in Kittle."

That was an exaggeration. Kittle had been crowded, but not a city. "Why is that important?"

"In a city it's harder to hide."

As though to prove the point, a short man dressed in a russet suit hurried up to them and begged their pardon.

"I'm sorry to bother you," he said, bowing briskly, "but I'd heard there was a Northerner in town. I could use your assistance, if you'd be so kind."

Sal's father looked nervously around them. "I really don't think--"

"It'll only take a moment, sir. Please, if you'll just come this way."

The man tugged Sal's father by the sleeve and led them back into the crowds. There, at a stall selling crystals and trinkets, the man held a honey-colored stone to the light.

"See here?" The man pointed at some marks on the crystal's base. "Can you tell what they are?"

Sal's father squinted at the marks, interested despite himself. "They're toa. I'm not sure where from, though. Leonora, maybe. Or Yamarna."

"Could it be a name?"

"It could be." He hefted the crystal in one hand. "But the name itself doesn't matter. It's not a fake."

The man in the suit expelled a small, tense breath.

"I told you," said a voice from the shadows of the stall.

"You did, but I couldn't believe it. I've been looking a long time for the missing piece." The man took the crystal back from Sal's father and handed over a large amount of money in coins to the stall owner. "Thank you, thank you both."

He nodded and headed off into the crowd.

"The missing piece of what?" asked Sal's father.

"I don't know exactly, but he seemed pleased enough to find it." The stall owner chuckled. "I owe you a small fee."

He leaned forward and held out a coin. As he did so, his face came into the light.

Sal gasped. It was Lodo.

"I couldn't," Sal's father said.

"Take it," Lodo insisted. "That's a sale I wouldn't have made without your help. Or not so easily, anyway. It's only fair, don't you think?"

Sal's father hesitated, then took the coin. "Well, I won't deny we could use it."

"Good." Lodo smiled warmly. "Would you care for a charm while you're here? I can't guarantee they'll work, but I'll give you the best price for a hundred kilometers."

Sal's father studied the trinkets arrayed on the table before him, while Sal stared at him in astonishment. What was wrong with him? There was Lodo right in front of him, tattoos standing out like a bushfire on grasslands. Why didn't he see?

Then Lodo turned to Sal and winked. Another face seemed to flow smoothly across Lodo's distinctive features-- that of a younger man with a gray-mottled beard and darker skin. It was this face Sal's father saw.

Sal stepped back, at a loss to know what to do. He opened

his mouth to blurt out what was going on when a voice whispered in his ear:

"Don't."

It was Shilly. He didn't need to look to work that out. He could smell her, all sweet rosemary and sweat, and feel her in his bones, standing just behind him. He closed his mouth into a thin line.

She touched his elbow. "Come with me."

He let himself be led a short distance away. As soon as he could, he shrugged off her hand. "What do you think you're doing?" he snapped.

"The old boy wants to take a look at your dad," she said. "Alone, and without being known for who he is."

"Why?"

"He's … sensitive. He can tell things by being near someone. He knew about you, for instance, the moment he saw you."

"Knew *what* about me?"

"He won't tell. But it was enough to warrant keeping an eye on you."

He glared at her. "You *have* been following me!"

"Ever since you arrived, almost, and luckily for you. No one else was going to stop Kemp from smashing you into little white bits." She smiled crookedly. "I did warn you, sort of. After the fact, yes, but--hey!"

He ignored her protest as he walked back to his father. Lodo looked up at him, then at Shilly behind him. A flicker of annoyance passed over the old man's true face.

Sal didn't care. He felt like an idiot. No, like *they* thought he was an idiot, which was worse. He wanted to get out of there, out of Fundelry altogether. Whatever his father needed Misseri or Lodo or whoever he was *for*, there had to be another solution.

"See anything you like?" Sal's father asked as though he had never left.

"No," he said curtly.

"I'll take this one." A small jar of brownish paste.

"Pearl shell and blood, sir? Are you sure? I doubt we'll be needing rain after last night."

"You never know." Sal's father handed over the coin he had been given and received half its value back in change.

"Thank you again." Lodo smiled as broadly as any satisfied trader as they moved away. "The best of luck in all your ventures."

They left the stall. Shilly fumed silently as they passed her. He could feel her stare burn into him like a blowtorch.

Sal's father shook the jar by his ear. "Probably full of ground bark," he said. "Still, I couldn't take all the money. It wouldn't have been right. I'm sure he needs it as much as we do."

They reached the podium end of the market. "I still haven't seen any signs of you-know-who. Have you?"

Sal shook his head in frustration and resisted the urge to say that he *didn't* know who.

"Oh well. We'll try another day. Where to now, then, do you think?"

Sal didn't care, as long as it was somewhere else, but at that moment a tall woman stepped up onto the podium and rapped loudly with a gavel. The crowd around them instantly hushed. His father stopped to see what was going on.

"Thank you," said the woman. She gazed across the faces staring up at her, smiling gently. Her nose was broad, and her graying black hair curled as close as a sheep's coat. "Welcome to the muster. Not a bad turnout this week; that's good to see. Does anyone have any urgent business before we move on to notices?"

A hand shot up at the front of the crowd. "What're the chances of fixing the weather, Iphi?"

"That's quite enough from you, Reed. I may be Mayor, but I can't work miracles. If you have a problem with the rain, you'll have to talk to the Wardens next time they pass through." She waited a second, then raised a sheet of paper. "I'll be quick. All jokes aside, last night's storm did cause some damage. Anyone with spare time or materials are welcome at Serafin and Balfort homesteads, where roofs came down. Anyone with serious crop damage or lost stock can report to the usual places; if the damage is severe enough, you'll qualify for compensation." She read a few personal messages for and from specific members of the crowd: birthdays, the death in the previous week of someone's grandmother, and an invitation from another town to celebrate an anniversary in three weeks' time. "Oh, and Alder Quinn asked me to remind you that Selection time is almost upon us. Application forms must be lodged by the end of this week. Anyone having trouble filling out the form can see me afterwards."

"Anyone having trouble filling out the form shouldn't be hoping for Selection," called someone in the crowd.

"Yes, well, that's not for me to decide." The Mayor looked around. "If there's nothing else ..."

A disturbance from the back of the gathering caught her eye. A short, very black man was pushing his way forward.

"Yes, Alder Sproule?"

"I'd like to say something," he said, his voice a light tenor with a sharp edge. But he wasn't content to address the crowd from the ground. He came all the way to the front and indicated that he would like to stand on the podium.

Sal watched him ascend with disquiet. He recognized the man's name from his conversation with Von. Hard to credit though it was, this black-skinned man was Kemp the albino's father.

"There's been a theft," he said. "One of my neighbors, Gai Kilmartin, had a sum of money removed from her premises last night. There was also a necklace and food missing when she woke this morning. Now, I know we all like to keep our doors unlocked, this being an open, trusting community, but be aware that someone has betrayed that trust and may do so again. If anyone knows anything about it, they can talk to me in private; I give you my assurance it will go no further. The same if the stolen goods are returned immediately. If not, as sheriff of Fundelry, I promise you that any further thefts will be dealt with severely." The Alder studied the crowd, his gaze lingering pointedly on the lighter-skinned strangers at the rear. "This is my first and only warning."

"Thank you, Alder Sproule," the Mayor said with a slight scowl as Kemp's father stepped down. "And on that cheerful note, may you all enjoy the rest of the day!"

A smattering of applause greeted her departure. Sal's father sighed as the crowd dispersed.

"He doesn't really think it was us, does he?" Sal asked.

"It'd be easier for him if it was. Better us than one of his own turning against the rest." His father looked resigned to it all. "It wouldn't be the first time as simple a thing as skin color has got us into trouble. And maybe that's why I didn't get any work today, even though there was all that storm damage to be fixed."

Sal's mind churned as they strolled back to the hostel. As if Lodo and Shilly and Kemp weren't enough to worry about, now Kemp's father suspected them of stealing. And the Selector was coming, according to the Mayor: that meant Sky Wardens. More than ever he was certain that Fundelry was the wrong place to be in, and he was no closer to a reason.

"Dad?"

"What, Sal?"

"Why don't we just leave?"

The question didn't seem to take his father by surprise. "We can't. Not yet. I'm sorry, Sal. There's something I have to do first."

"What?"

"You'll find out when I've done it. Hopefully not sooner."

"Is it dangerous?"

"I don't know. It might be." His father turned to face him as they walked, and attempted a joke. "Guess we'd better fix that buggy, eh? Just in case we have to make a quick getaway."

Not terribly reassured, Sal forced a tight-lipped smile and trudged on back to Josip's.

CHAPTER 5

A TEAR IN THE WATER

MRS Milka was a middle-aged woman with only two fingers on her right hand and a regular, singsong way of speaking that made Sal want to sleep. Not even the topic of her lesson could keep him alert.

"The Sky Wardens rule us, their subjects, only indirectly," she was saying. "Each village is run by a group of ten elected Alders, who in turn elect a Mayor. The Mayors then elect a Regional Governor, and these gather once every four years in the Haunted City to meet with representatives of the Sky Wardens to discuss governance of the Strand. The Alcaide, equivalent to a grand chancellor or highest judge, and the Syndic, the Alcaide's chief administrator, hear the requests of the governors and decide how best they can be met. That way all are heard, and all have a say in the future of our great nation."

Sal tried to concentrate. It was information he had been taught at various Schools in the borderlands--and no doubt his new classmates had heard it many times before--but listening to it was the easiest way to avoid looking at Shilly, who sat two seats across from him. They had been studiously ignoring each other all morning. It took a great deal of his attention.

"Similarly, we keep our villages small to ensure everyone receives the attention they deserve. Neither the weak nor the strong slips through the cracks. The former are given extra care by their community, while the latter are often Selected to join the ranks of the Sky Wardens themselves. This ensures the greatest well-being for all, and gives everyone the chance of attaining the highest possible level in the Strand. Are you following this, Sal?"

He nodded, thinking: what was the point of knowing your enemy if you didn't know *why* they were your enemy?

Mrs Milka pulled out a chart and began naming the various regional centers and important towns along the Strand. She gave a brief history of each of the major ports: where trading ships went to and arrived from; who the governors were and what causes they championed; which famous Sky Wardens had come from which place, and what great works they had performed. The chart was sketchy when it came to Interior geography, though, listing at least two major cities in locations Sal believed to be wildly incorrect. Geography was something he was relatively familiar with, thanks to the maps in the buggy's tool box.

"Does anyone remember the name of the current Alcaide?" the teacher asked, reverting to current events.

A half-dozen hands went up. "Yes, Manny?"

"Dragan Graham."

"Close. It's 'Braham' with a B. What about you, Sal? Can you guess the name of the Syndic?"

He didn't even try. "I've no idea."

Mrs Milka smiled patiently. "Well, that's perfectly understandable. The current Syndic is Nu Zanshin of Farrow. She was unanimously elected five years ago by an emergency sitting of the Conclave after the death of her predecessor, Salton Halech, in a freak accident."

So what? Sal wanted to ask, but he bit his lip. She was just doing her job and didn't deserve his disinterest--or his morbid fascination, either. He couldn't help imagining the Selectors rounding up children into nets with silver cattle-prods to feed the monstrous appetites of Alcaide Braham and Syndic Zanshin.

"Is it true, Mrs Milka," called a voice from the back, "that Stone Mages cut the heads off their kings when they've finished with them?"

The classroom fell silent. The teacher's eyes flickered to Sal, then away again. "What makes you ask that?"

"It's what my dad says." A poorly stifled snicker came from someone else at the back--and only then did Sal recognize the voice. He had been ignoring Kemp, too. "When their kings are too old or sick or gone mad, they cut off their heads and feed them to the dogs."

"Well," said Mrs Milka, "I hate to disagree with your father, but I don't think he's got it quite right on this count. First of all, the Interior doesn't have *kings* any more than we do. They're ruled by an Advisory Synod, made up of the most important Stone Mages in their land, which takes advice from the very best of their merchants, teachers, warriors, doctors and the like. Once every full moon they meet in a place called the Nine Stars to make or change the laws. They have a select group of Judges for casting final decisions on all matters, and officers who make sure that sentences are carried out. Although they do behead people who have committed particularly bad crimes, they never kill the rulers who fail them--just like us. There are better ways."

Sal kept carefully still, neither speaking up nor looking around.

"But my dad--"

"Your father and I were in School together, Kemp," Mrs Milka said firmly, "and I don't recall the Interior being his strong subject." She looked around the room. "If there are no other questions, I'll move along." She paused briefly, then went on. "As I was saying before, not all Sky Wardens come from towns like Fundelry. Indeed, most of them belong to three major families, or Lines, called Air, Water and Cloud. Newcomers to the Conclave may not initially belong to one of these Lines, but it's common for them to ally themselves with one. These alliances can be very strong, and are sometimes sealed by marriage. When a marriage happens between Lines, the resultant partnership belongs to the third line--so if a Cloud marries an Air, the couple and any children they might have belong to Water. This prevents aristocracies from forming, and spreads power evenly throughout the Conclave.

"The Interior has a similar system," she added, "but with Earth, Sun and Fire Clans. Is that right, Sal?"

"I guess," he said, knowing as little about the Interior as the Strand, except for what he'd picked up along the way.

"Now, although there is no present enmity between the Strand and the Interior, there has been in the past." She turned to the blackboard and began to write dates and names. "In the fourth century ..."

Sal's attention was already wandering when a spitball hit the back of his neck with stinging force. Ignoring another faint titter of laughter, Sal gritted his teeth and wiped it away, feeling his ears grow hot. He couldn't retaliate if he wanted to stay out of trouble. All he could do was hope to get through the day in one piece. After a while they would give him up as a lost cause and ignore him. Hopefully.

Then, perhaps, he could get on with finding out why he was here. That was his biggest problem. He *had* to find a way to get Lodo to speak to his father properly. The sooner he did that, the sooner they could move on. He didn't want to be stuck in Fundelry forever. The thought of that was too horrible to contemplate.

It wasn't Fundelry itself, though, making him feel that way. Although not much of a town, it was far from the worst he had seen. He had simply become used to a nomadic, ever-changing lifestyle. In a lifetime of travel, he had rarely seen any single town more than once, and never stayed anywhere longer than three months. He had watched his father work as a jeweler, a weaver, a manual laborer, a cook, an ironmonger, an alpaca herder, a fruit-picker, and even a gravedigger. He had seen many of the things he would otherwise only have been told about, like mountains, rivers, deserts, and now, perhaps, even the sea. He had met countless hundreds of different people, from the dark skins of Fundelry to people with coloring exactly like his on the edge of the Interior, and he had heard rumors of others much further away.

He suspected that he was more realistically educated, as a result, than Mrs Milka, whose cheerful zeal couldn't make up for the fact that she lived in a small town on the edge of nowhere. What she said certainly seemed too good to be true. In Sal's travels he had heard rumors of conflicts, slaves, torture, horrible crimes, some of them in the distant past, some more recent, all denied by the governments on both sides. He didn't doubt that some of the stories were true--they couldn't all be false--and it was ironic that some of Kemp's distrust of people from the Interior was probably justified. No doubt there were others like Kemp on the far side of the borderlands who felt the same way about people from the Strand, with as much justification.

Sal had no desire to be like Kemp, stuck in a little box of a world, no matter where that part of the world was. He wanted to get moving again, and if that meant nudging things along a bit then he would do it. How, though, was the question. He didn't want to nag any more than he already had, and putting his father and Lodo face to face hadn't helped at all. There had to be another way to break the impasse.

Unfortunately, the only other one he had thought of to date had led to a dead end.

After working with his father the previous afternoon, and dreaming all night of being chased by people hidden behind masks made of feathers, he had awoken early determined to get the day off to a positive start. Before School--which his father insisted he attend--he had gone to look for Lodo's underground lair. If Lodo wouldn't come to his father, maybe he could bring his father to Lodo. But even in the light of day, locating the entrance had proved to be impossible. All the dunes looked the same, and any footprints had been washed away by the storm.

He had stood for a long while on a large dune that seemed to be in about the right spot, looking for any sign at all. The bushes at its base hid nothing but sand and the odd shell. Shielding his hands against the sunlight, he had looked despairingly about him. Dunes marched off inland for a distressing distance before slowly merging with scrub. The coast stretched west to east like a winding ribbon; he could see two towns, one in each direction, blurred by distance. From his vantage point, he could see more of the sea to the south than he had at any previous time. It seemed to fill up half the world, gray and massive, yet flatter than any land he had ever seen. It looked completely unnatural to him.

The now-familiar feeling of being watched crept over him. When he looked around nervously, there was no one to be seen. No Kemp or his cronies. No Shilly or Lodo. And no strange-looking boys waving bells, either. He was alone.

Then a slight noise drew his attention to a seagull standing behind a patch of sea grass. They stared at each other for a second.

"I don't have any food," Sal said, feeling slightly stupid. The bird kept looking at him as though it understood what he was saying perfectly well and didn't believe a word of it. Its feathers ruffled in a gust of wind. The deep black eyes didn't blink. They made him uneasy.

"Garn!" He waved his arms and made shooing motions at the bird. It skittered sideways a step or two, cawed noisily, and finally flew away, its wings slapping into the distance.

Giving up on his quest, Sal had returned to the town proper and gone to School, where his worst fears of the day before had been realized.

* * *

Finally it was lunchtime. A bell rang to indicate midday, and Sal looked up to notice the bilby-faced boy looking at him. Both of them glanced hastily away.

Sal slipped out of the classroom as soon as he had the chance. He was unsure for a moment where to go, whether to retreat to the hostel or brave the square. As he stood outside the Senior School building, the weathervane on top of it caught his attention. It was distinctive, as Von's directions had suggested, despite its silver being tarnished almost black. Only its eye retained any gleam, winking down at him like a jewel. It was pointing east in defiance of the wind.

"It doesn't move," said a voice beside him. "Some say it's pointing at the Haunted City, but I think it's just stuck."

Sal realized that he was dumbly staring upward. "What?"

"The weathervane."

He looked down into the bilby-faced boy's large eyes. They were studying him closely. For a moment, Sal thought the boy might say that he'd seen Sal in the storm the previous night, but he didn't. Sal wondered if he should thank him anyway.

"You must have traveled a long way," said the boy.

"Yes. I have."

"As far as the Haunted City?"

"Maybe as far all up, but no, I've never been there."

"You'll go there one day."

"I don't think so." Sal felt uncomfortable; the boy seemed friendly enough, but he carried a hidden intensity around with him. Sal had noted that no one else in the class had spoken to him when leaving. "Dad wouldn't want me to."

"Why not?"

Sal was about to change the subject by asking about the bell-ringing the night before, when Mrs Milka came up behind them.

"Are you bothering Sal, Tom?" The teacher put one hand on each of their shoulders, even though she was barely taller than either of them. "I see you've met our star student," she told Sal proudly. "Tom will be Selected this year like his brother before him, if I'm any judge."

Sal looked at the boy in surprise. The boy--Tom--didn't seem any older than ten, and Mrs Milka had said that the Sky Wardens rarely chose anyone younger than twelve. Sal tried to imagine him robed in blue and wielding the Change like the giants in his dreams, but couldn't.

"It just goes to show what hard work can do," the teacher beamed.

Tom's eyes had clouded over. With a wordless shrug, he pulled out of her grasp and hurried off down the street.

Mrs Milka looked after him, her expression turning from pride to puzzlement. "He's an odd one," she confessed. "Rarely talks, even to his parents, and he doesn't have any friends. He did come and talk to you, though, didn't he?"

She looked hopefully at Sal, but he couldn't think of

anything to say. The look in Tom's eyes had almost been one of pleading. If Mrs Milka had seen it too, though, she was obviously as mystified as he about what the boy was pleading *for*. If she couldn't work it out, Sal didn't know what good he would be.

He made his excuses and went to find somewhere to sit.

He took a spot on a bench out in the open, where Kemp and his cronies couldn't sneak up on him. He wasn't hungry yet, being accustomed to meals only at the beginning and end of each day, and all the talk of Sky Wardens had unsettled him. No one made any move to sit with him. He thought idly about making an effort to find someone to talk to, but decided he was probably better off alone, anyway. Making friends and living on the road weren't terribly compatible pursuits.

Being alone proved more difficult than expected, however. One of the younger kids--a girl no more than three years old--wasn't as discriminating as her older school mates. She took a shine to him for no obvious reason. When he sat down, she was there looking up at him with a curious expression on her face.

"Hello!" she said.

"Hi." He wasn't used to kids at all, let alone ones so young. What was he supposed to say to her? "My name is Sal. What's yours?"

Instead of replying, she giggled and ran away.

That fixed that, he supposed. He scanned the square. Kemp was lazing on a bench in the shade, mindful of his pale skin, with a crony or two in attendance. Shilly was squatting on her haunches just like she had been when they'd first met. She seemed to be drawing. He was curious to know what her subject was this time, but when she caught him looking he turned away.

The young girl came back. "Hello!"

He wondered if that was all she could say. "Hello again. Are you going to tell me your name this time?"

She hid her mouth behind a hand but couldn't suppress a giggle. Then she turned and ran away again.

He'd become a game, he realized. It could have been worse.

He went back to watching Shilly. Her hands moved in swift, sure ways--poking here, scribbling there, erasing everything with a palm swept from side to side a minute later. She appeared to be doodling, drawing overlapping shapes that didn't mean anything. He noticed that nobody talked to her either, and wondered if her isolation was self-imposed. On the few occasions they had met she had acted like she knew everything and he knew nothing. While he would never argue that she did indeed know more about Lodo, Fundelry and the Change, he was sure there were things she didn't know: like how it felt to drive at speed on tarmac, or to see the desert fringes at sunset, or to fix an internal combustion engine. She shouldn't be so--

"Hello!"

He started. "Oh, it's you again. What do you want now?"

"Present." The little girl held out a flower.

"For me?"

She smiled wider, and nodded. The flower seemed to shimmer in her hand, as though it was made of gossamer. He'd never seen anything like it.

He reached out to take it, and a bright blue spark arced between their fingertips.

She laughed in delight.

He jumped. It didn't hurt him, but it did surprise him. And on the heels of that surprise came another. The flower disappeared into thin air with a golden sparkle and a faint "pop".

The girl shrugged and said, "Gone," in a resigned tone of voice, as though such things happened every day.

He clutched the bench beneath him for stability. The girl toddled off to find something else to do.

He watched her go, stunned.

"That's Elina," said a voice.

He looked up. It was Shilly, standing with the sun behind her head. Her hair seemed to glow around its edges.

"She's a source of wild Change, rather than a natural

talent. It's just as likely to burn out before she turns four, Lodo says, but in the meantime she's a great source of entertainment for herself, and those who can see." Shilly looked at him closely. "You did see it, didn't you?"

"The flower? Yes." He shook himself. "Was it something like Lodo's false face?"

"On a very basic level, yes. An illusion is nothing special."

"Can you do it?"

She hesitated, then said, "Not very well, but I'm learning."

Looking around her, she went on: "I was thinking of going for a walk along the beach. Do you want to come?"

He shuddered. "No."

"Oh, okay. If it's like that ..." She turned and started walking away.

"No, wait. That's not what I meant." He slid awkwardly along the seat, cursing the misunderstanding. Ignoring each other had been easier. "I don't want to go to the beach. Let's just sit here for a while instead."

She regarded him curiously for a moment, then came back. "Okay. I'm surprised, though. I'd have thought you couldn't get enough of the beach, being from the borderlands."

"It's not that simple." His father had always warned him away from water, scaring him with stories of drowning from a very early age. But there was more than just mortal fear to it. His father's attitude was part of it too--there was *something* about the sea that bothered him, and Sal knew it had to be more than just the smell of fish. It made Sal uncertain and nervous about going near the sea, in case he found out something he didn't want to know.

To change the subject he asked her the first question that popped into his head. "What are you doing at School? I thought Lodo taught you. Or are you following me again?" he asked, the idea occurring to him with vindictive relish.

She laughed. "Oh, it's nothing like that. I come to School three days a week, whichever three I want. Sometimes I'll skip the first day and stay home to do chores. Anything is better than listening to Mistress Em drone on. But when I need a break from the old boy, I turn up. He can be a bit dreary too, at times. Sometimes I think they'd be perfect for each other."

He smiled at the thought. "Is that why you picked today? To get away from Lodo?"

"Not really. To be honest, I figured you could use help with Kemp."

"I can look after myself."

"I'm sure you can, in your own way."

He bristled. "What do you mean by that?"

"Disappearing may be easier than fitting in, for you, but it's not going to work here. Kemp has already singled you out. You need to retaliate, not retreat."

"Like that's going to be easy." He remembered the strength of Kemp's big, pale hands and the humiliation he had felt lying in the dirt.

"And like I *said,* I figured you could use the help."

He fought an instinctive response to kick back. Shilly had an uncanny knack at getting a rise out of him. "Why?"

"Because we're both outsiders and we should stick together. I've copped a lot of flak from whitehead myself, and it isn't fun. This way we can spread it around a little."

"But why help me at all? You could just let me cop the lot and give yourself a rest."

"You're not going to be here forever, remember? It wouldn't really solve anything for me. Is that what you'd do in my shoes?"

He considered it. "No. It wouldn't be very nice."

"Exactly, my friend."

He looked at her, and realized she was looking right back at him. Her green eyes were no less startling than the first time he had seen them.

"We *can* be friends, can't we?"

Why? he wanted to ask. They weren't obliged to be anything. And just because she had made a move toward reconciliation didn't mean he had to return the compliment.

But everything she'd said about Kemp was true. He could use an ally. All thoughts of resistance crumbled at the thought of showing up the big bully, somehow.

"I guess so," he said.

"Good." She shifted on the seat. "So, what is it with the sea? Do you get seasick or something? Were you dunked as a baby?"

"Uh..." He was embarrassed at the thought of telling her.

"Oh, go on. It can't be that bad. If you tell me, I'll tell you what I think Lodo thinks about us."

He wasn't sure he wanted to hear that, either.

"Does it scare you?" she asked with a wicked glitter in her eye.

"I wouldn't know," he shot back, annoyed that she had seen through him so easily. "I've never seen it. Not close up."

She frowned. "What, never?"

"Never ever. In my whole life this is the closest I've come."

She leaned back, amazed. "Well, that wasn't what I expected. What a bizarre thought, to never see the beach." She suddenly stood. "Come on."

"What?"

"Let's go. You can't possibly come all this way and not look at it. Why not now?"

"Because..." He couldn't think of a reason she might accept. "What about School?"

"It's just over the hill, Sal. We can be back in two minutes. And if we aren't, so what? You don't live here and I don't care." She studied him closely. "What's the real problem? *Are* you afraid?"

He looked deep into himself. Not for the fear--he knew *that* was there--but for the inclination to confess to her about it.

"Tell me what you think Lodo thinks about us, first," he said, hoping to delay the decision.

"You and me?" Her smile became more of a smirk. "He thinks we're destined."

"We're what?"

"You know, *destined*. To be together, somehow. Maybe he means to live together and have babies!" She pulled a face like she had sucked on a lemon. "Maybe he means something else. I don't know for sure. But there's a weird look in his eye when he talks about you and looks at me. I know he's curious, and that's always a bad sign. Last time he took a *real* interest in my life it meant packing up and leaving everything I'd ever known, forever."

Sal must have looked as confused as he felt, because she didn't wait for him to ask.

"I'm an orphan," she said, "abandoned as a baby in a town a long way from here. Lodo adopted me when I was five, when I was like Elina and my fourth foster family didn't know what to do with me. I don't know why he wanted me, but they sure didn't, and I like to think he acted out of my best interests. If he didn't..." She shrugged. "Well, it's not as if I have anything better to do."

They stared at each other for a long moment. He didn't know what to say.

"So," she finally said, "how about that walk?"

* * *

He had no idea what to expect as they walked down the lane toward the sea. Glimpses over the dunes, combined with ominous hints from his father over the years, amounted to something more terrifying than he could imagine.

When he stood at the edge of the beach looking down on the shoreline and, beyond that, across the incredible ocean stretching all the way to the sky, all of it shimmering and in constant motion, churning and heaving as though at any moment it might suddenly surge forward and engulf him-- yet so massively substantial it was hard to conceive that it could actually be fluid--he almost turned and ran. It was too much, too alien, too incredible.

Shilly took him by the hand and he numbly followed her down the beach. The sand beneath his feet wasn't like desert sand. It was grayer, with bits of broken shells, smooth pebbles and drying weed everywhere he looked. He'd visualized the sea just coming to a stop: the grass and scrub continuing to the edge then drowning in water. In comparison to that, the beach looked completely sterile-

-a flat wasteland dividing wet from dry, on which nothing grew. Yet there were footprints everywhere.

Closer to the edge, the sea was no less threatening than from far away. The waves splashing on the shore startled him, and he tried to concentrate on the way they died--in fast-ebbing ripples on moisture-dark sand. These last dregs of mighty ocean surges were nothing to be afraid of, he told himself. When Shilly tugged him close enough so that a wave touched the tips of his toes, it felt cool and refreshing, just like a river or a lake.

But there was more to it than that. There was something else beyond the wetness and restless motion of the water, something strange.

It radiated a presence he couldn't define.

He was standing on the edge of a vast, living blanket covering more of the Earth than the land itself. If he wanted to, he could touch it, and that touch would reverberate around the world.

"How is it? Not so bad?"

Sal shook his head. He couldn't explain it. And he didn't want to let go of her hand just yet.

"Well, there's our claim to fame." She pointed, and he wrenched his eyes up out of the wavelets, almost lost himself in that impossibly flat horizon, then saw, further along the beach, a wooden jetty stretching far out to sea. Fishing boats were tied to one side, bobbing up and down in the water.

How did it survive? he wondered. Surely the water would smash it to pieces in a day. And the boats! Who would ever go out in such puny things on such a hostile surface?

"The longest for five hundred kilometers," she said, mock-proudly, like a tour guide showing off one of the world's seven wonders. "And a hundred years old if it's a day! We're actually at the center of a wide bay--see how the beach curves inward? If it had been a little less shallow, someone might've built a city here, once."

He stepped back and looked at the footprints around them, only half-listening to her. What did people *do* here? Fish? That was what the jetty was for, he assumed. Maybe they fished from the beach as well, although no one was doing it at that moment, from either the beach or the jetty. There was just one solitary person visible in the distance, not doing anything, just watching like Sal was. He had heard of people swimming in the sea, but he couldn't understand why they would do it. It would surely be too hard to get anywhere, with all the water moving and splashing around.

He took a deep breath of salty air and imagined its smell originating thousands of kilometers away, deep in the southern ocean where whales played and bred, according to legend.

"Are you okay?"

He shook himself, realizing how stupid he must look, gawping at everything like a small child.

"Do you want to walk now?"

"I guess."

"Let's go this way." She pointed along the beach towards the jetty. "No offence, Sal, but your hand is getting sweaty."

"Uh, sorry." He removed it and wiped it on his shirt.

"And roll up your pants," she suggested. "It'll stop them getting wet."

He followed her advice, and they walked off along the beach. They stayed close to the waterline, where the sand was firm and easier to walk on. He jumped every time a wave splashed near him.

Shilly asked him how he and his father had come to Fundelry, and where they had come from. He was so grateful for the distraction he forgot to be cautious about what he said.

"Gliem," he said, pointing inland and to the north. "We stopped there for a couple of days. Dad did some work to refuel the buggy. He must've asked around about Lodo too, although I didn't know it at the time. We came straight here afterward."

"By buggy, you say. Is that like a car?"

"Sort of. It runs on alcohol and isn't very comfortable. But it keeps on going, which is the main thing."

"Do you like traveling?"

"I suppose so."

"You don't sound very sure about it."

He shrugged. The question was one he hadn't bothered to think about before, since the alternative had never been an option. He hoped it still wasn't.

"This is the only place I remember," she said. "I've never visited Pounder or Butland." She pointed ahead of and behind them in turn, at the towns he'd glimpsed that morning. "Lodo sometimes goes away on business, but he always leaves me behind to keep an eye on things. He can be pretty paranoid about security and stuff."

Maybe with good reason, Sal thought, remembering Von's comment about Kemp's father wanting to run him out of town.

"What is he?" he asked.

Shilly thought about it for a long time. Then she said: "I don't know. You can see his tattoos, can't you?" He nodded. "Well, he won't tell me what they mean, and he keeps them hidden from everyone else, even his friends. He does it the same way he fooled your dad into thinking he looked different. Would your dad know?"

"Maybe. He called them 'rank' markings. But he doesn't talk much about important stuff, either." The more Sal thought about it, the more Lodo and his father had in common.

"I like to think he's a renegade Stone Mage, but he never tells me anything. It drives me crazy not knowing!"

She kicked viciously at a shell and it skipped into the distance. Sal confirmed his guess that she didn't like secrets. How she had endured this long with Lodo eluded him.

And that, he supposed, was why she was with *him*, now, not because she was pursuing some mysterious destiny or other. More likely she thought his dad might know something about Lodo, and hoped that by ingratiating herself with him he might tell her.

That was an ungenerous thought, though. She wasn't exactly pressing him for information. It seemed like nothing more sinister than a conversation to fill what might otherwise have been an awkward silence.

They had reached the jetty. He knew what she was about to say before her mouth opened.

"Do you want to--?"

"No way."

"It's perfectly safe, Sal."

"So *you* say."

"Why would I lie? We'd both get wet if I was wrong. I'd be with you, remember?"

He nervously studied the wooden structure. The single guard rail looked absurdly thin. He knew he should leave and walk back to School, but he was reluctant to make himself look any more of a fool than he already had. And she knew it, judging by the smile forming on her lips.

"Come on." She took his hand and gripped it tight. "Last one in's a rotten egg!"

Before he could protest she ran full-pelt toward the jetty, whooping and pulling him along with her. So intent was he on simply staying upright that he hardly noticed when the sand beneath his feet became wood, the beach fell away, and he was on the jetty itself.

She took him halfway out before he managed to dig his heels in and bring her to a halt. He took two steps backward, then stopped cold. He had caught a glimpse of the water through a crack between the planks. Shock had gone through him like an icy fist. He couldn't move; he could hardly breathe.

He looked up, saw the ocean all around him and closed his eyes; the presence of all that water was bearing down on him like an avalanche. From behind his eyelids all he could hear was the tiny splashes as the sea lapped against the base of the jetty, trying to suck it down into the depths. There was so much salt in the air he felt like he was already drowning.

He moaned in fear and fell to one knee. This was worse than anything he could have imagined.

"Sal? Oh, hell." Shilly squatted next to him. "I had no idea. Deep breaths, nice and slow. Take it easy."

He hadn't realized how fast he was panting until she mentioned it. She had an arm around him, squeezing. He opened his eyes a crack to look at her and was blinded by the sun. The world seemed to be turning: sea, sky, sea, sky ...

"I'm sorry, Sal. Honest. I shouldn't have made you do it. I just thought you were being silly. Come on--get up and I'll take you back."

"I can't." He was still frozen. His arms and legs felt like they weighed a thousand tons.

"Yes, you can." One skinny hand went under his armpit and tugged, but to no avail. "Shit. Well, you'll just have to stay out here forever, then."

The joke fell as flat as *he* wanted to. He went down on his hands and knees. Through two thick planks he saw gray-green waves dancing on the surface of what seemed an unfathomable depth like hands reaching up to drag him down. Bile surged in his stomach. He gasped and looked up.

A seagull fluttered over them, squawking. Shilly stood up and shooed it away, but it came back doggedly for another pass. Its wings seemed to graze them as it swooped overhead, then angled back to shore, its calls echoed by others. Soon the air was full of birds.

"Oh, no." Shilly clutched at him. They huddled together in the center of an avian maelstrom. Gulls came at them from all directions, pecking and scratching, squawking loudly.

One became entangled in Shilly's hair. She shrieked and batted at it with her free hand. Something burned inside Sal's chest, and a clear space momentarily opened over them, as though a gust of air was pushing the gulls back. Shilly staggered for a second, startled by the sudden respite, but soon took advantage of it.

"Bloody scabs," she muttered, tugging at Sal again with all her strength. "Come *on*, will you? I can't carry you back on my own!"

Sal did his best to stand up. He made it to his knees with Shilly's help. She put one of his hands on the guard rail and made him look away from the water. Staring at her eyes from close quarters helped. He was able to get onto his feet again, albeit a little uneasily.

Then the birds came back, attacking with renewed ferocity.

"Now, walk!" she ordered him over the racket, and he did manage a kind of controlled stagger. "That's it! One step after the other. All the way back. 'Cause if you don't--"

She didn't finish. From somewhere within him, he found the strength to move. Letting go of the rail, he pulled free of her. Waving his arms around his head he stumbled forward, beating a way through the birds, forcing himself through the swirling confusion. He didn't care where he was going, as long as it was *away*.

Feathers, beaks and claws parted in fright before him. Sensing that he was close to freedom, he broke into a run--

--and collided with someone tall and hard and smelling of sweat.

Sal recoiled, blinking.

"You again," said Kemp, his expression hidden in the shadow of a wide-brimmed hat. "Making a habit of this, are you, stone-boy?"

Sal staggered back a step and lost his balance completely. Shilly didn't catch him in time. His head knocked hard against the guard rail as he went down, and he saw stars, then black, then nothing.

The world lit up again the moment his head went under the water. There was a pain like white lightning coming from the ward in his ear. There was too much pain, everywhere. He didn't know what to do. There was no time to think.

Seawater burned in his eyes, nose and mouth. He choked, racked by spasms as his body fought for air but sucked in only more of the ghastly water. He couldn't see anything but bubbles; he couldn't tell which way was up. He was tumbling end over end into a deathly cold void, and was powerless to prevent it.

(And behind it all, he felt the same presence he had felt

in the storm; an unearthly eye searching from afar, through hundreds of kilometers of water that in an instant seemed to part like smoke. The pain in his head was like a beacon, signaling that eye. Mighty forces dragged their attention ponderously his way, and he thrashed about, as automatically afraid of those forces finding him as he was of drowning.)

His head broke the surface, and he seemed to hear people calling for him. He tried to swim but didn't know how to. There was little he could do but windmill his arms and kick his legs and hope for the best.

It wasn't enough. He went back under. The last dregs of air in his lungs escaped into the sea--and he was sinking, fading, drowning, falling.

(*"Sayed?"* a woman's voice called from the graying distance, growing fainter by the second. *"Sayed! Is that you?"*)

Then everything went black, and he was lost again.

PART TWO:

FINDING

CHAPTER 6
ON THE SURFACE OF THINGS

THE first thing Sal saw when he opened his eyes was the sky. It was blue, as blue as the eyes he saw when he looked into the mirror. He felt as though he was falling into it, dissolving like a cloud on a hot day. Then a gull wheeled across the heavens, screeching, and he automatically raised his hands to fend it off.

The movement triggered a spasm of coughing. His lungs were full of sand, or felt so; he could only gasp and choke.

A stranger leaned into his field of view, a balding man with heavy jowls and deep caramel skin.

"You're still with us, boy," he said, his voice resonant and deep. "That's a start."

"Whhh--?" Sal tried to rise and speak, but his throat was raw.

"Quiet, now. You'll be right as rain in a minute."

Sal fell back and felt the sand beneath him, his clothes sticking wetly to him--and remembered only then what had happened. The sea had pulled him down; he had been drowning; something about an eye, a voice ...

The man stepped away to talk to someone in a low, unhurried voice. Sal looked around for Shilly, but couldn't see her. A small crowd had formed, surrounding him with a ring of dark faces and looming bodies. He felt trapped, panicky. He wanted his father. He wanted to get away. He wanted--

A cool hand touched his forehead. "Are you all right, Sal?"

And there was Shilly, concern written across her face.

"What happened?" he croaked.

"You nearly drowned," she said. Her voice belied both her words and expression: light-hearted, almost joking. "When you hit the water, you went down like a stone. A heavy one.

I jumped in after you, but couldn't see you. You popped up and splashed about for a bit, but by the time I got closer, you were gone again, under a wave. I thought I'd lost you." She stopped for a second, and glowered across Sal's prone body. "Lucky for all of us, someone who knew what he was doing jumped in and pulled you out."

Sal followed her gaze, saw Kemp through the legs of a bystander, flushing furiously.

"What do you mean?"

"The big shit froze," she hissed in his ear. "I don't think he was trying to kill you, but he sure as hell didn't try to rescue you, either. He just stood there gawping while I did my kingfisher impersonation. I can understand him pushing you in for a joke, assuming you could swim, but once he saw that you couldn't--"

"He didn't push me in," Sal interrupted. "I fell."

"Are you sure? I couldn't see through the scabs."

"He startled me, that's all. I'm pretty sure--"

"Do you have a home, lad?" The heavy-jowled man was back. Now that Sal was more alert, he noticed the way the man's thinning, black hair lay slicked across his scalp and how his cream-colored tunic stuck to his broad chest and stomach.

"You pulled me out?"

"That I did." The man smiled and held his hand out for Sal to take it. "Euan Holkenhill, at your service once already and at any future time you should require it."

Sal felt Shilly stiffen beside him, but before he could think twice about taking the man's hand, he had done so and found himself tugged to a sitting position, spluttering again.

"You're obviously not from around here," Holkenhill went on, before Sal could thank him. "Maybe you're with one of the merchants, come in on a caravan perhaps. Is there--?"

"I'll take him where he has to go," Shilly said, kneeling close to Sal, her hand still on his forehead. Sal tried to pull free, but she held him close.

"Will you do that? Good girl." The man nodded, satisfied,

and clambered to his feet. He wiped both hands on his damp shorts and took stock of his surroundings. "There's nothing else to see here," he called to the small crowd. "Back to School and home, all of you!"

Holkenhill turned to Sal and winked. "Mind you stay out of trouble, now." To Kemp he added, with a deep scowl: "You too, boy."

He didn't need to add anything else--there was warning enough in his tone to make it clear what he thought had happened. Sal opened his mouth to protest that Kemp was unfairly accused, at least of pushing him off the jetty, but the older boy had turned away and begun marching along the beach, his hat back on to protect his pale face and neck from the burning sun.

Shilly tugged Sal to his feet, her gaze not on him but on Holkenhill's receding, round shape. "That was close," she said, taking her hand off his face.

The man was much shorter than Sal had realized. "He *really* rescued me?"

She glanced back at him. "Eh? Oh, yes. He sure did. Dived off the jetty like a seal, hard though it is to believe. Guess he could see you better from above than I could, in the waves. But that wasn't what I meant." Her gaze was sharp. "Come *on*, will you? We should get you changed. At the very least, this gives us a good reason to skip the rest of School today."

They trudged the short distance to the hostel in silence, Sal keeping his eyes firmly on the ground and trying to keep up. His body felt weak and bruised, as though it had been pummeled with hammers. He dreaded to think what his new School mates thought of him now. His mind was still reeling--and not just from his narrow escape. He couldn't shake the feeling that something *had* been looking for him through the water. Something a long way away. Something--or someone--that knew his real name: *Sayed.*

But that wasn't possible, he told himself. Only one person besides himself knew his heart-name, and that was his father. His oxygen-starved brain must have dreamed the voice calling him. He heard it again, replaying it in his memory: *Sayed! Is that you?* Certainly, it was unfamiliar--not Shilly's voice, or Von's, or any of the other women he had met in the previous days. His mother's voice? It might have been-- although Sal's father said that he had been much too young when she had left them to have any memories of her. Maybe he had made it all up in one last desperate pretence that he might know her before he died ...

* * *

When they arrived at the hostel, it was obvious Von was out; the lower floor was cool and dark, feeling unlived-in. Apart from some muffled noises upstairs--the other guest, Sal assumed, in the communal bathroom--the building was empty. Sal was glad for that, though. He wanted to catch his breath in peace and quiet.

They went to the room Sal and his father shared. He dug out his spare set of clothes, changed into them while Shilly turned her back, and set the wet ones out to dry in the light coming through the window. The memory of salty water flooding down his throat and into his lungs was still strong. He tried to think about something else.

"When you say scabs, you mean seagulls, right?"

She nodded. "That's one of their names. Around here, anyway."

"So why did you say I should watch out for them? They're just birds."

"Hello? Weren't you on the jetty an hour ago? They *attacked* us."

He remembered the blur of beak, claw and wing almost as vividly as he remembered the sea. It certainly seemed as though the birds had been united in their assault. "But *why?* And how did you know they would do it?"

She looked down at her hands. "I didn't. Not exactly. I just figured they might not like you. Or your kind--from inland."

"Why not?"

"They're more than birds, sometimes, although even as birds they're pretty dislikeable. They're scavengers--the rats of the sea. But they're sensitive to the Change and can be used as spies. The Sky Wardens like them, because the scabs extend their power onto land. They can fly a fair distance and they have no scruples. The scabs, I mean."

He went cold. "You mean the Sky Wardens made them attack us?"

"No." She looked uncertain, and he suspected she was as out of her depth as he was. "They might have been acting on instinct. Maybe they saw something they didn't like and tried to get rid of it."

She raised her hand as though to point, but the sound of footsteps approaching the door made them freeze. After the experience on the jetty, they were both jumpy. Sal didn't know what to expect next from Fundelry.

The footsteps came steadily closer, but passed the door without breaking rhythm. Sal--who had hoped it might be his father--assumed that either Von or her other guest had walked innocently along the corridor.

The thought of his father did give him some concern, though.

"Don't worry about him," said Shilly when Sal brought it up. "He'll hear soon enough, wherever he is. It's a small town and word travels fast. Will he be angry at you, do you think? At us?"

Sal lay back on his bed, glad for the warmth of the room. "No. He'll just worry. He's always told me to be careful of water."

Shilly eyed him crookedly. "You like your dad, don't you?"

"Yes, of course I do."

"Don't act like it's a stupid question. Lots of people don't like their parents. I never even knew mine. But I guess you don't have much choice, do you? There's no one else to talk to, out on the road. If you didn't get on, you'd go crazy."

A door opened and closed downstairs. The movements

around him were making him nervous. "So what do we do now?" Sal asked. "We can't sit around here all day."

She pulled a face. "I suppose not. People will *really* begin to talk. Perhaps I should get you away from here for a while. Show you around the area instead."

"I saw most of it the day after I arrived."

"Not the most interesting stuff, I'll bet." She bounced off the bed with a grin. "Yeah, that's it. Let's go."

Sal hesitated briefly, but sitting around was only going to give him time to dwell on what had happened. And it wasn't as if he had been hurt. Getting out would probably do him good.

He stopped to write a brief note for his father, telling him that everything was okay. As he bent over the yellowing scrap of paper, Shilly pointed at his ear.

"Right. And I'd take *that* off if I were you."

He put a hand to his ear-ring. "Why?"

"It might attract attention. You're getting enough of that as it is. If Holkenhill had noticed it, things might've turned out very differently."

Sal remembered the way she had clutched his head as he had recovered from his impromptu swim--not out of concern for his health, it seemed, but to hide the ear-ring. His *ward*, as Lodo had called it.

"Just who *is* this Holkenhill?"

"I'll tell you on the way." She opened the door. "Put the damned thing around your neck or in a pocket and let's get moving."

He found a piece of string thin enough to go through one of the three small holes in the silver arc of the ear-ring, yet strong enough to trust, and tied it around his neck so that the ward hung on his chest. It felt strange there, rather than in his ear. He felt oddly vulnerable.

Vulnerable or not, he followed Shilly out of the hostel and away from the square. At first Sal thought she was taking him towards the secret entrance to Lodo's workshop, and he memorized every landmark they passed, but as they left the town she took them in a different direction--inland

and northeast, not along the old road. Instead, she skirted several empty houses and their weed-choked yards on the edge of town. They scrambled through dense scrub until she reached the steep, crumbling walls of a dry riverbed, then led him along its sandy bottom. The air was still and hot, and within minutes he was sweating.

"Holkenhill?" he prompted her. Their voices were the only sounds apart from the buzzing of insects.

"Euan Holkenhill is our local Selector's representative," she said. "The Strand is huge, and each Selector has a large area to cover, so they appoint reps to look after districts of five to ten towns." She stopped at the look on his face. "You already know this. Okay. Well, Holkenhill is our local rep. He comes from Showell, three towns along, and sweeps by once or twice a year to make sure everything's in order, and to collect application forms, which he's probably doing at the moment. That's why you have to be careful. He's not a Warden, but he's not an idiot, either. He'll realize in the end."

The Selector's representative ... A shiver went through him. Euan Holkenhill was just one step away from a Sky Warden! Habitual fear cast the encounter in a completely new light. How close had he been to giving everything away?

Then annoyance stirred in him. *What* had he almost given away? Shilly obviously had some idea. Everyone seemed to know more about what was going on than him.

"Realize *what*?"

"You really don't know?" She looked at him sharply, suspiciously. "As I said before, I've got a feeling there's something going on. You and your father; your father and Lodo; Lodo and me; me and you. If I had a grain of talent in me, maybe I could tell. But I haven't, so I can't. All I can do is use my brain--and that's served me in pretty good stead so far in my life."

She picked up a fallen stick and swished it through a patch of tall grass, scattering seeds.

"Someone's up to something, and I'm determined to find out what it is."

"Maybe you're just being paranoid," he suggested, half-heartedly playing devil's advocate.

She flicked a stone at him. "Smile when you say that."

"No, really. Why should Holkenhill care about my ward? It doesn't mean anything. If it has any effect at all, it can't be that big. It certainly didn't work when I fell in the sea."

"It didn't save you from the sea because metalworking is a Stone Mage art, and the sea belongs to the Sky Wardens. Don't you know anything?"

He felt himself blush. "Not about the Change. That's *your* specialty, remember?"

"It should be everyone's. It's all around us. How can you avoid it?"

"Dad doesn't like talking about it."

"Is that so?" Her irritation turned to interest again. "Seems odd that he's looking for Lodo, then, doesn't it?"

Sal shrugged, finding the conversation uncomfortable. They walked for a while in silence, until he asked: "Where are we going?"

"Not much further."

"That wasn't what I asked."

"I know. But if you just *wait* you'll find out for yourself."

He rolled his eyes and kept on walking.

* * *

Shilly was true to her word. Barely had they walked another five minutes when he knew they had arrived. He noticed a slight change in the vegetation on the river banks; the trees became denser and the shadows between them darker. They rounded a sharp bend in the ancient river, and there it was.

He thought, at first, that it was a wall: a wall ten feet high blocking the riverbed, like a dam. But he knew it couldn't be a dam. Clearly, no water had run along the riverbed for years, and it had probably never been enough to warrant damming even when it had. Also, it stood taller than the banks, and stretched out of sight in either direction without curving, the left side markedly higher than the right. There were marks in places that looked like faded writing, at an angle of nearly ninety degrees to the horizontal, but he couldn't read them even though he tried.

Shilly stopped and held out her hands to frame the sight. "Here you go. Worth the wait?"

"It's a Ruin, isn't it?"

"It is indeed." She led him closer to the right-hand bank. "People in town know about it, but they avoid it on the grounds that it's supposed to be haunted. It's not, but we don't discourage them from believing it. Lodo and I come here when we don't want to be interrupted."

"Has it been surveyed?"

"Yes, a long time ago. I don't know what they found, but there's nothing interesting left. Except the place itself."

She climbed up the embankment, following the line of the wall. There she held out her hand to help him up. He could see where steps had been worn into the wall's crumbling brickwork. They led over the top.

"After you," she said. "Be careful of your footing when you're up, though, and don't wander off. I'll show you where to go."

Wondering what he would find, he clambered up the steps, eleven of them in total, and onto the top of the wall. There he straightened, and looked down.

The wall marked the side of a building, a building that seemed to have tipped over onto its side and now lay half-buried in the earth around it. Instead of a roof, Sal saw another wall stretching a good thirty paces before him, and then at least as much to either side. Whereas the wall he had just climbed up seemed to be intact, this one had sagged and collapsed in a wide circle that gaped like a mouth full of rotten teeth, open to the sky. What had once been interior walls and floors chopped the dark circle into segments; some of these had fallen in, but many remained intact. A large tree grew from the far side of the hole, its thin trunk snaking upward to the light and sprouting a dozen frail-looking, feathery branches that waved in a breeze Sal couldn't feel.

Someone had laid planks across the gaps between the

intact interior walls. They marked out a zigzag path from one side of the hole to the other.

Shilly scrambled up beside him. "What do you think?"

He didn't know how to describe what he felt. "It's amazing."

"You can feel it? Around us?"

He nodded. "The air is--is *buzzing.*"

"Like bees?"

"No, not exactly." His head was light, as though he'd been breathing too quickly. "When someone plays a didj, if you touch the wood you can feel the sound in your fingers. This is like that, but without the sound."

"Interesting." She raised her eyebrows, then lowered them. "I see it in the light. It twinkles here--everything's a bit sparkly around the edges. Lodo says he smells it. Maybe there's no right way to describe what we're picking up." There was an excitement in her expression that he had seen before: when she had lit the fire in Lodo's workshop. "It's the Change, Sal--or a remnant of it, anyway. You've never felt it before?"

Sal shook his head.

"Well, you're going to love it."

Sal inched further onto the "roof" of the structure. He wanted to explore the contents of the hole to see if the Sky Warden surveyors had missed something, but at the same time he was nervous. What if the surveyors *had* left something behind, and it turned out to be dangerous? There were stories about people who had met horrible deaths in ruined cities and buildings not dissimilar to this one. He had never believed any of them before--but here, feeling the weirdness in the air, he was no longer so certain.

"Come on. Let's go down." Shilly stepped carefully across the rough, stone surface, heading for the nearest of the wooden planks. "Watch carefully, and only step where I step. If you fall, you'll die. The bottom of this thing is a lot lower than the ground around it."

Sal swallowed his nervousness and followed. If she could do it, so could he, and this time there wasn't any water to be afraid of--only height. He followed her to the edge of the hole, then out across it, waiting until she had crossed the first of the planks before stepping out after her. It wobbled slightly beneath his weight, but was wide and didn't bend much. Both ends of the plank were firmly anchored onto stone, the far end fixed to a wall scarcely wider than his two feet end to end. It was quite solid, though. What had looked like a dangerously haphazard arrangement from a distance turned out to be a relatively safe fixture of the place, perhaps maintained by Lodo and Shilly, he thought.

Even though he knew it might be a bad idea, he couldn't resist looking down as he crossed the next gap. The space below was like a canyon, with sheer walls dropping straight down and extending some distance to either side of him. He could see ledges further down that had probably been more walls, and a hole that might once have been a stairwell, although there were no stairs to be seen any more. The very bottom was invisible: the tops of trees, similar to the one he had noticed growing out into the sunlight, overlapped, creating a dense mat that light couldn't penetrate from above.

Coolness and birdsong radiated from the depths as he walked the plank. It was like stepping over another world.

They crossed two more plank bridges, the last angling down to a rubble-strewn platform inside the fallen building itself. From there, through what had once been a doorway but was now a hole, a rope ladder descended into the darkness.

"Wait until I'm down, then follow me."

Shilly swung herself into the hole and climbed down without hesitation. Sal still couldn't see the bottom. With each rung she slipped further away from the daylight, losing first color, then definition. The buzzing in the air was much stronger.

Then he realized that he was *feeling* the buzz, on his chest. When he slipped the ward out of his tunic and held it to his ear, he could actually hear a tiny hum.

The jiggling of the ladder ceased, and Shilly stopped

shrinking. He assumed she had reached the bottom, although he couldn't see what she was standing on.

Her voice floated up to him. "Okay, your turn!"

Sal took a deep breath and did as she had done. The ladder was more stable than it looked, the rope dry and rough on his hands. He couldn't look down so he looked up instead, taking one careful step at a time, not letting go with either hand until he was completely certain of his footing. The rectangle of sky above him slowly shrank as he passed through fronds of trees then climbed below even them, into darkness.

Then her hands gripped his waist and steadied him down the last few steps. He tore his gaze from the rectangle of blue and looked around, his eyes slowly adjusting to the gloom. He was standing on a rough stone floor in what looked like a cave. The last few rungs had taken him through a wide gash in the floor of the fallen structure and into the natural earth. The remaining lip of wall acted as a rough ceiling, under which deep shadows hid all details from sight. In the dim light filtering down from above, Sal saw tree roots snaking in and out of the dirt, forming a rough circle around a large, angular chunk of rock protruding from the floor.

The chunk of rock looked like an altar. Had there been no light at all, he would still have known it was there: the hum was strongest in the rock, as though it was the source. On it lay several oddly shaped stones, varying from one of Sal's knuckles to his clenched fist in size. They didn't look like the sort of ancient artifact that would hurt anyone.

The way Shilly was watching him, though, as if waiting to see what he would do next, her eyes glittering in the gloom, made him nervous. Her dark skin blended into the shadows a little too perfectly.

"Why did you bring me here?" he asked.

"Because..." She hesitated. "Well, there's more than one reason, although none of them really add up. Lodo tells me that instincts are no substitute for learning, but that neither is any good without the other. I'm following an instinct now." She picked up one of the stones on the altar-like rock. "This is a special place. There are things he can teach me here that he can't at the workshop. We're closer to the bedrock, as well as the old times. If I'm ever going to tease a bit of the Change out of the background on my own, it'll be here."

She offered him the stone, and he took it. A single groove ran around the stone's entire surface, beginning in a deep indentation at the top and ending similarly at the base. It was heavier than it looked and seemed to vibrate, like his ear-ring.

"How old are you?" she asked.

"Twelve," Sal replied. "Almost thirteen."

"I thought it would be something like that. You're due, then."

"Due for what?"

"Thirteen is the age when successful male applicants are Selected by the Sky Wardens; girls tend to be a little younger. I'm a little older than you. Lodo waited for a sign that anything at all might come from me, but it didn't arrive, even though he'd been teaching me to be ready if it did. I think he'd suspected all along, really, but made me his apprentice anyway. He needs someone to clean all his stuff." She grimaced. "But not you. You're full up. Aunty Merinda saw it straightaway, and so did Lodo, when she told him. The scabs feel it too. Even I can feel it. You're full up and starting to brim over."

"Full of *what*?"

"The Change, of course."

His face felt hot. "That's what you think is going on, is it?"

"Yes. You saw Elina's flower. You saw Lodo lighting the globes, and you saw his face through the illusion. That's more than most people. And when the seagulls attacked us--do you remember? I was angry. We were touching, and something happened. The birds scattered for a second; I felt something go through me like a hot wind. Like when I use Lodo's talent, except Lodo wasn't anywhere nearby. There was only you, and I was holding onto you to stop you falling.

You have to touch someone to use their talent. So it had to be you."

"But--"

"Don't bother saying you don't know anything about it," she interrupted him. "That's the way it happens to most people outside the Sky Warden Lines--or the Clans, I guess. It just appears. Like it or not, you have the Change, or you're getting it. My advice to you is to like it. I'd kill to be in your shoes."

Her eyes were intense, even in the gloom. He turned away, looking for something to sit down on. His legs felt weak. He had the Change? Impossible. It just couldn't be. He couldn't create fire out of nothing, as Shilly had, or call light from glass like Lodo; he couldn't alter the weather, summon fish or fowl, or do any of the other things he had heard about the Sky Wardens. He wouldn't know what to do with it, even if he *did* have the Change.

He found a thick root and eased himself onto it, subconsciously moving away from the rock altar but still holding the carved stone in his right hand.

"You don't believe me," she said. It wasn't a question.

He shook his head.

"I could be wrong," she admitted. "There's really only one way to find out. Well, two ways. We could wait for your voice to break and puberty to really kick in; by then we'll know for sure. You'll either have it or you won't, and any flutters that come or go beforehand will have settled down for good."

"I'll be long gone by then," he said, hoping against hope that it was true.

"Exactly, and I'm impatient. I want to know now."

"You want to use me," he said.

"No. I want to test you."

"By using my powers."

"They're not *powers,* Sal, and they're not *yours.* The Change just *is,* and you can be part of it sometimes. If what I think is right, anyway."

"How can I have the Change and it not belong to me?"

She shook her head. "That's not the way it works, Sal. It's a gift, not a thing you can own. It's a responsibility too, Lodo says. I don't know what he means half the time but I think I understand that. I want it, but can't have it. If it could be got, could be owned, I'd have a found a way. Lodo would've shown me. This isn't something I'd happily miss out on, no matter what it costs."

"And what if I'm not like you--if I don't want it?" he asked.

"Don't you? Really?"

That was another question with no easy answer. Sky Wardens and Stone Mages were legendary figures looming over the Interior and the Strand. Few people met more than one or two in their lifetimes, and then only briefly, when Selection time came, but their deeds and histories were foremost in the cultures of both countries. Even a lowly weather-worker or seer lived a better life than most, given just a little talent. He would be a fool to say no, given the choice.

Instead of speaking, he reached out to take her hand. As soon as their skin touched, he felt a strange sensation thrill through him, as though something simultaneously cold and hot had slid down his spine.

Shilly stiffened and took a deep breath. She closed her eyes, and the cave-like chamber beneath the ancient building suddenly felt much darker. In Sal's other hand, the carved stone seemed to grow in size. The deep hum from the altar swelled in his mind, in his bones, until it dominated the entire world around him. There was only the hum, the throbbing stone in one hand and Shilly's skin in the other. He couldn't even feel himself breathing.

Shilly's fingers tightened on his, and a light flared in the darkness.

With a soundless explosion, the rock in his fist blossomed like the sun. Not pale blue like the fire in his memory, *this* was white and bright, flaring through his fingers as easily as though they were air. Beams of light cast the shadows aside, throwing every nook and cranny into sharp relief. Sal saw the crumbling former wall sagging above them, shedding dust, and thick roots lacing the earth below. They met in oddly regular niches all around them, tiny spaces difficult for even a child to crawl into--and from each glinted the white of bone. Dozens of animal skulls stared back at him, wide-eyed, from the recesses of Lodo and Shilly's secret space.

He gasped and pulled free. Instantly the darkness returned, and he was blind behind a bright purple after-image.

"What?" asked Shilly, her voice annoyed. He knew why: the last thing he had seen before killing the light was her face, eyes tightly closed, smiling, reveling in the Change.

He opened his mouth to describe what he had seen, then shut it. Oddly, the thought of all the dead animals around him didn't bother him. They were part of the place, and he wasn't threatened by the place as a whole. He had just been startled by the sight. If she knew they were there, they obviously didn't bother her either.

"Nothing," he said. "It was just too bright." He squeezed the rock in his hand. It was warming slowly to the temperature of his fingers but was otherwise unaltered.

He couldn't say the same about himself. He felt flushed and confused. Changed *himself,* somehow, in a way he couldn't define. He had no idea what, exactly, Shilly had done, but the feeling that had passed through him, into her, tugged at him. Although he was nervous that he might be doing the wrong thing, part of him wanted to try again, very much wanted to try again.

He could feel her uncertainty, her fear that he would ask to leave. She wanted to try again, too.

"Maybe you should go a little easier next time," he said, giving in.

"Easier? I wasn't even trying."

"Well..." He couldn't see her face. "Try something different, then. An illusion, like Elina's, perhaps? You said you were learning."

He felt her nod. "Can you draw?"

"No."

"Well, that's okay. I can do that side of it. Know any bird calls, then?"

"What's that got to do with--?"

"Don't worry about it. We'll make it up as we go along." She moved away from him, and he heard her rearranging the stones on the altar. "Come over here and let's see what happens."

He stood, but didn't obey immediately. The memory of the light--its potency and purity, its sheer power--made him hesitate.

"Are you sure it's all right to do this?"

"Yes. Positive."

If she was at all uncertain about that, she kept it carefully hidden from her voice.

CHAPTER 7

A MEETING OF SORTS

THE sun was sinking by the time Sal and Shilly left the cave under the Ruins and headed back to Fundelry. A light breeze rustled through the scrub, bringing with it scents Sal was used to--dust and leaves rather than salt and fish. He was, for several minutes, quite disoriented. The smells reminded him of the life he had always taken for granted, whereas everything he had seen under the Ruins, still hanging fresh in his mind, came from another world entirely.

He had not expected how easily the Change in him had been harnessed to Shilly's will. Far from being a simple demonstration of what she had learned, the illusions she had called forth from the darkness had unnerved him completely. Birds and beasts, snakes and insects, solid or ghostly, brightly colored or drab--all had materialized at her mental command, and vanished just as readily. Without any volition of their own, they were perfectly docile and obeyed every spoken instruction. The only thing they lacked was sound: whether it was horse or python, dog or red-breasted robin, not one of the illusions ever made a noise.

All it had taken was a rough sketch in the dirt floor, an imitation call, or even the vaguest outline drawn in the air, and out they had poured: an endless series of animals that had seemed, at times, to startle Shilly just as much as Sal.

Perhaps strangest of all was the dolphin Shilly had drawn with dust on one of the low banks beneath the overhanging "roof" of the cave. He hadn't realized what it was at first, thinking it to be a person lying on their side, asleep. Animated, the dolphin had circled them silently through the stone walls as though swimming through water, one eye fixed always on them.

Later, when Shilly *had* tried to create the illusion of a person, the figure had refused to come to life, hovering on the edge of drawing and reality as though seen through a heat haze, then suddenly vanishing into nothing at all.

Shilly was silent on the way back, her expression one of concentration. Sal was tired and his chest was still sore, but Shilly showed no signs of fatigue--and hadn't once in the cave. If anything, she could have stayed longer. Had it not been for his father and a lingering sense of guilt, she might have insisted.

"Don't you see?" she had asked him, gripping his arm tightly to maintain the link between them. Her skin was hot, feverish. "This is what life is about. The Change is everything. Without the Change, there's nothing."

Her intensity had frightened him a little. He had been relieved when she had eventually agreed that they'd explored enough--and confirmed her suspicions about him, which is what they had set out to do.

He felt dizzy just thinking about it, as though he was back on one of the wooden planks, teetering over the drop. *He had the Change*, or the beginnings of it, anyway. There was a flicker of something in him that he had never suspected before. Even if it faded away, later, it deserved to be explored. That much at least he agreed with Shilly about.

He wondered if that was why his father had brought him to Fundelry, and why he was looking for Lodo. Perhaps he too had seen it building in his son and hoped to find a way to use it.

But if that was the case, why had he kept all knowledge about the Change hidden from Sal--not just throughout his life, but even now, on the brink of its emergence in himself?

The breeze stiffened, throwing dust into his eyes. He shook his head, clearing it. There was no point guessing blindly, he told himself. He would have to ask his father. And if what he and Shilly now knew turned out to have no relation to why they were in Fundelry, it might yet prove useful ...

They were met by Lodo on the edge of the small town. Shilly saw him first.

"Uh-oh," she said.

"What?"

"The old boy's upset about something."

Sal peered ahead and saw Lodo walking towards them at a rapid pace, his arms swinging wildly. He was too far away to determine his expression. "How can you tell?"

"I just can." As the old man came into earshot, she glanced at Sal from under the tangle of her fringe and hissed: "Here's hoping it's not over us."

The deep scowl visible on Lodo's face as he came closer didn't put Sal's mind at ease. When he spoke his annoyance was clear:

"What have you two ...?"

He stopped in mid-sentence and mid-step, and sniffed the air. "No, Shilly, tell me you haven't!"

Shilly put on an innocent look. "Haven't what?"

"You know what I'm talking about," Lodo snapped. "Of all the stupid things to do. I expect much better of you than this!"

"Why?"

Sal was lost until he recalled what Shilly had said about Lodo smelling the Change, rather than seeing or hearing it. Lodo could tell what they had been doing, and his glare was terrifying. Sal felt as though he was being physically struck as those dark gray eyes were turned full on him.

Lodo ignored Shilly's question. "Where?" he asked.

"The Ruins," she answered. For the first time since Sal had met her, she sounded defensive and uncertain. "I thought--"

"Ah, well!" To Sal's surprise, Lodo's wrinkled face broke out into a relieved grin. "Thank goodness. Even if you didn't know what you were doing, you did it the best possible way. Come on. We might yet salvage something."

He stepped between Sal and Shilly, grabbed each of them by their upper arms--his fingers digging deep into their flesh--and led them into Fundelry. Wincing, Sal could do nothing but let himself be led. He received the distinct impression that Lodo was keeping him and Shilly apart as much as making sure they came along quietly.

"Your father is waiting for you, boy," the old man said, his tone more calm than before, but still urgent. "Von has had a hard time of it, making sure he stayed put until you got back. I don't know what he'd rather have done, but he hasn't liked waiting. You should do your best to reassure him that nothing untoward has happened."

"Nothing has," Sal asserted. "Has it?"

"That depends entirely on where you're standing." He shot Sal a stern look as he dragged them through the quiet streets toward the square.

"Look, Lodo," said Shilly, "if anyone's at fault, it's me--"

"I agree, but that doesn't mean you're to blame. You didn't know that what you were doing was dangerous." Lodo thought for a second, then asked: "What *did* you do, exactly?"

"Just illusions."

"That's all?"

"I swear."

"Good were they?"

She nodded.

"I thought they might be. Ah." They stopped, having reached the rear of the hostel, where Lodo finally let go of their arms. "Now, Shilly, I want you to go back to the workshop and continue with your exercises." He raised a hand as she started to protest. "I know you think you've already done enough for today, but don't argue. I'll tell you what happens here when I get back."

The struggle was plain on her face, but in the end she did as she was told. With a silent glance at Sal, she turned and hurried back towards the dunes.

"You, Sal," Lodo said, "are going inside to talk to your father."

"What about you?"

"I'll wait out here."

"No." Sal shook his head. "I want you to meet him, properly, to see if you're the man he's been looking for."

"Why?"

"Because..." He hesitated, having no good reason to think that putting Lodo and his father together would actually be for the best. He simply wanted to do it to get rid of that part of the puzzle.

"Because," he said instead, "you've been checking *him* out without him knowing, and he deserves the chance to return the favor."

Lodo nodded slowly. "I suppose that's fair. You go in first, though, and I'll join you later. When the light appears in your room I'll know it's safe to talk in private." He indicated the setting sun. "I have work to do."

Sal glanced at the reddening sky--remembering the globes and the light Lodo called forth from them at the end of every day. That it could be nightfall already struck him as ridiculous. It seemed only an hour had passed since he had woken on the beach, choking for air, and he wondered where the afternoon had gone. *In dreams*, he told himself.

Taking a deep breath, he walked around the corner of the hostel and up to the front door.

"Sal!" His father was out of the kitchen before the door had shut with a gentle click behind him. "You're finally back! Where have you been?"

Sal stopped in the hallway as his father approached. There was a look in his eyes he hadn't seen before: part fear, part anger, part something Sal couldn't immediately identify. It threw him.

"I wasn't feeling well, so--so a friend took me for a walk."

"A friend? Who?"

"It's okay," Sal said, hoping it was. "She's just someone from School. I left you a note--"

"You did, but you didn't say where you were going or who you were with."

"We didn't go anywhere much. Just around." Von had followed Sal's father and stood leaning in the kitchen doorway. Her face was expressionless. "I'm feeling better now, anyway."

"Are you sure?"

"Yes, Dad, really."

"I hope so." His father looked like he didn't know whether to come closer or move away. "I was mending a fence out of town when I heard you'd fallen off the jetty. I came as soon as I could, but you weren't here and no one knew where you'd got to. I thought--well, I didn't know what to think. I was worried."

Another emotion took the dominant place in his father's expression: concern, deep and overriding.

"Don't do this again, son."

Sal was already regretting everything he had done that day. He didn't need to be asked. "I won't, Dad, and I'm sorry. I didn't mean to--"

"You don't have to apologize, Sal." His father approached, put both hands on his shoulders and squeezed. Although there was a difference in their heights, Sal felt as though they were looking eye to eye. "It's not your fault. I trust you. And you *did* leave a note. It's just..." A flicker of pain passed through his father's brown eyes. "I'm over-reacting, I guess. That you're safe is the main thing."

Sal didn't know what to say. There was more than just concern of his near-drowning behind his father's reaction, he was sure of it. But if there was more to worry about--if he was in any danger--why didn't his father just *say*?

But rather than pursuing the subject, his father let him go and turned away. "So, you've made a friend."

"Kind of. I think."

"Good, good. Are you hungry? I've paid for a meal. You can tell us where you went while you eat."

Sal hadn't eaten since breakfast, but Von's expressionless eyes were watching him. "I'm tired more than anything."

His father shrugged. "Then we can put it on credit for tomorrow. You'll wake up hungry, I'll bet." He turned to Von. "Is that okay?"

"Fine." The manager of the hostel turned her back on them and disappeared into the kitchen.

His father's palm between his shoulders guided Sal up

the stairs, to their room. The hand was large and strong, and had always seemed to Sal to be as steady as a rock, but now, for the first time, he thought he felt it tremble.

"Are *you* okay, Dad?"

The slight pressure disappeared. "Yes, of course. I had a shock when I heard about you. You won't go near the sea again, will you? You don't know how to swim. It can be dangerous."

Sal remembered the insistent tug of the current around his body and the burning in his lungs. He heard again the ghostly call of a woman who, in his dreams, he imagined might be his mother. "Wild camels couldn't drag me back."

"Good."

Sal opened the door of the room, noting that there was still no sign of the other tenant in the long, narrow hallway. An oil lamp was already burning low on the chest holding most of their belongings. Sal walked into the room and increased the flame from a yellow flicker to a steady, white column. Through the window he caught a glimpse of one of Lodo's glass globes shining in the night--its light as white and pure as that which Shilly had called forth in the cave-- but no sign of the old man himself.

Dark shapes wheeled across the sky: a flock of seagulls heading to a nesting ground.

Shivering, Sal pulled the blind down, confident that the lamp's light would shine through it. Lodo would know it was safe to come, if he was as good as his word and watching from somewhere out of sight.

Then he sat on his bed and took off his shoes. His feet were aching and his skin stung as though burned. He wanted to lie back on the bed and shut his eyes, to rest, just for a moment, but he forced himself not to. If Lodo *did* show up, he wasn't going to miss it.

On the other side of the room, his father was doing exactly what Sal wanted to do. Never one to delay sleep, if possible, for long after sunset, he had already slipped out of his shoes and work-shirt and put his feet up on the bed.

"I don't think Von likes me very much," said Sal. Anything to keep his father awake.

"Oh, I wouldn't say that. Maybe she's a little cautious, but you know what small towns are like. Everyone's suspicious of strangers at first. That's the way it goes."

Sal remembered the pronouncement made by Alder Sproule, Kemp's father, at the fair and the look of suspicion he had cast upon them. "Have there been any more thefts?"

"Not that I'm aware of." His father looked at him from under a raised eyebrow. "Why? Have you got a guilty conscience?"

"No."

"I didn't think so." He relaxed against the wall and closed his eyes. "And I know you'll keep it that way. Remember what happened to Polain the butterfly merchant."

Sal leaned forward. "Tell me again."

"You've heard it a million times."

"But not for ages. Please, Dad?"

"Well..." He opened his eyes and sighed in resignation. "All right. But you let me get some rest afterwards, okay? I've got a lot of work to do tomorrow."

Sal nodded and sat cross-legged on the bed to hear the story. Although he knew it by heart, he was glad for the opportunity to keep sleep at bay.

"In the times before the Change," his father began, "there was a man who sold butterflies. His name was Polain-- Polain the butterfly merchant. He lived in a metal and glass city that was larger than any built before or since, and beautiful in a way we don't see any more. There were many things to do and see in the city, but the butterflies bred and sold by Polain were numbered among the greatest. Buyers came from all around the world to purchase eggs and larvae, confident that each caterpillar and butterfly would be unique. For that was Polain's Guarantee: never once did any of his creatures repeat a pattern, no matter how fervently some of his competitors hoped that they might. And hope they did, for if it happened even once, Polain's reputation would be tarnished forever.

"Needless to say, it was difficult to maintain such a Guarantee. The harder Polain worked and the more years went by, the more butterflies he sold and so the more difficult it became to be absolutely certain that each was a true individual. In order to do so, he kept a record-- detailing the number of spots, the shading and hue of the colors, the precise shape of the wings and antennae, and the total mass at maturity--of each one, and the number of records mounted rapidly. As his popularity grew, people came in boats and cars and flying carriages to purchase his wares, some intending to breed from them or keep them as specimens, but most sporting them as badges of wealth- -trifles to flitter about the house until the butterfly died, giving delight for a short time only, and quickly forgotten.

"Ten years into Polain's career--after beginning with a single, humble stall and a small stack of notebooks--he had three separate rooms full of records. At the time of this story, he had rented a small warehouse and employed five clerks to maintain and conduct searches through the catalogues. Sometimes it took more than a day to ascertain that a single promising butterfly was indeed one of a kind. Literally one in a million.

"With no understanding of or concern for their patron's situation, his insects bred without check. In vast glasshouses next to the warehouse full of records--with temperature and humidity kept constant by machines the like of which we have long lost--eggs were laid, caterpillars hatched, pupae were woven and butterflies emerged, limp and fragile, into their new world. Many were redundant, repetitions of ones that had existed before; many *might* have been new, but time didn't allow a thorough search through all the minuscule nuances on file. Only the most dramatically different were chosen, the ones that stood out as being brilliant in some novel and pleasing way. Only these were sold.

"Naturally, Polain's output dropped steadily through this time. Demand had not fallen, however, for butterflies live far shorter lives than their fanciers, and in the city of glass and steel little true color remained. Also, as word spread that Polain's handiwork was becoming scarce, it increasingly became a sign of prestige that one should possess an example of it. Polain could ask more and more money for each creation and people would still buy. As his clientele became richer and more discerning, his sales dropped to a handful a month, then a handful a year. Long gone were the days when he would sell butterflies by the jarful on a street corner to anyone who passed.

"All in all, Polain was proud of his achievements, even though he knew it couldn't last. The demand for butterflies would drop in time, to be replaced by some other fancy requiring a fortune. This thought didn't bother him. He was becoming tired of the endless checking and re-checking. He wanted to retire. One of his competitors could take his place, and he would go back to breeding butterflies for fun, not profit.

"Now, it happened that in a matter of weeks of him arriving at this decision, the queen of a distant and powerful country was due to visit the city. He publicly announced his impending retirement with a promise to present this queen with the last truly unique Polain butterfly in the world. It would be his masterpiece, and he would devote all his efforts to its creation. She would take it home confident in the knowledge that she was carrying a piece of history. Nothing like it would have existed before. That, after all, was his Guarantee.

"And so he set to work, mingling strains in time-proven ways in some glasshouses, and cross-breeding new strains in others. Hungry caterpillars devoured leaves by the million, swarming in green and brown tides across veritable forests. Thousands of butterflies were born and died with a shiver of wings, their individually inaudible rustlings adding up to a cacophony, deafening the feeders who tended them and the clerks who studied them. It was a symphony to Polain's ears. He would make a butterfly fit for a queen, no matter what it took. All he needed was one to put into the special bell-shaped jar he had constructed for it.

"Just one."

Sal's father paused in the telling of the ancient tale in the same place he always did. For him, Sal knew, the pleasure lay in building the world, setting the scene, rather than the story itself. "You know what happens."

"Yes." Sal nodded, feeling as though he was out on the road and much younger, listening to the tale by the light of a camp fire. It was a great relief to return to a world where Sky Wardens didn't exist, even if it was an imaginary one. "It's not as easy to find the one butterfly as he'd thought it would be."

"No. In all the millions he breeds, beautiful though they are, the last unique one eludes him. Too many have matches in the catalogues. Some are beautiful in ways that excite the eye. Others are flawed, or do not mate well, or die too young, sickly and weak from inbreeding. As time passes, Polain becomes anxious. He stays longer and longer in the glasshouses with the feeders and clerks, pacing up and down through the feather-soft fluttering, and seeking, always seeking, for the one he knows must come. It has to. If it doesn't, he will be humiliated in front of everyone--the queen, the people of the city, his competitors.

"As the deadline approaches, the fear of failure mounts in him as it never has before. What if the right butterfly *doesn't* come in time? What if he has exhausted every possible variety and no new ones remain? What will he do? He wouldn't dream of substituting a fake--a butterfly modified in order to present a unique coloration. No matter how clever a forgery it was, it would be discovered eventually. He would be ruined in his finest hour. All his past work would be forgotten, and only his shame would survive.

"All too quickly the appointed time looms and still he has nothing. His dreams are filled with nightmares: he is mocked, taunted, jeered at as he arrives at the queen's reception holding in his hands nothing but a dry and dusty moth.

"Then, with just two days to spare, Polain is inspecting the butterflies in one of his auxiliary glasshouses when he spies an empty cocoon with unfamiliar spiral markings.

The cocoon is paper-thin and gray in color, except for the spirals which are soft pink. Polain raises it to his nose and sniffs. It has only recently been vacated. The butterfly that crawled from it can't be far away.

"He searches the branches and ground nearby. If he finds it in time, it will still be hardening its wings, anchoring itself against a stone or a twig to practice fluttering before joining the great throng above. Polain creeps carefully through the enclosure, wary of stepping before he has made absolutely certain that nothing is underfoot. His heart beats a little faster as he thinks: *Maybe this is the one. Maybe at last, at the last minute, my search will be over.*"

A knock at the door brought Sal's father abruptly out of the tale. He blinked as though unaware what had interrupted him, then put his feet over the side of the bed, ready to stand.

"Yes?" he called.

"May I come in?" said a male voice. "I understand you've been looking for me."

Sal's father stiffened. Sal sat straighter on his bed: the voice was Lodo's. He had become so wrapped up in the familiar tale that he had quite forgotten about the old man.

"Are you...?"

"I am Misseri, yes--although how you know of me is a mystery. No one has called me by that name for ten years or more. Would you care to tell me how you heard of it?"

Sal's father stood, wiped his hands on his pants and reached for the door handle. Story forgotten, he hesitated for a second, then opened the door.

Lodo stood, undisguised, in the hallway. His gray hair was held back from his dark forehead by a bronze clasp behind his ears, exposing the blue spirals tattooed on his temples and the pale gold rings high in his ears. His expression was patient, almost indulgent, but he looked much older than Sal remembered.

"It *is* you," said Sal's father.

"I'm glad to hear it." Lodo smiled. "But that leaves us with another mystery, I'm afraid. As far as I can recall, we've never met, yet you know me by sight. How is that?"

"No, no, we haven't met." Sal's father seemed to remember himself, and waved Lodo excitedly inside. "Not formally. But I know of you, and I did see you from a distance, once. It was a long time ago. I--" He stopped, swallowed, and continued more soberly. "I've been following your reputation."

"Oh?" Lodo's smile widened. "Now I have a reputation. What on earth did I do to acquire one of those?"

"You know very well ... what you were accused of, anyway."

Lodo's eyes narrowed. "And what do you know of my accusers?"

"That they lied, mainly. I didn't believe it at the time, and I don't believe it now, to see you here, in such firm spirit. But old charges stick, and they have followed you. Your presence in this region is known by some in high places-- perhaps even sanctioned, but not without a word or two of caution. It was a simple matter to inquire after scandal or rumors of scandal. People will happily talk about the misfortune of others. From there, it was just a matter of persistence. No matter how well you try to hide, your past will always follow you."

Lodo sighed. "You're right. I'm scarred by those years in the Haunted City. And if the Wardens continue to paint me in a bad light, then so be it; I return the favor often enough. But I'm no bigot, and no fool, either. The past I can accept-- but you? Who are you and what do you want with me? Tell me now, or let me get back to forgetting things better left forgotten."

Sal's father looked uncertain for a moment. To gain time he indicated that Lodo should sit on the bed, but the old man declined the offer, moving instead to lean against the windowsill between the two beds. Sal's father shut the door, glanced at Sal, and sat down.

"I need your help," he said, looking down at his hands as though frightened by the thought of what he might see if he looked up.

Lodo nodded. "Ask, then."

"No, it's not that easy." He spoke haltingly. "In fact,

coming to you is one of the most difficult things I've ever done--and I've only done it because you're the one person I'm prepared to trust. Not that I have much choice. No one else but you has the knowledge I need and, I hope, the inclination to use it in the way I need. The way *we* need..." Again he paused.

"You want me to train your son," said Lodo.

Sal's father looked up, eyes wide. Sal mentally chalked up a correct guess. "No--I mean, yes. In a sense. But for you to ask that, that means you can feel it. Already? Have I left it too late?"

Lodo raised a hand. "Not so fast." The old man shot Sal a fleeting look that said as clearly as anything: *patience.* Sal felt the tension leave him in a rush, and only then realized that he had been sitting on the edge of the bed, so intently focused on what was happening that he was as rigid as a board.

"Take it slowly." Lodo folded his arms. "Yes, I can feel the boy's talent. I felt it the moment he arrived in town. I've been watching you both since then, waiting for the moment to introduce myself, if that seemed the right thing to do." Another glance at Sal warned him to keep quiet about everything else that had happened. "When I heard that you'd been looking for me, I began to get curious. What do you want with me, if not to train your son? Innocent enough, I suppose, on the surface. But why me? Why now and not sooner? What do you mean by 'in a sense'? And who *are* you? You still haven't answered even that most basic of questions."

"No, and I'm sorry." Sal's father exhaled heavily, so heavily he seemed to deflate. He shook his head. "I don't know how to tell you everything you need to know--not right now. We're too vulnerable."

"You're in trouble?"

"Maybe. It's been a long time. I don't know. But I fear..." Sal's father stopped, searching for words.

"The past has talons in someone else, I gather," said Lodo with a grimace.

"Yes."

"So let's start with what I can guess. You haven't taken the boy to the Wardens. There must be a reason for that."

"Yes." Sal's father spoke very quietly. "Years ago, I took something from the Sky Wardens. Something they wanted to keep very much. They say I stole it." Sal thought immediately of the ward in his ear, but his father's gaze didn't drift anywhere near him. "To stop them getting it back, I ran as far as I could, to the very edge of the Strand, where I thought I was safe. But they found me, anyway. The Wardens took it back--and perhaps only luck saved me and my son from them, too." He did glance at Sal then, briefly. "I've always feared they'd come after me, so I've been careful. I swore never to let them take anything of mine again. That's why I won't go back to them now."

Lodo rubbed his chin. "The boy is powerful; there's no denying that. They'll want him, given the chance. But are you sure they'll still want you, too? You say this happened years ago. People forget, times change--"

"I'm not prepared to take that chance."

"You're already taking a chance, coming so deep into their territory."

"I know. Surely you are, too?"

"Sometimes it's easier to hide in a crowd than alone."

"I know. That might be our last hope."

"Indeed." Lodo folded his arms. "But it will become increasingly difficult to conceal the boy's potential. Uncontrolled talent is like a flare, shining for all with eyes to see. The gulls have noted him already, and only quick thinking on the part of my apprentice kept him from more probing eyes this morning. Next time you won't be so lucky."

Sal's father nodded. "I understand what you're saying, although I didn't realize how obvious it was becoming. I don't have any talent myself, so I can't see what you see. But there is still a chance we can do something about it."

"I wouldn't be so sure of that. Your timing is bad. The Selector will be here in just two weeks. Her representative is already in town."

"I'm aware of that. But that should be long enough."

Lodo's eyebrows went up. "To teach someone the Change? You must be joking. Even if I devoted myself completely to his training, you're talking about a job that would normally take years! And as I do already have an apprentice to deal with, at a crucial point in her training--"

"I'm not asking you to teach him *everything*--"

"That doesn't alter the fact that I'm an old man. Two students would be a handful, even with no deadline--not to mention the risk of getting on the wrong side of the Wardens. Again. So I'm sorry to have to say this, but I don't think I can give you what you need."

Sal's heart sank, and his father looked beaten. All the years of running radiated from him like grief.

"Is that your decision, then? I've come here for nothing?"

"Not necessarily." Lodo raised a finger and examined the nail. "I suppose I *could* take him on for a couple of weeks only, to teach him the basic principles of how to use his talent. What happens after then we can deal with when the Selector is gone. Would that be acceptable?"

Sal looked to his father, his hopes revived.

But his father shook his head. "You misunderstand me," he said. "I don't want you to teach him how to use it. I want you to teach him to *hide* it."

"They are much the same thing--"

"Not in effect. When Sal was born, I prayed that he would be like me. Now that I know he's not, we have to deal with it before it becomes a problem. If he doesn't know how to use the talent, and he can hide it from others, then we can get on with our lives--*safe*. We're better off without the Change. I don't want him to know anything that might hurt him."

Lodo studied him closely. "I fear that decision might not be yours to make."

"I have no choice but to make it, Misseri. It was taken out of my hands years ago."

Sal watched the two men debating with a feeling of dismay. The Change might not be something he owned, like a pair of shoes, but it was still his, while it lasted. He was certain he could learn to use it in ways that weren't harmful to anyone. Didn't *he* have a say?

But neither of them seemed to notice him. After a moment's thought, Lodo clicked his tongue and said, "Well enough, I suppose. First of all we should at least deal with the formalities. I'm not called Misseri any more, as I thought I'd made clear. It's Lodo."

Sal's father inclined his head. "I'm sorry, Lodo. I'll take more care in future. And we are--"

"No need to tell me. My new student is Sal and you prefer to be called Gershom--an unlikely use-name if ever I've heard one. I'm guessing you picked up the custom on the run and figured it would be good for maintaining your anonymity." His eyes took on a cunning glint. "'Exile' is a little too obvious for my tastes. I would have gone for something more subtle like 'adulterer'. Eh?"

Sal didn't entirely follow what Lodo was saying, so his father's reaction came as a surprise. His gaze didn't leave Lodo's face, and his tan skin went pale. He looked like a man who had just been challenged to a duel.

"Irrespective of that," he said, visibly pulling himself together, "the important thing is to keep Sal safe. That dunk in the ocean was one too many for my liking. How much will his tuition cost, and when will it commence?"

Lodo waved a hand dismissively. "Money isn't important to me here. I have everything I need close at hand. And as far as lessons go, I run to no fixed schedule. I'll have my apprentice, Shilly, come for Sal when we're ready. Until then ..."

Lodo stepped away from the windowsill and reached into his pocket. With a tinkle of red and yellow beads he produced a complicated charm and handed it to Sal.

"Wear this wherever you go, Sal. Around an ankle would be ideal. It's designed to anchor you more closely to the Earth, to the bedrock. It'll ground any stray discharges and make you harder to detect, protecting you from the gulls if nothing else."

Lodo folded the charm into Sal's outstretched hand and

closed Sal's fingers around it. He felt the expected tingle of the Change, followed by an odd sensation, as though everything around him had become dull and muted, even though to his eyes it looked the same.

Something of his surprise must have shown on his face, for Lodo nodded and said: "You've just lost your perception of the background potential. Don't worry about it. Six months ago you probably didn't even know it existed, and you won't miss it now. We'll remove the charm during lessons, and when you know how to contain yourself. Until then, don't take it off. I'll know if you do."

Lodo turned back to Sal's father. "I'll leave you for now. Goodnight."

"Thank you," Sal's father said, opening the door. "Dream well."

"Sleep is for lizards," said the old man, and left them alone.

Sal's father returned to his bed looking cautiously relieved and exhausted.

"Why--?"

"No questions, Sal. Not yet. Just do as he says and we'll see what happens. If there's another way out of this, we'll think of it in time, I'm sure." His frown belied his words. The lines on his forehead were deep in the yellow light of the lamp. So were the bags under his eyes.

"I'm sorry, son, but we'll have to skip the rest of the story."

"That's okay." Sal genuinely didn't mind. He knew well what happened to Polain on his quest for the last perfect butterfly--and the story had served its purpose, anyway.

His father slumped back onto the bed with a sigh. "Turn down the lamp, would you? We should've been asleep hours ago."

But Sal could tell that his father was far from sleep. As he too lay awake, he knew that what occupied his father's thoughts was not what he and Lodo had talked about, but all that had been left *unsaid* between them. Sal knew what an adulterer was, but why that word should have such an effect on his father, he couldn't guess. Perhaps it had something to do with the mother he had never met, or the thing Sal's father had stolen from the Sky Wardens.

But that didn't make sense. There was no reason for him to be so afraid of the Sky Wardens. They'd already taken the stolen object back, hadn't they? The matter was dealt with now. Old news.

And even if it wasn't, that was no reason for Sal to ignore his talent. It didn't make sense to turn down a gift some people would kill for.

He thought of Shilly, then, and wondered how she would react when she found out that they both were to be apprenticed to Lodo. Maybe she would be happy; maybe she wouldn't. Either way, he would've paid a fortune to see her face when she found out.

CHAPTER 8
VOICES ON AN ILL WIND

"STONE-BOY! Hey, stone-boy!"

Sal looked up from his book and immediately regretted it. Kemp and his gang were crossing the clearing toward him, shuffling like a single entity with many gangling limbs, a dozen staring eyes and six identical leers. If he hadn't acknowledged them by looking, they might just possibly have walked by. Now he had no choice but to respond.

"Hello," he said, cautiously rising to his feet.

"Have you dried out yet, stone-boy?" Kemp, for once, wasn't doing the talking. The ribbing came from a stocky youth sporting a dark, shaved scalp that gleamed brightly in the sunlight. "I hear you sank so fast they had to dredge you out of the harbor."

"Sank like a stone," added another voice.

"Yeah," jeered the first. "Isn't that right, stone-boy? You've got rocks in your head?"

Sal wished he could use the Change and blast the lot of them into nothingness. Not that blasting would be necessary. Just a small display would demonstrate that he shouldn't be trifled with. After all, he might be a nobody now, but in years to come, if his talent was encouraged, he might become someone important. And he would *remember*.

But that was just a fantasy. He had no idea how to tap into the Change as Shilly had and therefore nothing to defend himself with but his mouth.

"All I've got in my head is brains," he said. "What about you?"

The bald youth's grin vanished. "I think we should conduct a little experiment," he proclaimed to the group, eyes narrowing. "Let's throw him in again and see what happens. If he goes down, we'll *know* he has rocks in his head--but if he comes up, his head's empty. That's what I call using my brains."

Sal's insides froze at the thought of going into the sea a second time, without anyone around to save him. They would make sure of that, this time.

"You wouldn't--"

"Hold it, guys," said Kemp, shouldering his way to the front. "Why are you wasting your time with this piece of dirt?"

"He said I was stupid!" The bald youth affected a look of hurt and consternation.

"Well, he's got a point. And you're ugly, too." Kemp smacked the youth lightly across the back of his skull, and the gang snickered at this reversal of fortune. "We're throwing him back, but only metaphorically. There are bigger fish for us to fry."

Sal stared as his tormentor backed down and away, leaving Kemp before him, his expression aloof and almost friendly.

"Thanks," said Sal, meaning it--although the sudden change of heart mystified him.

"Think nothing of it."

As the rest of the gang moved away, muttering among themselves, Kemp's expression changed into a sneer. His white face leaned close. The gap in his teeth loomed like a black cave.

"You'll get yours, stone-boy," he hissed. "You're mine."

Then he was gone, loping at the rear of his group like before--a warlord surrounded by his bodyguards, looking for prey elsewhere--and Sal was left behind, even more mystified than ever.

He had been reading *Battles Along the Kartinyeri Border*, an account of numerous clashes between the Sky Wardens and Stone Mages over a particularly contentious stretch of land. He had liberated it from the storage space under Von's stairs in the hope that it might keep him occupied. It was interesting enough. In his one School session so far, Mrs Milka had stated the official line that there was no conflict between the Interior and the Strand, despite the fact that the two countries had been squabbling on and off for centuries. Sal had heard of a memorial to the dead in the Haunted City as large as five Fundelrys, and of warrior caste Sky Wardens clad in blue ceramic and copper armor. He doubted such a long-held hostility could evaporate overnight and would have liked to talk to someone who knew more about it. Maybe Lodo. He made a mental note to ask him when he had the chance.

Unfortunately, Shilly hadn't appeared that day to take him to Lodo as he had hoped. Why she hadn't, he didn't know. He would have thought that, with only two weeks to go before the Selector came to town, his education would be a priority, but the old man obviously thought differently. Sal couldn't even feel her nearby.

There was no School that day, it being the weekend and the last day of the Fundelry market. The air was very hot-- thick and suffocating like the inside of an oven. The close of the market was celebrated with musical concerts and other amusements staged by local performers on the podium in a clearing at the town end of the stalls. Sal had gone to watch, finding a place in the shade nearby and trying to keep as low a profile as possible.

He had thought he was doing a good job. The crowd was full of ordinary people enjoying the break from the normal routine: bakers, fishers, carpenters, cooks; no different from people anywhere, except for the uniformly dark color of their skin. The amusements had been adequate for the most part, despite the heat, and the book interesting when they weren't. No one seemed to notice him in the shade, apart from the odd scathing look every now and again. He overheard someone talking about more thefts, so perhaps that explained it. But nothing had been said to him and he hadn't been harassed--until Kemp and his gang had come along, anyway.

As though they had broken the bubble of silence around him, Sal had barely sat back on the scratchy grass when he was joined by someone else.

"Do you know how to play Advance?"

The voice was familiar. Sal looked up into the blinding sun at the person bending over him. Squinting, he recognized the distinctive silhouette of Tom's ears.

"Not very well," he replied. "Dad taught me a long time ago, but we don't have a board or the proper pieces. I have to relearn the rules every time we get the chance to use someone's set."

"Would you like to play me?" The boy held out a flat leather case. "People around here don't find it very interesting."

Sal could see no reason to say no, and if he said yes, he might find out what Tom had been doing two nights ago, ringing a bell in the storm.

"Sure. Do you want to sit here, or--"

He stopped as Tom dropped down next to him and opened the case on the ground between them. Leveling it with a stick under one edge, he unrolled a leather parchment to reveal molded pewter and brass figures in two neat rows. Flattening the parchment on the case's wooden interior provided a playing field with a ten-by-ten array of squares etched in black and red ink, faded from long use. Although it had been lovingly cared for, Sal could tell that it was very old.

"This is beautiful," he said, reaching out to touch one of the pieces, a disc-shaped peon. It was surprisingly heavy for its size--about the size of his thumbnail--and carved in the likeness of a flattened helmet.

"It belonged to my grandfather, and his grandfather before him," Tom explained, as he lined up the rest of the pieces on the field: a rank of peon at the front; superior grenadiers, cavalry, samurai and bastions behind them; and, as it was a Sky Warden set, the Alcaide and Syndic ruling all from center rear. "It belonged to my brother for a while. Now it belongs to me."

"What happened to your brother?"

Tom didn't answer, just finished laying out the game. "I like to play silver. Do you mind playing gold?"

"No." Sal wondered idly if Tom's brother had died, but didn't press the subject. "Gold goes first, right?"

"Yes."

Sal dug deep in his memory for the rules. If he recalled correctly, a peon could cross either one or two squares on its first move, but he wasn't willing to push his luck just yet. Selecting the piece in front of his Alcaide, which was stern and upright in brass, with a heavy sword representing the law held diagonally across his chest, Sal moved just one square.

Tom responded with an immediate two-square move from a similar position, confirming Sal's guess. Advancing a grenadier, then a peon to expose his left cavalry, Sal thought hard to remember the rules and rituals of approach and combat. Advance was hard enough to learn, and even harder to play well. The unfolding fact that Tom had taught himself to play *very* well didn't make it any easier.

Only a handful of moves passed before Sal's Syndic was backed into a corner, her upraised horn no match for the twin samurai Tom had sent to dispatch her. Once she fell, defeat for Sal's Alcaide didn't take long. And when he, too, had fallen, the game was over.

Sal leaned back and wiped his hands on his shirt. He had forgotten how much he enjoyed playing, even against someone much better than him.

"You sacrificed your bastion too early," Tom said. "That exposed your flank."

"What else could I have done? You had my cavalry under threat."

Tom's hands danced across the board, recreating that moment of play from memory. "You're right, but you could have distracted me." He pointed at the other side of the board. "Here was my weakest point. A single peon in the right spot could've unraveled my defense--and you had one, here, perfectly placed. If you'd moved it like this, I would've had to back away from your bastion and defend myself."

Sal struggled to visualize the play Tom was describing. "I didn't think of that."

"It's not the sort of thing an inexperienced player would notice. They tend to overlook the subtle for the obvious, never thinking that a peon can be used for serious attack. In Advance as well as real battle, sometimes the smallest thing makes the greatest difference."

Sal couldn't help but stare as the boy swept up the pieces and began arranging them in their proper places.

"Another game?" Tom asked, without looking up.

"Yes," he said. "Thanks for the tip. I'll try harder, this time." And he promised himself he would, simply because Tom was not patronizing or berating him for being a poor player, but because the boy really wanted him to learn to play better. While he didn't enjoy losing, the fact that Tom didn't act as though he was enjoying winning made it easier to stomach. Tom seemed to be more interested in training a potential competitor than gloating over his skill. Sal doubted that many could play as expertly in such a small town, where there were few accomplished teachers, if any at all.

They played a second time. Sal thought he performed a little better than before, but he was still roundly defeated. This time he had advanced too slowly, resulting in his senior pieces being trapped when Tom inevitably broke through his defensive wall. Again Tom made sure he learned from the experience, pointing out how Sal could have attacked more effectively as well as demonstrating what mistakes had led to his downfall. Sal swore he wouldn't make the same mistakes again.

Soon he stopped worrying about losing so much. The pieces moved in a dance beneath their fingers, sparkling in the sunlight coming through the leaves of the tree above them. Sal almost became hypnotized by the ebb and flow, sensing his own awkwardness in the way his pieces stumbled and bumped into each other, whereas Tom's slid smoothly and elegantly on their deadly errands. Slowly, Sal's moves attained a measure of Tom's grace, but he knew he still had a long way to go. Even if he played every day for a year, he doubted he would ever be as good as Tom.

He certainly wasn't as focused on the game. Every time Sal tried to raise a different subject, Tom brushed it off and returned to Advance. Even when they packed up the set to get a drink from one of the stalls, Tom talked about nothing but strategies and end gambits until they returned to their place in the shade and commenced again. Sal wondered if Tom's obsessive interest in the game hid something, or whether Tom was just obsessive by nature. Or both.

After his twentieth or thirtieth defeat--he had long lost count--he rolled onto his back and said: "No more! My brain is going to explode!"

Tom blinked large eyes at him, apparently mystified. Then he recovered: "I'm sorry. I've kept you too long. Do you have somewhere else to go?"

"Well, no..." From some other person Tom's words could have been a jibe at the fact that, patently, Sal *didn't* have anything to do, otherwise why would he have been lying around in the shade? But Tom meant the question innocently.

"I'm tired, I guess," Sal said. "Maybe we can just talk."

"About what?"

"Anything. Whatever comes to mind."

Tom nodded and looked blank for a minute. Then he suddenly came alive again, as though someone had flicked a switch. "I saw you talking to Kemp before. Are you helping him, too?"

Sal suppressed a bitter laugh. "That depends on what you mean by 'helping'."

"School work. Assignments. History. That sort of stuff."

"Why would I do that? He's a pain."

"I tutor him," Tom said. "He's not stupid, you know. He's good at mathematics and languages. Even without me he'd be bright enough to skip School some days and help the Alders. His dad's an Alder. Did you know that?"

Sal nodded dumbly, surprised by this quite different portrait of the town bully.

"He's old enough to be of use on the boats," Tom went on, "but Alder Sproule wants to keep him studying as long as possible. He's hoping Kemp will be Selected. I think he might, if he keeps working right up to the examination."

"All thanks to you," Sal said.

"I'm only doing what Mrs Milka doesn't have time for. Besides, it keeps me on Kemp's good side."

Sal thought it a very pragmatic solution to what might otherwise have been quite a problem. Young, intense Tom would have been no match for Kemp under any other circumstance.

"What about you?" Sal asked. "You're going to be Selected too, I hear."

"Yes. I'll be Selected. They'd be mad not to take me. I've had the highest standard test results in this area for fifty years."

"Wow," Sal whistled, genuinely impressed. "You're really bright, aren't you?"

"Maybe." Tom looked down at his hands, brooding again. He didn't seem particularly excited by the thought of being Selected, Sal thought. Or was he hiding something?

Instead of finding another topic of conversation, Sal let his gaze drift idly across the crowds of people milling through the marketplace and around the common ground by the podium. He recognized a few faces from his short time in Fundelry. Most seemed to be having a good enough time. Shilly wasn't around, though, despite the return of the odd feeling in his gut that she was near, somewhere.

On the far side of the clearing stood Euan Holkenhill, the representative of the Selector, doing little to alleviate his weight problem with a meat roll in one hand and a tankard of beer in the other. Sweat dripped from his exposed skin. Sal hunched down slightly in the shadows for fear that the man might see him, but Holkenhill wasn't looking his way. He was laughing at a comment made by a woman at his side, then stuffing his mouth full of food.

As Sal watched, though, Holkenhill's expression grew puzzled, and he cast his eyes upward. Intrigued, Sal followed his gaze, wondering what he had seen or sensed in the sky.

Far above the market hung a tiny speck of silver. It moved slowly across a wispy cloud, then disappeared for a moment. A second later, it reappeared, brighter than before. Squinting, Sal could just make out the shape of a bird around it, as though a star had sprouted wings and was descending toward the earth.

Black and white feathers fell into focus as it grew nearer, flapping steadily to reduce its speed. The light reflecting off it faded as its angle to the sun changed, and it revealed itself to be an ordinary seagull gradually coming in to land. It seemed to be wearing something around its neck--a necklace or band--from which the light had gleamed. As it flapped to a halt a few meters above the heads of the crowd in the market, others noticed its approach. It looked around briefly before gliding down. Someone gasped as it came to a perfect landing on the outstretched arm of Euan Holkenhill.

Instead of reveling in its appearance, though, Holkenhill moved purposefully through the crowd and away from the markets, his face serious, the half-eaten meat roll and ale left behind in the care of his friend. The bird didn't move at all as he walked. When Holkenhill disappeared from sight, it was still balanced on his arm, like a statuette.

Sal was left with an uneasy feeling, as though something bad had happened--or was about to happen.

A premonition? Just his imagination, he hoped.

He sensed Shilly standing behind him a moment before she spoke.

"Interesting." She was leaning against the trunk of the tree shading them. "Hi, Sal. Hi, Tom."

"Hello, Shilly."

The younger boy looked up at her and nodded curtly. Gathering the shining pieces with rapid, practiced motions and putting them back in the leather box, he stood and walked away.

"Thanks for the game," Sal called after him, without receiving a reply.

"Bye, Tom."

Sal stood and turned to face Shilly. She watched with her arms folded as Tom hurried away.

"Don't worry about him," she said. "That's probably the friendliest he'll ever be."

"He was fine before."

"Well, I did notice that you got to see the precious Advance kit."

"Yes." The note of disdain in Shilly's voice bothered him. "He's very good."

"That's no excuse for being antisocial." She shrugged. "But who am I to talk? He's got Kemp in the palm of his hand, and that's no mean feat."

"What happened to his brother?"

"Tait? Oh, he was Selected three years ago. He and Tom were very close, apparently, and the family tried to keep Tait back an extra year so Tom could get used to the idea. But the Sky Wardens insisted it was either then or never. Tait, naturally, chose to go. Tom's never quite gotten over losing him. He was always a bit … *dependent*."

Sal saw how it fit together, now. He was certain Tom had always been bright but this need to join his brother would account for his urgency to pass the Selection exams quickly. For Tom to be in such a hurry, his love of his brother and his grief at losing him must have been very great.

Sal felt bad for him. He wondered if Tait, Tom's older brother, knew just how much sorrow he had left behind.

"He's hoping to follow in his big brother's footsteps, I presume."

"Maybe." Shilly's expression was sly. She was relishing the story. That much was obvious. "There's more. You've met Aunty Merinda, our local seer?"

Sal nodded, remembering the ugly old woman in the market the day after he arrived in town.

"Well, she's not as much of a fake as some people think. Lodo will admit that, if you ask him. Tom's family went to see if she could do anything for him--help him get over Tait, whatever. They didn't want a reading, just a tonic to help their boy sleep. Aunty Merinda did what she could for them,

and sent them away. That was the end of it, she thought--
until the middle of that night, when Tom appeared at her
window. He'd snuck out of bed after a nightmare and come
to her on his own for advice. It turns out he'd been having
prophetic dreams ever since Tait went away, and *they* were
bothering him just as much as being alone."

"Prophetic dreams?" Sal echoed, confused.

"Visions of things that haven't happened yet--but when
you're asleep, not awake. Not many people get them, and
they're hard to tell from real dreams. They usually recur,
but not every recurring dream is prophetic. Anyway, Tom's
were, and in them, among other things, he saw Tait coming
home to Fundelry in the middle of a storm, guided by a
bell. Or something like that. Dreams are always confused,
prophetic or not, and the only thing Tom was sure about
was that it was important he should be ready. So, every time
there's a storm--"

"He's standing in the rain ringing a bell, hoping to guide
his brother home." Sal shook his head at the thought.

"How do you know that?" Shilly asked, annoyed at
having the punch line taken from her. "Oh, the other night.
You saw him, did you?"

"I *wondered* what he was doing."

"You're not the only one." She rolled her eyes. "We all
wonder, at times."

Sal ignored her jibe, concentrating instead on Tom's
peculiar gift.

"What else does Tom see?" he asked.

"Eh?"

"In his dreams. You said he sees his brother coming home
in a storm--among other things."

"I don't know. You'd have to ask him. You seem to be
great mates, now."

Sal nodded distantly, remembering the day Tom had first
spoken to him, under the School's fixed weathervane. They
had been talking about the Haunted City, the Sky Warden
citadel. *You'll go there one day*, Tom had said.

Sal shivered. He had never believed in prophecy before--

but he had never really believed in the Change, either, since his father had kept him away from it all his life. Now he had the Change himself, who was he to say prophecy wasn't rubbish too?

He wanted to ask Shilly if any of Tom's prophecies had come true, but he was afraid of what her answer would be. He didn't want to go to the Haunted City. He didn't want to have anything to do with the Sky Wardens. He just wanted things to stay the way they were.

"Anyway," Shilly asked, interrupting his thoughts, "are you ready?"

"For what?"

"For your training to begin."

Sal's stomach turned. "I guess I'm as ready as I'll ever be."

"Good. Let's go." She reached down a hand to help him up. "Lodo's waiting."

He brushed grass off his backside. "Do I need anything?"

"Just your wits." She smiled--maliciously, he thought--and led him away from the marketplace.

CHAPTER 9

TRIAL BY FIRE

THE moment Lodo removed the anklet charm, Sal felt the background potential rush through him, as welcoming and vital as an eager puppy. But at the same time he felt the teeth and claws buried in the sensation. They weren't properly there yet, but they would be, given time.

Not a puppy, then. A wolf. And wolves sometimes bit their handlers ...

"You feel it?" Lodo rose to his feet with the charm in one hand and looked Sal up and down. "Yes, you do. It's practically making your hair stand on end. The second thing we have to do is dampen your sensitivity to the background potential by better means than a simple charm."

"What's the first thing?"

Lodo didn't answer. He turned away and began rummaging through items in his workshop. Sal watched curiously as the old man lifted rolled-up parchments, jars and bags of pebbles. The air, as always, was thick with heat. Three round stones, protruding out of the chamber's rough-hewn walls, glowed yellow-red to provide indirect lighting. Shilly knelt on a cushion in one corner of the room with her hands folded in her lap, apparently ignoring them.

"Ah, here." Lodo turned back to Sal with a smile on his wrinkled face. His eyes were bright. In his left hand he held a section of rope one meter long. It wasn't ordinary rope, though. The intertwined fibers were much coarser than usual and had threads of metallic blue and red wound among them. One end terminated in a silver cap, and Lodo gripped the other by a black leather handle, lending it the appearance of a short whip. When Lodo moved it through the light, it glittered strangely.

Again, Sal felt the faint buzz that accompanied an object or place heavy with the Change.

"I don't expect you've ever seen one of these before," said the old man. "Few people have. It's sometimes called the Scourge of Aneshti. Every great teacher of the Change has had something very much like it, be they Sky Warden or Stone Mage. I'm not saying I'm a great teacher, mind." He waved the scourge experimentally through the air. "But I did listen to what my own teacher taught me, a long, long time ago."

Sal watched the scourge, hypnotized by the shining threads. "What does it do?"

"It's not a magic wand, if that's what you're thinking. It's not a weapon, either, despite its name. It's more like a magnifying glass, or a telescope. It *reveals*." He held it out before him. "Take the end opposite the one I'm holding."

Sal did so. The silver cap was icily cold, and the cord squirmed in his fingers like a snake. Startled, he almost dropped the end, but grabbed it tightly with both hands and fought the urge to let go. Lodo was watching him even more closely than usual. If this was a test, he told himself, he wasn't going to fail.

"That's good," Lodo breathed. "But this isn't the sort of test you *can* fail."

Again, Sal almost dropped the scourge. "You--what?"

"Quiet." Lodo closed his eyes and pulled the rope tight between them. "I'm concentrating."

Sal barely had time to think--

He's reading my mind!

--when suddenly the ground was pulled out from underneath him, and he was falling--

--or flying--

--down into the molten heart of the Earth--

--or up through the incandescent eye of the sun.

He let go of the scourge. He felt its coarse weave slip through his fingers, and he shrieked with fear. But he couldn't get it back, no matter how he clutched. He was being pulled away from it--

--or someone was pulling *it*--

--and the heat was burning, burning, all around him, sucking the air out of his lungs.

The shriek died on his lips as the pain hit harder than anything he'd ever experienced, more piercing than a thousand knives, flaying him until his nerve endings were bared, then flaying each of them in turn: burning and burning and burning until he thought his mind would shatter like glass and explode into a million tiny fragments--

--yet he *could* think that, and that surprised him.

"Good," said Lodo as the flames sucked him back down--

--or up--

--and the pain was gone. The heat was gone. All he felt was coolness, as though he had been dunked in a cold lake, except there was no water. Only air, thin and wintry, curling around him, embracing him with chill limbs, holding him tight. As the heat radiated from his skin and he felt ice leaching in, he realized that the cold hurt as much as the fire. His skin seemed to peel back and shed tiny crystals, eroded layer by layer until his bones were exposed, cold and hard and frozen like rock, right down to the core--

--right down to his heart, which stopped in mid-beat.

And everything was still for a single, timeless moment. There was no light, no dark; no cold, no hot; just a single, deep note humming far off in the distance, like the sound a sleeping mountain might make turning over ...

"Again," said Lodo. Sal's heart beat once more. He gasped for breath, took two desperate gulps of bitter wind deep into his chest--

--then the air was gone.

--there was dark. Something wrapped around his face and throat--and his shoulders and chest and arms and stomach and waist and thighs and knees and feet--and gripped *tight*. He was being squeezed by a giant, rock-hard fist. He couldn't move his jaw to open his mouth, let alone his chest to inhale. The stone was rough and warm against his skin, and as implacable as granite. He would never be able to shift it a millimeter, let alone dig his way out. He would die encased in rock like a living fossil, a modern dinosaur to puzzle future miners--

--but again he wondered how that could be. If there was no way out, that meant there was no way in, either--

--and if *that* was so, then he wasn't there at all.

"Very good," said Lodo, into his head. "Now, this is the last one."

Suddenly his mouth could open and his chest move. He gasped for air, but only water poured into his lungs, thick and choking, filling up every oxygen-starved corner of his chest. He jackknifed, vomiting fluid out of his throat and sucking still more back in. This was worse than when he had fallen off the jetty. Here, there was no light and no way up. His body went into spasms and his mind recoiled from the realization that unless something happened soon, unless someone saved him again, he would surely drown.

Yet somehow, through the panic and the pain, a bubble of calm appeared and began to grow, enveloping him. It numbed the pain and the panic; it soothed him, drew him down, deeper, into serenity and darkness. He accepted the descent with gratitude. Somewhere, he knew, his body's spasms were becoming weaker; its resistance was ebbing-- but *he* was safe. *He* was no longer afraid. *He* was--

--at peace. There was only him and the distant hum--and as time itself faded away, he began to doubt that even *he* was real.

* * *

"Wake up," said Lodo.

Sal's eyes jerked open. For a moment he didn't understand what they were showing him. The messages of his senses, too, he could hardly accept. All felt wrong--as though the world around him had become translucent and he could see behind it to another reality. Another reality that faded as his mind cleared, leaving behind tantalizing fragments like scraps of fog boiling away at sunrise.

He was standing upright in Lodo's workshop holding the silver end of the scourge in both hands.

"Welcome back," said the old man.

"What ...?" Sal let go of the scourge and ran his hands over his face. His skin was tingling all over. He remembered the pain of burning and freezing, being buried alive and then drowned, as vividly as though it had actually happened to him. Yet it so clearly hadn't. He was alive and unharmed. He hadn't even moved.

"The Change comes from one single source," said Lodo. His voice was firm, an anchor on which Sal fought to find stability. "What that source is, we don't know, but it is no different in a Stone Mage than in a Sky Warden. There are simply different ways to teach it--at least two--and which path a student takes depends to a large degree on the student's temperament.

"Like a river on its journey to the sea, the Change is guided by the shape of the banks and the strength of its source. The scourge helps us determine the former, at least. Without measuring your temperament, I wouldn't know how best to proceed."

Sal's legs were beginning to tremble with delayed shock, but he forced himself to stand still and silent.

"In the first examination, your heart chose air and your head chose fire. In the second, your mind revealed a natural predilection for stone over water. This surprised me, I'll admit." Lodo smiled slightly. "But it is good news. I can guide you along the path of fire and stone.

"Shilly, you might be interested to know, is the other way around in both cases. If she had the Change, I would have been forced to finish her teaching by a completely different method. As it is, she can use my power in ways that I cannot, and is unable to do some things I find simple."

Lodo stopped and frowned. "Are you feeling all right?"

Sal tried to keep his voice level. "Yes."

"Don't be ridiculous. You can barely stand upright. Sit down before you force me to catch you."

Sal stumbled to a cushion and collapsed gratefully into

it. His muscles were weak and his eyes heavy. Lodo brought him a lukewarm drink that tasted faintly of limes, and he felt better almost instantly. The memory of the scourge began to fade.

When Lodo spoke again, his voice was firm. "Let this be your first lesson, Sal. Don't ever be afraid to speak your mind, because I can only read it on odd occasions and it's a chore to do your thinking for you at *any* time. I want a pupil, not a puppet. Understood?"

Sal nodded.

"Good. Now, where was I? Oh, yes. Your temperament. A bad beginning leads more often than not to a bad ending. Even though I'll probably never complete your training, it's important to begin the right way. But one thing the scourge can only hint at is your lineage. Given what I can guess about your parents, I'd say you're an odd blend of Earth Clan and Cloud Line, with the Cloud coming from your father."

"But Dad doesn't have the Change."

"Are you sure about that?"

"Yes."

Lodo's gaze evaded his. "Well, he may not, but he must carry the trait, even if it's recessive. Otherwise you wouldn't have it. It takes two with the trait to make a Change-worker, you see, and one must always be active. Two latents are no good. All you get then is another latent, weaker than either parent. There are occasionally throwbacks, yes, but never as potent as you seem to be. You're a true match if ever I've seen one. Your mother, I suspect, was very potent indeed."

Sal absorbed this. Among the many things his father had been silent about was the possibility that the Change ran in his family. It was an odd thought, to be related to the Sky Wardens he had been afraid of all his life, since that was what it meant to belong to one of the Lines. And Lodo thought he belonged to a Stone Mage Clan as well! The thought seemed too bizarre, at first, to accept, an impossible mix of bitter ice and searing fire.

"What about Shilly?" he asked, seeking to draw attention away from himself. "Does she come from a Line, too?"

Lodo shook his head. "No. She's a free latent talent--an Irregular, as some people call them--sprung out of nowhere and bearing no sign of Line or Clan. I took her in because, as a toddler, she exhibited enough flashes of the Change to disconcert her foster parents. They didn't know what to do with her, and I doubt anyone else in her village would have, either. Her talent burned out before she was seven, but the pathways are still there, getting more sophisticated every year. Whoever and wherever her real parents are, they don't know what they're missing."

Sal glanced at Shilly, who was still pretending not to listen, and thought of Elina, the child who had given him the illusory flower. This was the first time he had heard Lodo compliment Shilly, and he thought she looked faintly smug.

"She told me," Lodo went on, "about what happened in the Ruin. I'd like to hear it from your point of view. What did you feel when she used your ability? How did you feel afterward? Did you feel that you could do it on your own at any point? Were you ever afraid that you might lose control of the Change?"

Sal thought to recall everything he had experienced. He described the way the air had seemed to buzz, and how something simultaneously hot and cold had crawled up his spine when Shilly had called forth light from the carved stone. The illusions had been less of a strain, but had left him exhausted afterward. Not physically exhausted, or even mentally. He didn't have the words to describe how he had felt. As though he had become *thinner*, perhaps, less substantial. As though, every time he used the Change, a piece of him was taken with it.

Lodo nodded at that. "That's the truth of it, more or less. Having the Change won't give you access to boundless reserves of energy. All you have is as much as you are, and no more. Take too much, and you risk losing yourself. You'd become like a ghost, or the opposite of a ghost: a body without true life, a shell of yourself. A *golem*, as some call them. Many Wardens and Mages have fallen into this trap over the centuries; some still exist, and they can be dangerous. Empty vessels can sometimes be filled by other things. Most Change-workers are aware of the risks and take precautions. There are places and times when reserves can be replenished, when the ambient Change is strong and can be drawn upon. This ambient level, the background potential, can also get in the way, however, by interfering with the senses, as it did for you at the Ruin. It is therefore both a resource *and* a nuisance. You must learn to control it before you can learn to control yourself."

Sal nodded slowly, hoping he understood even half of what the old man was saying. He could feel the Change all around him, yes, but had no idea how to tap into it, or to ignore it.

"Give me your hands." Lodo leaned forward. Sal placed his hands in the old man's, noting the callused, leathery skin, and the blood-red jewels where Lodo's littlest fingernails had once been. In the roughly circular space enclosed by their arms, a cloudy white glow appeared. It had no definite form or shape, but stirred restlessly.

"This is a simple, contained version of the background potential," Lodo explained. "It's easier to control than the real thing, and easier to study your effects upon it, since you can see it. Ultimately, you must learn to intuit the Change, rather than use your normal senses. First, I want you to find this cloud with your mind and make it part of you. Can you feel it?"

Sal frowned, concentrating. "I'm not sure …"

"Be sure, either way. I can't describe how it will feel to you, because everyone is different in that respect. But you may sense it through sound or balance. A buzzing, like at the Ruin, perhaps?"

Sal closed his eyes. Yes, he could sense something. Like a noise on the very edge of hearing, or the touch of a mosquito's legs. There was *something* …

"Good," he heard Lodo say, and he opened his eyes. There was a dent in the top of the cloud, as though a finger had poked into it. He gasped with surprise, and the invisible finger withdrew. But it had been there, and he was encouraged by that fact.

"Try again."

This time, Sal kept his eyes open. As he found the sensation again, he saw the cloud deform once more, this time on its upper left flank. As Sal concentrated on the sensation, the dimple drifted across the cloud, as aimless and jittery as the floaters visible in his eye when he looked at the sky. If he concentrated harder, he could make the dimple bigger, but he was apt to lose control of it that way. When Lodo asked him to try to poke right through the cloud, the dimple flailed wildly left, then right, then disappeared entirely.

"Never mind," said Lodo, in response to Sal's crestfallen look. "It happens to all of us, the first time. Shilly, come and join us."

Without a word, Shilly unfolded herself from her cushion and joined them in the middle of the room. Lodo let go of Sal's right hand, and she filled the gap.

Instantly, the cloud expanded to fill the larger space enclosed by the three of them.

"There's a simple game new Stone Mages learn," said Lodo. "They call it Blind: Double Blind with two players, Triple Blind with three, and so on. The object is to pin down your opponent's will using nothing but your own. Shilly and I will demonstrate."

Instantly, two tendrils of fog appeared, rearing like snakes on the surface of the cloud. They danced around each other, pulling forward and retreating, until one of them struck the other--or attempted to. The second tendril retreated back into itself, turning inside-out in the process. Transformed into a mouth, it engulfed the striking tendril and closed shut around it.

Shilly grimaced. Another tendril appeared, this time terminating in a circular loop, like a lasso. A copy appeared on the far side of the cloud and swept around to meet it, pulling free at the last moment and attempting to jump through the loop of the first. The first ducked nimbly aside,

and tried to jump through its opponent's loop as it returned
to the cloud. This maneuver failed too, so they went back to
circling each other, with Sal watching their every move.

The rules of this particular engagement seemed to be less
permissive than the first, in that the loops never transformed
into another shape, but flexed and dodged in order to avoid
an attack. The melee was therefore more intense, as each loop
fought for an opening in the other. The end came when one
of the loops--Sal couldn't tell whose it was--feinted a jump
to the left but instead jumped to the right. The opponent, for
a split second taken off-guard, then crouched down to avoid
the leap, and leapt up to pass through the hole of the loop
jumping over it. The victor instantly doubled in size, while
the loser vanished.

Shilly pulled another face. Her hand in Sal's clenched a
little tighter.

"Have a go, Sal," Lodo said. The winning loop sank
back into the cloud, leaving the featureless pseudo-sphere
between the three of them. "There are no rules in free-form,
which is the way Shilly and I first played. Your goal is simply
to capture or subdue your opponent any way you can. Show
us what you can do."

Sal concentrated, searching for the cloud hanging before
him with his mind--or whatever sense it was that registered
its presence. Instead of simply prodding it, he tried to draw
part of it away from the rest. He visualized teasing a yarn
out of a bale of raw wool. To his amazement, something
very similar happened on the surface of the cloud before
him. By concentrating harder, he found he could make a
vortex the size of his thumb stand out from the rest.

But it wasn't going anywhere. It just wobbled unsteadily
to one side of the cloud. Sal willed it to move--any direction
would do--but nothing happened.

Then, from the far side of the cloud, a wave swept over
his vortex and swallowed it whole. Sal felt as though he
too had been swallowed. The part of his mind controlling
the vortex was tugged away from him, and he staggered
forward, his balance thrown.

Lodo and Shilly steadied him with their hands. The cloud wobbled for a moment, then firmed.

"Sorry," Shilly said with an evil grin. "I'll go easier on you next time."

Sal fumed to himself and went back to concentrating. The vortex popped up again, a little stronger than before. This time Shilly's wave encircled the vortex and began to close in on it. He could feel her mental wall contracting around him, and he struggled to escape the only way he could. Squeezing its base, he managed to detach the top of the vortex from the cloud an instant before Shilly's ring slammed shut below. The remainder of his vortex, now a rough ball, hung in the air above the cloud, skittering nervously every time Sal tried to move it. When Shilly's wave reappeared, this time as a mouth reaching up to gulp him down like a fish snapping at an insect, Sal's panicky mental impulse sent his sphere swinging around the cloud. It survived two attacks that way, but was captured on the third. Again he was tugged forward when she swallowed him. This time he was ready for it and managed to stay upright.

"Okay," said Lodo. "You're improving. Now we'll make it a little more interesting."

Sal wondered what he could mean, but was completely unprepared for what happened. The three stones illuminating the room abruptly went black, plunging them into darkness.

"I asked you to make the cloud part of you." Lodo's voice came strongly from nearby. "That's what I want you to do now. Don't *see* the cloud. Feel it. *Be* it."

At first Sal was completely lost. Feel the cloud? Thrown off-balance, he could barely feel himself. The darkness was suffocatingly warm; his hands were clasped tight by Lodo and Shilly. All he could see was a blotchy after-image. All he could feel with his mind was the background potential, chaotic and confusing. When he tried to sense the cloud, he received nothing in return.

But then he did feel something. Out of nowhere, he was nudged by someone else's will. It tapped him gently, then darted away. He tried to follow it, caught a fringe of it as it fled, and was bumped by another, this time more firmly.

He smiled to himself, recognizing the second touch as Shilly's. It was blunter, less refined than the first--which could only have been Lodo's. They were trying to draw him out.

Gradually he learned how to follow them. It was like trying to catch flies with his eyes closed, but he did get better. And gradually, out of the darkness, he began to feel the cloud as a whole. Its presence hung before him, vague in outline but definitely there. How he knew, he couldn't exactly say. He just *knew*. If he clutched that knowledge too tightly, it slipped away and the cloud was gone. He simply had to accept that it was there, and move on.

Moving on, in the context of the game, meant trying to touch Shilly or Lodo back. Or so he supposed. But he wanted to surprise them with what he had learned, so he waited until the touch belonging to Shilly darted closer to poke him, and then he pounced.

His will sent the cloud ringing like a bell. Vibrations rippled through its surface and sent echoes deep into its core. Sal staggered back, alarmed by the strength of the cloud's reaction but gratified by two things: the sudden, startled squeeze of Shilly's fingers, and the fact that her mental touch in the cloud was gone.

Lodo laughed, and the light returned.

"Good work, both of you. I don't mind you competing as long as you both learn something in the process."

Sal blinked, blinded. He could still feel the cloud before him, even through the light, but less clearly than before, as though the light were getting in the way of a new form of sight opening to him.

Lodo brought his hands in and linked Sal and Shilly together, alone. The cloud shrank and flickered, but didn't vanish.

"I have to activate the town lights," he said. "You two keep practicing. Sal, quick thinking will get you further in Blind than brute strength. Shilly, don't be afraid to dig deep.

I think our new friend needs to be reminded that his talent has limits. I'll be back before long."

Lodo picked up a long, wool coat and draped it over his shoulders. Various implements, some very peculiar-looking, peeked out of pockets on the inside. Nodding at both of them, he went to the tunnel leading to the surface.

"But remember," he said, turning on the threshold. "No mucking around. I'll be watching."

Then he was gone.

"What did he mean?" asked Sal. "How could he see us?"

"I don't know." Shilly shrugged. "But he can. I only ever tried to go behind his back once. It didn't work. He can see everything in here, no matter where he is."

"How?" Sal asked again.

"You ask him. He won't tell me."

Sal looked around the workshop. There was only the one door, and no windows.

"I know what you're thinking," Shilly said. "I've looked for ways he could spy on me. There are no ways in or out of this place except the tunnel, and up there."

She nodded her head to indicate the ceiling. Directly above them in the stone was an inverted funnel, leading into a chimney. Sal craned to look up it, but saw no light at the top. Yet he doubted that the chimney was closed; the air in the workshop didn't smell at all stale.

"How far underground are we?" he asked.

"I don't know."

"It can't be far, I guess. The tunnel doesn't drop for long before it levels out. The chimney must have a kink in it."

"I'll bet we're further down than you think," Shilly said. "When Lodo took me in, we lived in another town. The entrance to his workshop was in a cave visible only at low tide. We moved here three years ago, when the market picked up--but I'll swear this is the same workshop. Only the entrance has changed."

Sal studied her face. She didn't seem to be joking. "That's impossible."

"How would I know what's impossible and what isn't?" she shot back. "You can do lots of things with the Change."

If Sal disbelieved her, then the proof was right before him, within his outstretched arms. But still he couldn't tell if she was having him on. He simply couldn't credit the idea of a moving workshop, or short tunnels that actually covered great distances. And was Lodo really able to spy through walls of solid rock? If he could, it would be an incredible ability to have--but if he couldn't, there was no reason not to experiment. Lodo might have been lying simply to make Shilly think twice.

"Are you sure you don't want to try something different?" Sal asked Shilly. "I mean, you must be bored with this game and know plenty of other tricks--"

"For now," she interrupted him, "we do only as we're told."

She looked cautiously around her, and that convinced him. Under any other circumstance he doubted she would be so obedient. It seemed they didn't really have a choice in the matter.

But when her gaze returned to his, there was a look in her eyes that clearly said: *Later.*

CHAPTER 10

NIGHT AND ITS SECRETS

IT was late at night when Sal finished his third lesson with Lodo. He had been in the workshop since midday, patiently listening to everything the old man said and doing everything he was told. There was no moon, but he thought it might be after midnight. He was exhausted and long overdue for sleep. Even Shilly had fallen asleep in a corner before Lodo had finished with him.

He had learned the way to and from Lodo's workshop well enough to travel it in the dark with or without the light visible from the town square. He could feel the door buzzing softly in the dunes behind him, even through the dampening effects of the anklet. Had he been lost in a storm this night, he could easily have found his way back to Lodo's. And he now knew how to open the door. Shilly had told him the day before.

"When you know you are in front of it, within two paces, find it with your mind and give it a push. The sand opens up, and there it is."

"That's how *you* do it?"

"Well, no ... unless I'm channeling the Change through Lodo. If I'm on my own, I have to touch two particular rocks together under the bush behind it. That works too."

"How does it know you're you?" he had asked. "What if you were someone trying to break in?"

"I don't know, but I doubt if it would open. I can't imagine Lodo making it so easy."

Privately, Sal agreed. The old man wasn't the sort to leave much to chance in anything. Sal hadn't tried to open the door; he didn't know what it would mean if it rejected him.

On the way back to the village, he reviewed everything he had been told to remember for his next lesson. He had some mental exercises to perform--visualization and meditation, mostly. What the odd shapes and symbols he had been asked to concentrate on meant, he didn't know yet, but he assumed they would turn out to be important. There were a couple of exercises requiring the Change, but he was under strict instructions not to try them in or near Fundelry, unless he was in the controlled environment of the workshop, or the Ruins. He was hoping to get to the latter the next morning. He hadn't been able to make a carved stone glow in the workshop, but he was sure he could do it given time to practice on his own.

Some of what Lodo said was starting to make sense to him. As well as improving his skills at Blind, he was beginning to grasp how a person with the Change could detect another from a distance. When Lodo let down his guard, Sal could feel his mind nearby, firm and strong like an anchor. The old man said that this recognition of minds could be used to allow communication between--and, in some extreme cases, influence and control over--Change-workers, but Sal hadn't been taught anything about that. Much of his training had been simply to educate him on how vulnerable he was. The anklet could protect him from distant minds, but if those minds came closer, or if he exposed himself by using the Change out in the open, then the charm would be about as useful as hiding behind a tree in a bushfire.

So far, Sal's lessons had served mainly to make him nervous. He had learned little of any use, except that his father had good reason to be afraid that he would be discovered. It was only a matter of time before he slipped up, or bumped into a Sky Warden. Indeed, the Selector's gathering was only eleven days away. That was no time at all to fool someone adept in the Change that he was no one worth looking twice at. Although Sal's father let him go about his lessons without interference, Sal could tell that he was concerned, and as nervous as Sal was. They were caught between the threat of the Sky Wardens and the abilities of Lodo. Sal hoped they would cancel each other out.

And he couldn't forget the eye searching for him in the storm and in the sea, and the voice calling for him ...

On the way back into town he stayed strictly to inland roads and avoided those that ran parallel to the coast. As he wound his way through the narrow streets in the dark, moonless night, he heard the sound of footsteps ahead. Not wanting to be caught out, he slowed to a halt and listened closely. The footfalls were faint and stealthy, and coming nearer. He looked around, saw a dark alcove under a nearby verandah, and ducked for cover before the owner of the feet could stumble across him.

Hunkering down in the shadows, he held his breath and waited. It surely couldn't be Tom; the night wasn't stormy. The only person Sal could think of was the thief. There *had* been other thefts, because he had overheard people talking about them. If he was quiet, he might be able to see who was behind them. Knowing who the real thief was would go a long way to clearing his and his father's names of any suspicion. With the culprit caught, even Alder Sproule would have to leave them alone, no matter how much he disliked the color of their skin.

But as the person slowly came into view, moving surprisingly lightly and rapidly along the street in spite of his size, Sal knew it wasn't going to be that simple.

It was Kemp.

When the big bully had passed, Sal eased out of the alcove and followed, keeping carefully to shadows and treading as lightly as he could. He avoided the gravelly road surface, following the sandy verge instead. Kemp didn't look back. He seemed to be concentrating on where he was going rather than what lay behind him. He gave Sal the distinct impression that he was returning rather than heading out.

Sal followed Kemp toward the sea, swallowing his reservations. He hadn't gone down to the beach since the day he had nearly drowned. That one visit had almost given him away to the Sky Wardens, and he wasn't about to try again. The only good thing was that the steady booming of the waves was likely to cover any sound he might make.

The quality of the houses and streets improved as the two of them went through the night. At the end of the last road Kemp took, a cul de sac overlooking the sea, a gas lantern shone yellow against the darkness.

Sal stayed back as Kemp approached the pool of light. The big albino seemed to glow as he passed it and turned into the driveway of a relatively large house. Stone-built, like Von's hostel, it squatted on a high point of the coast, exposed but sturdy enough to withstand rough weather. When Kemp went around the house and in through a back door, Sal knew that it had to be the Sproule household. Kemp had come home.

But where had he been? Just because he had been out at midnight didn't necessarily make him the thief. He was old enough to be sneaking off with a girlfriend. Or he could have been out with his gang, getting up to a different form of mischief. There was more than one possible explanation.

Sal waited, but no light that he could see came on inside the house. Kemp's parents probably didn't know he had gone out, then.

As Sal retraced his footsteps back into town, he pondered what he should do. He would have to check with Shilly to make sure the house *had* been the Sproule household. If it was--and even if Kemp wasn't the thief--Sal now had something to blackmail Kemp with. But Sal doubted he would ever be able to use his knowledge. Who would believe him? Not Alder Sproule, that was for sure.

And if Kemp *was* the thief ...?

Sal didn't know what it would take to bring the boy to justice, but he swore that he would do it if he had to. He didn't want to take the blame for someone else's crimes. If some of the people in Fundelry believed that the color of a person's skin was a good indicator of guilt, then he thought it was about time they took a look much closer to home.

He slept poorly, and woke feeling as though he hadn't slept at all. He blamed that partly on his father, who had stirred when he'd slipped into their room and called out an unfamiliar name in his sleep: "Seirian! Seirian, don't!"

The name haunted Sal in his dreams, in many different guises. She was the queen of a far-off land with jet-black hair and skin like gold. She stood, face hidden behind a blood-drenched helmet, over a field of bodies. She ran, clad only in a shift, along the bank of a river, hairless and pale, crying in despair. She stared stubbornly back at him with features as black and broad as those of a Strand native. He never once heard her speak.

Who *was* she? She might have been anyone, but the more he thought the more convinced he became that the name belonged to his mother--that mysterious member of the Earth Clan who had given birth to him, then disappeared. If, as Lodo suspected, she was a potent Change-worker, maybe even a Stone Mage in her own right, then it was her legacy that had brought his father to Fundelry. Her talent, passed on to Sal, was the reason his father had searched for Lodo, and why Sal was dreaming of her now, even though he didn't know what she looked like.

But he still couldn't understand why his father was so afraid. What did the Sky Wardens want so badly? Why should Sal hide from them? Why had his father never told him anything of his past before?

The lack of understanding only reinforced Sal's trepidation. Not knowing, he imagined the worst, even though he knew it was irrational. He couldn't help being swept up by his father's fear and carried along with it, wherever it was taking them.

He tried some of the visualizations that Lodo had given him in the hope they might put him to sleep again. The complex shapes--triangles upon triangles, circles overlapping and multiplying, squares within stars within other angular shapes--did little to ease his mind, although at some point he must have succumbed to exhaustion. Dawn came all too soon, glaring through the window and waking him.

His father said nothing about a nightmare in the morning. But the day soon went from bad to worse. Von watched

Sal balefully over breakfast, as hostile as a glowing coal. Sal's father didn't notice anything because she replied to his questions in her usual gruff manner and saved the daggers for Sal. Sal didn't know what he had done to incur her wrath. Maybe he had woken her other guest coming home the previous night, and he had complained. But why, then, wouldn't Von deal with the problem head-on? There was no reason that he could see for her to keep it a secret.

When, finally, breakfast was over, Sal escaped outside. The day was already warm and promised to be very hot. There was a baked, dusty smell to the air, as though it had traveled a long way from deep inland. It gusted powerfully through the streets, kicking up sand and stinging Sal's unprotected face and eyes. The sky to the north was a dirty brown color. The small town huddled around itself like a snake in its burrow. The weathervane on top of the school building hadn't moved.

He saw Mrs Milka on the other side of the square rounding up a couple of young children and bringing them in out of the sun. She saw Sal, but looked away. Sal wondered if his lack of attendance had offended her. But she hadn't said anything to his father that he knew of, and she didn't seem the sort to give up on a student so readily. There must have been more to it.

But he had more important things to worry about, such as Kemp and what to do about what he had seen. Sitting in the shade of the hostel's verandah, he could feel the small of his back tingling, as though he was being watched. Part of him wanted to reach out with his mind and see if it was someone he recognized. He didn't, but not just because Lodo had warned him against using the Change. He already knew who it was.

"Waiting for something?" Shilly asked from behind him.

"Not any more." He smiled, wondering what she would think of his sixth sense concerning her proximity. Why it happened, he didn't know--maybe it had something to do with studying the Change together--but he doubted it had anything to do with them being "destined."

She looked refreshed and well-rested, and smelled again of rosemary.

"What are you doing this morning?" he asked.

"As little as I can."

"Fancy a trip to the Ruins, then?"

"When?"

"How about now?"

"Sure."

Sal stood up. "Thanks. I need to practice."

"You sure do." She sounded as ungracious as always, but Sal was sure she was glad he had asked. "This time we'd better not stay too long, or Lodo will kill us."

They walked together across the square. Sal caught another odd look from Mrs Milka, hurriedly bustling her students ahead of her into a classroom as though afraid that Sal might try to join them.

"Did you see that?" he asked Shilly.

"Mistress Em? Don't worry about her. She's mad."

"It's not just her. Everyone's acting like I've done something wrong."

"Have you?"

"I don't think so, unless hanging around you and Lodo counts."

"In some people's eyes it might." She shrugged. "But they don't matter. I don't care what people think about me. I know what I'm doing, and that's what counts."

Sal nodded, despite the fact that he found her response unsatisfying. Of course it mattered what people thought of you. Even if he was only just passing through, he didn't want to leave anyone with the impression that he was a bad person, however they had arrived at it. It wasn't fair, and if he had a chance to change it, he felt he should.

Whether he had the chance or not was the question. He didn't dare hope that Shilly would be able to help him.

They left the town behind them and headed up the dry riverbed. The day was steadily getting hotter. The air was thick and heavy, like an oven. Sal could feel sweat dripping down his back and the sun boring into his skin. He tried to stay in the shadows to prevent being burned.

When they reached the Ruins and clambered up onto the top, Sal looked longingly down into the shadowy depths where the fern-trees grew. The air was buzzing softly to itself, setting his nerves tingling in a vaguely pleasant way. As soon as they were at the bottom of the rope ladder, he removed the anklet charm and let the background potential wash through him.

They began as before, with Shilly lighting the carved stone using Sal's talent. Together they explored the many niches in the cave, staring at the skulls and wondering what animals they had come from. Some seemed to be very old, blackened as though burned, or crumbling in the light; some had holes or cracks in them, possibly where their owners had been injured. Sal found himself drawn to one with a split from top to bottom, as if it had been cracked in half. What would do something like that? And why had it been preserved in the cave?

No matter how close he and Shilly came to the skulls, though, they didn't touch them. Even the ones within easy reach radiated a sense of distance, as if they didn't quite belong in the light.

Then it was Sal's turn with the stone. He held it in the dark, after she had extinguished it, and tried his best to ignore the feel of it in his hand--the alternating smoothness and roughness of its carvings, its solid weight. Instead he concentrated on its presence in his mind. He could sense the promise of light deep within it, like a star at the bottom of a well. All he had to do was lure that star toward him, out of the well and into the world. He wanted to see how much he could do on his own before he asked Shilly for her help with Kemp.

It wasn't as easy as he had hoped, and it took him over an hour to coax a weak glow from the stone, even with Shilly's encouragement and guidance. By then he had a headache. As the glow flickered and went out, he closed his eyes and leaned back against the altar stone in the center of the cave, exhausted.

"Well," said Shilly, squatting down next to him, "you're getting somewhere. How are the visualizations coming along?"

He shrugged in the darkness. "Okay, I guess, although I don't see what good they'll do."

"Don't you?" She exhaled sharply once, like an aborted laugh. "They're the whole point. Without them, you won't be able to use the Change properly."

"Why not?"

"Because..." He felt her gesticulate but couldn't see. "Because ... Oh, it's hard to explain. Lodo says it's all to do with tools and why people need them."

"How?"

"Humans are pretty good at doing lots of things, right? But we can't do everything the best. If we want to dig a hole, we could use our hands, and our ancestors probably did, years ago. But today we can use a shovel, and that's better. The difference is the tool--the shovel. And it's the same with most things. You could tear vegetables apart with your hands before you eat them, but a knife makes it easier. You could walk from town to town, but your dad's buggy is quicker. Where there's a will to do something, there's usually a way to do it better--and with people, that way usually involves a tool. Are you following me?"

"I think so."

"Tools don't have to be physical things, of course. They can be like fire, which makes vegetables taste better. Words can be tools, too; they communicate ideas, and ideas can change the way people see the world. That can make some things easier in the long run. So Lodo says, anyway."

Sal wasn't sure he followed that. "What does this have to do with the Change?"

"Well, the Change requires tools just like anything else. This stone is made to call light. Using it is easier than summoning light from nothing. You *could* do it, if you were powerful enough and trained properly, but the stone is simpler and better. There's no reason to take the hard way if you don't have to. It's the same with Lodo's globes, or the Scourge of Aneshti.

"Some things, though, require a different sort of tool. There's nothing to hold on to; there's no shovel. It's all in the head. A lot of the Change is like that. The symbols you're learning are the tools you'll need to do more than just call up light and heat. If that's all you want to do, then you just need the stone. It'll do what it's made to do well enough, and you'll master it eventually. But if you want to make your own stone, or change the way this one works, you need to think properly. You need to see *into* things. That's what you're learning, even if you don't know it."

"I am?"

"Yes. That's all I can really do. I learn the shapes and use them through you or Lodo, when you'll let me. They may seem meaningless at the moment, but there is a kind of pattern to them. Some are purely symbolic and have to be memorized, others are sounds that aren't really words and are tricky to get right, but there's a whole class of imitative patterns that are easy to learn. They're the older ones, usually, and can be a little clumsy."

They were drifting again from the subject Sal was interested in. "Such as?"

"Well..." She thought for a moment. "Remember how I did the illusions, last time we were here? It all begins with something representing the thing I want to call up: a picture of the thing, say, or the sound it makes. If I can't get that, I have to use a visualization based on what it looks like or sounds like. So, the secret lies in imitation, however you do it. You pretend it's there, and then it is, after a fashion."

"What else can you do?"

She hesitated again. "Nothing much, really. Just tricks."

"That Lodo taught you?"

"Some. I talk to Aunty Merinda, the old woman at the markets. She tells me things, too. Some of her charms work better than others, she says. She can find something that is lost if she knows you well enough, and she can purify water. Small scale stuff."

"Can she read the future?"

"I don't think so. She says that telling the future is as hard as telling the past. Telling the present is easier."

"Has she told you how to do it?"

Shilly nodded. "It's not hard. You focus on a particular person and you can see what they're doing."

"So you could use it to spy on someone."

"Exactly. In theory, anyway."

"Maybe that's how Lodo keeps an eye on the workshop while he's not there."

"Maybe. I've never been game to try it around Lodo, or ask him about it. I don't think he'd like me learning this sort of stuff before I'm ready. Aunty Merinda did tell me that it doesn't work well through rock, so I'm not sure if that was what he's doing. He might have a better way."

Sal mulled all this over for a moment, then said: "Do you think it would work down here?"

He heard the smile in her voice. "I thought you were fishing for something. It might. Who do you want to spy on? Your father?"

"No. Kemp." He told her what he had seen the night before. She listened closely, fascinated, as he described how he had seen Kemp sneaking through the streets of Fundelry after midnight.

"That's his home, all right," she said, when he described the big stone house by the beach where Kemp had gone inside. "I haven't spoken to anyone this morning, so I don't know if there was a theft last night--but it wouldn't surprise me. There has been at least one every night for over a week now. You and your father are the main suspects, of course. Everyone has pretty much made up their minds about that."

Sal's stomach sank to hear it confirmed to his face; no wonder people were looking at him suspiciously.

"Kemp wasn't carrying anything that I could see," he said. He could only act on the assumption that Shilly, at least, thought he was innocent and would need all the information he could give her.

"That doesn't matter. Big things aren't being stolen. It's more like money or trinkets, stuff that could fit easily into a pocket. Stuff that Kemp might actually steal. It's not as if he's poor and needs food or tools or anything obvious."

"So it could be him."

"Theoretically. Ignoring the problem of motive..." It was Shilly's turn to think it through.

"We could *try* spying on him," said Sal.

"Wouldn't hurt, I guess." She sounded uncertain but determined to press ahead. "Aunty Merinda didn't warn me not to do it."

"There you go, then. What do you need?"

She looked around. "A picture of the person we want to watch--I can draw one in the dirt--and something he has touched recently. I'm not sure what we can use for that."

"What about me?" Sal suggested, thinking of the day on the jetty.

"That was a while ago now." She frowned. "But we don't have much choice, I guess."

She stood up and, by the light of the glowing stone, began sketching in a soft patch of the cave floor. Sal watched over her shoulder, amazed at how well she could draw. With an economy of lines, she managed to capture everything about Kemp that made him who he was: the large brow and chin, the wide-spaced eyes, the thin lips. When she had finished, she dusted pale ash across the drawing to make it stand out from the brown earth.

"Not bad," she said, dusting her hands. "Right. Stand on the picture, and give me your hand. And remember: I've never done this before, so it might not work. Even if it does, we might not learn anything. Don't get your hopes up."

"I won't," he promised. He was more excited simply to be trying something new with the Change. The prospect of seeing someone from afar was much more interesting than making a rock glow.

Shilly closed her eyes and concentrated. Her fingers

tightened around his, and he felt once again the odd sensation of something shifting inside him--something his normal senses couldn't interpret.

At first it had seemed both hot and cold at once; now it seemed simultaneously hard and soft, or sharp and blunt. There was no defining it, except that it was there.

Then, through the link between them, Sal caught a glimpse of what Shilly was visualizing. He saw a tunnel of glowing, crimson rings snaking into the distance. The end was invisible at first but, as Shilly imagined herself moving down the tunnel, it slowly came into view. Sal saw the picture she had drawn of Kemp growing nearer.

Faster and faster they moved, until they were falling down a red-hot pipe. The rings blurred. Kemp's face grew larger. For an instant, Sal felt like they were about to crash into it--

Suddenly, it was gone. The tunnel was gone. A rush of images washed over and through him, disconnected and confusing, but vividly real. Kemp's images.

School. Mrs Milka mouthing words in front of her blackboard. Not really paying attention to what she was saying, though. Gaze drifting across the backs of heads in front of him. Thinking.

(the face of a girl Sal had seen in Kemp's gang but whose name he didn't know)

...BEWARE...

Yawning.

(a dark corridor, an unlocked door)

Someone nudging him in the arm. Shrugging it off with a grunt of annoyance.

...THE GOLDEN TOWER ...

(a slim, silver chain coiled in the palm of one hand, as light as a feather)

Remembering.

(Sal's face up close)

Dreaming.

...BEWARE ...

(a slim, wooden box with a dragon carving on the lid, hidden in a drawer)

(a jewel as clear as a diamond and as tiny as a fish egg)
...THE GOLDEN TOWER ...
Planning.
("You'll get yours.")
Smiling.
...BEWARE THE GOLDEN TOWER!

Then, just as suddenly, Sal was pulled backward, out of Kemp's mind and along the red tunnel. Rapidly at first, gradually slowing, he felt himself ease back into his body, through Shilly. It was the most peculiar sensation he had ever felt.

When he could feel himself again, his hand was clutching Shilly's for support, and she was clutching him back just as hard. Both of them were breathing heavily.

"Wow," she said. "That was amazing!"

"You saw it? You saw what he was thinking?"

"I sure did. He's definitely up to something."

"Something to do with me?"

"He *hates* you. Did you get that?"

Sal was startled by the intensity in her voice. "No, not exactly."

"He does. It was frightening." She let go of him and ran a hand through her hair. Her eyes avoided his. Sal wondered if some of Kemp's feeling had rubbed off on her.

"What was all that about a golden tower?" he asked.

She frowned. "I didn't get that."

"It was really strong, but from a long way off. Just a feeling to stay away from it--from a golden tower. No images or thoughts came with it." An idea struck him. "It seemed to come from *outside* him."

"Maybe it was the future. His future." She did meet his eyes, then. "The only golden tower I know of is in the Haunted City."

"Do you think that's what it means?"

"I don't know, Sal." She looked nervous then. "He's out to get you. That's all I know for certain."

She slumped down to the floor, and he sat next to her. They thought in silence for a long while, each examining what they had experienced in Kemp's head. Sal wasn't at all reassured. They had seen some suggestive images, but nothing actually confirming that Kemp was the thief. Similarly, they knew Kemp was plotting something, but they didn't know what it was. Without knowing what it was, they couldn't do anything to avoid it. If anything, Sal was feeling more frustrated than before.

"Maybe Tom knows what's going on," Sal eventually suggested.

"You can ask him if you like, though I doubt he will. He lives in his own little world."

"We could break into Kemp's house, then, see if we can find anything we saw. They must've been some of the stolen goods: the necklace, the jewel, the dragon box. If he has them, that'll prove he's the thief."

"And what if we're caught doing it? Everyone will think *we're* the thieves!"

"Well, there must be something we can do!"

"Maybe." Shilly put her head in her hands. "At the moment, I don't care. I just want to get the taste of him out of my mind."

He realized then that pushing her wasn't going to help. He hadn't understood just how deeply being inside Kemp's mind had affected her. It would be better to wait for her to recover from the experience before discussing what to do about it.

He leaned against her, and she leaned back into him. Putting his arm around her seemed the most natural thing in the world. In the gloom of the cave under the Ruins, he held her in silence and waited for her to come back to herself.

CHAPTER 11

THE CONSEQUENCES OF DESIRE

WHEN they emerged from the shelter of the Ruins, the heat hit Sal like a sledgehammer. They retreated to Lodo's workshop, where even the usual stifling warmth seemed cool in comparison to outside.

The old man had them work together on more visualizations while he kept busy with his own projects. He seemed distracted and unaware that they had done anything untoward. Perhaps they hadn't. Sal wasn't about to ask Lodo about it. He had enough to worry about already.

Shilly was distracted, too. Even challenging her to a game of Double Blind didn't elicit much of a response. She still won, but not by as great a margin as Sal had expected.

Eventually, Lodo threw what he was working on down onto the bench and straightened with a snort.

"It's no good! I can't concentrate. Something is distracting me, and I'm not going to find it here." His gaze swept the room, settled on Shilly and Sal. "How would my two apprentices like to dine on the beach this evening?"

"Ah..." Sal didn't know what to say.

"What's the matter?" Lodo's eyes held a mischievous twinkle. "Nervous of falling in again?"

"Yes," supplied Shilly.

"Well, then. This will be a good test of your concentration. Come on."

The old man struck a long, brass cylinder hanging from the ceiling with a small hammer, making it ring with a deep, vibrant note. As Lodo gathered up Sal and Shilly and led them out of the workshop, it was still humming.

The afternoon was fading. Sal was surprised, as he often was, by how much time had passed in the workshop. The day was only a little cooler, though, if at all. The air lay heavy and thick over the dunes, sucking up sound. The sun hung low in the sky, fattening as it descended toward the horizon. There was little respite in the shadows it cast.

The town seemed dead when they arrived. Everyone was either inside or still out on the fishing boats. Red dust puffed up under their feet as Lodo marched up to the hostel and banged loudly on the door.

It was opened immediately. "So," said Von from the relative cool within, her voice as ragged as ever. "You're putting in an appearance, are you?"

"Aye. If you'll take me."

"Would that I wouldn't, old man."

"Not so old, hag, and you know it."

Von smiled at that; her rough voice softened slightly. "You're a bitch as well as a witch, "she said." That's good. At least I know you're not a golem. Come in, come in."

She waved Lodo inside, then Shilly. The hostel owner's smile faltered when she saw Sal waiting to come in too, but she sniffed and let him past.

They filed into the kitchen. There Sal saw Lodo touch a miniature version of the brass cylinder he had struck in the workshop, stifling its faint vibration. The old man's expression was one Sal hadn't seen before: part amused, part chastened.

"I was considering a picnic," Lodo said, taking a seat at the heavy wooden table. "By the sea."

"For how many?"

"Ten, perhaps. We don't want too large a group."

Von shrugged. "It won't be anything fancy."

"We're not royalty. The less trouble it is to you, the better."

"Then I think I'll manage well enough."

Lodo turned to Sal. "Your father is invited, if you think he might like to come."

Sal was about to say that he wasn't sure, when Von said shortly: "He's upstairs."

"I'll go ask him."

Von stared at him, then turned to Lodo. "Yes. You go too," she added to Shilly.

Sal left the room, glad to be away from Von's odd looks. Shilly followed him, her tattered blue dress whispering as she brushed the wall.

"Did you notice anything weird about Von?" Sal whispered.

"Where do I start?"

"No, seriously."

"Back at you. She's an odd one. They make a nice pair."

"What, her and Lodo? Really?"

"No, not really, but I think she'd be interested. He helps her out and she cooks us meals sometimes. Like tonight. The menu is pretty dull out at the workshop, in case you hadn't noticed."

Sal hadn't seen Lodo eat at all. But there was no time to pursue that topic. They had arrived at the door to the room Sal shared with his father. He knocked once and went in.

His father was seated on his bed, digging through the contents of his pack. Dull brown and weatherworn--not dissimilar to the man who carried it--it sagged limp in his lap. Sal thought he saw something thrust hastily back into it as the door opened, but couldn't be sure.

"Oh, Sal, it's you." His father put the pack aside and folded it shut. "Hello, Shilly. Sal's told me who you are. You can call me Gershom." He held out his hand. Shilly took it, shook once and let go. "Finished lessons for the day?"

"I guess so." Sal explained that Lodo had invited them to an impromptu picnic on the beach. Initially, his father looked uncertain, but acquiesced when Shilly said that she thought it might have something to do with Sal's training.

"Know the enemy?" he asked with a smile. "I guess that makes sense. You two go on down and I'll follow in a second."

Sal did as he was told--but noted his father reaching back into the pack as they left the room.

As they came down the stairs, they caught a fragment of conversation from the kitchen.

"Don't be ridiculous," Lodo was saying. "You can't seriously think that he's--"

"I know what I've seen," retorted Von, her voice soft but intense. "And heard. Everyone--"

She fell silent at the sound of footsteps on the corridor's wooden floorboards.

"Well?" Von snapped as they walked in. "Is he coming?"

"Yes."

"Good. My food won't be wasted, then."

"What about your other guest?" Sal asked, trying to be helpful. "Shall I see if he'd like to come too?"

"No," Von said, casting Lodo a quick glance. "I don't think he'll fit in with this lot."

If Lodo knew what she was talking about, he made no sign. "Well," he said, "if you don't need a hand, perhaps we'll meet you there.

"No trouble. Where exactly is 'there'?"

"Around the bluff, I think, where it's sheltered."

"And out of sight of town." Von nodded understanding. "I won't be long."

Lodo smiled and bustled his apprentices ahead of him again, out of the room and out of the hostel.

There was no turning back. Sal's nervousness rose in direct proportion to the proximity of the sea. He remembered the way it had moved, the constant turmoil just below the thin skin of its surface. He remembered the feel of that skin closing over his head and sucking him down.

"Wait, Lodo." He reached out and grabbed the old man's arm. "What did my dad mean when he called the sea 'the enemy'?"

"Well, he has reason, I guess." Lodo looked around. "The sea isn't your enemy, Sal. It's dangerous, and it can be deadly, but it bears you no ill-will. Not personally."

"Then why ...?"

"The *sea* isn't your enemy, Sal. It's the people who use it you have to be careful of."

Sal was more confused than ever. "The fishermen?"

Lodo laughed. "No, but that's a fair guess. Look, let's keep moving and I'll explain as I go. Don't worry about the sea tonight. You'll be safe with us as long as you keep your anklet on."

Sal looked up into the old man's face and knew he had little choice. There was kindness in that expression, but determination also. And sympathy, although Sal wasn't sure what for.

They walked on, Shilly trailing at a leisurely pace, kicking at stones.

"The background potential," Lodo explained, "is like a well-spring. It trickles forth slowly but surely, and those with the Change can use it if they know how. But since, as you have learned, some places have more potential than others, the trick often lies in finding such places that are suitable for your needs. Not all well-springs are the same; different skills require different flavors, different sources. Now, this knowledge is more important than it sounds. On it lies understanding of the great rift that divides the Stone Mages and the Sky Wardens. It explains why the Strand and the Interior are the way they are--and why, even though skirmishes are common between both nations, one has never succeeded in taking over the other."

"Why's that?" Sal asked, intrigued.

"Because we can't use each other's reservoirs," Lodo said. "It is that simple. The Stone Mages draw forth the background potential from bedrock and store it in fire. Sky Wardens, on the other hand, weave into the air what they take from the sea. The sea, in short, is their reservoir. It may not obey their will, but it is theirs nonetheless. They can tap into it and read its humors; when they bathe in it they absorb some of its vitality; and when they die, they are cast back into it, to sink slowly into its depths and become one with the water."

Understanding dawned. Shilly had once said that the sea belonged to the Sky Wardens; Sal hadn't realized that she had meant that more literally than he had thought.

"So being near the ocean," Lodo went on, "places us near the Sky Wardens as a whole. You see, the Haunted City might be the metaphorical center of the Strand, but the sea is its heart. Without it, the Sky Wardens would just be people like everyone else, the Syndic and Alcaide nothing but fancy titles, and the Conclave a privileged upper class destined for bickering and impotence." Lodo's expression was almost a sneer; his gaze focused on a distant place. "Away from it, the Sky Wardens are nothing. Yet it is as nothing to the Stone Mages, who cannot use it. This is the barrier that keeps the nations apart."

Sal was less interested in a political discussion than learning about his own situation. "If being near the sea is the same as being near the Sky Wardens, what happens when you're *in* it?"

The old man seemed to return to himself. "*In* it? Oh, I see. Well..." He shrugged. "It might mean nothing more than that you had an impromptu swim. But only time will tell. I'm keeping my fingers crossed. Ah, look."

The road they were following had hit a sharp bend.

"Almost there," said Lodo, and strode on ahead as though grateful for the interruption.

Sal lagged behind, not wanting to face the ocean again. The last time, it had held an unearthly gaze searching for him through the water. Had its owner seen him? Did it belong to the Sky Wardens? Would they catch him if he fell in a second time? He imagined an ice-blue figure poring over a crystal telescope, one end in the ocean, the other held to its piercing, burning eye.

Shilly's elbow in the small of the back nudged him forward.

"Don't worry," she said. "You're not going anywhere without me down there."

He didn't want to remind her that it hadn't helped last time.

They followed Lodo around the bend and between two shoulders of weathered sandstone--a natural gateway to the beach. One moment the sand and ocean were just suggestions on the wind: the smell of salt and fish, the sound of waves and gulls. Then, suddenly, there the sea was before them, even bigger than Sal remembered and twice as terrifying.

And yet, at the same time, it wasn't. The surf wasn't as strong. In fact, it seemed to be in retreat.

"We've missed high tide," said Shilly. "That's something."

"Yes." Lodo looked around, pointed to a slight hollow in the sandstone shelf. "There will do nicely. We'll sit and wait for the others."

Sal did as he was told. The white sand was soft--almost oily--between his toes as he stepped across the beach. He concentrated on the stone ahead of him rather than the sea at his back, but he could still feel the waves reaching for him like out-flung hands, trying to drag him into the ocean's depths.

And all around him, even through the anklet's deadening spell, he could feel the Change buzzing.

They sat in a close circle in the shade, facing each other. Shilly immediately began sketching, sweeping her index fingers through the sand with sure, rhythmic strokes.

"The most important thing you have to learn," said Lodo to Sal, "is to close yourself off from the background potential. That is the way others will detect you. Think of yourself as an island surrounded by water. If people on another island nearby can build a bridge across the water, your island and theirs can be joined. Sometimes this is a good thing. In your case, it is most likely to be bad. So you have to stop that bridge being built."

Sal nodded, even though he had no idea how to do such a thing.

"Another way to visualize it is as if you are a castle surrounded by a moat. Someone outside wants to cross the moat, so you make the moat wider and wider until no bridge can cross it. If you think of it this way, the background potential is everything on the other side of the moat. You must learn how to distance yourself from the outside. You must learn the art of solitude."

Shilly finished drawing with a satisfied nod. Lodo regarded her work with a pleased expression, and Sal tried to understand what it was, exactly, that she had drawn. It looked like a complicated series of interlocking circles. From one angle, the circles seemed to be looping around each other in a chain; from another, they seemed to be converging on the center. Then, if Sal blinked, they seemed to move into another configuration, as though they were alive.

"This is called a Cellaton Mandala," said Lodo. "It is designed to simultaneously shield you and confuse attack. The rings are only an analogy to the actual processes involved, but an analogy is all we need when dealing with minds and the Change. An advanced student learns how to visualize them as spheres, completely enclosing themselves. For now, this will have to do." Lodo's eyes didn't move from Sal's. "I want you to attempt to hold the image Shilly has drawn in your mind's eye. Let it hang there, moving as it wills. Concentrate on it as closely as you can. You will have to learn to hold the image at the back of your mind while you go about your everyday thoughts and activities, but for now we won't try anything so complicated. Do you think you can do this, Sal?"

Sal nodded, even though he was uncertain about the entire process of visualizing anything. He could try, at least. He settled back into a comfortable position and focused on the drawing before him. Unblinking and not looking away, he tried to inscribe the complicated arrangement of circles onto the surface of his eyes. It was hard, though; they seemed to slip away from him. He knew it was an optical illusion, but that didn't make it any easier.

After a couple of minutes, he closed his eyelids. The circles remained, etched in red against black. Their movement only seemed to increase, though, and he flailed mentally, and fruitlessly, to stop them from spinning away into the darkness. The pattern fragmented and dissolved, and he heard Lodo chuckling as he opened his eyes for another go.

"Many people rich in the Change have this difficulty," said Lodo. "It's always easier to use a power than *not* to use it."

Sal clenched his jaw and concentrated harder. This time,

when he closed his eyes, he retained control of the spinning circles long enough to feel a difference. The buzz of the sea ebbed for a moment, and the constant tickle that told him where Shilly was faded to nothing. He was, just for a split-instant, alone.

His success surprised him so much that he lost control of the Mandala again. When he opened his eyes, he saw Lodo smiling.

"I did it!"

"You took a step forward," said the old man. "A small one. If you are going to hide from the Sky Wardens when they come, you will need to do much better for much longer--and without the anklet to help you. Keep practicing."

Sobered, Sal tried again. He never quite achieved the complete isolation of his second attempt, but his control over the circles did gradually improve.

He could tell that Shilly was getting bored when, from around the curve of the sandstone wall, he heard a voice calling them.

"Over here!" she yelled, standing up and brushing the pattern away with her feet.

"Ah." A slender man came into view. It was Josip, the mechanic. "Von told me you'd be here."

"We are indeed," Lodo said. "I'm glad you could come."

Josip was carrying a wicker basket, which he set down on the sand between them. Nodding to Sal and Shilly, he squatted down on the beach and looked around.

"It's going to be a clear night," he said.

Sal agreed. The sun was sinking to his left, and the sky was deepening in color. Rich blues and indigos crowded together, bursting into reds and yellows closer to the horizon. Despite the lack of clouds, the sunset was going to be magnificent.

A moment later, Sal's father joined them, followed by an old woman Sal recognized as Aunty Merinda, the white-haired market seer, and Von, carrying another basket and a folded mat. Moving people aside and clearing a space, Von unfolded the rug and opened the baskets. Within was a variety of breads, salted meats, cheeses, and some brightly colored salad vegetables.

Two other people Sal hadn't formally met before joined them for the meal. One was a short, stumpy man by the name of Derksen who made charms for the local fishers. He carried a small guitar in one hand, strung with seven thin wires. Sal couldn't recall where he'd seen Derksen before, until he remembered the man in the russet suit at the market who had asked his father about the toa marks on the bottom of a crystal. Derksen acknowledged Sal with a wink.

The other was a woman about Sal's father's age who made a living divining for springs in the area. Her name was Thess, and she wore a long, blue smock over her advanced pregnancy. When she arrived, Aunty Merinda ran her hands across Thess's stomach and nodded with satisfaction.

"Beating strong," the old woman declared. "He'll be a tough one, like his father."

Thess rolled her eyes, and gratefully eased back onto the mat.

"Thanks for heeding my call," said Lodo when everyone was seated and introduced. "It's good to see you all in one spot again."

"Our pleasure, I'm sure," said Josip, to a murmur of agreement. "Any excuse will do, ill or otherwise."

"You feel it too?" the old man asked.

"A twitching in my joints," Aunty Merinda complained. "Something's up."

Thess nodded. "I assume you know what it is," she said to Lodo.

"No." The old man shook his head. "But I think we'll find out soon enough."

"Then there's time to eat," said Von, passing around plates and stoneware mugs. From one of the baskets she produced flasks of fresh water and wine. "The Earth's blessing be upon this food and all who eat it."

Lodo nodded. "Agreed. And thanks especially to you, Von, for providing it."

Von looked uncomfortable, but accepted the thanks and

indicated the trays of food. Sal felt his stomach rumble, and reached for meat and salad. Shilly ate only salad, bread and cheese, as did Lodo, who picked at his plate like a bird at seed. Sal's father ate awkwardly at first, but unwound as conversation flowed around him. Sal didn't participate much, for the most part watching the adults as they talked.

They were an odd group, centered mainly around Lodo or his work: Josip had his charm necklace, unusual for so deep in the Strand; Derksen wore a bronze ring in one ear; a delicate tattoo snaked around one of Thess's fingers. Aunty Merinda had the Change in common with him, if not the same methodology. Von seemed to like Lodo for himself. And then there were Sal and his father, drawn from the borderlands by the promise and threat of the Change, caught in the net.

The sun set in a wash of reds. As night fell and a slight breeze sprang up, the sea became easier to ignore. Overhead, flocks of seagulls fluttered restlessly to and fro, making Sal nervous. They looked like bats in the growing darkness, but they never flew too close to the group on the ground. Derksen found a large, round stone further up the beach, which Lodo set aglow by holding it between his hands and concentrating upon it. It cast no heat, just a light much like campfire embers, softening the faces of those sitting around it.

"What about the town lights?" asked Thess.

Lodo waved a hand. "They can wait for once. Fundelry will survive without me."

"No doubt," agreed Derksen, "but it wouldn't be half as entertaining."

"I'm amazed you practice your craft so openly here," said Sal's father.

Lodo shrugged. "I'm useful. The *source* of my usefulness is irrelevant to the people here."

"Don't the Sky Wardens worry you, though? I can't imagine you hiding when the Selector comes to town."

"No. I'm not frightened of them." The old man looked down at the glowing stone. "Power is like a rope bridge, with the highest at either end and the lowest in the middle. The ones in the middle--always jostling for position and setting the whole thing rocking and swaying, threatening to tip everyone off--they're the ones I'm afraid of."

"That's why you jumped?" Sal's father asked.

Lodo's gaze didn't leave the glowing stone. "Yes."

Josip cleared his throat into the awkward silence that followed. "A moment ago we were speaking of entertainment ..."

"Ah, I thought you'd never ask." Derksen reached for his guitar and took a heavy draught of wine. "Any requests?"

"Something in tune," suggested Aunty Merinda. "For a change."

"No use asking for miracles," said Thess.

"Come now," Derksen admonished them. "This isn't a court in the Haunted City. You only get what you pay for. What about our new friends? Do you have any requests?"

Sal's father looked startled. "Me? No, play what you like. I have no preference."

"Well, so I shall." Derksen plucked strings and twiddled knobs experimentally. With the sound slightly improved, he launched into a bawdy ballad Sal had no memory of hearing before. Aunty Merinda laughed and joined in on the chorus, not adding much to the tunefulness of the performance. Lodo shook his head and rolled his eyes at Shilly and Sal, but did nothing to stop them. Sal paid habitually close attention to the melody, thinking that it might be worth something at the next town they visited.

Thess leaned back against a sandstone outcrop with one hand on her stomach. When Derksen finished, with a bow to Aunty Merinda and Josip's applause, she asked for something quieter.

"Little Gil doesn't like the loud ones," she explained.

Derksen shrugged good-naturedly and tried an instrumental tune that Sal vaguely recognised, a piece he'd heard called "The Mountain Rondo". Neither Derksen's guitar nor his playing was the equal of it, however, and Sal saw his father wince every time a note fell wrongly.

When it was over, Derksen wrung his hands and apologized for being out of practice.

"That's been your excuse for as long as I've known you," chuckled Lodo.

"Yeah, well."

"Do you know the Marchiori Cycle?" Sal asked.

Derksen looked surprised at the question--but not half as much as Sal's father.

"A tune or two," admitted Derksen. "Do you?"

"I know I like them," said Sal. "I've heard fragments, but never the whole thing."

"Well..." Derksen thought for a moment, his fingers idly stroking the strings. "Let's see. I think this one's part of it."

Once again he began to play, this time a soft introduction to a melody that managed to seem beautiful even through his rough playing. Sal had heard it before, in a town far away, but then it had had a vocal accompaniment. He couldn't remember much about the lyrics, except that they were very old: something about loss, perhaps, or regret ...

When it was over, the notes reverberated in the air for a moment before a wave drowned them out. The glowing yellow stone shone in everyone's eyes--but in Sal's father's most of all, his gaze fixed on Sal.

"Lovely," said Lodo, breaking the spell. "That brings back memories."

"I've never heard it before," said Thess. "Was it written for someone?"

"A place, I think. Or a time." The old man shook his head. "I'm not certain."

"You played it very well," admitted Aunty Merinda.

"I won't take any credit for that," said Derksen. "It's one of those tunes plays itself, if you know what I mean."

The words seemed to stir Sal's father from his spell. "The last line wasn't right. Close, but not quite."

"You know it too?" Derksen didn't seem to be offended at the criticism; in fact, he looked almost relieved, as though he wasn't used to praise.

"I ... yes."

"Can you play it?"

"Once, but--"

"Here." Derksen extended the guitar. "Show me. I can always use a lesson."

"I'll second that," said Aunty Merinda.

Sal's father hesitated, then took the instrument and swung it onto his lap. His fingers hovered over the strings, as though nervous, then stuck the correct notes in perfect, fluid time. Sal was amazed: he had never heard his father play anything before.

Then suddenly the full tune was coming from the guitar, so pure and sweet it seemed to bear no relation to what Derksen had played. Sal listened breathless as his father played the passage through once, his face expressionless and the music flowing like silver clockwork, then repeated it, this time with the accompanying words sung in a smooth, tenor voice:

"I stand amid the roar
Of a surf-tormented shore,
And I hold within my hand
Grains of the golden sand--
How few! Yet how they creep
Through my fingers to the deep,
While I weep--while I weep ..."

When Sal's father ceased singing, this time even the sea seemed to have fallen silent.

"Now *that's* playing," said Derksen, once the last note had faded away.

"I'll say," said Aunty Merinda. "Wherever did you learn to play like that?"

The spell broken, Sal's father looked awkward and defensive. "I learned a long time ago, a long way from here. I haven't played for years." The last was addressed to Sal, as though in apology. He offered Derksen the guitar, but the would-be minstrel waved it away.

"No, I wouldn't dream of embarrassing myself further. Play something else, please."

"I'd rather not." Sal's father kept the guitar at arm's length, as though it might cut him.

Derksen took it with a shrug. "Okay, but it seems a waste."

"A story, then," suggested Josip. "You promised me one the other day."

Sal's father looked relieved. "Yes, I did."

"Well, I'd call that a fair trade."

"Aye," said Lodo, nodding. "Your time in the spotlight isn't over yet, son."

Sal's father and the old man exchanged a long look that Sal couldn't interpret. It was as though they were playing a game of cat and mouse no one else could join.

"What story, then?" Sal's father finally asked.

"Something new," said Josip. "We don't get many inlanders through here."

"What about Polain the butterfly merchant?" Sal suggested.

"Yes." His father nodded. "A good choice--if no one here has heard it, of course."

No one had, so Sal's father settled down into a more comfortable position and began the tale.

Sal listened with half an ear. Not only had he heard the beginning just four days before, he was still stunned by what he had just learned about his father. He had had no idea he could play the guitar, let alone so well. Sal couldn't have been more surprised if his father had unscrewed his head and booted it into the sea. Again, he was at a loss to understand why such knowledge had been kept from him-- especially when music was something he had pursued with interest throughout his travels. If he had known his father had shared that interest at all, it was something they could have explored together ...

But gradually the tale of the merchant's quest for the last, unique butterfly in the world succeeded in dragging him in, as it always did.

"He searches the branches and ground nearby," his father was saying. "Polain creeps carefully through the enclosure, making absolutely certain that nothing is underfoot. His heart beats a little faster as he thinks: *Maybe this is the one, the last unique butterfly in the world. Maybe my search is over.*

"And when he sees it, perched on a branch with its wings upraised, still soft from birth but beating the air with increasingly sure strokes, he knows. Its coloring is pale green across its abdomen and thorax. Its antennae have an orange hue with yellow highlights and are curled in a tight spiral. Its wings are black, lightening to blue around the edges, with a subtle cross-hatch pattern in silver visible only as the light reflects off them. In the center of each wing is a single, pure white circle.

"Polain has never seen its equal. Backing away, wary of startling it, he calls hoarsely for the butterfly feeders. Sensing his excitement, they come running. One of them has the forethought to bring a silk net. Polain snatches it from her and swoops up the butterfly with a swing more delicate than a gentle breeze.

"He cradles the captured butterfly in both hands and takes it to the main enclosure, where a special habitat has been prepared and kept ready. There, the specimen is examined for flaws and signs of ill-health. None are found. It is weighed and its markings are recorded. The clerks dive into the vast bookcases, the catalogues, following themes of shape and hue in search of a match. This is the most nerve-racking time for Polain. All he can do is wait impatiently for word to come that his venture has not been in vain. It is too late to breed another with this butterfly in the hope that a similar but unique creature will result. And the chances are infinitesimally small that another will be born in the one day remaining. It is either this butterfly or none at all.

"The night passes sleeplessly. Still no word comes. He joins the clerks at dawn to supervise their quest and promises them substantial bonuses if they work without rest until they are satisfied. Midday comes, and the queen's departure is only hours away. One of the clerks declares in exhaustion that he is sure that, judging by the shape of its wings, the butterfly is unique. Polain sends him home, relieved to a small degree but still anxious. Two hours pass, and another clerk, specializing in abdominal markings, similarly declares satisfaction. She too is dismissed with thanks. The third and fourth clerks--wing markings and head/limb composition-- are certain by five o'clock that their work is done. Only then does Polain begin to feel anything like joy. These two clerks are sent home with smiles and a shot of liquor burning in their bellies. Just one remains, an elderly man specializing in the relatively small field of antennae.

"With just two hours left, Polain hurries about the business of preparing the butterfly in its presentation jar, dressing himself in his finest suit and composing a short speech of thanks--to the queen, for accepting the gift, and to the people of the city, for buying his butterflies in the past and permitting him the indulgence of his vocation. Without them, he might have been a street-sweeper or postman or something as insignificant. Instead, his name will be known forever as the greatest butterfly breeder who ever lived.

"As he puts the finishing touches to his bow tie and his speech, a soft knock is heard at the entrance to his chambers. When he opens the door, he finds the elderly clerk waiting in the hallway outside.

"'What?' Polain snaps, angered by the interruption to his train of thought.

"'I'm sorry to bother you, Master Polain,' says the clerk, 'but I thought you should know immediately. I've found a match.'

"Polain's heart freezes. 'No, that's impossible. The others are satisfied, and I myself don't recall another butterfly like it. How can it be?'

"The elderly clerk holds a large book open in both hands. He raises it as he explains: 'I, too, thought I was certain until I happened across an obscure morphology in an old record- -one of your own, sir, made before I joined you. A tight, clockwise spiral not dissimilar to the one we have before us.' He indicated the glass-bound butterfly, which flapped its wings innocently. 'I followed the record backward, through several generations. The chances were slim that I would find one with not just the same antennae but the same coloring, shape, legs and features--but I did, sir. Here. I'm sorry.'

"Polain looks down at the open book with something approaching horror. There, sure enough, is a picture of a butterfly identical in every respect to the one in the jar. A note in his own handwriting refers to its purchaser, a banker from a neighboring province who had paid a fraction of its true worth many years ago, before Polain's name had become known. The butterfly may have only lived a day or two in the hands of such an ignorant carer, but it *had* lived. That is the important--and tragic--thing. There is no escaping the fact.

"'I'm sorry, sir,' repeats the clerk. 'I can't imagine how you must feel.'

"'No,' says Polain. 'You can't.' He takes the book from him and considers smashing it down upon the glass jar and its fragile occupant. Such has his life become. One hour remains until the presentation--until failure and ruin, public humiliation and mockery. Despair fills him.

"Or ... need it be so? Polain's mind seizes a possible solution. Yes, an identical specimen had once existed, but who knew of it? Its owner had been no one in the butterfly world; such a man would never remember a token bought for a lover or mother so long ago--and even if he did, who would believe him? The chances are exceedingly slim that the butterfly itself has been preserved--and if it hasn't been, there is no evidence at all. The remains would be nothing but dust, worn down by time.

"Polain decides to present the second butterfly to the queen anyway--and accept the accolades of the crowd--confident in the knowledge that his deception will go undiscovered.

"There is only one problem.

"'What are you going to do now, sir?' asks the clerk.

"Polain looks at him with cold calculation. The record he can destroy as easily as tearing it from the book and throwing it in the fire. But the clerk knows the truth, and he will not be easily bribed. Money and prestige are not important to him. A man obsessed with antennae associates only with those like him, when he associates at all. He will let the secret out before long. It is inevitable. Who would miss a man with such an obscure fascination?

"Polain resolves to get rid of the clerk, otherwise his plan, and his life, will come to ruination. It is the only way.

"So he does."

Sal's heart always went out to the aged clerk, whose life held only his beloved butterfly antennae and whose reward for diligence was nothing but a violent death. He didn't know if the story of Polain was true, but even if it wasn't it still had the capacity to make him sad. The first time he had heard the story, many years ago, he had cried for so long his father had thought he might never hear the end. This time, he kept carefully quiet. The only sound was the relentless breathing of the surf.

"Polain kills the clerk and goes to the presentation. The queen accepts the butterfly with a gracious smile and the crowd farewells him with a loud cheer--although neither matches his expectation. The queen smiles far wider at the thought of going home, and the crowd cheers more for the fireworks and streamers than him. Even his own heart, he must confess to himself, isn't really in it. He is already planning how to dispose of the old clerk's body by burying it in the soil of the various glasshouses.

"So he leaves behind the gaily colored pennants and goes home to finish his work. He dismisses the feeders to prevent his grisly deed from being discovered. He burns the treacherous record and catches up on his sleep. Soon, he promises himself, he will be alone with his butterflies. He will be content then. Breeding has always been his first love, not the endless competition and cataloguing. With no need of money, he will be happy for the rest of his life, once the unpleasantness is forgotten."

Sal's father paused to clear his throat and take a sip of water.

"It can't end here," said Thess.

"No." Sal's father smiled at her comment. "Life is never

so simple. First, the clerk's body putrefies in the soil and emits a powerful stench. No amount of perfume will hide it. It fades only with time, and leaves behind an unexpected boon: patches of explosive growth where the plants in the glasshouses have taken sustenance from the old man's decaying flesh. The flowers are beautiful and large, and the butterflies seem to favor them over the others, so Polain is pleased enough. But their association with his crime is not so easy to expunge, and he is ill at ease around the flowers.

"Then the police call to ask him questions about the dead man. The clerk's absence was noted after all, by a granddaughter whose birthday he had never before missed. Polain feigns innocence. Yes, the last time he had seen the clerk was just before the queen's departure. He had worked all his staff hard in the days leading up to the presentation. Perhaps the clerk had worked *too* hard and had had a heart attack on the way home. Is it so unlikely that the body of an unidentified old man might go unnoticed by the medical system?

"His evasion doesn't entirely satisfy the police, but they leave him alone; they have, after all, no firm evidence to suspect him, and no motive. Still, Polain's conscience is troubled, and will not let him rest. That night he dreams that the queen has rejected his gift and returns it to him with a disgusted expression on her face. He looks down into the crystal jar and sees a spider swimming in a puddle of blood, trying to escape.

"He wakes screaming and goes down to the glasshouses, seeking solace. A new generation of butterflies is being born, slipping from their pupae and inflating like balloons. He watches in awe: their colorings are striking, their patterns unique. All of them have the same corkscrew, orange-yellow, antennae of the butterfly the dead clerk identified. It seems almost like a tribute to the clerk, as though somehow his essence had been leached into the soil from his body, fed the plants upon which the caterpillars ate, and reached a strange expression in the resulting insects.

"Polain shivers, unnerved by the thought, and tells himself

not to be a fool. He has never been superstitious. Why start now? It is just a coincidence.

"He watches them for hours, hypnotized by their seemingly aimless motion. They are very beautiful creatures, with their angular markings of silver on blue that hint at familiarity but never reveal themselves. Every glimpse of every wing trembles on the brink of recognition, but never allows itself to be known.

"A bell rings late in the afternoon, and he stirs himself to answer the door. The police are back with more inquiries. They want to inspect the grounds, and even though they do not have a warrant, Polain lets them. To deny them access would only make them suspicious, and the chances of them uncovering anything are slim. The stench of decay is now gone. Without digging, they will find nothing but flowers and butterflies.

"Only as he shows the policemen the glasshouses does he realize what the patterns on the new breed remind him of. He was too close to them, before. From a distance he can see that each marking is a letter, drawn in the minuscule, reflective scales of the butterfly's wing. As they fly by, they spell gibberish through the air, meaningless jumbles of consonants and vowels that distract him from what a policeman is asking him.

"The policeman repeats his question, and Polain snaps himself out of his reverie to answer. What does he care that none of his neighbors saw the elderly clerk leave that fateful evening? He had more important things to worry about-- and besides, they were all jealous of his success, or were spies for his competitors. He would expect them to incriminate him whenever possible. And why would *he* lie? He has a reputation and a very successful business to maintain.

"Even as he says this, though, a swarm of butterflies lands in a line on a branch behind the policeman and spells out the words: 'NEMDO. CONFESS.'

"Polain stammers to a halt. 'Nemdo' was the name of the dead clerk. Noticing his fixed stare over their shoulders, the policemen turn to see, but their motion startles the butterflies. They fly away to another branch, where this time they just spell 'CONFESS', once again out of sight of the policemen.

"Polain suppresses an angry snarl. He knows what the butterflies are trying to do. They want him to own up for the crime. But he won't. He has no reason to. It is over, finished. The clerk was old, anyway, and near the end of his life. What had he to live for? The policemen are only tying up loose ends, and can't seriously be concerned for a lost geriatric.

"Still, 'CONFESS' say the butterflies, waving their wings at him and twitching their antennae.

"He picks up a rock from the dirt floor and throws it at them. The rock scatters them, and sails through the glass behind them with a loud smash.

"If the policemen are unnerved by that, there's worse to come. As a cloud of butterflies sail out through the hole, the policemen press Polain for an explanation of his bizarre behavior. It's nothing, he stammers. Nothing but reasonable distress at being interrogated in such an unseemly fashion. Who are they to insinuate that he is lying, that he knows something about this absent octogenarian? It's none of his business, or theirs, and they should leave immediately.

"But even as he speaks, the cloud of butterflies that escaped through the hole have not flown away to freedom. Instead, they settle on the roof of the glasshouse and proceed to spell out another word in shadows against the sunlight.

"'CONFESS!' they cry.

"Polain staggers backward, shielding his eyes from the sight. Alarmed, the policemen back away as the deranged butterfly breeder trips over a protruding stem and falls into a patch of enormous flowers. Butterflies go everywhere in a panic, filling the air with dark blue and silver flashes."

Sal was distracted by a faint disturbance on the other side of the dunes. It sounded like someone shouting, or calling, but his father didn't allow it to interrupt.

"Polain sees them all around him, in clumps and flocks, tormenting him. 'NEMDO' exclaims one group; 'CONFESS' yet another. His guilt presses in upon him, suffocating him. Keening, he clutches at the soil for a stick to arm himself with and swings at his tormentors. Swarms of butterflies part before him, sending fragmentary 'EMDs and 'ONFs and other syllables in all directions. But they always regroup, no matter how he batters them. Broken wings fall out of the air and soft bodies squash against stiff branches. His hair becomes entangled with broken antennae and legs. His eyes sting with butterfly blood until he can no longer see--and the fight goes out of him like air from a punctured ball."

The shouting was louder. Behind it, Sal could hear the slap-slap of bare feet running toward them.

"And so the police find him, clutching the trunk of a tree, bespattered with the crushed carcasses of his former wards, his face--"

Sal's father stopped as a boy skidded around the corner of the road and onto the beach before them. Through the darkness, Sal recognized him as Tom. Breathing heavily, the boy pointed back the way he had come.

"The hostel..." he gasped.

Von was instantly on her feet. "What about it?"

"The Alders ... Sal ..."

The look of alarm on the boy's face was instantly echoed on Lodo's and Sal's father's. Sal felt his stomach roll.

They ran with Tom back to Fundelry, the night rushing by them in a blur. Sal couldn't imagine what had happened to drive the boy into such a panic--but he began to get a better idea when they reached the square.

A crowd had gathered around the hostel verandah, at least thirty men and women all craning their necks to peer inside. Lodo pointed and shouted a single word. The two nearest globes flared into life, casting a bright white light over the scene. The crowd fell away before them, blinking and muttering in surprise.

"What's going on here?" demanded Von.

"They're inside," said one man, pointing at the open door.

"*Who's* inside?"

"Alder Sproule, of course."

As they hurried up the stairs to the verandah, the black-skinned Alder appeared in the doorway. He was dressed in his formal robes and held both hands closed around something close to his stomach.

"Ah," he said upon seeing them. "Here we are, like rats returning to the lair."

"What is the meaning of this?" snapped Von. "Why are you on my property?"

"I am here in the interest of the public good," replied the Alder. "You have nothing to fear, Von--but your guests have some explaining to do."

"We've done nothing wrong," said Sal's father.

Von stepped aside as the Alder approached Sal and his father. His gaze swept over them like an icy wind.

"No?" he asked, showing them the contents of his hands. "We found these in your room."

Three flashes of memory swept through Sal's mind:

(*a slim, wooden box with a dragon carving on the lid*)

--but now the box was open in Alder Sproule's hands, revealing--

(*a slim, silver chain*)

--and--

(a jewel as clear as a diamond and as tiny as a fish egg).

Sal felt a look of shocked recognition form on his face, even as he realized that such a look would only be taken as proof of guilt.

"These items were stolen from three different houses in this area in the last week," Alder Sproule stated, raising his voice slightly so the crowd could hear. "I think we can call that mystery closed, now."

"But I've never seen these things before," protested Sal's father over a growing mutter of voices. "I certainly didn't steal them!"

"You or your son or both of you--it makes no difference to me."

"It makes a big difference to *us*!" Sal had never seen his father so angry. "I demand a fair trial!"

"And you will get one," said Alder Sproule. "When the Selector arrives, you will be judged."

"But that's over a week away! What are you going to do with us until then? Lock us up? You don't have any evidence--just a few trinkets anyone could've planted."

"Ah, but we *do* have witnesses." Alder Sproule's eyes narrowed. "Another tenant in this establishment has heard someone leaving your room on a number of nights, at a time when decent people are asleep."

"And you believe this person? How do you know *they're* not the thief?"

"We can safely rule out that possibility." Alder Sproule straightened. "Anyway, you won't have to wait long for a trial. We should have this all sorted out in two days at the most."

"But you said--"

"Yes. The Selector will try you. Her visit has been put forward. We've just heard that she will arrive the day after tomorrow."

A cold more piercing than Sproule's triumphant stare stabbed into Sal's gut. *Two days!* He would never learn how to hide from Sky Wardens in that time.

Judging by the expression on his father's face, he wasn't the only one thinking it.

"No." Two large men moved in to bind their arms and take them, but Sal's father shrugged them off. "This is a travesty. I will not allow it."

"You don't have any choice, I'm afraid," said Alder Sproule.

"I have as much choice as I ever had," Sal's father said, elbowing the officer behind him in the stomach and pushing him backward, into the crowd. He ducked a swing from the second officer and pushed him off-balance into Alder Sproule. Then he grabbed Sal's hand and dragged him through the chaos along the verandah, ducking the outstretched arms that reached for them from all sides.

They made it off the verandah and into the square before Alder Sproule bellowed: "After them! Catch them!"

Footsteps clattered on the worn cobbles behind them. They sprinted away as fast as they could. Sal let go of his father's hand and concentrated on running.

They went inland along the main street. Sal knew where they were going but doubted they could possibly make it in time. If they could split up or cause a distraction, maybe-- but the feet behind them were too close, too loud, and too many.

Through the burning of his lungs and the growing ache in his muscles, Sal was reminded of the other time he had been chased along this road, by Kemp's gang. Then it had been daylight and he had been alone, but the feeling of being hunted down was the same. The road to Josip's workshop hadn't looked so perilous the day they had arrived in Fundelry.

"The key is in the ignition," Sal's father gasped as they rounded the last turn. "I'll hold them up while you go on ahead and start the engine."

"But--"

"Don't argue! There's a spare key under the mattress in our room if something goes wrong."

Sal was about to protest, then they rounded the corner. Ahead lay Josip's workshop, and the shed in which the buggy had been hidden. He felt his father slow down beside him and instinctively did the same. He didn't want to leave his father behind, even if he had been told to.

But that wasn't why Sal's father was slowing and why he jogged gradually to a halt, shaking his head. Only then did Sal realize what had gone wrong, why there was no point in running any more.

The doors to the workshop shed hung open. Inside were nothing but boxes. The buggy was gone.

Sal's father hung his head as the pursuing footsteps reached and overtook them. Suddenly the night was full of shapes. Hands grabbed them and pulled them apart. Sal felt rope loop around his wrists and tighten into a knot. He bit his lip to stop himself crying out as he and his father were knocked to their knees and forced to listen to Alder Sproule's breathless pronouncement.

"I arrest you in the name of the Shire of Fundelry on charges of theft, deceit and attempting to evade justice. You and your son will remain in custody until brought before the Selector of this region, two days from now."

Behind the Alder, Sal could see Lodo watching sternly from the sidelines, holding Josip's shoulder with one gnarled hand. The mechanic looked like he wanted to kill someone. Behind them it seemed the entire town had gathered to watch.

Alder Sproule concluded: "If found guilty, you will be sentenced under the laws of the Strand. Anything you say now may be used in these proceedings against you."

"What would be the point?" spat Sal's father, his voice thick with bitterness.

Alder Sproule snorted. "Only the guilty have no defense," he pronounced. "Take them away."

The hands holding Sal's arms jerked him upright and away from his father. There was nothing he could do to resist them. He felt like he was caught up in the current of a wild, dark river, unable to understand how he had come to be so trapped, and equally unable to escape.

The last person he recognized before he was taken to the cells was Kemp, watching quietly from one side with an expression of cold satisfaction on his face.

PART THREE:

CHANGING

CHAPTER 12

THREE ON THE HORIZON

FUNDELRY had four small cells to call a prison. Each would have held six adults at a pinch, with bed space for just two. Sal and his father had one cell each, on opposite sides of a short corridor cutting the chamber in half, and none of the others were occupied. If they had stuck their arms through the bars and reached across, they might have just touched fingertips.

There was an officer seated outside the room's only door--one of the big men who had tied them up at Josip's and half-frog marched, half-carried them away. Any disturbance would bring him in to "restore order". That was what he had called it when Sal's father had resisted being placed in a separate cell. A large splash of blood on the stone floor testified to what had happened next.

"Are you all right, Dad?" Sal kept his voice low.

His father sat hunched on one of the benches in his cell, the mess of his nose hidden in the shadows. By the light of the single smoky candle they had been allowed, Sal couldn't tell if he was even breathing.

He stirred just as Sal was about to repeat the question. "As well as can be, given the circumstances." When he looked up, Sal saw blood crusted on his upper lip and spilled down the front of his tunic. His nose was crooked, and his eyes seemed to drift in and out of focus. "What about you? Did they hurt you?"

Sal tried to keep his voice light. "I'm all right. They just untied me and put me in here."

His father nodded slowly, then rested his head back down on one hand. "I'm sorry, Sayed. It wasn't supposed to go like this."

The use of his heart-name made Sal's eyes prick. "I know, Dad. It's not your fault."

"Some of it is. I should have told you before now, but I didn't want you ever to have to know about it. I still don't."

"Will you ever tell me?"

"Do you want me to?"

"I'd like to know the truth." Sal thought for a second. "I'd like to know about my mother." *And you*, he wanted to add, thinking about the music he had heard his father play on the beach. There were a thousand questions he could ask. "I'd like to know where I come from."

His father sighed. "I wouldn't know where to start, let alone where it's going to finish."

Sal could hear the despair in his father's voice and was momentarily torn between pushing for answers or offering reassurance. "There's still time, Dad."

"Two days." His father snorted. "Not even that."

"You never know what will happen."

"No. That's true." He looked for a moment like he was about to say something else, but instead he lay back on his bench and shut his eyes. In less than a minute, his breathing was regular and slow, if a little ragged from the injury to his nose.

Sal considered calling for the officer guarding them. If his father had concussion, sleeping would be the worst thing to allow. But it seemed like normal sleep. He resolved to wait up as long as he could, listening for any change and practicing the Cellaton Mandala. That was probably the only hope they had left.

When exactly he slept that night, he didn't know, but he never forgot the dream he had.

He was standing alone at the base of a wide bowl with deceptively shallow sides, like the bottom of an empty dam. He couldn't tell how far away the lip of the bowl was, but it seemed a long way. The sun hung distant and high above him, casting no heat, and the sky looked misty rather than cloudy.

Sal shivered. He felt terribly exposed and vulnerable under that sky. But it was the horizon that made him the most nervous. Shadowy shapes seemed to be lurking just over the edge of the bowl's lip, sensed behind him but unseen when he turned. When he tried to run away, in any direction, the lip behind him failed to recede; if anything, it only came closer, all around him. When he stopped running, he was back in the center again, a little bit more trapped than he had been before.

So when he turned and finally *did* see something, it came almost as a relief.

A person had appeared on the lip of the bowl, standing silhouetted against the sky. Sal could tell the figure was female, but could discern little more than that. Not tall, but imposing all the same, she wore a hooded robe and held a staff upright with one hand. The top of the staff glinted in the sun, as though it was made of crystal. She didn't move at all.

He was debating whether to walk toward or away from her when another movement caught his eye. He turned to find that someone else had stepped over the lip. Another woman, taller than the first but wearing an unhooded robe and holding no staff. Her hands seemed to be clasped in front of her, although whether in a gesture of nervousness or hope, Sal couldn't tell.

The two women were spaced far apart but not quite opposite each other. Sal had to turn his head to look from one to the other. They didn't acknowledge each other in any way Sal could tell. They simply stood immobile, like statues, facing him.

Then another tingle in his spine told him someone else was standing behind him. He spun around and, sure enough, a third person had appeared on the lip. Less a woman than a girl, this one wore a simple dress. Her arms hung loose at her sides in an attitude of uncertainty.

Sal's first thought was that this third person was Shilly. But he couldn't feel her, and she didn't seem to recognize him. Concerned, he reached out with his mind, using the

Change to see if it *was* her--and suddenly felt the gaze of the other two women converge on him.

A chill rushed through him as their invisible eyes locked on where he was standing. He turned and saw that their robes had begun to shift as though in a breeze. Their arms rose high above their heads. They grew larger and he realized that they were coming closer. The horizon was contracting around him on all sides. He was frozen in the middle, uncertain what to do.

Faster the two women came, reaching for him. They were racing each other, fighting to get to him first. Fingers splayed, still silhouetted in perfect black against the sky, they rushed forward to engulf him--while behind him, forgotten, the smallest of the three faded away into nothing ...

He awoke surrounded by shadows that seemed like the fluttering of cloaks or the wings of a dark-feathered bird flapping at his face. He flailed at them with his hands--and finally realized that they were an illusion and that the three women had been a dream. A breeze was blowing through the cells, making the candle flame gutter and cast strange shadows on the wall.

He collapsed back onto the bed, gasping. He didn't want to sleep again; a lingering sense of panic wouldn't leave him. Just like in the dream, he could feel nothing when he reached out for Shilly. Her absence disturbed him. He had become used to her being there, on the edge of his mind. Was that what the dream had been about, then? Perhaps, he thought, but it didn't explain the identities of the other two women.

Uncertainty over the dream distracted him from Mandala practice until he almost despaired of ever getting it right. How he would maintain the defense while going about seemingly normal behavior was beyond him--even though he knew he had no choice but to try. Besides, he had little else to do until someone came into the room, either to release them or to continue their persecution. He didn't even know what time it was. Days could have passed, for all he knew; the Sky Wardens might have come and gone, leaving them alone forever; it might all have been a terrible mistake.

Then his father began to stir and he guessed that it was around dawn. That was when his father would normally wake, sun or no sun. He sat upright on the bench and waited to see what would happen next. His father's sleep became increasingly restless, but didn't break.

The door clattered open not long after, bringing with it a shaft of light. His father groaned as someone stepped into the room. Sal's heart beat a little faster. It was Lodo.

"Good morning," said the old man to Sal, who rose to meet him at the door to his cell, not daring to hope. Lodo looked tired. "They told me to give you this."

He passed a flask of water through the bars. Sal gulped at it gratefully as the old man crossed the room and tugged at solid shutters opposite the door. They resisted for a second, then swung aside with a clatter, letting in still more light. Sal held his hand over his eyes until they adjusted, then put the flask back into Lodo's waiting hand.

Sal's father stirred again. He clutched the side of his bench and his eyes fluttered.

"You're lucky, you know," Lodo said, leaning as close as he could to Sal's father's head and speaking loudly. "You haven't got the headache I earned from arguing with the Alders all night."

The sound of Lodo's voice snapped Sal's father awake. Blinking, he sat up and looked around, confused. "What?"

"Here." Lodo thrust the flask through the bars, and Sal's father took it. "And listen. Euan Holkenhill, the local Sky Warden's representative, announced yesterday evening that Selection will take place earlier than usual this year. He apologized for both the inconvenience and the late notice, but he has no choice but to do his superiors' bidding. They follow their own counsel."

Sal's father sat up straighter, and winced. "How does he know they're coming?"

"He received word of the possibility several days ago, by gull, and had it confirmed the same way yesterday."

Sal recalled the day at the markets, the gull alighting on Holkenhill's arm and the way he had suddenly left the festivities. He thought of the Sky Wardens--looming ice-blue giants he had hoped never to see in the flesh. "Why is she coming early?" he asked, unable to keep a faint tremor from his voice.

Lodo turned to face him. "Because of you, my boy. They know you're here, and they're coming to get you before you escape."

"You're certain of that?" asked Sal's father.

"As certain as I can be, under the circumstances. Holkenhill doesn't know much, really, but he says that more than the usual one Selector is coming. That much he *has* been told. Why would they bring the date forward *and* send more Sky Wardens, if not for Sal?"

"How did they know I was here?" asked Sal. "Was it the seagulls?"

"To begin with, perhaps. The scabs notice free talents and report them. Just being here might have got their attention--but I doubt that would have been enough on its own."

"The eye, then," said Sal. "The eye in the storm, and in the sea. That *was* them."

"It seems so." Lodo nodded wearily. "I had hoped they might not have seen you, or that they couldn't tell with any precision where you were. But I fear the sea was your undoing. In their domain, you could not possibly remain hidden for long. They have obviously spent the time since preparing for your capture. Now they are ready to act."

Sal's father planted both fists on the bench, on either side of his legs. "It was always a risk, coming here."

"Yes, and boldly taken. All is not yet lost."

"But they've taken the buggy and made sure we can't get away. They've got it all covered."

"No. That's an unrelated matter, nothing to do with the Sky Wardens. Alder Sproule has little doubt that you're guilty of the thefts and saw no reason to leave you with a chance to evade justice. I can see his point of view, even though I don't happen to think he's right." Lodo stopped for a second, then asked Sal's father: "He *is* wrong, isn't he?"

"Yes. We earn our way, wherever we go."

"That is the most sensible thing to do if you want to stay unnoticed--but I had to check. You do have a case to answer, unfortunately."

Sal's father shook his head. "It can't be much of a case. We haven't done anything wrong."

"What about the stolen goods they found in your room?"

"We didn't put them there. There must be another explanation."

"And the witness? He says he has heard someone leaving and coming back to the hostel late at night, on several occasions."

"Well, that's true enough. Sal has been going to and from his lessons at all hours."

"True or otherwise, it is suggestive."

"Can we discredit him?"

"I doubt it. He's Euan Holkenhill."

A light dawned in Sal's mind. The witness who had heard him moving around at night had been a guest of the hostel. Euan Holkenhill, the regional Selector's representative, was in town to get things ready. Where else would he stay but at the hostel? He and Von's mystery guest were one and the same.

Sal had simply never put the two together before. When he thought about everything that had been said in the room he and his father shared, he realized just how lucky he was that Holkenhill hadn't seen or heard more than he had.

But the concept of luck was relative in this case.

"So it's our word against Holkenhill's," Sal's father said. "You're right. We're in trouble."

"Even *without* Holkenhill, you'd be in trouble. Sproule doesn't like you, and there is the material evidence. If we could find out how it got there, maybe we'd have a chance."

"I can guess," said Sal. "Kemp put it there."

Lodo's eyebrows went up. *"Kemp?"*

Sal nodded. "He's trying to set me up."

"Why?"

"He doesn't like me. I guess he figures that if he can get us convicted of stealing, we'll be kicked out of town."

"At the very least. Can you prove any of this?"

"I know it's true." He told Lodo and his father about what he had seen two nights before, and what he and Shilly had subsequently uncovered with Aunty Merinda's charm.

Lodo still looked uncertain. "It's not that I don't believe you, Sal, but even if you had evidence I doubt we'd convince Sproule. He's never going to accept that his son was behind it. It would ruin his reputation."

"I don't care," said Sal's father, getting up and pacing the cell. "If that's what it takes to get us out of here, then I say we should do it. Anything to keep Sal safe."

Lodo gestured for calm. "Yes, I thought you'd feel that way. That's why I'm keen not to rock the boat just yet. You see, I've managed to broker something of a deal. Hence my headache."

Sal's father stopped pacing. "What sort of deal, exactly?"

"Well, you've seen some of the work I do in Fundelry. The lights, for instance, and hot water. I fix pottery and settle foundations. There's a lot of stuff in any town that Sky Wardens are no good at, and I fill the gaps here. That has increased the town's standing in the area, as well as given the Alders a little extra comfort. I simply threatened to take it all away from them--for the visit of the Selectors, if not permanently--unless they gave me what I wanted."

"And that was?"

"I wanted you both out on a good behavior bond. With the buggy hidden, there is no way you'd run. But they wouldn't give it; letting you both go didn't set enough of an example to other would-be thieves. So I settled for just Sal. He won't be going anywhere without you, and if they have you here, safe and sound, they figure he won't get up to any mischief either."

Sal's father stared at Lodo and Sal for a long moment. "Sal goes free?"

"He leaves with me now, if you agree."

"And I stay here."

"To be tried by the Selectors, when they arrive."

"Where will Sal be then?"

"That depends on how well I can hide him." Before Sal's father could ask, Lodo raised a hand. "And it's best you don't know, for now."

Sal's father resumed pacing. "You're asking me to let go of Sal, to trust you completely. In here, I won't know what's going on. I won't know if you turn him over to the Sky Wardens the first chance you get. I won't have any idea until it's too late."

"Not that you could do anything from in here, anyway."

"That's not the point. If Sal was in here with me, at least we'd be together."

"Hung up like pigs, waiting for the butcher's knife."

Sal grimaced at the metaphor. "I don't want to leave you here, Dad."

His father looked at him, and sat back down on the bench. He rubbed at his eyes and winced when he bumped his swollen nose. "I don't think we have a choice, son."

"You don't," said Lodo.

"But that doesn't mean I have to like it!" The stare Sal's father cast at the old man, then, was filled with a dark emotion. "I don't have to like any of this. Why can't they just leave us alone? Why won't they let us get on with our lives? Why *us*?"

"You know the answer to those questions, Dafis Hrvati."

Sal's father nodded in resignation, then looked up in surprise. Sal, too, was startled. Dafis was his father's heart-name, known only to a handful of people. How Lodo had learned it, he couldn't guess.

Nothing was said for a long moment. The two men just stared at each other, as though daring the other to speak.

Then footsteps came from the doorway.

"I think that's long enough," said a voice. Sal turned to see Alder Sproule standing just inside the room, dressed in his black Alder's cloak. "Do they agree?"

Lodo brushed down his tunic. "I think they do."

"We agree," said Sal's father, casting a baleful look at the Alder.

Sproule grunted and produced a key. He crossed the room and unlocked the door to Sal's cell.

"Get out, white boy."

Sal did as he was told and waited as the Alder locked the cell behind him. "The slightest trouble and you're back in here, understand?"

Sal nodded.

"You too." That was directed at Lodo. "He's only free on your recognizance. You don't want to give me the chance to put you away as well, old man."

With one last scowl at the three of them, Sproule turned and stomped out of the room. An officer took his place, indicating that Lodo and Sal should come with him.

Sal hesitated. His father looked very small in the cell, still bloody and exhausted.

"Take care, son," he said. "Visit if you can."

"I will." They clasped hands through the bars. Sal didn't trust himself to say anything else.

"Never underestimate the power of light and hot water," said Lodo, gripping the man's shoulder briefly before leading Sal away.

CHAPTER 13
OLD TRUTHS IN A NEW LIGHT

"FROM now on," said Lodo, as he led Sal out of the prison cells, "you don't leave my sight."

Sal tried to ignore the hostile stares greeting him. The antechamber to the cells seemed to be full of Alders and their officers, all watching him closely. He had no doubt that none wanted him to leave, or that Lodo was bearing a large part of their animosity for forcing them into it. He had a lot to be grateful to the old man for.

But all he could think of was the man he was leaving behind--trapped and powerless, in the dark.

"I'll need your signature here, Lodo," said one of the officers, holding out forms. The old man stopped to scrawl in the spots he was supposed to, then herded Sal out of the room. The bony hand digging into Sal's back wouldn't accept argument.

"Don't say anything," Lodo added as they exited the station into the full light of day.

Outside, a small group of people waited. Sal didn't recognize many of them, but they knew who he was. Upon seeing him, they booed and hooted. One threw a stone that missed Sal's ear by a millimeter. Sal turned to see who had thrown it, and saw the boy--younger than him--drop the next stone he intended to throw with a cry of pain. He clutched his fingers to his chest as though he had burned them.

Lodo hurried Sal up the street, away from trouble. The group didn't follow them, but only because some of the Alders' officers kept them back.

"Idiots," Lodo muttered under his breath. "They won't go away if you ignore them, but at least they won't get any worse."

Sal's voice had left him. He was afraid to open his mouth for fear of what might come out--be it a scream, a sob or vomit.

Lodo moved quickly. No one got in their way as they crossed the town square, although more than a few stared, and a couple even voiced their displeasure at seeing the "white thief" freed so soon. Sal tried to ignore them, but he still felt angry--and undeservedly ashamed at the same time. His ears were burning and he kept his head down.

Lodo didn't even have to knock. The hostel door opened before they'd come up the steps.

"You're doing yourself a disservice, old man," said Von as she let them in.

"Do you think I'd be doing this if I thought they were guilty?" he snapped back.

"That'd depend on what you thought you could get out of it."

"My survival instincts are still good."

"That's not what I'm saying."

"I know." He headed up the stairs with an irritated shake of his head.

"You won't find their stuff up there," she said.

He stopped on the stairwell with Sal behind him. "Where is it, then?"

"In here." She sighed and showed them to a ground floor room hidden behind a locked door. Sal realized it was her own room. There was a large, messy bed, a wardrobe filled with old clothes, a candelabra covered with wax, and--most startling of all--a wig resting on a stand that was the exact same shade and style as the hair on Von's head.

In a pile in one corner lay Sal and his father's packs.

"Go through them," Lodo ordered. "Make sure it's all there."

Sal did as instructed, smoothing out the clothes and repacking them as neatly as he could. The small supply of coins was missing from his father's possessions, as was a cotton rug he used for warmth, but otherwise everything seemed to be there, including the small jar full of pearl shell and blood mixture that they had bought from Lodo at the market, and the buggy's spare key his father had said was under the mattress.

In the base of his father's pack Sal discovered a flap of leather that could be tied down to form a false bottom. He had never known it was there before, and might never have known had he not seen it now. The space beneath the flap was empty.

"They found the stolen goods under your mattress," Lodo said. "They also found this." He held out a thin, leather pouch, creased from repeated folding. "As it wasn't listed as missing, I demanded that they return it."

Sal sat on the ground and unrolled the thin leather. Inside he found a silver clasp that might once have closed a light cloak or gown. It was tarnished almost black, but the work was very fine. The silversmith who had crafted it had folded silver threads in layers around a central, hemispherical device. It looked fragile but held its shape well. It was firm between Sal's fingertips and showed no signs of ever having been bent out of shape.

"The motif symbolizes the Earth," said Lodo. "I'd have to guess it was your mother's."

Sal had never seen it before, but knew it must be what his father had kept in the hidden space at the bottom of his pack. That knowledge tipped the balance. His throat constricted, his face screwed up and there was nothing he could do to stop the sob that came with the thought that his father had carried this memento of his mother everywhere he went, for almost as long as Sal had been alive.

Lodo didn't touch him while he cried, and for that he was grateful. Distantly, he was aware of Von leaving the room and coming back a moment later. When he was able to look up again, he found a glass of water beside him on the floor. He wiped his eyes and washed the taste of tears from his mouth.

"I never met them," said Lodo, "but I heard about them." The old man took a seat on the bed and sat staring at his hands while he talked. Sal didn't interrupt. "Your mother's family came from Mount Birrinah in the Interior. Her grandparents had formed a powerful Clan alliance between Sun and Fire, making them part of the Earth Clan. But something went wrong a generation before your mother, some scandal or other involving her parents, and they left the Interior. They resettled in the Haunted City and formed new alliances there.

"Against the odds, your grandparents arranged a union that would bring their Clan together with the Cloud Line. Such a union wouldn't have been unique. There have been marriages between Clan and Line before, but this one promised a lot more than just political advantage. You see, your mother's family had a talent for the Change, which was why they'd been allowed into the Haunted City to begin with. And, at the time, several members of the Cloud Line had risen very high in the Conclave, increasing the chances that any offspring would be talented. Theirs was the most anticipated union of the decade."

Lodo stopped and thought deeply for a moment. "I've never had a reason to tell this story before, and it surprises me how clearly I remember it. Maybe I sensed that I would brush against it, one day. You see, I too am an exile of sorts, from two worlds. My skin is brown; by right of birth, I should have been a Sky Warden. But my talent lay with the fire of the Stone Mages. I rejected my early teachers and abdicated to the Interior, to the Desert Ports. My years there were productive. I learned and achieved every goal I set for myself. I was never happy, though--I missed my home. In the end, I returned to the Strand and sought a position in the Haunted City."

He shrugged. "I didn't understand at the time why I so threatened the establishment there. I didn't fit in, and moved from place to place before realizing that I would never be welcome. Before I left the City, I stood briefly on the fringes of your parents' story. It was one of the few times when scandal pointed *away* from me, and I'll admit to being glad of it for a while. When I did leave, I left voluntarily, and not a day too soon."

Again he paused. "I'll tell you this, Sal, then return to your parents. I think you'll understand--later, if not now--although so many haven't over the years. The Change doesn't sit well with everyone. It's a powerful gift and a terrible responsibility, that's for sure, and big things don't mix well with little people. I prefer the small magic, the magic of the everyday, and I came here to Fundelry because the beach has its own magic, a magic that is neither water nor earth, neither fire nor air, but a mixture of them all--malleable, wild, subtly vital. Unique." He looked up and met Sal's red-rimmed stare. "You haven't come into your full power yet. I know that. When you do, I want you to remember the words of a tired and old man. Here, on the edge of one world, I have found a bridge between two."

He looked back down at his hands. Sal waited with increasing restlessness as Lodo collected his thoughts.

"Your mother's name was--"

"Seirian."

"Yes. You've heard her name before?"

"My father called it out in his sleep."

Lodo nodded. "I told you earlier that she was of the Earth Clan. She had your coloring--same hair, skin and eyes--but you're already taller than her. You take after your father there. Her family name was Mierlo, but she and her husband took the new name of Graaff when they wed."

"That's not the name you called my dad."

"No, for one important reason: Dafis Hrvati is not the man your mother married."

Sal's stomach sank; he could see now where the story was going and how the word "adulterer" fitted in.

"Highson Sparre--later Graaff, then Sparre again--was a high-ranking member of the Conclave. Young and ambitious, he sought in your mother an alliance with an unknown political power. Her family was unlikely to be a threat, and there was a chance they could be an asset to add to the many he already possessed. Seirian was clever and had a raw talent in the Change. Also, she was beautiful, and talented children would increase his prestige. Her pale skin didn't perturb him. He, like many in the Haunted City, had ancestors who cross-bred, and his skin was only slightly darker than hers.

"But he wasn't the only one whose thoughts were more on politics than love. Your mother's family sought induction into the Conclave, and Highson Sparre would give them that. There was talk that he might one day become Alcaide, if his rise continued unchecked, and Seirian herself responded to that thought. He was handsome, influential and sophisticated; he could teach her how to control her talent so perhaps she, too, could make her presence felt. So they wed and became Seirian and Highson Graaff of the Rain Line, one of the golden couples of the Haunted City." Lodo's eyes stared off into the distance, remembering brighter places. "Neither of them reckoned on her falling in love."

"With my father," Sal prompted.

"Yes. Dafis Hrvati was a journeyman apprentice to one of the senior Sky Wardens of the day, a woman named Esta Piovesan who died not long after I left the Haunted City. Her position brought him into regular contact with Highson Graaff. Despite their age difference, they became close friends and frequent companions. Seirian, your mother, apparently didn't like Warden Piovesan, Highson's new friend, and sought company of her own. The journeyman was an obvious choice, for their free times frequently coincided. He, like Highson, had learned a great deal about the methodology of the Change, although he had no talent of his own. He also knew some of the more worldly arts, particularly those of music and storytelling.

"No one knows exactly when they become lovers, or when Highson found out. Suffice it to say, the scandal was enormous--not least because the lovers refused to desist. Such liaisons happen often enough in and around the Conclave, but usually they end swiftly and are never discovered, or are ended upon discovery, with no great loss of face. But not this time. Seirian requested an annulment of her marriage to Highson and sought permission to wed Dafis Hrvati instead."

Sal's spirits rose, hearing of his parents' love for each other. Lodo went on: "Perhaps the greatest error on anyone's part occurred at this time. Falling in love is never a mistake, whatever the circumstances. We err only in how we deal with it. Both families could have accepted the reversal easily enough, but neither could without the other's willingness. Seirian's family had a great deal to lose: if she backed out of the marriage, they risked public humiliation and loss of status; they would be back where they started when they arrived in the Haunted City. So they refused to grant their daughter her wish, and Highson's family had no choice but to back them. Seirian's formal options were reduced to just two: to stay married to Highson and end her affair with Dafis, or to seek annulment without the consent of her family or her husband, a process that could take years to proceed through the Conclave.

"So they took a third option that hadn't been offered them. They ran away. In the middle of the night, with the help of two friends who went to jail rather than confess how they had done it, the two lovers were spirited out of the Haunted City and into the Strand. There, they disappeared. No trace was ever found of them beyond the City's outer precincts. The search was massive and thorough--and utterly fruitless. Highson himself led the final sweep. He turned up nothing. Your mother and her lover were gone forever.

"At least, that's what it looked like. Clearly they went to ground somewhere, and kept moving to avoid suspicion. Your father, like Highson, has relatively light skin, so it made sense that they would go to the borderlands for a while, at least until the fuss settled down; it was probably there your father obtained the buggy, since such machinery isn't used widely in the deeper Strand, near the Haunted City. That's my belief as to what happened, anyway, even though Highson found no evidence that they had passed near or through any of the usual border crossings. Only your father could tell you for certain. Beyond that point, for me, the story ends.

"Until now." He looked up from his hands and fixed Sal with his storm-gray eyes. Sal thought of what his father had said about stealing something from the Sky Wardens. "When your father turned up looking for me, I had an inkling who he might be. When I saw your ward, I was certain. I had never known about a child--but why couldn't there have been one, later? And any child of your mother was likely to be talented, especially if its father had some form of talent, latent or otherwise. At least it would solve half the mystery: the whereabouts of Dafis Hrvati is bound to be something Highson Sparre would dearly like to know. I can understand why Dafis Hrvati is still running.

"But the mystery doesn't end here. *I'd* like to know where your mother is, and what caused her to leave you and your father. How *do* the Sky Wardens know about you and why do they want you so badly?" Lodo got up and ran his hands through his hair. "And why did your father pick *me* of all people to solve this particular mess?"

"I don't know," said Sal.

"No, I know you don't, and it's not your fault." Lodo tried to smile, but it was obviously forced. He reached down a hand and helped Sal to his feet. "With time to prepare, we could have hidden you easily. You would have worked on your concentration until you were ready to face the Selectors. If you hadn't been subjected to their full scrutiny, there's more than an outside chance they would have overlooked you. If we'd only had *time*."

"But we don't."

"No." Lodo looked back down at Sal. "And what's happened with Sproule isn't helping us at all. We're going to have to take an enormous risk if we're to have any chance whatsoever. Will you do what I tell you, no matter what it is?"

Sal nodded. "Yes."

"Good. Then I can help you, with luck."

"And Dad?"

Lodo's hand gripped his shoulder. "I don't know, Sal. It all depends on who they send."

* * *

Sal put his mother's silver clasp in his bag and stowed the clothes back in their correct places. When he was finished, Lodo bade Von farewell and they headed out into the world. The square contained only school children, busy playing. No Kemp, Sal was relieved to see.

"I apologize for Von's suspicion," Lodo said as they walked through town, toward the dunes. "She has learned not to trust people--with good reason, I'm afraid."

"What happened to her?"

"Several years ago one of her guests robbed her, then tried to destroy the evidence. She was burned very badly in the fire, and would have died but for a healing technique I learned from my old teacher. The experience taught her to be too careful at times. But it did open her eyes to Stone Mage techniques, and that helped my acceptance here."

Lodo put his hand on the amulet hanging around his neck.

"There's another storm coming," he said. "A big one."

His gaze turned inward, then, and Sal let him think. He tried to concentrate on the Mandala while he walked but was too distracted by what he had learned about his parents. He couldn't picture his father as a journeyman in the Haunted City; it was too strange, too *wrong*. Similarly, he could barely conceive of his mother as errant heir to a Stone Mage family. It contrasted so totally to the life he had shared with his father. What did a man who traveled in a buggy for a living know about courtly ways and the Change? More than he had ever guessed, obviously.

When they arrived at the workshop and he saw the stone fire in the center of the room, he wondered if the nagging thought it had prompted--that he had seen such a thing before--might not have something to do with this.

But there was no time to ponder it. Lodo put him through

an increasingly complex series of exercises designed, it seemed, to put all extraneous thoughts out of his head. He barely had time to notice that Shilly wasn't there and was, in fact, still absent from his senses. His mind filled with images of spirals, cubes and pyramids until they all seemed to merge into a horrible, uncontrolled mess.

As though Lodo could sense his state of mind, the old man soon called a halt to that exercise. He set Sal the task of calling forth light from a stone, while he went about other duties.

"If you strain hard enough," he said, "you might dull some of the shine off you. Or it could do the opposite ..."

Sal tried not to let thoughts of his father or the Selectors get in the way of this new task. He focused on what Shilly had told him in the Ruins--to summon the light from the dark heart of the stone as though drawing water from a well--and did find some small success. The light he called up looked weak compared to the flasks of frozen fire scattered through the workshop, but it was progress and, afterwards, he did feel exhausted. The effort combined with lack of sleep left him yawning compulsively.

Lodo looked up from his work and noticed him struggling.

"I have to go out," the old man said, standing up and scooping a handful of small objects off his workbench and into a pocket. "I'd prefer to take you with me, but you should be safe enough in here. Keep up with your exercises as long as you can, then get some rest. I won't be long."

Sal nodded, waited until Lodo had gone, then found a pile of cushions in a corner and fell instantly asleep.

He was woken what seemed only minutes later by a hand at his shoulder shaking him roughly.

"Wake *up*, Sal!"

He twisted onto his back and jerked his eyes open. "What? What?"

"You're on my bed." It was Shilly, crouched scowling over him. "Where's Lodo?"

"I don't know." Sal blinked, disoriented, and tried to get his bearings. "Where have you been?"

"It's none of your business."

"You've been at the Ruins." The realization came to him in a flash. *"That's* why I couldn't sense you."

"So what? I don't have to tell you where I am." Her expression darkened, and he thought she was about to say something else, but instead she turned away and strode angrily through the workshop to get a drink.

"What's wrong?" he asked her.

"Nothing."

"There is. Something's happened."

"You happened," she spat back at him.

"Me? What've I done?"

"'What've *I* done?'" She mimicked him with sarcastic venom. "I'll tell you what you've done. You've messed everything up, that's what. Before you came along, Lodo and I fitted in perfectly. We did the jobs we were asked to do and stayed out of everyone else's way. We were comfortable enough. We were even happy. Now you're here and everything's going wrong. Alder Sproule is threatening to kick us out; the School won't let me back in; no one will talk to me--or even look at me without making the sign of the evil eye. It's one thing to be ignored, quite another to be actively shunned. And it's only going to get worse. With the Selectors and the Goddess knows who else on the way, there's no doubt who's going to get the blame. You've ruined my life, Sal!"

He gaped at her for a second. "I didn't mean to--"

"Well, *that* makes it all right then."

"No, Shilly, listen to me--"

"Why? You can't tell me this isn't your fault. Your damned father came here *looking* for Lodo. Are you going to deny that? No? So stop pleading innocence. Whatever curse it is you're dragging around after you, I didn't ask to be part of it. Don't expect me to be grateful. Just stay out of my way until it all blows over, and maybe--when Lodo and I have finished picking up the pieces--I'll forget about you. All right?"

Sal got up and went to go to her, but she stopped him with a look.

"I know what you're going to say. *Don't.* You go through your life as though nothing's your responsibility. You're like a hermit crab letting himself be picked up and moved around without taking charge. You can't do that forever, Sal. You have to join the real world at some point. Maybe when you've done that it'll be easier to be around you. Until then, just leave me *alone.*"

Hurt and bewildered, Sal retreated to another niche of the workshop. There, out of her sight, he tried to concentrate on the exercises Lodo had given him. It was hard, even with his eyes tightly shut. He could hear Shilly moving around the room as though she was trying hard not to break things. He could understand her point of view. Up until his father's arrest, none of it had seemed real; it had felt more like a game. Reality had hit home hard for both of them.

The echo of her words still stung in his mind. He didn't know what a hermit crab was, but he got the idea. Maybe she was right. He did tend to go with the flow. He let his father decide where they would travel and he spent most of his time trying to avoid trouble rather than confronting it head on. But what else could he do? He wasn't especially strong or smart; he trusted the people around him to do what was best. That had usually worked for him.

Or had it? If, now, his father stayed in jail, where would that leave him? His father's decision to keep him in the dark had brought them to a situation that could only be described as unsatisfactory. Perhaps if he had spoken up sooner things might have turned out differently ...

Somehow, as though his mind unconsciously needed to distract him from the mental turmoil, the Cellaton Mandala took shape in his mind and remained firm. The circles seemed to rotate around their central point as smoothly as the stars at night, each engaging its neighbor in a complex dance that never repeated itself once. As his conscious thoughts fell away from him, Sal let himself become entranced by the dance. Concerns for his father, the sting of Shilly's words, nervousness over the Selectors' imminent arrival, even his sense of time, all faded. What he experienced was better than sleep: more controlled and peaceful, yet more free and invigorating at the same time.

There was just him and nothing else. He was unsurprised to learn that he liked it that way.

Lodo returned some time later looking satisfied. Sensing the tension in the room, he sent Shilly out to gather ingredients for the evening meal--"*Make* them listen to you. Tell them I'll clog up their chimneys if they don't."--while Lodo tested to see if Sal had improved at all.

"Could you really do that?" Sal asked as they settled into position around the central stone.

"What?"

"Clog up the town's chimneys?"

"No, not really. A Sky Warden might be able to make them smoky, since it's an air problem rather than stone. I could only make one or two fall down. That'd be enough, though." Lodo smiled at Sal's puzzled expression. "Small magic. Remember that. If someone's throwing stones at you, don't throw a bigger stone. It's always better to make them not want to throw stones at all, however you go about it."

Sal remembered the boy who had burned his fingers on the rock he had been about to throw that morning, but didn't ask. He figured he already knew the answer.

Lodo tested Sal's control over the Mandala and declared it much improved. "Still not good enough, though. We'll have to work together. I'll make some charms overnight for you to wear. They'll smooth out the dent you make in the background potential. The *physical* you we'll hide using illusion and good old psychology. We'll start by making you look a little different--darken your skin a little, and your eyes--but not much more than that. The key to this will be to keep you out in the open, where everyone can see you."

Sal's expression gave away his alarm. "But--"

"This is the only chance we have, Sal," Lodo said. "Hiding in a crowd is easier than hiding alone. If everyone takes you for granted, why shouldn't the Selectors? They'll be expecting you to be hidden away somewhere, out of sight, so they'll be looking in exactly the wrong places."

Sal didn't argue, although the plan seemed foolhardy. He had promised to do whatever Lodo said and he would honor that. He had no other suggestions anyway.

Shilly returned with a bag of provisions and retreated to her niche on the far side of the workshop without saying anything. Lodo kept Sal practicing, testing his defenses at every opportunity, to isolate weak points and shore them up. Sal had lost all sense of time so had no idea how long this went on. It felt like days. Still, he was surprised when Lodo called a halt to their exercises and declared that he had to activate the town lights.

"Got to keep my side of the bargain." He put on his many-pocketed coat, and gestured for Sal to get up. "Come on. It'll do you good to get out of here."

Sal wasn't sure about that--the thought of bumping into Kemp in the dark was a concerning one--but he didn't argue. Shilly said nothing, just watched, looking slightly hurt, as they left. Sal wondered if Lodo ever took her on his evening expeditions. Was that something else she would resent him for?

The evening was still warm, but becoming humid and unsettled. Clouds were sweeping across the sky, gathering more deeply to the east, and strange gusts of wind darted along the empty streets. The sun was setting in an explosion of reds and yellows, a foreboding of violence the following day.

"Yadeh-tash never lies," said Lodo, also studying the sky. He took Sal's hand and placed it on the worn amulet around his neck. Sal distantly heard a high-pitched voice whispering words he couldn't quite understand.

"How does it know?" Sal asked.

"I have no idea." Lodo shrugged. "It's very old, and its maker had far greater skill than I. My teacher gave it to me, along with the scourge."

"Why?"

"Why did he give them to me?" Lodo's voice was sharp,

and for a moment Sal regretted his curiosity. Then the old man sighed, as though releasing a burden. "He had high hopes for me, Sal, and I let him down. It was that simple. By returning to the Strand, I turned my back on everything he had taught me and all that he stood for. I was too busy burning my bridges to notice. He knew better than I that you can never go back."

They reached the first of the light poles. It stood on a crossroads Sal vaguely recalled passing on his first full day in Fundelry. If Lodo hadn't stopped at its base he might easily have walked past it without noticing.

The old man put both hands around the pole and closed his eyes for a second. The pole seemed to be made out of iron, its surface dark and rough, but it hadn't rusted anywhere. The spherical globe, as large as a baby's head, sat in a bracket not much higher than Sal's hands would reach, balancing on the points of five tapering claws. It wasn't transparent; the fading light of the sky didn't pass through it even slightly. It seemed to be made of a cloudy gray crystal with no visible flaws.

Lodo opened his eyes and raised one hand to touch the globe with his right index finger. Instantly, a glimmer of light appeared in its depths, flickering faintly.

"Look away, Sal," Lodo warned with a smile.

Sal obeyed barely in time. Light blossomed from the globe brightly enough to leave an after-image even out the corner of his eye. Night turned to day in a pool around them. Details stood out sharply, as though every stone or footprint had become somehow more real. Despite that, it cast no heat.

"It looks easy, doesn't it?" Lodo guided Sal down the street, away from the globe atop its pole. "Took me years of practice to get it right."

"Could you teach me how to do it?"

"Given the chance, maybe. Not many people have the knack, and I think you'll find an outlet more suited to your talent, eventually. But as an exercise it would be interesting."

They walked unhurriedly from pole to pole. No one paid

any attention to them, not that there were many people about. With the storm coming, and the Selectors, the town seemed to have huddled in upon itself. It was going to be a busy morning.

Sal gradually realized that the lack of interest in them went deeper than the villagers they had other distractions, though. They weren't just ignoring Sal and Lodo; they weren't even seeing them. As the lights went on, they blinked and looked up in acknowledgment, but not once did they see the two people standing in the light's full glare.

"It's a glamour," said Lodo when Sal asked. "The opposite of an illusion, if you like. It won't work on anyone with talent, so it won't be of any use tomorrow, but it is useful at night. I like to keep a low profile."

The glamour was eerily effective, but Sal remembered the way he had seen through such a trick in the marketplace, even when he hadn't known then that he had the Change. It was a double reminder: of the old man's skills and his limitations.

Lodo's path from pole to pole led them to the heart of town. The night was almost full by then, and the gaps between each light darker. The ever-present grumble of the sea seemed to be getting louder, too. All in all, Sal doubted he would ever remember nights in Fundelry with any fondness.

One of the globes rested near the School hall with the weathervane atop its roof. Sal couldn't be sure, but he thought the silver arrow might have moved slightly, tending more south-east rather than just east. Maybe it was just stuck, as Tom thought, and not pointing toward the Haunted City. A strong gust of wind could easily have knocked it aside marginally so it pointed in a new direction.

Then it was on to the square itself, with its eight globes on their poles. The hostel was dark apart from one light on in an upper floor room. Holkenhill, Sal reasoned, boning up for the big day. They circled the square, lighting each globe in turn, Sal conscious of his exposure. Again, though, no one noticed them. It was as though they were ghosts drifting through the streets, as ephemeral as mist.

Sal was wondering how many more could be left when they exited the square and headed for the prison. His heart lifted at the thought that he might be able to visit his father, but he didn't let himself become too hopeful. Lodo hadn't mentioned anything about the possibility, and he didn't doubt that it would be difficult to organize. But it felt like days since this morning in the cells; he wanted to know that his father was all right.

Standing alone directly outside the entrance to the prison was a single pole, complete with unlit globe. He hadn't noticed it that morning, distracted as he had been by the crowd that had booed them. They had, of course, dispersed, lacking further excitement to egg them on. He felt slightly ill, returning to the scene, but didn't hesitate as Lodo walked past the pole, opened the entrance and guided Sal inside.

There was one officer seated behind the wide counter. He was instantly on his feet when he saw Lodo and Sal walking in the door. Evidently the glamour didn't work in the light, or Lodo had removed it.

"I thought I'd find you on this shift," said Lodo.

"And I thought I'd see you before long." The officer didn't smile, but there seemed to be no overt hostility between the two men. They clearly knew each other.

"How is he?"

"Quiet. He's slept a lot."

"Can we ...?" Lodo indicated the door.

"Not until tomorrow. Sproule's orders."

"When tomorrow?"

"After he's met the Selector."

"What about the boy?"

The officer shook his head. "There's nothing I can do."

Sal's stomach sank.

"I could ask the Mayor," Lodo persisted.

"Don't bother. She's up to her eyeballs getting ready for tomorrow."

Sal felt tears prick his eyes. He hated the thought of being so close to his father but unable to communicate with him.

"You won't let me in?"

"I'm sorry, kid, I really am. He's asked about you. I'll tell him you were here, if you like."

Sal turned away to hide his disappointment.

"Thanks, Cran." Lodo put his hand firmly on Sal's shoulder. "We'll get out of your hair, now."

Sal didn't want to leave. Anger and frustration strained within him to be set free. Part of him resented the fact that Lodo didn't try harder--but he knew that wasn't fair. There was little Lodo could have done. The officer had orders he wasn't going to break. An old man and a boy couldn't convince him otherwise, let alone overpower him and force their way past him and the probable reinforcement beyond the inner door.

Knowing didn't help, but it did make it easier for him to succumb to Lodo's tug toward the door, acutely conscious of his father just meters away, through a stone wall or two. It also took the edge off Shilly's words, remembered afresh: if he *was* like a hermit crab that was only because he had no choice. He was powerless to do anything.

Outside, the fresh air stung his face, drying the tears that had trickled down his cheeks without him noticing. He wiped his nose on his sleeve and watched Lodo.

The old man had turned to the pole. Instead of grasping it like he had the others, he stood looking up at the globe for a moment, studying it.

"I thought so," he said. He pointed. "Can you see it? There, on the left."

Sal squinted. "What is it? A crack?"

"Exactly. I felt it earlier today. Someone damaged it." Lodo stepped back. "See if you can get it down for me."

Sal stepped forward and reached up on tiptoe. He managed to get his fingers under the globe and push, but it wouldn't budge. It was firmly anchored in place.

Moving him aside, Lodo plucked the globe out of its bracket with a single long-fingered hand.

"Tricks of the trade," he said by way of explanation, and held the globe up to the light coming through the prison's front window. To Sal's untrained eye, the damage seemed superficial. Lodo, however, looked decidedly unhappy.

"Ruined," he muttered, putting it into one of his voluminous pockets. From another he produced a replacement. Lifting it above his head, he set it in place. Activated, it shone with a dim red light.

"Hasn't had a chance to absorb anything," he said. "It has been in the workshop for weeks. Give it one good day's light, though, and it'll burn as brightly as the others."

He nodded satisfaction and headed up the street. Sal looked over his shoulder as the prison receded, mentally wishing his father a goodnight, whatever he was doing, however he was feeling. He couldn't remember another night they had spent apart in his entire life.

That seemed to be the last globe, because they headed by a roundabout route for the sandhills, avoiding lit areas and keeping to themselves. The wind had picked up in the hour or so they had been lighting the globes. It whipped around Sal in sudden flurries, wrapped Lodo's coat around his legs, then dropped back to nothing just as suddenly.

As they walked, Lodo reached into his coat and produced a leather-wrapped bundle. Giving it to Sal, who was surprised by its weight, the old man indicated that he should unwrap it.

Inside lay a smaller version of one of the globes, clouded gray like the others but half their size.

"When we get back to the workshop," Lodo said, "slip it into your pack. Make sure Shilly doesn't see. I don't think she'd understand at the moment. But I want you to have it, anyway. It'll come in handy one day, I'm sure."

Sal protested that he couldn't. "It's much too valuable."

"A thing is only as valuable as the need it fills," said Lodo, pushing it back into Sal's hands. "That's what my teacher used to say. A trinket designed for storing light is useless to me. I have many such things, and could make more if I needed to. But you, I think, will need a little light in the future, wherever you go."

Sal resisted a second longer, then gave up. He could feel

the globe buzzing in his hands, as though it was alive. If nothing else, it would give him a reason to pursue his study of the Change; without such mastery, he would never be able to make it work.

"What was your teacher's name?" he asked, as they left town and passed through the patchy scrubland leading to the dunes.

"Skender van Haasteren. He's probably dead by now." Lodo put his chin down on his chest. "Everyone I've ever known seems to have died, over the years. The load gets heavier, the fewer there are to share it."

They walked in silence over the dunes. The night was deep and dark, the sky obscured by clouds and the wind strengthening, carrying with it the smell of rain. Sal thought of Tom. He wondered if the boy was ready for the night ahead--another night waiting for his brother to return. For the first time, he could imagine how it might feel to experience such a loss.

He put the thought out of his mind and called up the Cellaton Mandala. This night was all that stood between him and the arrival of the Selectors. Lodo seemed worried about it, but not afraid, and Sal tried to emulate the old man's frame of mind. If it was going to be his last night of freedom, he wasn't going to waste it on fear.

Together they walked into the coming storm.

CHAPTER 14

A BONE FROM THE SEA

THERE was no dawn the next day.

Sal woke early, before either Lodo or Shilly, and was surprised to find the workshop still lit. He had assumed that the lights would go out while their owner slept, but they glowed with a warm, red light, like embers. He found it comforting for a while, until he remembered what the day held for him.

Tossing aside the light rug under which he had spent the night, sleeping fitfully at best, he climbed the tunnel to the entrance in order to relieve himself outside. There, he opened the portal as Shilly had showed him several days earlier: by placing his hand on a protruding spear of rock and willing the wall to part. It did so, dissolving into sand that fell with a hiss to either side, leaving a narrow space in its wake. Water instantly poured in, and he forced himself through the gap as quickly as he could.

The rain was heavy and fierce. Nearly blinded, Sal stumbled away from the door and into the lee of a large dune. It didn't make much difference. The storm raged around him like a living thing, worse than the one he had become lost in on the first night he had come to the workshop. Even though he knew his way around now, he still felt threatened.

Part of that was, again, due to the feeling that someone was looking for him. The sensation was hard to define. It was not literally as though there was a giant eye in the sky staring down at him, although that was how he thought of it. He simply knew that someone was probing through the clouds, through the wind, through the rain, clutching for any sign of him--and coming closer, as though they already knew where he was.

He called up the Mandala he had practiced all night and felt the gaze of his pursuer slip over him and away.

Staggering back to the door, relieved on two counts, Sal realized that he didn't know what time it was. It might have been dawn or afternoon, for all he could tell. The storm had erased all evidence of the sun. Without his father to wake him up, he had no idea when the day had begun.

An enormous crack of thunder followed him back into the workshop, where he stood, shivering, by one of the heat-emitting stones to dry.

Lodo rolled over on a bed of pelts and opened an eye in Sal's direction.

"Not long now," the old man croaked. "I feel them battering at our hatches like never before."

"What about the storm? If it's too rough to travel--"

"They'll be here. Don't worry about that. You can say what you like about them, but they always keep their appointments." The old man smiled. "By the way, there's a privy in that alcove." A finger emerged from under the covers and pointed. Sal could have kicked himself for going outside when he didn't need to.

Shilly stirred with a groan on the other side of the room. "It's too early for talking, you two."

"No." Lodo sat up with a grunt. "It's too late, if anything."

"Exactly my point. What difference will it make what time we get up?"

Lodo ignored her and got out of bed. He slept mostly clothed and only removed his tunic to wash from a copper bowl. Sal kept his eyes averted, but the old man didn't seem to mind if anyone watched or not. There were tattoos on his back that Sal hadn't noticed before: thick, angular patterns reflected on either side of his spine. He hummed tunelessly as he freshened up, then offered Sal the bowl.

Any self-consciousness Sal had experienced before was nothing compared to what he felt when it was his turn to wash. Shilly's eyes were on him all the while, peering darkly from under a flap of her covers.

"The first thing to do," Lodo said, busying himself at a

workbench, "is to adjust the way you look." He came over
to Sal, holding a selection of charms and pastes in his hands.
Before Sal could dress, the old man applied them one at a
time to odd places on Sal's body. "Skin. Your hair's about
right, so we'll leave that. Eyes. Build." The thong Lodo
wrapped around Sal's chest was tight, but not painfully so.
Next came a dab of ochre on forehead, chin and each cheek.
"Face. We'll keep the charm on your ankle for the time being.
It won't hurt." Lodo eyed Sal critically. "Now, put your top
back on." Sal did so. "Not bad. Here, look."

Lodo indicated a silver mirror and Sal stepped forward
to see. It was startling--and off-putting. At first sight he
saw a thin, tall boy with brown hair, skin and eyes. But
a second look showed the real him beneath. The two
appearances seemed to flicker in and out, as though fighting
for dominance. When he looked down at his hands, they
appeared normal.

"From a distance, you'll pass. Maybe even close up, if
no one looks too carefully. In a crowd you should be okay.
Just be sure not to wander off alone or draw attention to
yourself." Lodo nodded in satisfaction. "Now for the tricky
part." He produced two bracelets and wound them around
Sal's wrists.

Sal felt as though his hands had been dipped in icy water-
-a feeling which rapidly spread up his arms and through the
rest of his body.

"Don't take these off, whatever you do," Lodo warned.
"Unless I say so--or unless you desperately need to use the
Change, I suppose. But as the whole point is to hide the fact
that you have the Change, and given that you've hardly had
time to learn *how* to use it, stick with the first rule. These
bracelets do not come off. Got it?"

Sal nodded, although his skin seemed to be covered with
invisible ants.

"Right. Now, try the Mandala."

Sal concentrated on bringing up the spinning circles and
holding them in his mind's eye.

"Good." Lodo nodded slowly. "Good. Well done. Can you feel him, Shilly?"

"No," she yawned, rolling clumsily out of bed and heading for the privy alcove.

Sal felt his ears turn red at the thought that it would be her turn to strip and wash when she returned. He cleared his throat and desperately tried to find somewhere else to look.

Lodo's smile was perceptive and amused. "Whatever lies ahead of you two," he said, "I hope I'm there to see it."

When they were ready, the three of them left the workshop in waterproofed skins and walked through the rain into town. Shilly hadn't wanted to come, but Lodo insisted. There was a chance he and Sal might become separated, and she would need to keep an eye on the charms. She saw the sense in it, but didn't like it. The wind was coming off the southern ocean, bringing with it sheets of water barely less dense than the sea itself. It wasn't cold, exactly, but it did chill. The constant barrage penetrated even the deepest reserves of warmth and dryness.

Surprisingly, there were a lot of people about in Fundelry. Small crowds had gathered along the main route to the square, more than Sal had expected; he supposed that some of them had come from neighboring towns. Decorative ropes crisscrossed the street, snapping overhead. The main bell was tolling erratically, as if allowed to swing in the wind. Lodo's globes still burned, although the light they shed didn't go far through the rain. There were a lot of children, waving sodden bunches of blue and white ribbons or playing in the water.

Sal remembered that this was a special occasion for those in this area of the Strand. The Selectors only came by once a year, offering the town's hopefuls a chance to high jump out of the backwaters and into the prestigious circles of the Haunted City. Some might be destined to become administrators under the Alcaide, others representatives of the law acting with the authority of the Syndic. A select few might even graduate to become Sky Wardens, the Strand's rulers and caretakers, remote and blue and cold as ice.

It was odd, in the middle of a crowd with a lot to gain, to be the only one with everything to lose. His stomach churned from nerves.

Lodo found a position halfway along the route. Sheltered by a tall shed, the crowd was large enough to blend into. There they waited. Sal kept wanting to step back behind the onlookers, but Lodo wouldn't let him.

"Act like everyone else," the old man hissed. "Remember, you're supposed to be one of them."

But Sal noted Lodo breaking his own rule. He seemed anxious and unsettled. Although the crowd kept their gaze expectantly on the route out of town, the old man's attention wandered back toward the square.

"Is something wrong?" Sal whispered to him after enduring it for half an hour.

"I don't know. I just have a feeling ..."

But he didn't get any further than that, for a growing buzz up the road drew the attention of the people around them. A clamor of bells and rattles had started up and wasn't easing. Cheering, joining in with the racket, the crowd craned forward to see what was coming down the road towards them.

Sal couldn't help but do likewise. Even Shilly didn't fight it. The mood of the crowd was infectious.

And it wasn't disappointed.

Through the bobbing of heads, they saw a group of men and women, some on horseback and some in a cart, coming slowly through the streets. Maybe twenty in all, they wore a mixture of uniforms, from the black of the Syndic to the gray of the Alcaide. They seemed to be the source of most of the ringing, tolling away on bells small and large to announce their arrival. Even the horses had bells on their harnesses.

At the front rode a man and a woman, both dressed in blue slicks stained dark from water. The woman was older, in her fifties, but still firm in the saddle, while the man looked to be around thirty years old. Through gaps in their cloaks Sal could see glistening crystal around their throats: insignia of the Sky Wardens.

His heart skipped a beat. He fully expected them to stand up on the cart and point at him, their eyes and fingers burning him to a cinder where he stood. But they didn't. They looked like ordinary people. The man's skin was rich and dark, while the woman's was paler, more exotic. Both were smiling and waving at the people who had gathered to welcome them. Behind the smiles, both were definitely scanning the crowd, but they hadn't seen him. They weren't the all-seeing giants he had always imagined them to be.

Sal fought the instinct to hide, even so, and forced himself to wave along with the others while concentrating on the Mandala. So intent was he on acting naturally that he didn't notice the pair who led the progression on foot until they were almost past.

Walking slowly at the head was a young man of about seventeen years dressed in blue and gray, with narrow, handsome features and a dense mat of black hair. He was beaming and smiling as much as anyone. Beside him, holding his hand and looking up at him as though unable to believe what his eyes showed him, was a younger boy with ears that stuck out.

He nudged Shilly without thinking. "That's Tom, isn't it?"

"Yes. And to forestall your next question, that's his brother, Tait. As cute as ever."

Sal watched in amazement as the pair strode past. Tom's dream had come true, more or less: his brother had returned in the midst of a storm accompanied by the sound of bells, and he had been there to greet him.

Then the rest of the parade was passing. He felt the gaze of the Sky Wardens glance over him, and keep going. He hadn't been aware of Lodo's hand on his shoulder until then, but he was glad it had been there. Otherwise he might have fainted with relief.

The ordeal wasn't over yet. As one, the crowd around them moved onto the road to join the other locals following in the wake of the carts. Everyone was shouting over the noise of rain. Some people danced in the mud and puddles. Sal tried to join in the merriment--or to pretend to--but he was aware of a certain distance maintained by the crowd around them. Despite the charms, they still seemed wary of him, as if they could feel the truth lurking beneath his new face.

Also, he could hardly take his eyes off the backs of the people they were following deeper into town. He had seen his first Sky Wardens--and survived! It hadn't gone anything like he had imagined. The two on the cart looked strong and handsome, not frightening and shadowy, as he had expected. And these were the people who had come to take him away.

It all depends on who they send, Lodo had said. The man in blue wasn't old enough to be Highson Sparre--his mother's jilted husband who had personally hunted the fleeing lovers, and whom Sal had been half-dreading all day. "Do you know who they are?" he asked Lodo.

"The younger of the two I don't know," the old man replied, "but the older is Amele Centofanti, senior Selector of this region. She isn't powerful, being more an administrator than an inquisitor. We have nothing to fear from her."

Sal knew better than to be relieved at that news. Lodo certainly wasn't looking relaxed. "What about Tait? Is he a Warden too?"

"No, just a journeyman, according to his insignia."

Someone jostled Sal from behind. He turned, saw the person who had bumped into him look puzzled for a second, then return to dancing a one-person jig on the road as though nothing untoward had happened. "Where do they stay when they're in town?"

"The Mayor puts them up," Lodo said. "If things go the same as they always do, there'll be an official welcome in the square followed by a tour of the town. Then the Selectors will meet the candidates for examination and hear any grievances held over for them to judge. Tonight is usually reserved for the Alders' Feast, open to anyone and paid for by the town. Tomorrow, the real business gets done: the lucky are chosen from the applicants and the unlucky are judged and sentenced. There's another short party, if there's time, then the Selectors move out before nightfall. They don't waste any time, if they can help it."

Sal absorbed this with a sinking feeling. The Sky Wardens would hear the local grievances--including the one involving his father--that afternoon. It could be all over as soon as that.

But Lodo had more to say. "I usually meet them about the same time as the candidates."

"*You* do? I thought you'd stay well clear of them."

"Not at all. We're on fairly cordial terms, despite our differences. They're practical people out here, for the most part, and they want what's best for their constituents. They listen to what I have to say about the candidates. Whether they act on what I say, though, I don't know."

The parade turned the last corner and reached the square. The carts jangled to a halt in a semi-circle facing the sea while the crowd spread out and around the square, rapidly filling it. On a small, covered podium erected in the center of the square, covering the pump, stood the Mayor and her Alders, all wearing their ceremonial robes, and Euan Holkenhill, round and cheerful despite the weather. The clouds over the sea were black and ominous. The rain still fell, thick and heavy. As everyone settled into position, some under umbrellas or tarpaulins but many simply accepting the weather and letting it batter them, Sal caught sight of one white face amid the dark throng: Kemp was watching from the sidelines, looking nervous.

Sal continued to keep a low profile, despite what Lodo had said and his own awareness that Kemp probably had much more important things on his mind. The bully was hoping to be Selected, Sal remembered. That meant more than getting even with the new kid in town.

A bolt of lightning struck nearby, followed by a crack of thunder that was frighteningly loud. Mayor Iphigenia stepped to the front of the podium. She spoke loudly and clearly, but Sal could only snatch the occasional word from the wind. She seemed to be promising to keep things brief and welcoming the visitors at the same time. The two Sky Wardens climbed down from their horses and, to much cheering and clanging, ascended the steps to the podium. They shook out their slicks, splashing the Alders, then made a big show of apologizing and shaking hands. Holkenhill embraced Centofanti with a broad smile.

"The young one's name is Shom Behenna," Lodo shouted over the storm. Rain had plastered his hair flat. Heavy droplets lay on his cheeks and forehead, occasionally joining forces to trickle down his weathered, tattooed skin. "Or something like that. It's hard to read lips from this far."

"I've never heard of him," Shilly shouted back.

"Neither have I. I wonder--"

Another lightning bolt split the sky and thunder boomed. The lead Sky Warden, Amele Centofanti, raised her hands to address the crowd, but her words were almost inaudible. She frowned and shook her head, and her younger companion put his hand on her shoulder.

Instantly, a warm, female voice was heard throughout the assembly.

"Our thanks to you, people of Fundelry, for your kind welcome. Your hospitality warms us, especially on such short notice. As always, we are glad to be here."

A cheer went up from the crowd. Centofanti paused to acknowledge it before continuing.

"We are particularly delighted to bring one of your children home with us. Tait has traveled well with us as a journeyman, and we commit him to you as Selector's assistant this coming year. His return gives us as much pleasure as it does him, and we are sure it will lead him to greater things in times to come."

This time the cheer was louder and more prolonged. Tait, though, seemed uncomfortable with the praise; he shrugged off attempts to shake his hand and the embraces of two older people Sal assumed were his and Tom's parents.

"Lastly," Centofanti went on when she could, "there is something I must tell you. I'm sorry to keep you out here any longer than is necessary, but I know you'll be as delighted as I am when you hear the news. This visit was put forward to coincide with an exciting development in this particular region of the Strand. Never before have I heard of anything like it, and I am proud to be part of it here, today. We are--"

Another bolt of lightning crashed down, seeming to crack the sky in two. It struck a nearby building, provoking a gasp from the crowd. The bolt was earthed safely, but it made Lodo frown. He stared at the building, as though its survival bothered him.

"We are not the only--"

A second bolt of lightning struck the building and Lodo gripped Sal's shoulder as though he had just realized something.

"Look!" he hissed, pointing.

Sal squinted through the rain. The top of the building glinted in the dim light. He vaguely recognized it as the School building, the gleam on its roof coming from the weathervane. It was this, clearly, that attracted the lightning.

But that wasn't what Lodo meant.

The weathervane was pointing *south*--over the heads of the crowd and out to sea.

"We are not the only visitors you can expect to see today!" boomed Centofanti's voice over the storm, even as Lodo tugged Sal and Shilly through the crowd, around the podium and toward the seaward edge of the square. The sky was rapidly becoming a constant sizzle of lightning, and the rumble of thunder continued far beyond what Sal thought was possible. But still the voice persisted. "We are just the vanguard, the welcoming party sent to make sure everything is in order! My friends, we are honored to--"

A barrage of electricity descended from the sky, along with a torrent of water and gale-force winds. Centofanti gave up and waved for the Mayor to dispel the crowd, just as the podium's cloth roof tore away and vanished into the sky. The crowd began to disperse on its own, alarm over the power of the storm outweighing any patriotic fervor that might have remained. People scattered in all directions.

Lodo alone moved into the wind, dragging Sal and Shilly with him. He pushed them under cover behind a low wall, from which vantage point they watched the Alders getting drenched and the Sky Wardens' horses whinnying in fear. The Sky Wardens themselves didn't seem worried, though. The two blue-clad figures calmed the horses and led them out of the square, along the road leading to the beach, past the place where Lodo, Sal and Shilly were hiding. Holkenhill, the Alders and the Mayor followed them, looking as puzzled as Sal felt.

Lodo, Shilly and Sal stayed out of sight behind the wall until the group had passed. Then the three of them emerged and followed, keeping off the road and using the low dunes as cover. As carefully as they could, they peered to see what the Sky Wardens were doing.

They were heading for the sea. The storm had whipped the water into a feral rage unlike anything Sal had imagined in his wildest nightmares. But that wasn't what first caught Sal's eye as he turned his gaze further southward.

A white ship, sails full to bursting, rose out of the darkness and pounded forward on the ocean, propelled by the fierce winds. Its masts were hung with blue and silver pennants snapping at right angles to the masts; its decks were slick with water. Foam crashed from its bow as it rode the waves toward the shore, rising and falling with stately yet impatient grace. Lightning struck the sea all around it, surrounding it in a cage of white fire. The tips of its straining masts burned with an unearthly light.

It grew perceptibly larger, and Sal feared that it would crash on the beach and tear itself asunder.

The Sky Wardens, the Alders and the Mayor struggled upwind to meet it.

"*Os!*" Lodo shouted.

"What?"

"That's its name: *Os*, the ship of bone." Lodo seemed stunned. "I'm a fool. They came by sea!"

Somehow, the ship managed to turn. Its crew scurried frantically about on its deck, tying ropes and reeling in sheets as though their lives depended on it. And they probably did, Sal thought. One miscalculation could throw them overboard into the mercy of the storm. A series of them could wreck the entire boat.

Incredibly, it looked as though they were going to risk tying to the end of the jetty. Its sails came down and disappeared below deck; members of the crew jumped overboard, onto the jetty's rain-dark boards as it came broadside on; ropes followed and were wrapped quickly around poles before snapping taut. Sal could almost imagine the little jetty groaning under the weight of the ship--and all the ocean behind it--as the ship was dragged reluctantly to a halt. Then it was still, somehow, apart from the surging of the waves beneath it.

At that moment, the fury of the storm peaked. A mighty gust of wind roared over the watchers and the beach and into the dunes, knocking them to the ground. The sea rose up and crashed down on the beach, sending spray flying in sheets. There was one last clap of thunder that seemed to go on forever.

Then everything was still.

Sal lay face-down on the sand with his hands over his ears, convinced that he had gone deaf. He rolled over when a hand gripped his arm, and he saw Shilly's awe-struck face leaning over him. He scrambled to his feet to join Lodo, who stood with his hands on his head, watching the great white ship rocking on the waves.

"Whose is it?" Shilly asked over the easing wind.

"It doesn't belong to anyone," the old man replied. "It belongs to the Strand."

"Who travels in it, then?"

Lodo didn't answer immediately. With a snort that could have been either despair or defiance, he led them off the beach and out of sight.

"Lodo?" Shilly prompted.

"*Os* sails for just two people," he said, "and both their pennants are flying from its mast. I never would have believed it possible, but there's no point doubting it. They're here and we have to deal with them if we can."

Shilly grabbed his arm and tugged him to a halt, tired of his evasiveness. "*Who*, Lodo? We have a right to know."

"You'll find out soon enough." His voice held a bitter note Sal found disturbing--but nowhere as disturbing as the information Sal had that Shilly lacked.

"The only people *Os* sails for are the Alcaide and the Syndic," he said. "It was in a story my father told me years ago. I thought it was just a legend."

Shilly's eyes seemed to bulge, and for once she was speechless.

CHAPTER 15

ON THE POINT OF THE SWORD

"SO what happens now?"

Shilly sat at the table in Von's kitchen with her hands lying flat in front of her. Her wet hair hung in a limp ponytail that dribbled water down the back of her clothes. An air of urgent pragmatism had replaced her previous bad mood--and brought her voice back--as though the new development had pushed her through resentment and out the other side. Sal didn't understand that; he would have predicted precisely the opposite effect, since the threat to her security had just grown exponentially.

"Patience," said Lodo from the laundry, a square, slate-floored room abutting the kitchen. Sal didn't know what he was doing in there, exactly. He was using a lump of chalk to draw a complicated design on the floor, but to what end Sal had no idea.

All this went on with Von fussing in the background. She had ten new tenants, all belonging to the contingent accompanying Centofanti and her assistant. The Mayor's home would house only the Sky Wardens themselves. It wasn't known yet where the Alcaide and Syndic and their retinue would bunk down for the night.

Sal tried to keep out of everyone's way. Lodo had whisked them off the beach and into the hostel before anyone had left the white ship, so he had yet to see the new arrivals. The thought that the two most powerful Sky Wardens in all the Strand had come for him and his father seemed unlikely at best. Insane at worst. It just didn't make sense.

He sat at the table opposite Shilly, concentrating on the Mandala as best he could. Even through the tingling of his skin and the charms--the ones that hadn't washed off his skin--he could feel a growing pressure from all around him, as though the air itself was trying to crush him. Outside, the main fury of the storm appeared to have abated, although the rain still fell, heavy and damp.

"There must be *something* I can do." Shilly got up to look in the laundry. Lodo's hands appeared, shooing her away.

"Wait until I'm finished," he said, "then you'll have plenty to see."

She stomped back to the table and leaned against it with arms folded. Her gaze wandered the room, then settled on Sal. "Do *you* know what's going on?"

He shook his head, startled to realize that Shilly hadn't participated in any of his conversations with Lodo regarding his parents. She was as much in the dark as he had been a day or two ago.

"I hear they're looking for someone," said Von while she chopped vegetables. "And if you really wanted to do something, you'd give me a hand."

"What sort of someone?" Shilly asked, ignoring the hint.

"Someone important who doesn't want to be found, I guess." Von's sour look matched the younger girl's. "Why don't you go ask them yourself?"

"That won't be necessary," said Lodo, emerging from the laundry with a satisfied expression and chalk dust on his hands and thighs. "If we could be alone for a while, Von, please. Sal, Shilly, through here."

Sal followed Shilly into the small room, careful not to smudge the lines Lodo had drawn on the ground. The pattern resembled a compass, with four large points of a cross superimposed over a circle, but there the similarity ended. A tight spiral traced a complicated design around the edge of the circle, while interlocking triangles of many different shapes and sizes formed complex patterns within. In the center was an empty circle, within which Lodo instructed Shilly to stand.

"You'll be our anchor," said Lodo to her. "Your lack of natural talent will confuse attempts to trace us--not that they'll be expecting anything like this out here."

"*Who* won't expect *what?*" Shilly flapped her hands in frustration, resembling a bird caught in a trap.

Lodo removed Sal's bracelets and placed him at one of the points.

"Alcaide Braham and Syndic Zanshin." Lodo seemed to be enjoying her irritation. "Yesterday, remember, I visited the Mayor to discuss Sal's father's case. While there, I planted some charms I thought might come in handy--if not now, then another time." He took a position one point around from Sal and closed his eyes. "A moment, please. I need to concentrate."

Sal, vulnerable to any movement of the Change by the removal of the bracelets, felt a swirl of energy brush past him, as though a breeze had blown through the open door. He reached behind him to pull the door shut, and Lodo's eyes snapped open.

"Yes, a good idea," he said, when he saw what Sal was doing, "but then don't move from that spot. Don't even reach out. It's not safe."

Lodo closed his eyes again and Sal ignored a *What do you think you're playing at?* look from Shilly. Again something invisible brushed by him; it was soon joined by another. The air in the room seemed to be moving in patches in a circle around Shilly.

A burnt-orange light began to glow in the floor beneath Shilly's feet, casting shadows across the walls and ceiling. It too rotated, but in the opposite direction. Sal was starting to feel dizzy and noted that Shilly had closed her eyes. He did the same--

--and suddenly found himself in another place: a room at least three times as large as Von's kitchen, containing only a desk and four empty chairs. There was no one in the room. Lodo and Shilly had disappeared and, when he glanced down, he couldn't see himself either.

Sal looked around in amazement. His eyes were closed but he was still seeing. That wasn't possible. It couldn't really be *seeing* as he was used to seeing. This was something to do with the Change. And Lodo.

"Ah, yes." The old man's voice was perfectly clear, although Sal didn't seem to be hearing with his ears, just as he didn't seem to be seeing with his eyes. Lodo himself was still nowhere visible. "I thought we might get away with it. This far, at least."

"Where are we?" asked Shilly from thin air.

"In the Mayor's office. That's what we're seeing, anyway, through the charms I placed. We're not actually there--and neither is Iphigenia, unfortunately. Hold on."

The view dissolved into gray. For a dizzying moment Sal heard the deep hum that had filled the spaces between the scourge's visions--then everything settled down and they were elsewhere.

This time the room was much larger, with curtained windows, carpeted floors, a high ceiling and several tables around the walls. A dozen or so people--Alders and other officials--stood in attitudes of deference around two seated figures. These two were both dressed in white and old enough to be in their sixties: the Alcaide and the Syndic, Sal guessed. They weren't monsters, just ordinary people. A buzz of voices surrounded them. Sal felt exposed, even though he assumed no one could see him. He was a bodiless spirit, unable to move but at least able to watch.

"We understand perfectly," said the blue-clad Amele Centofanti. "If you choose to deny the imposition--"

"Nonsense," said the seated man. His face was rectangular and strong, topped with a thin stubble of gray-black hair, and his features were regular and handsome. No decorations of any kind marked his light-brown skin. Apart from a crystal choker around his throat, he wore no ornament at all. "We are the ranking officials on this expedition and we must follow form. Isn't that right, Nu?"

The woman beside him inclined her head. She was narrower, darker and older-looking, with pepper-gray hair tied back in a severe bun. She looked uncannily like the Syndic piece in Tom's Advance set. "Yes, Dragan. Everyone knows we're here. To *not* see them would be a slight. We would never sanction such rudeness at home, so we will not be part of it here."

Sal frowned. He recognized the Syndic's voice, although he didn't understand how that could be. Where he had heard it before, he couldn't imagine.

"If you're certain--"

"We are." The Alcaide gestured economically with his right hand. "Bring them in."

Centofanti nodded once and left the room, closing the door behind her.

"And the other matter?" prompted someone Sal instantly recognized.

"It can wait a moment, Alder Sproule," said the Alcaide, his expression benign and patient. "There is no need to rush things."

The door through which Centofanti had vanished opened again, and seven teenagers filed into the room. It was clear from their nervous expressions that they were the candidates for Selection, brought in to meet their examiners. Kemp led the way, followed by five others Sal recognized by face rather than name. Tom, the smallest, brought up the rear. Only he seemed unfazed by the thought of being examined by the Alcaide and Syndic themselves. He just looked tired. Sal imagined that he would be, having been up with the storm the previous night, then welcoming his brother back home.

"Hello, children," said the Alcaide, leaning forward on his chair as though he was about to stand up, but not doing so. "It's a pleasure to meet you. I hope we're not too intimidating."

"We're honored, sir. I mean, sir and madam," said Kemp, with a quick glance at his father. Alder Sproule frowned at the slip as though Kemp had uttered a profanity. "We never dreamed *you* would come to Fundelry."

The Alcaide glanced at Zanshin beside him. "Neither did we, to be honest, but it's nice to be here. We wish we could stay longer."

"Well, there's not much to see," Kemp said, seeming to relax slightly, then stiffening when he realized what he had said. His father's scowl deepened. "That is, for someone like yourself, this must seem a very small town, and--"

The Alcaide laughed good-naturedly and raised a hand to stop Kemp in mid-back-pedal. "I understand what you meant to say, and I disagree. Towns like Fundelry are the backbone of the Strand. Without them, we would have nothing to govern. The Haunted City would be at the center of a terrible void. The first thing we learn when we reach the heights of the Conclave is to treasure the details. Fundelry may be small, but it is none-the-less important--or pleasing--for that."

"Bah!" snorted Lodo, but Kemp was clearly relieved. The Alcaide had turned a potential slight on Fundelry into a compliment.

"You must be Kemp, the Alder's son," said the Syndic. "We've heard about you."

"They comprise a fine group, all of them," put in Mayor Iphigenia from behind them. "We're hopeful at least two will return with you."

"With Centofanti," the Syndic corrected her. "There is no room aboard our ship."

"And no need to frighten anyone unnecessarily," added the Alcaide, rolling his eyes. "*Os* is an uneasy ride at best. I will never grow accustomed to it."

The Syndic leaned forward and pointed at Tom. "You. Do you wish to ask a question?"

Sal, like most of the people in the room, hadn't noticed Tom's raised hand. The boy had a way of slipping into the background.

"Is my brother staying here?" he asked.

Both the Syndic and Alcaide looked confused for a moment, until Centofanti stepped in.

"He's referring to Journeyman Tait," she explained. In response to Tom's question, she said: "More or less. He'll act as an apprentice to Euan Holkenhill for a year, so he will be in the area."

"Then I wish to retract my application for Selection."

A startled whisper rippled through the room, but Tom seemed oblivious to the reaction his announcement provoked.

"*What* do you wish to do?" asked the Alcaide.

"Retract my application for Selection, sir," Tom repeated. "I no longer wish to apply for--"

"I know what it *means,* boy, but I still don't understand you. Why would you ask such a thing?"

"My brother is home, so now I don't need to leave. I want to stay here with him."

Braham and Zanshin exchanged glances. "Well, this has never happened before, to my knowledge. What do you think, Nu?"

"I think the decision is in *our* hands, now, Dragan, not the boy's. He has applied and must see it through. If he is capable or talented, the best place for him is with us. Why would anyone genuinely want it any other way?"

"Agreed." The Alcaide looked satisfied with the administrator's ruling. "The application remains open for consideration."

"We will hear the cases for the applicants in detail later this evening and judge them tomorrow," the Syndic said. "You will know then which way we have decided."

Sal caught a fleeting look of alarm cross Tom's face, but it was quickly buried as Centofanti took the hint. With hurry-up gestures, she gathered the applicants and led them from the room.

The Alcaide and Syndic conducted a brief, whispered conversation between themselves that Sal couldn't overhear. More than ever, something about the woman's voice seemed familiar, but Sal still couldn't place it.

"How are you doing this?" asked Shilly. "Are we there, or still in Von's laundry?"

"I'll explain later," said Lodo.

"You always say that."

"Quiet, now."

Alder Sproule had addressed the seated pair again but the brief exchange between Shilly and Lodo had obscured it.

"Very well," said the Alcaide to whatever Sproule had said. "Bring him before us."

Sproule smiled and nodded to a door attendant, who left the room. A moment later she brought back Sal's father.

Sal gasped at the sight, and wanted to run to him, but he couldn't move independently. All he could do was watch as his father was led, bound, to the center of the room. He was wearing the same clothes he had been left with in the cell; the bloodstain on his chest was still there. Unshaven and unwashed, his nose broken and eyes bruised, he looked barely civilized.

Sal remembered the beautiful notes he had heard from his father's fingers and throat and felt like crying.

"And this is...?" prompted the Alcaide.

"My apologies, sir," said Alder Sproule, stepping forward again to address the pair. "This is the miscreant we discussed earlier, the thief and vagabond calling himself 'Gershom' who, with his son, took advantage of the trust and generosity of our people."

"Give me specifics, Sproule, not rhetoric," interrupted the Syndic.

Sproule bowed. "They arrived in town ten days ago and took lodgings in a local hostel. Immediately thereafter a number of thefts were reported, occurring solely at night and persisting despite public warnings and offers of clemency if the stolen goods were returned. Two nights ago, acting on information I received in the course of the investigation, I inspected the room in the hostel where the two were staying and found the missing property."

"All of it?" asked the Syndic.

"The greater part, hidden under a bed. The remainder must have been sold at the markets."

The Syndic nodded. "Continue."

"Upon realizing that we had discovered their crimes, the pair attempted to flee in their motorised vehicle, which I had the forethought to confiscate earlier. They were arrested and placed in custody pending the arrival of the Selectors, at which time they would be judged."

"Indeed," said the Alcaide, nodding. "And what is your opinion in this matter, Alder Sproule?"

"I advise you not to be clement." Sproule sneered at Sal's father as though he were something revolting. "I have seen thieves like this before, and they are rarely to be rehabilitated. We don't want their kind here, and would be well rid of them."

"Transportation, then, is what you request?"

"Yes, sir. Effective immediately."

"I see." The Syndic leaned her chin on one hand and nodded. "I have a couple of questions, though, if you would be so kind. From where did you obtain the information that these people might be in possession of the stolen goods?"

Sproule looked uncomfortable for a moment, but quickly recovered. "From my son."

"And how did *he* know?"

"Apparently the thief's son had been bragging about it at School."

"Ah." The Syndic leaned back in the chair, as though that explained everything. Sal bit down on an outraged retort. "We should add brazenness to our charge, then. Shouldn't we, Dragan?"

"Yes, Nu." The Alcaide flashed a brief smile.

"And this son of his," the Syndic asked. "Where might he be?"

"He was released on a good behavior bond." Sproule's expression showed that he hadn't been entirely happy with the agreement. "His whereabouts are presently unknown."

"I see." The Alcaide leaned forward, turning his attention to Sal's father. "You--'Gershom', wasn't it? What do you have to say about all this?"

"That I am innocent." Sal's father's gaze was on the Syndic to the Alcaide's left, and didn't leave her.

"Of course he would say that," countered Alder Sproule.

The Alcaide waved a hand. "Please, let him speak."

Sal's father seemed to be keeping a tight rein on his emotions. "I have nothing else to say."

"Really? I find that hard to believe. Perhaps the crowd

is putting you off." The Alcaide looked around. "Mayor Iphigenia? Mayor? Oh, there you are. Have the room cleared, please. We wish to address this man in private."

The request took everyone by surprise--from Alder Sproule, who looked startled and suspicious, to Sal's father, who winced but didn't drop his eyes.

The Mayor looked puzzled, but was happy enough to oblige. "Of course. At once." She gestured around her, and people headed for the doors.

Sproule lingered. "Are you certain this is wise? I mean, someone should remain to ensure your safety."

"We are eminently able to defend ourselves, Alder." The Alcaide made a shooing gesture, his eyes sharp. "Out, please. We will summon you when we have heard his side of the story and are satisfied with it--or not."

The Alder bowed and strode out the nearest door. The door shut behind him with a click, leaving Sal's father alone with Dragan Braham and Nu Zanshin, the highest ranking Sky Wardens in the Strand.

There was a moment's silence. It seemed to last forever, like a nightmare without end.

Then the Alcaide cleared his throat and stood. Upright, he was much taller than Sal had expected, and solid with it. He looked like the sort of person who would command an army, not rule a decadent court. He made the Syndic beside him seem almost fragile.

"So it comes to this," he said to the man before him. "Arrested for petty theft in a backwater town, thousands of kilometers from home and with no one to defend you. How far you have fallen, Dafis Hrvati."

Sal's father met his stare with a look of contempt. "Yet I still tower over you, Braham."

The Alcaide laughed. "Is that what you think? I admire your persistence, if nothing else. Few people have the strength to maintain beliefs of such demonstrable falsity for so long."

"Listen to you two," interrupted the Syndic with a weary

tone to her voice. "You could be brothers sparring, or father and son."

"Spare me," said the Alcaide.

"No, I'm serious. You're much more alike than you care to realize."

Sal's father flexed his bound wrists. "Our circumstances couldn't be more different."

"That's my point!" said the Alcaide, his voice rising. The Syndic touched his arm, and he shrugged her off. "Don't shush me! They can't overhear us--the doors and walls are charmed. And I'm entitled to a little annoyance, don't you think? After all he's put us through."

"After all *I've* put *you* through?" Sal's father shook his head in disbelief. "I knew you'd be unreasonable, but--"

"Stop it!" the Syndic snapped. "You two can fight it out later if you want to. I have no desire to watch it. Where is the boy, Dafis?"

"What boy?"

"Your son. Isn't that what they called him?"

"I have no son."

"There's no use lying. Sproule says you came here with him. There will be other witnesses."

"I came here with a companion, yes, but he's not my son. He's just a waif I picked up a couple of years back and let travel with me in exchange for labor. He's good enough company, I'll admit, and he does have some latent talent that might one day be put to good use, but that's all."

"A waif with some talent, you say," the Alcaide said. "So you still practice, then?"

"No, never."

"She says you used to."

Sal's father couldn't hide a slight wince. "By 'she' you mean Seirian, I presume?"

"Of course. That's how we know there was a child."

Sal's father paused to take a deep breath, as though composing himself. "There <u>was</u>. He died, long ago."

"Where?"

"In the Broken Lands, between stops. He had a fever I

couldn't treat. I buried him near Yor. You'll find his grave there, if you look hard enough."

"The Broken Lands are thousands of kilometers across. Do you expect us to search the entire wasteland in the hope of finding a grave that might not even exist?"

"I don't expect anything."

"No, but it would amuse you to watch us try, I suppose. It would gain you time."

"I'm out of time, and you know it, Braham. I don't expect you to let me go, now you've found me."

"You flatter yourself. Without the boy, you're useless. And if you're telling the truth--"

"If he's telling the truth," the Syndic snapped, "this trip was a complete waste of time."

He turned on her. "It was you who said you sensed something. You who *insisted* we come! Don't blame me if it proves fruitless."

Her gaze narrowed. "I felt him, Dragan. I felt his mind. He was here."

"And now? Is he here now?"

She looked away. "I don't know. If he *is* here, he is well hidden."

"Impossible. He should stand out, for his skin if nothing else."

"My young friend is of Interior stock," said Sal's father. "He would fit the description in that respect."

"How convenient," the Alcaide sneered. "And where is he, Dafis? Produce him, prove to us that he is not the one, and we'll let you go."

Sal's father shrugged. "I'd do as you say, were I able to. Unfortunately, due to the fact that I've been in prison, I have no way of knowing where he's got to. He might not even be here any more--and I can't say I'd blame him for running. Your constituents aren't very hospitable in these parts."

"No." The Syndic allowed herself a tight-lipped smile. "They aren't, are they? I suspect Alder Sproule would find even *your* skin uncomfortably light, Dragan. Under different circumstances, perhaps you too would find yourself accused of trumped-up charges before the likes of us."

The Alcaide waved aside her comments and sat back down. "This is getting us nowhere," he grumbled.

"Indeed," said Sal's father. "This entire vendetta is pointless."

"My nephew would disagree." The Syndic pulled a face.

"No doubt. How *is* Highson these days?"

"He fares well enough." She met his gaze squarely. Even Sal could tell she wasn't telling the whole truth, but that was nothing compared to the revelation he had received. His mother's jilted husband was a relative of the Syndic! No wonder Sal and his father were in so much trouble.

"And Seirian?"

"She's dead," the Alcaide spat.

Sal's father blanched. "No, she can't be."

"She is. She died five years ago--of grief, some say. She missed her son too much to live without him."

"Is this true?" Sal's father appealed to the Syndic, his eyes shining.

"It is true," she admitted. "Seirian is dead."

Sal felt something in his heart break. He had never known his mother, nor known what had happened to her, but he had always hoped that one day they would meet, somehow. If what the Syndic and Alcaide said was true, however, now they never would.

"You killed her." Sal's father strained at his bonds, his grief turning to rage. His face was red. "You killed her!"

"Far from it," said the Alcaide calmly. "We made a mistake at the time, separating her from the boy. We admit that much, even though, until it was too late, we had no way of knowing that there was a child at all. When we tried to put things right, you had gone. Vanished again. And this time there was no finding you--no clues, no subtle traces to follow. You were wise not to use the Change, Dafis, otherwise we would have found you instantly. But your *wisdom*"--he almost snarled the word--"led to Seirian's death. As time passed and the scent became increasingly cold, she gave up hope. She died despairing of ever seeing her child again-- because you had hidden him from her. How does that feel?"

Sal's father wept openly at the Alcaide's words, belying his words: "I don't believe you."

"Believe it. You killed her as surely as we did."

"She wouldn't have wanted him found. I know it. She didn't want you to have him."

"Are we so heartless?" the Syndic asked. "We can sympathize with your plight, Dafis. Give us credit for that, at least. After all, it wasn't us personally who hunted you when you fled. We didn't even order it. Who is to say that we don't think our predecessors over-reacted to the situation? We wouldn't be alone, you know, if we did. The idea of the star-struck lovers fleeing their families in order to spend eternity together is enticingly romantic. It has popular appeal, even if it is not the whole truth. We are only human, Dafis."

"We simply can't understand why you're running from us." The Alcaide frowned deeply, his puzzlement plain. "What do you think we want to do to you?"

"Not to me."

"Sayed, then. Whoever."

"You tell me, Braham. Why are you so desperate to find him? What *is* it you want? Why was Seirian so afraid of you?"

"Me?" The Alcaide raised his eyebrows. "She had no reason to be afraid of me. Now you really are imagining things."

The tears on Sal's father's cheeks had dried. His expression was one of repressed fury.

"I've seen what you can do," he said, his voice soft but intense. "I know what you are. You say you care, but you don't. You don't feel anything for people like me, for the little people. Democracy and Schools--they're all really only there to safeguard your own survival, to ensure replacements when you don't breed true!"

The Syndic looked horrified. "How can you say that?"

"Because it's true. Do you deny it?"

"Of *course* I deny it!" the words flew from the Syndic's

lips. "You're raving, Dafis. You're insane. You won't accept the truth so you wrap it up in lies and throw it back at us!"

"Really?" His lips were white, his eyes slits. "You stole a mother from her child without a second thought. You killed her more surely than I ever did. I don't want my son growing up believing that sort of behavior is acceptable."

"Enough," growled the Alcaide, standing with his fists clenched. "Enough!" he roared, and for a moment Sal was afraid that the Alcaide might strike his father. Instead, he swung aside and crossed the room. "Pah! We have wasted enough time with this fool." He banged on the door. "Get in here! Take him out of our sight!" Their retinue rushed in, followed by the Alders and other local attendants. The room suddenly seemed very full, the Alcaide and Syndic much smaller.

Sal's father was swept up in the tide of limbs and led toward the door. "You won't get away with this, Braham!"

"Won't we?" The Alcaide turned his gaze on Sproule, waiting expectantly before him. "Congratulations on apprehending a dangerous criminal, Alder Sproule. We have been seeking him for some time. We will not break tradition by announcing a sentence before the proper time, but I think you can safely say that he will soon be out of your hands."

The Alder bowed deeply. "Please accept my thanks, sir. Your commendation honors me."

The Alcaide waved him away and gestured for the Mayor to come closer. His expression had changed now that he was in public; he looked older, more tired than before, benevolent under pressure. It contrasted completely to the look of anger and annoyance he had displayed just moments before.

"We are growing weary," he said to the Mayor. "Our long journey has taxed us, and we must rest. Could we impose upon you for a short period in which we will not be disturbed? An hour at most is all we need."

"Of course. Anything you wish." The Mayor waved, and an attendant approached. "I'll arrange a room. Warden Centofanti can continue in your place until you are feeling better." She turned away to speak to the attendant, who rushed off to do her bidding.

"Thank you," said the Alcaide. "Your hospitality is as fine as we had heard." He stood with a sigh and a hand on his back. Another attendant appeared to show him the way. He waited until the Syndic was also on her feet before following.

"Oh, there's one more thing." He waved for Sproule's attention as they left the room. The Alder was immediately at his side. "Find me the boy that man came here with."

"As you wish, sir."

"We sail tomorrow. I would be very grateful if you could do it before then."

The two men exchanged looks. "Of course. It will be done." The Alder turned away with a determined look and hurried off.

With a slight smile and the Syndic on his arm, the Alcaide left the room.

CHAPTER 16

THE ART OF SOLITUDE

SAL opened his eyes. He couldn't take any more. He couldn't stand aside and watch while his father was accused of killing his mother. It wasn't right, and it wasn't fair!

He opened his eyes not on the laundry he had expected but on a terrible gray void swirling like water in a drain all around him. It was pulling at him, sucking him down. He flailed for balance but the floor beneath his feet had vanished. He felt himself falling--

Then a hand grabbed his wrist and pulled him away. The gray dissolved. The laundry formed around him. Lodo had Sal's wrist clasped tightly in both his hands. He looked relieved and angry at the same time.

"I told you not to move," he snapped.

"You did, but I thought..." Sal stopped in mid-protest. He *hadn't* thought. He was dealing with people and powers he knew next to nothing about. He had to do as he was told. "I'm sorry," he said.

"We nearly both were. I don't know how I would've explained to your father--not to mention the Syndic--that I'd lost you for good." The old man brushed hair back from his forehead and looked down at the chalk diagram. It had been heavily scuffed by their feet. "Hmm. It'll be a while before I can repair the damage. It's probably quite timely, anyway. This sort of work is very taxing."

He guided Sal out of the laundry and into the kitchen. The room was empty apart from the smell of simmering stew.

"Are you going to tell us *now* how you did it?" Shilly asked, following them with her hands on her hips.

Lodo produced an elaborately carved, shell-like stone

from his pocket and held it up to the light. Its carvings matched those on the laundry floor. "This is one of the charms I planted yesterday. They act as eyes to people who have learned how to see through the Void Beneath. Their range and usefulness is limited, and they can be detected quite easily if someone is looking--but, as Fundelry is hardly the sort of place one would expect espionage of this sort, clearly no one *was* looking, and we got away with it."

"Wait. The Void what? I've never heard you mention that before."

"There's a lot I haven't told you about, Shilly. The Void Beneath, the Weavers, the man'kin ... A whole lifetime isn't enough to hear it all."

"It'd help if you started *somewhere*," she said, glaring.

The old man sighed. "True. Well, the Void Beneath is that which stands between a person in one place and a point in another place when that person uses the Change to connect the two places. When you look anywhere using the Change--be it into the past or the future, or into someone's mind, or just to another place--you send part of yourself in the process. If the connection is severed, you may never get that part back. When that happens, it falls into the Void Beneath and is never recovered."

Sal swallowed at the thought of how close he had come to disappearing into that place. He would never forget the terrible, gray emptiness that he had glimpsed.

"But what is this void?"

"Shilly, I don't know, and I doubt anyone does. It just *is*." He looked very tired. "If you have no further questions, I think we should return to the matter at hand. Sproule is going to be looking for Sal much more closely than he's looked before, along with the Alcaide and the Syndic. Now--"

He stopped as Sal suddenly clicked his fingers and said: "*That's* who she is!"

"Who?" Shilly asked.

"The Syndic! I knew I recognized her voice from

somewhere. She's the one I heard in the sea that day, calling me!"

"Syndic Zanshin?" asked Lodo, coming round to look at his face. "Are you sure?"

"Yes. It was definitely her. She called me by my real name, which made me think it might have been my mother. But the Alcaide knew my name, so the Syndic would too. My mother must have told them. They said that she…" He stopped. The enormity of what he'd heard was still creeping up on him. "They said that she's dead."

There was an uncomfortable silence until Shilly said: "Yeah. I'm sorry about that."

"It's okay." He took a deep breath and tried to keep his voice steady. "I never knew her."

"That doesn't matter. If I found out *my* parents were dead, whoever they were, I'd still be upset. They're my parents regardless."

"Thanks, Shilly."

But Lodo wasn't listening to them. "Why would Syndic Zanshin be calling you? Why not some underling better suited to this sort of far sensing?" He rubbed his chin. "This is very strange."

"What about the Highson Sparre she mentioned, the man Sal's mother married?" asked Shilly. "He's her nephew. Maybe he has something to do with it."

Lodo turned to face her, one finger raised and his mouth open to speak. Then he stopped and turned back to Sal. "Yes," he said softly. "Yes, maybe that's it."

Sal had had enough speculation for the time being. The two of them would stand around talking all day while the Sky Wardens wrapped the house in charms. "What have they done with Dad?"

Lodo seemed to shake himself out of a deep thought. "What? Oh, he'll be back in prison by now."

"I want to see him."

"Yes, I can imagine--"

"Lodo, I need to see him." Sal couldn't find words to express the ache he had felt upon seeing the vision of his father before the Alcaide: broken, despairing, and very alone. "We have to find a way to get him out of there."

Lodo nodded firmly. "We will, I promise. And you'll talk to him soon. But now isn't the right time, Sal. Later, during the Alders' Feast, I'll take you there. It'll be dark and everyone will be occupied. You'll be safer then."

Sal looked out of the kitchen window. It was barely midday. Evening seemed a month away.

The kitchen door burst in and all three of them jumped.

"Are you still here?" demanded Von, her face red and flustered. "I've got twenty people to feed!"

"Of course, I'm sorry." Lodo retreated across the room with his hands raised. "I'll get out of your way, now. Thanks for being so patient. While I'm gone, I'll leave these two here to give you a hand, to make up for the inconvenience."

"What?" Shilly looked as surprised as Von. "But--"

"Don't argue. I'm going to meet with Centofanti." Lodo shrugged away a look that might have been nervousness. "Best to get it over with, I think. In the meantime, you two make yourselves useful. Stay back here and clean out the laundry if you get a chance. The less seen, the better."

"I suppose." Shilly didn't try to hide her unhappiness. "But that's the last time I do your dirty work for you."

He nodded. "If I'm not back in two hours, perhaps you should start to worry."

Sal did as he was told without qualms. Von didn't seem overly enamored with the idea of looking after Lodo's two apprentices, but she did put them to good use--so much so, there wasn't time for talking or thinking. They chopped, mixed, stirred and washed under her watchful gaze. After an hour, Sal's hands felt like wrinkled leather, but at least it was all done. A solid meal was ready for all of the hostel's guests. Von took the steaming bowls and platters out into the common room, and left her impromptu assistants alone with a small portion of food for themselves. Sal shut the door carefully behind her, nervous of the voices they could hear just down the hall. The guests weren't Sky Wardens, but they were still too close for comfort.

"We shouldn't be here," said Shilly, wringing her hands and pacing the room. "I feel like we're trapped."

"Lodo said to stay." Sal took a seat and picked at the stew they'd made. It tasted salty, like everything else in Fundelry, and he was too nervous to be hungry. "It's all part of his 'hiding things in the open' plan, I think."

Shilly uttered a *humph* and went to find a mop to clean the laundry floor. Barely had she gone when a high-pitched scratching at the window made Sal look up with a start--right into the eyes of a huge seagull flapping at the glass, cawing for attention.

Sal ducked under the table and called for Shilly. She came back into the room, saw the bird and slammed the blind shut.

"Did it see you?"

"I don't know." Sal eased out from under the table, feeling like an idiot.

"I don't care what Lodo says, it's a bit *too* open for me in here." Shilly gathered up a bread roll and some cheese and put them in a bag. "I'm not sitting around waiting for them to find us."

"But--"

"Don't worry. I'll leave a note." She found the piece of chalk Lodo had used in the laundry and scribbled some symbols on the back of the kitchen door. "*Not safe. Gone to workshop. See you there.* That should do it." She put the chalk into her pocket and looked at Sal. "Well? Are you coming?"

He looked around. "What about the laundry?"

"It can wait. Who's going to look in there anyway? Come *on*." She took his arm and approached the kitchen door. "Most of your charms are still working," she hissed. "Put your bracelets back on, concentrate on the Mandala, and be quiet!"

Sal did as he was told, feeling the tingling safety net creep back over his skin. Shilly eased open the door and peered through it. The corridor was empty. She inched out of the kitchen one step at a time, looking both ways and up the stairwell. When she was satisfied no one was coming, she hurried for the front door, trailing Sal behind her. Her hand clasped his so tightly he had no choice but to go with her.

The door clattered as she opened it, but she didn't stop to bemoan the fact. They were outside in the gray daylight and hurrying across the porch, not pausing even momentarily to look who might be there. Sal concentrated on not being noticed. If Shilly was right and the charms were still working, he hoped their confusing influence would help them escape attention.

They made it to the side of the hostel without anyone sounding an alarm. When they were a block away, Sal started to look around. The sky was dark, but at least it wasn't raining any more. The streets were muddy and relatively undisturbed. Not many people were about, and few of those appeared to notice the two young people hurrying past them.

Of greater concern were the specks circling high in the sky, swooping lower here and there to look at something more closely. Sal saw birds poking their beaks into dark spaces under houses and behind sheds; some were even going through open doors and looking inside. Their squawks filled the air all around him, urging him on. Individually, the birds didn't worry him, but the entire flock was a concern. As a whole, it had too many eyes. It could look too many places at once. The lone gull at Von's might have been confused by the glass and the charms, but it was only a matter of time before another saw through the illusion and realized who he was.

All he and Shilly could do was hurry. The squawking never changed pitch around them. Gradually, Sal began to think that they might actually make it. He could tell from the way the gulls were swarming that they were concentrating their search on the town. Once he and Shilly made the safety of the dunes, they could relax slightly.

Their breath came heavily by the time their feet touched the soft sand of the dunes.

"Not far now," Shilly gasped, clutching her sides.

Sal struggled to keep up. It was much harder running in sand. They tried to keep to the valleys between the dunes to save going up and down their slippery sides, but that wasn't always possible. Every time they crested a new dune, Sal felt horribly exposed and slid down the far side as quickly as possible.

They were more than halfway there when they heard the sound of crying from nearby.

Shilly raised a finger to her lips and slowed her pace. They crept around the next dune rather than over it, and found a small figure hunched in its shadow.

"Tom?" Shilly slapped Sal's arm for speaking, but he couldn't help himself. The small boy looked utterly disconsolate. "Tom, are you all right?"

The boy looked up with a start. His eyes were red; his face was blotchy. He looked so startled Sal thought he might bolt. Then a look of confusion passed over him.

"Who...? Is that *you*, Sal?"

Sal came closer. "Yes, it's me."

"You look strange."

"Don't worry about that. You're crying."

The boy didn't bother denying that he had been crying, like a lot of boys might. He simply shook his head.

"Can I help you?"

Tom shook his head again. Shilly made an exasperated noise.

Sal turned to her. "If you're so impatient to keep going, feel free. I'll catch up."

She shook her head. "I can't leave you alone. Lodo will kill me."

"Then be quiet and wait." He turned back to Tom. "Tell me what's wrong. I'm in a hurry, but I don't want to leave you like this."

"It's just..." The small boy stopped to wipe his nose on his hand. "I don't understand. What's wrong with Fundelry?

What's wrong with me?" He looked like he was about to cry again, so Sal squatted down in front of him and put a hand on his shoulders.

"Take it easy. There's nothing wrong with you."

"There is. Tait says so. He says I'm an idiot for not wanting to be Selected."

Sal thought about what life would be like for a bright boy like Tom in an out-of-the-way town like Fundelry. Sky Wardens or not, at least he would have more opportunities in the Haunted City. "Well, he might have a point--"

"No! I don't want to leave. I like it here!"

"Because Tait's here now?"

"Yes, although..." He shook his head, scattering tears down his cheek. "I dream strange things. I'm afraid." Tom put his head in his hands. "I don't want him to go!" he wailed.

"Who says he's going anywhere?" Sal did his best to comfort the boy, nervous of the noise he was making. Behind him, Shilly kept a close watch on the sky.

"*He* does." Tom sniffed. "Tait says he never wanted to come back. He doesn't want to be here. He wants to be in the Haunted City, with *them*." It was clear from Tom's tone just how much he resented "them". "But they won't let him, and that makes him angry. He's not like he used to be. He wants to go, but I want him to stay. And if he stays and *I* have to go ..."

Sal squeezed the boy's shoulder while he sobbed. "They can't *force* you to go, can they?"

"Not officially," said Shilly, "but they could make it difficult for Tait."

Tom nodded. "He says I'm making him look like an idiot. He says *I'm* an idiot. I don't know what to do. I'm so afraid!"

"What are you afraid of, Tom?" Sal asked, but Tom didn't answer. He just shook his head and pulled away from Sal. His thin legs scrabbled for purchase in the sand, and suddenly he was gone, vanishing over the dune and out of sight.

"A complete waste of time," said Shilly, shaking her head.

"Will you get a move on now? And can we ignore any other losers we stumble across on the way home?"

Sal didn't respond to the gibe, although annoyance at her flared inside him. Instead he just nodded and they set off again. He didn't want to fight with her, as she was doing a lot to help him and putting herself at risk in the process. Even if her efforts weren't remotely good-natured, he still owed her his gratitude.

It was with a feeling of intense relief that they made it back to the workshop unscathed. Back in the familiar surroundings, he was able to remove the bracelets and let his guard down for a time. The Mandala had left a permanent imprint on his mind; he still saw the circles turning when he closed his eyes. Maybe that was a good thing, he thought, but it was unnerving. He didn't know how long he could live like this.

Then he remembered his father, and all the years *he* had been running. He wanted to talk to him so much it was like a physical ache. It was so frustrating that he couldn't just reach out with his mind as Lodo had hinted might be possible by using the Change, and talk to him by thought alone.

From the other side of the room, Shilly looked up from where she had collapsed on her bed. "I felt that. What are you doing?"

"Nothing." Sal was as startled as she looked. "I was just thinking about my father."

"I felt you calling him--and it must have been strong for me to hear it, even in here. Did you know you were doing it?"

"No." A chill swept through him. "Do you think anyone heard?"

"I doubt it. It couldn't have been *that* strong. Lodo has the workshop pretty well shielded. It'd take a decent punch to get through. You did well for a first try, though," she added, looking impressed despite herself. "You really *do* have the knack, you lucky sod."

He didn't respond. An idea had come to him. "Where did you say this workshop is, really?"

"What?"

"You told me the other day that it was the same when you lived in another town, that you thought only the entrance had changed. If the tunnel stretches from door to door but the workshop stays where it is, the workshop could be anywhere. Nowhere near Fundelry, in fact."

"Yes. So?"

"So if I did try to call my father from in here, and if it *was* loud enough for the Alcaide and the Syndic to hear..."

He got no further. She straightened bolt upright. "If they heard, they'd think you're where the workshop is--and it could be hundreds of kilometers away. Sal, that's brilliant!"

He was thrown by her response. He hadn't expected anything so enthusiastic. "It is?"

"Of course! They'll be thrown right off the scent! We should try it right now."

He was even more unnerved by that suggestion. "What about waiting for Lodo?"

"Why? The sooner we do it, the better. Anyone who's seen you with me would guess what's going on. They might have got the truth out of Von--or Tom. Lodo could be in trouble. We have to help him before it's too late." She jumped up and crossed the room to where he was sitting. "Come on, Sal! What are you waiting for?"

He was waiting for a good reason, albeit half-heartedly. He knew she was only exaggerating--and he knew *she* knew--but her excitement was infectious anyway.

"Do you think it's safe?"

"Sure. What's the worst that could happen? If they don't hear you, we've lost nothing. If they do hear you and they can't tell where we are, we've at least confused them. And even if they do pin us down precisely, wherever the workshop really is, they still won't be able to find the entrance. We have nothing to lose, and a lot to gain. No?"

Sal thought about it. The way she put it, it did seem foolproof. "Okay, I guess. What do I do? I've never tried this before--not properly. I was just wishing when you heard me earlier."

"There's not much else to it, really. I've only tried it a couple of times myself, and then only using Lodo's talent to talk to Aunty Merinda from across the market. I probably shouldn't help you much--otherwise they'll know it's not just you--and I don't know exactly how far away we are from your dad..." She got up and looked around. "The first thing we need is something to draw with."

Sal was getting used to this. Shilly, being a natural artist, needed visual clues to pin down the Change. Sal, on the other hand, knew that he would have no trouble conjuring up a mental image of his father. He could see him in his mind's eye all too easily, still scruffy and roughed-up by the prison officer. He could also hear the sound of his voice and smell his sweat. Every detail was fixed in his mind from years of close contact, a lifetime of travel together.

When Shilly returned holding parchment and charcoal, he shook his head and took her hand. With the image of his father filling all of his mind, he let her in to show him what to do.

"Yes, perfect," she breathed. "Relax. I'll show you the visualization." Straight lines danced in front of his eyes-- white on black, rotating around a common center. "Try to bring them together into one line. When you have that line, the link is open."

Sal concentrated on the lines. They spun like pieces of falling straw, tumbling end over end through space. He was reminded of the Void Beneath and wondered what would happen if he opened a connection between him and his father only to have it broken by the Sky Wardens. What part of him would he lose? The part that knew and loved his father?

But he didn't stop to worry about that. He had to bend the lines to his will. He *had* to. It was the only way to talk to his father--his father, locked in his stone cell; bloody, dirty, tired; alone...

Slowly, but inevitably, the lines did respond. He felt

as though his mind was being stretched--stretched and squeezed at the same time, like he was trying to force his head through a rubber sheet. Something was resisting him; maybe the defenses of the workshop, he thought. But despite that, part of him *was* moving. He was definitely making progress. He could feel the kilometers between the workshop and Fundelry contracting like leather drying in the sun.

"That's good, Sal," said Shilly softly, her hand gently on his shoulder. "Good. Almost there..."

Finally, the lines were one.

Dad? Can you hear me?

He waited, but there was no response. He shot a questioning look at Shilly, without breaking his concentration, and she gave him an urgent thumbs-up. It was working, even if there was no response.

Dad? What's happening to you?

The silence echoed back at him like a cave.

Dad? Are you there?

Shilly frowned. "He must be able to hear you. It's hurting *my* head and I don't even have the Change."

"Neither does my father."

"Oh, well--"

She got no further. A reply came out of nowhere, loud and strong.

Sayed! It was a woman's voice: the Syndic's. *Sayed, is that you? Where are you? Sayed, speak to me!*

Sal recoiled from the woman's mental touch as though it had stung him. The lines dissolved back into tumbling straw, and he felt a distant part of him snap back with a thud. The shock of breaking the connection so suddenly knocked him flat for a second--not unconscious, but overloaded. His mind couldn't withstand the backlash, so it took the only action it could: it blanked out completely to avoid it.

(And for a timeless moment there was nothing but a distant hum all around him--embracing him, drawing him back into the Whole.)

When he could see again, Shilly was bending over him.
"Are you back?"

"I--think so." He tried to sit up and was overwhelmed
with dizziness. He lay back for a moment with his hand over
his eyes. "You heard her? The Syndic?"

"Yes, and I guess that means she heard *you*." Her dark
face was gray, and she sounded slightly nervous, as though
belatedly regretting the experiment.

"Now what do we do?"

"We wait and see, I guess." She sat down next to him and
tapped his arm. "Are you feeling any better?"

"Yes. Why?"

"I'll give you a game of Blind to pass the time, if you like."

They didn't have long to wait. Just as Sal was about to pin
down one of Shilly's elusive tendrils, they heard the entrance
to the workshop hiss open.

"Are you two here?" they heard Lodo bellow down the
tunnel.

The fog cloud vanished as their concentration shattered.
They sprang apart as though caught doing something
forbidden.

"We're here," Shilly answered cautiously.

"Ah, I thought so." His footsteps thudded rapidly toward
them. Sal waited nervously to see what expression the old
man was wearing, but when he appeared he had the same air
of pent-up energy as always. Upon entering the workshop,
he didn't stop until he was right on top of them, then he
crouched down and took their hands in his.

"Well done!" he said, and his face broke out into a wide
grin. "You clever things!"

"You heard us?" Sal almost wet himself with relief.

"Yes, and it's thrown them into complete panic." Lodo
held their hands clasped tight. "I only wish I'd thought of it
myself."

"What happened?" asked Shilly.

Lodo settled back onto his haunches. Sal distinctly heard
his hip pop. "As it turned out, I was meeting Centofanti at
the very same time. She'd kept me waiting more than an

hour while she dealt with some request from the Syndic, and when she finally let me through all we did was talk about the applicants for Selection. I could tell her mind wasn't really on the topic, though. It wasn't until she worked around to asking about the new apprentice of mine that she seemed to be interested at all in what I was saying. Someone has obviously been asking around.

"Anyway, I said pretty much what your father told them, Sal. That you were from out of town, somewhere in the borderlands, no one special, and she seemed to half-believe me, even though she'd obviously rather I was lying. It would be a big boost to her career to be the one who found you." Lodo winked at Sal.

"And then it came. I felt your call go through me like a sledgehammer. It was very well done, Shilly--I presume you helped Sal with it." She nodded, looking pleased. "Even though you'd aimed it at your father, the fringes spread enough for anyone nearby to hear it, and the Mayor's offices aren't too far from the prison. I panicked for a second, wondering what on earth you two were up to, until I traced the call back to its source, and realized."

He stopped and folded his hands in his lap. "Seconds later, the building was in turmoil. Every Sky Warden in the place had heard it, apart from Centofanti. She's obviously even less talented than I thought. Everyone was running around, trying to find the Syndic before you disappeared. But *she* had heard it well enough, and she appeared a moment later, screaming for everyone to be quiet. By the time you sent your third call, she knew where you were and she was ready to reply. She had enough composure for that, at least.

"And then you were gone again. You couldn't have timed it better! The Syndic was beside herself. She cursed everyone she could think of: your father, the Mayor, Centofanti. She even cursed the Alcaide. And that got him in a rage, too, for it was she who had led them to Fundelry. And so it went.

"So things aren't currently looking too rosy for the local officials. First, Holkenhill almost let you slip through his fingers--and he was practically sleeping in the room next door!--then Centofanti didn't hear your call. I slipped out while people were still arguing about what it meant, just in case they asked me for my opinion. I'm quite happy for them to continue thinking of me as a well-meaning charlatan. You get more work done that way."

Lodo looked very pleased with them. He ruffled their hair and clapped his hands together. "And there you go. We're not out of the swamp yet, but the end is in sight. The last I heard, they're thinking of hauling anchor early and heading off to Tumberi, the town nearest the workshop. That's over a hundred kilometers west. I built the workshop there when I first left the Haunted City, in a place unlikely to be disturbed but strong in background potential." He indicated the walls of the workshop. It was weird to think that they were, in truth, nowhere near the town just a kilometer or two away. "At the very least, their attention will be focused there, not here--or the other way around. Whatever, that makes the rest of our job that much easier."

Sal nodded. "We have to get Dad out of the prison before they leave."

"Or convince the Alcaide to let him go." Lodo nodded. "I said I'd take you to see your father during the feast, and I'm as good as my word. We'll go once everyone is occupied. If they're as distracted by the Tumberi lead as I hope they'll be, that will definitely work in our favor."

"And what then?" asked Shilly. "Do you have a plan?"

"I have several. Whether any of them will work is open to debate." He held out one hand and ticked off his fingers with the other. "First, we have to distract the Sky Wardens. Second, we have to get Sal's father out of jail. Third, we have to get both of them away from Fundelry. Fourth, we have to stop them from being followed. The last two will be easiest if we can find the buggy, so we'll call that five. All up, that's a pretty tall order for anyone." He put his hand down, his expression sober again. "If we could talk the Alcaide into letting him go, that would solve everything, but I'm not pinning my hopes on it. Just getting a chance to talk to him will be difficult, let alone getting him to listen."

Sal was silent for a moment. Lodo had no good reason to help him, and saying "thanks" seemed woefully inadequate. Even worse would be to ask *why* Lodo was helping him. He simply had to accept it, for good or ill.

"Soon," he said, "I hope you'll see the end of my parents' story."

"Of Dafis and Seirian?" Lodo smiled. "I hope so too--or the Goddess knows it'll be the end of me."

CHAPTER 17

A HEART LOST...

THE afternoon passed in a blur of preparation. Lodo had Sal concentrating on the Mandala technique while Shilly helped him make charms. Sal had become very good at holding the Mandala in place, even while he did other things. Now, given the one task to do, and with a terrible urgency driving him on, he was pleased to see just what he could accomplish--especially when, not even a week ago, he had not had much of an idea about the Change at all.

What Shilly and Lodo were making, he didn't know. Sal received the distinct impression that Lodo was trying to cover as many contingencies as possible. Since he didn't know exactly what they would need, he made a little of everything. Shilly too seemed to be out of her depth, but she had stopped complaining and did as she was asked.

Finally, everything was ready, and Lodo judged that the feast was about to begin. He struck the brass cylinder with its miniature hammer. "I've summoned the others," Lodo said. "They'll help us blend in and will keep an eye on what's going on."

"'The others'?" asked Sal.

"The people on the beach," Shilly explained. "The ones we can rely on."

Sal nodded, remembering guitar-playing Derksen, and Thess, her stomach swollen with child. Josip, Von and Aunty Merinda had been there too. He was glad they were on his side, but didn't think much of their chances against the Alcaide and the Syndic and all their entourage.

"Surprise will be the key," said Lodo. "Their attention will be diverted. They'll be in a hurry to wrap things up and move on while the trail is fresh. While their minds are elsewhere, or on trivia, we'll find a space to act."

Sal nodded. Lodo sounded like he knew what he was talking about. There was just one thing still bothering him. "Why do they want me so badly?"

Lodo paused in his preparations and met Sal's gaze. "When we first met, I thought I knew. I thought they just wanted to bring the vendetta to an end. If they brought your father in to face justice, they would solve the mystery of what had happened to him and Seirian. But there's obviously more to it than that. Your father talked as though they had taken your mother away from him, and they didn't deny it. And once they found out there was a child, it was *you* they were after, not your father. There's something about you that's special, Sal--or they think there is--and I'm not sure what that might be."

"He's very talented," said Shilly, studying them both with watchful eyes.

"Could it be just that?" In the short time they had known each other, Sal had never seen Lodo look so uncertain. "Maybe I'm overestimating them. They simply may not like the idea of another wild talent flaring up without warning."

"Another what?" asked Shilly.

"That's a long story," said Lodo. "Later. Suffice it to say that, if that's what they're trying to prevent, they're going about it completely the wrong way."

The old man shrugged into his coat, which hung even heavier than it normally did. "Bring your packs, Sal. We might not have time to come back to get them. Shilly, you wear his father's."

Shilly rolled her eyes, but slipped her arms through the worn leather straps and hefted the small pack onto her shoulders. Sal put his on with a grunt, the unexpected weight of the globe hidden inside taking him off-balance for a second. He recovered and hefted it into a better position. He could manage it. With the bracelets back on his senses were once again deadened to the Change.

"Right." Lodo looked them over as though inspecting troops for battle. "Good enough. Let's go."

The square was filling with people when they arrived. It was a warm, muggy night, perfect for an outdoor event. Lodo did a quick tour of the town to light the main globes, but he didn't light them all. Sal assumed that he was in a hurry, or didn't want to stand out for too long. Either way, they soon joined the rest of the town around a number of large trestles containing baked fish, broth and bread free for all to eat. In the center of the square, both the Alcaide and the Syndic sat on the podium with their attendants close at hand, the ranks of black and gray and blue uniforms making them look like soldiers. Alder Sproule and the Mayor were with them, as was Amele Centofanti, looking sourly at the crowd. Holkenhill, the rest of the Alders and the town officers were forced to mingle with the villagers, although most didn't seem to mind.

Sal was horribly nervous, despite the charms and the Mandala. He just wanted to get away, but Lodo wouldn't let him.

"Eat first," the old man insisted. "You'll need your strength."

Sal accepted a plate piled with food from Thess--who, with the rest of Lodo's friends, was always nearby--and forced down as much as he could. He could feel the food sitting heavily in his stomach and tried to think about something else.

Shilly nudged him and pointed to someone on the far side of the square. "There's Tait," she said. "He doesn't look happy about things either."

"Who doesn't?" Lodo asked.

She described their encounter with Tom in the dunes that morning: Tom's disappointment at his brother's reception, and Tait's unwillingness to come home.

"Yes," said Lodo, nodding. "I wondered about that. It's not usual for a trainee to be sent home so soon. They rarely are at all, in fact. Sky Wardens are mostly posted to distant regions to make sure they don't get too comfortable. Tait must have done something wrong, or failed quite badly, for them to want him out of the way."

Lodo's words gave Sal a better inkling of Tait's position. It must have been galling to fail in the Haunted City and be sent home, only to find that his little brother had done better than he ever did. In such a light, it was easier to understand his callous treatment of Tom, even if it wasn't forgivable.

Wine flowed freely among the adult members of the crowd. Spirits lifted steadily. Word was spreading that the Selectors would make their announcement early the next morning, rather than in the afternoon, in order to move on to more pressing business. Sal worried that that might not give them enough time, but Lodo didn't seem overly concerned.

Finally, the old man looked around to judge the mood of the crowd, then turned to Sal and said: "It's time for you to see your father."

Sal put his half-full plate on a trestle and wiped his hands. His heart beat a little faster. He followed as Lodo spoke to his friends one by one, giving them each a small splinter of brown stone. Thess kissed Sal on the cheek; Aunty Merinda smiled toothlessly and wished him luck; Josip and Derksen tried to lighten his spirits by joking; even Von looked sympathetic. When it was over, Sal was relieved.

Lodo, Shilly and Sal slipped safely out of the crowd and into the shadows. The sound of talking and laughing faded behind them but didn't quite disappear as they wound their way through the streets toward the prison. The knowledge that a large number of Sky Wardens were only a short distance away was forever with him. Sal hadn't seen any of them drink much, so he didn't dare hope that they would be too drunk to respond to an alarm. It was just as important as ever to be inconspicuous.

Sal had been wondering how they were going to get into the prison, and received the answer when they approached the front entrance. They stopped under the low-hanging branches of a tree and held a brief whispered conversation.

"We're not going in the front door, are we?" asked Shilly.

"You aren't, Shilly. You're standing guard out here." He gave her one of the thin slivers he had given the others. "If someone comes, snap this in two. Otherwise, don't do anything. Just stay under cover and wait. Understand?"

She nodded. "But the officers--"

"Don't worry about them. There will be just two at the most, and I can handle them." To Sal he said: "You follow me and don't say anything."

Sal swallowed. "Okay." He let himself be led out of the shadows and toward the front door. Their feet crunched on the road surface. Behind them, he heard a slight scuffling sound as Shilly took cover. When he looked over his shoulder, she was nowhere to be seen.

The door approached all too quickly. Lodo eased it open and walked right in. Sal took a deep breath and followed.

The same officer from the previous day was on duty. "Hello again, Lodo," he said from behind the wide, wooden counter.

"Good evening, Cran. Can you let us through?"

"I don't know. Our orders were never changed. Alder Sproule--"

Cran never finished his sentence. Lodo reached into his pocket, produced a handful of white sand and threw it into the officer's face. Instantly, Cran's face went blank and empty.

"You didn't see us come in," Lodo said. "Resume your duties as before."

Cran didn't respond. He simply turned and went back to his seat. He didn't look up as Lodo guided Sal--with one finger to his lips--past the counter and down the corridor on the other side to the cells.

None of the interior doors were locked. It was almost too easy, Sal thought. If they could get the key to the cells they could easily sneak his father past the hypnotized Cran ...

"Hey, where did you come from?" boomed a voice from behind them.

Sal turned, his throat in his mouth. Another officer had entered the corridor.

"We're here to see the prisoner," said Lodo calmly. "Cran sent us through."

"Did he, eh? He should know better. I'll--"

Another puff of white sand brought his objection to an end.

"We were never here," Lodo said. "Do what you have to do, and forget about us. The prisoner does not need to be disturbed."

The officer went back up the hallway with a slight frown on his face and disappeared around a corner.

Lodo wiped his forehead. "Pray to the Goddess there are no more than two. I'm not sure how many of them I can hold at once."

Sal nodded, even though he didn't believe in the Goddess Lodo occasionally mentioned. He was pretty sure the old man didn't, either. It was more likely a figure of speech than a genuine appeal to the supernatural.

They made it to the cell room with no more incidents. Lodo eased the door open and peered inside, then waved Sal through.

"I'll keep an eye on things out here," he said, "and call you when we've run out of time."

"Aren't we getting him out?"

"Not yet. This is just so you can talk to him."

Sal slipped through the gap and into the room. The shutters were closed again, leaving the air inside uncomfortably warm and bad-smelling. It was very dark, apart from one candle burning in the center of the room. Sal's father had been put in a different cell and sat with his back against the bars, facing away from the door.

Sal took a few steps, until he heard the door close behind him.

"Dad?"

His father straightened, looked up, then turned to look behind him. "Sal? *Sal!*"

Sal ran forward. His father was instantly on his feet, arms passing through the bars to clutch Sal to him. For a moment it was almost as though the bars weren't there at all. His father's arms were around him and Sal could feel his breath on his neck. The scent of him was strong and comforting.

But the reality of the cage was undeniable. It dug into their flesh, driving them apart.

Sal's father finally pulled back, but not entirely. His hands clasped Sal's forearms and wouldn't let go. There were tears on his cheeks.

"Sal, it's really you! How did you get in here?"

"Lodo brought me." Sal found it hard to speak, the lump in his throat was so large.

His father looked over his shoulder. "Where is he?"

"Waiting outside. He's doing everything he can to help us. We're going to get you out of here--"

A finger to his lips stopped him talking. "You have to save yourself. Get away now, before they find you."

"No. I'm not going to leave you behind." The certainty was hard and cold inside him, like granite. "Anyway, they think I'm somewhere else, a long way away. When they leave, we can run away again. They'll never find us."

"Where will we run to, Sal? We can't run forever." Sal's father looked as though he had aged a hundred years in the cell. "I've been thinking about things--about what happened to your mother, and what might happen to you. I dreamed that you were trying to call me, earlier. You sounded frightened."

Sal opened his mouth to say that it *had* been him calling, but again his father silenced him and went on: "It made me think, it made me realize, that I have no right to put you through this. You're nearly old enough to make your own decisions. I can't hold on to you any longer."

"But you're not holding on to me, Dad. I *want* to be with you!"

"I know, Sal, but you haven't seen the alternatives. I saw the way you listened when I played the other night. I can see how much you love music, and how good at the Change you could be. Who am I to deny you this? You could have a wonderful life anywhere you liked, if it wasn't for me and my fear for you. Keeping you from that makes me worse than the Sky Wardens themselves."

"No," Sal said, shaking his head furiously. "That's not true."

"It is, Sal, and I don't want to be like them."

Sal turned away. This wasn't what he wanted to hear. It was all going wrong. He'd wanted reassurance that everything would soon be the same--that all they had to do was get away from the Sky Wardens and life would return to normal. He didn't want anything more than that. It didn't seem too much to ask for.

But if even his father was denying it...?

"Tell me about my mother," he said, turning back to face the bars. He didn't know how much time they had: he had to make it count.

"Your mother?" His father sat down on the bench as though his legs had suddenly run out of strength. "Why?"

"She's behind all this. She's what brought us here--and I don't know her. It doesn't seem right."

"What have you heard?"

Sal nodded. "Her name was Seirian, I know that much. Lodo told me about Highson Sparre." His father winced but didn't interrupt. "He told me how you ran away from the Haunted City and hid where no one could find you. But he didn't tell me about *her*. He didn't tell me what she was like. I don't know anything about her at all."

His father nodded, his gaze on a place far away, behind the tears. "I remember her as though we met yesterday, Sal. I still see her in my dreams. The first time we spoke, I knew that I loved her, but I didn't dare tell her. She was married to Highson, and I was just a journeyman. A good journeyman, to be sure, but nothing more than that. Esta trusted me, and she was Highson's friend." He stopped, swallowed, and continued. "Seirian and I were companions; it was nothing more than that at first. We spent a lot of time together, while Highson and Esta were busy, and I kept my emotions to myself. Then she confessed one day that her feelings had grown deeper, and I didn't know what to do. To reject her would have been a lie against my own feelings. To act upon those feelings ... Well, I guess you know what happened. It was a disaster. We had no choice but to flee. It was the only way we could be together."

Sal tried to imagine his father in love with a woman Sal could not remember. It wasn't easy. "Were you happy?"

"Yes, Sal, very. It didn't matter where we traveled, what names we used, or how poor we were. We made a small living from the Change, enough to keep us moving. Seirian had a strong innate talent but hadn't learned to use it yet. I had the tricks I'd learned from watching Highson and others. Together we tended dry or contaminated wells; we called weather for farmers; we even made charms to catch fish, when we dared to come that far into the Strand. We tried to help the people around us so they would remember us fondly and be less inclined to betray us if ever anyone asked.

"That's how we stayed hidden for so long, I guess. A year, maybe more. You came in that time, and our travels slowed for a while. We had to work harder, and your mother was tired more often. For a while I worried that she was sick, but she seemed to recover perfectly well. Then, one night ..."

He stopped and looked away. His lips were pressed tight together. "One night, I woke up and she was gone. The bed was empty beside me, and you were crying. I knew what had happened the moment I woke and realized she was missing. She hadn't left us. She had been stolen. Somehow Highson and the Sky Wardens had tracked her down and taken her back. I could smell their stink in this, even though I don't have the Change. They hadn't even had the courage to confront us directly. Like thieves, they invaded our home with their damned charms and tore it apart."

Sal imagined his mother spirited away by the Change: one moment there, asleep beside the man she loved, and the next, gone, the sheet falling empty to the mattress.

"At first," his father went on, "I didn't know what to do, except to get moving again. Before dawn, we were back on the road--you and I, alone. I had to move quickly before they found out about you. I had no choice. Once they found out about you--and there was no way Seirian could have kept you a secret--they were sure to want you as well.

"I swore to be very careful, this time, hiding every aspect of my past life to prevent the slightest chance of recognition. I had to lose everything that had once been me in order to stay free. I stopped playing music. I sold my guitar. Most importantly, I avoided the Change.

"You see, I eventually worked out how they must have found us. Despite all our other precautions, Seirian and I had been careless in using our joined talent. The Sky Wardens had picked it up, somehow; it was the only way they could have known. So I never used the Change again, and kept it from you, too. There was a chance you could have inherited it from your mother, and I thought that keeping you away from it might stop it appearing. I was wrong, in the end. It came out naturally anyway, and there was nothing I *could* do to stop it. But it did give me a focus, back when you were young. And as soon as it did start coming out, I came here to find out how to hide it properly. Otherwise the Sky Wardens would have found us before long. I had no choice."

"You keep saying that," Sal interrupted, conscious of time passing outside the cell. "Was there really no other option?"

His father looked at him with red-rimmed eyes. "No, not now--and not then, either. It was wrong that they took Seirian from us--from you especially. You should have known your mother. She was kind and loving. You would have loved her as much as I did--and I loved her more than anything. But when she was taken, I had to choose: would I try to get her back, or would I save you? I know which she would have wanted, but it was still a difficult choice. And although I know I chose well, no matter what they say, living with it is the hardest thing I have ever done.

"I hope," he said, putting his hand through the bars and clutching Sal's arm, "I hope I haven't made a terrible mistake--for your sake. I no longer care what happens to me. If Seirian is really dead, then my last hope dies with her. For although we ran, you and I, as hard as we could to get away from the people who had taken her, I still hoped that

I would be with her again one day. No matter how long it took, no matter where you and I fled, she was still there in the Haunted City. Without her there, in my imagination..." He shrugged. "Without her, my heart is dead."

Sal felt a coldness welling within him at those words. He wanted to say: *What about me? I'm still here!* But the words wouldn't come.

"Lose a heart, gain an eye," Sal said instead, quoting an old proverb.

His father looked up and snorted back an unexpected laugh. "Indeed. I taught you that, didn't I?"

"You taught me everything I know."

"You poor kid." He shook his head. "I should've listened to you when you asked if we could leave."

Their hands found each other and gripped tight. The coldness melted away. Sal knew that, regardless what happened in the next twenty-four hours, his life with his father would remain untarnished in his mind. It was a precious thing few people ever had: to travel, free, with someone you could trust until the end of the Earth. He would cherish it as long as he lived.

His father still loved him, there was no denying that. And his mother had loved him too. It was better to have had that love and lost it than never to have had it at all.

The door squeaked open, startling them both. Sal turned to see Lodo easing himself into the cell room.

"Someone's coming," he whispered, waving for Sal to follow him into an empty cell. Sal did as he was instructed, even though there was no way they could hide there. The moment someone walked into the room, they would be seen.

Sal's father lay back on the bench as though asleep. Lodo and Sal sank back into the rear corner of the cell, backs flat against the rough stone walls. Sal felt Lodo's right hand descend upon his head and grip it tight.

"Stand perfectly still," Lodo said. His left hand gestured and the sole candle guttered out, its flame smothered by the Change.

An instant later the door opened. A shaft of blinding light cut across the room, striking the exact spot Sal and Lodo were hiding. Sal braced himself for cries of alarm, but none came. The light seemed to burn right through them, without even casting a shadow.

"On your feet," ordered one of the officers. "They've called for you."

"Who?" Sal's father rose slowly to his feet, blinking.

"Who do you think?" The officer's keys rattled as he walked to the cell.

"But they're not supposed to make judgments until tomorrow!"

"I guess they can do whatever they like." The door swung open. "Now, out--before I have to come in and get you."

Sal's father obeyed. His gaze swept the cells but clearly saw no sign of Lodo or Sal. The officer's beefy hand clamped around his upper arm and led him out of the room.

CHAPTER 18

...AN EYE GAINED

S AL watched in a silent uproar as his father was led from the cell. He had to do something! But Lodo's hand was firm on his head, holding him still. It wasn't until the door swung shut and they were back in darkness that he was able to move and dared to speak.

"What are we going to do?" he asked, pulling free. "We can't just let them take him!"

"For now, we have no choice." Lodo brought the candle back. His face was heavily etched by shadow in the flickering light, darker even than his tattoos. "We'll wait to see what decision they've come to, and then act. Who knows? We might not need to act at all. They may have decided he's not worth worrying about."

Sal didn't dare hope for that and he knew it would only solve their problems in the short term.

"So what *do* we do?"

"We follow them and see what happens. No matter what they decide we'll have time to react. They can't just leave in an instant. Derksen is watching the ship. He'll let us know if they make any sudden moves."

"How?" Sal asked.

Lodo produced one of the stone slivers from his pocket. "Everyone I trust has one of these. If they snap it, I feel a pinprick on the back of my neck. That's how I knew that someone had come for your father. Shilly broke hers not long before the officer walked in."

Sal nodded. "So let's go after my dad and see what's happening." He made for the door, but Lodo grabbed his arm and brought him back.

"Wait. There's something I have to ask you first."

"But we have to hurry!"

"Not yet. This is important, Sal. We must make time for it."

"What?" The old man's expression was very serious, making him dread the question.

"It's about what your father said."

"About my mother?"

"No. Before that. You *are* almost old enough to choose for yourself. If you go with the Sky Wardens of your own volition, a lot of strife could be avoided. You certainly have the right to ask for training, and your father's captors seem keen to exercise it. What's stopping you from just going along with their wishes?"

"What's *stopping* me?" Sal could barely believe what he was hearing. "They stole my mother. They hunted us!"

"They said they made a genuine mistake. That as soon as they knew about you, they tried to reunite you with your mother. You heard them say this, and it could be true. Certainly if your mother *did* die because your father kept you hidden, that might explain their continued resentment of him. They may not mean ill."

"But ..." *How could that be true?* "But you don't like them either."

"That has nothing to do with you, Sal. You can't take my word for it, or your father's. It's *your* decision, your decision alone, and the time has come for you to make it."

Sal leaned against the wall, thrown off guard. For a moment, despite the urgency, he couldn't answer. All of his life he had been afraid of the Sky Wardens, and he could see why now. But under other circumstances, maybe he would have been tempted to join the Sky Wardens. Most people, like Shilly, would be glad to have his talent. Did he have the right to turn his back on it?

Yes, he thought, he did. For all their power in the Strand, Sky Wardens led a life full of responsibility. If he surrendered himself to the Alcaide and the Syndic, that was what he would be condemned to. He would much rather live the way he always had: as a wanderer, with his father. There were other ways to learn.

He told Lodo this as best he could, and the old man nodded.

"It's one thing to be given an opportunity, quite another to have it forced upon you. But what about this: if we *can't* rescue your father, would you join them then? Would you follow him voluntarily into their hands? Or would you do as your father asks and keep running?"

Sal's first thought was to shake his head. He didn't trust either the Alcaide or the Syndic. He didn't believe their version of events, no matter what Lodo said. But to let his father be taken, and maybe never see him again …? The thought was utterly galling.

"I don't want that to happen," he said. "I want to rescue my father, no matter what it takes."

"I thought you might say that," Lodo nodded. He seemed to grow older and smaller in front of Sal's eyes.

Sal tried to read from Lodo's expression what the old man was thinking. "I won't kill anyone, though, if that's what you're about to say."

"No. It shouldn't come to that." Lodo drew himself up. "Very well. You have decided, and I will help you to see it through. That is *my* decision, and I'll stick to it. And now," he concluded, "it is time to hurry."

Shilly was waiting for them outside, hopping from foot to foot with nervousness.

"I thought you'd never come out!"

"Getting out wasn't the problem," said Lodo. "There's no one left in there, now their prisoner is gone. Which way did they go?"

"They headed for the square." She pointed up the road, toward the sound of cheering in the distance, and they walked briskly in that direction. "I almost died when they appeared. I thought you'd been caught for sure."

Sal shook his head, still impressed with the way the old man had hidden them. How far his talent extended, Sal didn't know. Maybe he could have made the stone walls of the cell fade away, or softened the iron bars so his father could've slipped through. The fact that he hadn't didn't necessarily mean that he couldn't.

"What are we going to do now?" asked Shilly.

"I'm going to give them one more chance," Lodo said. "There's an easy way out of this for all of us, and they'd be fools not to take it. If they'll see reason, we can get Sal's father back before midnight and the Sky Wardens can go on their merry way. Sal can stay here if he wants and continue his training, or move on. Moving might be safer. The Mandala will keep him covered for a while, until he is older and has more options, perhaps. But you'd be welcome here if you wanted to stay, Sal." The old man's gray eyes were softer than Sal had ever seen them. "Life has certainly been more interesting since you arrived."

"You can say that again," said Shilly with a crooked smile.

There was no more time for conversation. The square was quiet when they arrived. Standing on the podium, its cloth roof newly repaired after the storm, Mayor Iphigenia was making a speech about the town's pride at having such distinguished guests and how overjoyed she was at their generosity. Most people looked cheerfully uninterested.

Lodo, Sal and Shilly slipped into the crowd's outer fringes and waited patiently. Moments later, Thess appeared at their side.

"You've missed the Selection. Tom and Kemp made it through."

Sal peered to see the faces on the podium. Tom was standing behind Amele Centofanti, looking so exhausted and strained he might collapse at any moment. Kemp's face glowed with triumph.

"Have they passed judgment?" Lodo asked her.

"Not yet. After this speech, I think."

"Good. We're not too late, then." He turned to Sal and Shilly. "Wait here for me to come back. If things go wrong and we're separated, make for the weathervane building. I'll meet you there."

Lodo vanished into the crowd. Sal couldn't see where he was headed. Without the old man around, he felt exposed and nervous but tried not to show it. Concentrating on the podium didn't help much.

The people around him muttered among themselves as the Mayor's speech meandered on. Sal suspected the speech was more for the guests' benefit than for the people who lived there. When it was over, a rowdy cheer went up. Sal craned his neck to see what was happening. Amele Centofanti's younger companion approached the front and stood patiently, waiting for the noise to settle. Centofanti was still seated, looking annoyed. Why she wasn't doing the talking, Sal didn't know.

"Thank you, Mayor Iphigenia," said the Sky Warden Lodo had called Shom Behenna. His voice was warm and smooth; he didn't need to strain to be heard. "As your new Selector, I thank your Mayor for her kind words."

Sal understood, then. Centofanti had failed to detect Sal's call, and her substandard talent had not gone unnoticed by the Syndic.

"I am glad to say that my visit here has some time yet to go," Centofanti's once-assistant went on with a smile. "I leave tomorrow, at the customary time. Our other guests, however, must leave much earlier. I'm sure they envy me my continued enjoyment of your hospitality."

He bowed, and the crowd clapped. Sal found his performance irritatingly insincere.

"But before they depart, I will ask them to conduct one last duty. Your Alders have been resourceful enough to apprehend a thief who has been plaguing the area for some time. The case has been brought before my ultimate superiors, and they are pleased to make judgment. If you would please welcome, this time, the Alcaide Dragan Braham."

The crowd clapped uproariously, and Sal forced himself to join in rather than stand out. Shilly, at his side, just mimed the action. The Alcaide, wearing another white outfit, waved the crowd silent.

"This isn't a cause for excitement," he said in a chiding tone. To Sal, he sounded mildly intoxicated. "This is a very serious moment, and one which I, the person in whom the judicial system of our great nation ultimately places its trust, have the sad duty to oversee. While it is all very well to enjoy our clean streets and safe lives, the punishment of those who break our laws must be strictly observed. Any faltering of our desire for justice will act as a widening crack that threatens to bring down our entire social structure." The Alcaide waved to the side of the podium. "Bring out the accused."

Sal's father was led onto the podium to a round of catcalls and boos. He didn't struggle or shout, but he didn't look beaten, either. He faced the Alcaide squarely, and refused to turn toward the crowd.

"I won't bore you with the details," the Alcaide went on, as though he had been through this routine many times before. "The case against this man has been put to us by your Alders, and we have heard him speak in his own defense. We have weighed the facts as carefully as we can and come to a judgment concerning his innocence or guilt." The Alcaide paused for effect, then said: "We find this man guilty of the crimes with which he has been charged. His sentence will be transportation, enacted immediately. He will return with us to the Haunted City and there pay recompense for his crimes."

Sal bit his tongue on a cry of dismay. But the cheer the announcement received wasn't loud enough to drown out a dissenting voice.

"Stop!" Lodo's cry came from close to the podium, loud enough to be heard by everyone. Sal peered but couldn't see him. "Your judgment is wrong, and you know it!"

The Alcaide, too, seemed to have trouble locating the heckler. "Who said that?"

"Does it matter? The truth remains. This man is innocent and you are about to do him a great injustice."

"How dare you question our judgment?"

"I dare because I know the truth!" The voice seemed to move among the people at the front of the stage. Sal saw heads turning, looking for the source. A growing mutter rose from the crowd. "This man has done no wrong. He is the victim of prejudice. Visitors to our town should not be treated so poorly, according to the color of their skin."

The Alcaide guffawed at this. "Are you calling me a bigot, whoever you are? I, who am lighter by birth than most of you before me? I, who has chosen a child of pure white skin to attend us in the Haunted City?" Behind him, Kemp shuffled his feet, clearly disliking being the center of attention at that moment.

"Not you," responded Lodo. "One of the Alders of this town, and the people who support him because they fear or desire his authority."

"That is a serious allegation, friend. I trust all of Fundelry's Alders absolutely, and I trust the people who elected them."

"Of course you do. In the same way you trusted your Selector and her representative. Everyone is fallible."

The Alcaide scowled, no doubt thinking of Centofanti and Holkenhill's inability to find Sal. He seemed to be sobering rapidly. "What are you suggesting?"

"That you shouldn't place your trust in officials who take ten days to catch a so-called criminal, and then act only on the word of a boy."

The spectators either hissed or cheered at this, depending on their relationship with Alder Sproule.

"Quiet, please!" The Alcaide took a deep breath to compose himself. He looked like he was about to explode. "Again I ask what you're suggesting. Stop making insinuations and speak plainly."

"You know what I'm saying, Alcaide Braham. I ask you to rescind the transportation order and set this man free."

"I can't do that."

"Why not? Can you possibly believe that this man is guilty beyond reasonable doubt? Would you ask all your people to be treated with the same casual justice? What sort of precedent are you setting?"

The Alcaide fumed for a moment. A heckler shouted: "Let him go so I can get another drink!" The Alcaide silenced him with a look.

"My justice is not casual," he said.

"Prove it to be so, then. Set this man free, or at least give him a public trial."

Sal held his breath. The time it took the Alcaide to decide stretched forever.

In the end, it was the Syndic who spoke.

"Impossible," she said, her voice ringing out across the gathering.

"It is not your place to decide," Lodo shot back.

"Yet I *have* decided!"

"And I stand by her decision." The Alcaide looked relieved that someone had backed him up. "My authority is not absolute, and I respect the words of my advisers."

"Too much, I think." Lodo's voice sounded resigned. "Syndic Zanshin perpetuates a feud that has stretched too long and resulted in one death already. She is not acting in the best interests of the Strand, and her advice should be disregarded."

"Ridiculous!" The Syndic took two steps to the front of the podium and glared down at the crowd, seeking the source of the voice, again without success. The crowd stared back at her, hypnotized by what was unfolding before them. "Where are you, old man? Show your face!"

"No. I have no faith in your ability to listen to reason. I do not wish to suffer the same fate as the man you have wrongly convicted tonight."

"I assure you that you will come to no harm."

"Is that what you told Seirian Mierlo?"

The Syndic went as pale as Kemp behind her. "Who?"

Lodo didn't bother to answer. "Why do you lie? Lies can never cover the truth. You yourselves have denied the Selected passage on your ship, yet you deign to take a criminal in their place. Does this not say something of your motives? This man is not the one you want. He can't help you find the boy. Let him go and your conscience will rest easy. The people listening to this conversation will never need to know the rest. Let time heal what you cannot undo. That is the best course of action open to you now."

The Syndic's hands clutched each other in front of her

stomach. She seemed to be warring within herself. The Alcaide, too, no longer looked quite so self-righteous.

"He may have a point, Nu."

"He speaks nothing but lies!"

"This man is not guilty," Lodo reiterated. "He's just caught in the middle. If you leave him here, he'll never trouble you again."

The crowd was becoming increasingly confused, judging by the whispers Sal overheard.

"Perhaps we should reconsider," said the Alcaide, wiping his palms on the front of his white robe. "There may be a case for appeal. We don't want to act too hastily."

"No," the Syndic hissed. "It's a trick."

"To what end, Nu?" The Alcaide was growing impatient with the way things were turning out. Sal could tell he wanted to end it, either way. "Dafis is no one special. He didn't seek us out; we tracked *him* down. Why wouldn't he just fade into the background once we're gone? It's not as if he could do anything to harm us."

"I think we're underestimating him," she shot back. "Look at the harm he's already done."

"And what is that?"

"He lied about the boy--"

"To him, he's just raising a child away from interfering elements. He's being over-protective, but that's all. I can almost sympathize with him, at times, as should you. Everyone wants the best for their family." The Syndic shot him a dark look, but he went on: "We have better things to do than stand here arguing. The boy has slipped through our fingers, if he was ever here at all. Our time is better served going after him than condemning one man to a marginally greater hell."

"What happened to justice being served, Dragan?"

"Who decides what is justice and what isn't? That's my job, if I recall correctly."

The Syndic opened her mouth to respond, but Sal never found out what she was going to say.

There was a disturbance in the crowd as someone pushed

forward to the front. "The boy you're talking about," called a voice. "Is that the one *he* came here with?" A finger stabbed up, pointing at Sal's father.

The Alcaide sought the speaker, and found him. "Yes. He's gone. Do you know where?"

"He's gone nowhere. He's been here the whole time. He's probably still here, somewhere."

A buzz went up in the crowd and a dagger of ice stabbed deep into Sal's gut.

"Where?" asked the Syndic, her voice as sharp as that dagger. "We last sensed him a hundred kilometers from here."

The owner of the new voice clambered onto the podium. The dagger twisted when Sal recognized the blue uniform and handsome face of Tait, Tom's older brother.

"I don't know where exactly," he said, looking nervous but resolute. "But he couldn't be that far away. He made friends with my brother. Tom saw him in the dunes just this morning, charmed to look different."

Sal shook his head in horror. Behind Tait, Tom mirrored the gesture.

"Interesting," said the Syndic. "Our thanks, journeyman Tait. You have done well. Perhaps we should reconsider our decision regarding your placement here."

Tait's face lit up.

"And what do you say to that, old man?" she asked the voice from the crowd. "Don't think I don't know who you are. You've meddled in the Strand's affairs one too many times, I think, Payat Misseri!"

Her face was a mask of rage. The crowd echoed it instinctively, calling for justice, or at least a show of it. The Alcaide moved toward her.

"Nu--"

"Enough, Dragan! The boy is here, and I want him found! We're not leaving here until he's on the ship and heading back to where he belongs!"

Sal tried to shrink into himself, torn between running and trying to rescue his father. Around him, the crowd was becoming agitated, roused by the emotions on display before them. Shilly's hand on his arm held him still, but it was only with the greatest act of will that he forced himself not to pull from her and run.

Then he felt the eye boring down upon him again with renewed pressure and weight. He collapsed to the ground with a cry, clutching his head. He felt as though the charms Lodo had given him had caught fire. His wrists burned as though they had been bound in shackles of molten glass. The ward on its string around his neck burned red-hot.

"No!"

He dimly recognized his father's voice, but could do nothing to answer.

Then there was a flash of light so bright he could see it through the arm across his face. A rush of energy passed over him like a wave, sweeping the eye aside. He heard screams all around him, and a sound like glass shattering. Shilly dropped to the ground beside him and clutched his back, trembling. Feet kicked them as people ran in a panic around them. They were both moaning with fear, but couldn't hear their own voices over the terrified crowd.

Then hands reached out of the chaos and shook their shoulders. "Quickly! You must run!"

Sal opened his eyes. The voice belonged to Josip. His nose was bloody, and half his face was red, as though it had been burned. He helped them to their feet and pointed over the heads of the people running around them, toward the silver weathervane. "He'll meet you there! Go!"

Shilly collected herself first and did as she was told. Sal, dragged along by her hand grasping his, looked over his shoulder. The podium was emptying rapidly, along with the square. The Alcaide stood at the front, his hands raised as though calling for calm, but his expression was thunderous. Sal's father was nowhere to be seen.

Sal heard another muffled glass-smashing sound from his right, on the far side of the square. A flash of bright light made him flinch automatically as a cloud of what looked like dust rose above the crowd. People ran away from it as fast as they could. Some were bleeding from small cuts and grazes.

Then Sal realized: the town's light globes were exploding one by one, releasing all their stored energy in powerful bursts. One near him must have exploded first, hence the blast of light and energy that had deflected the searching eye. He had been protected by being down on the ground already.

The crowd was running in the same direction as them, so it was easy to move. No one seemed to be actively looking for him yet. The people of Fundelry were more interested in getting away: things had become much more chaotic than they could, or wanted to, deal with. The Alcaide and the Syndic would resolve the problem, whatever it was--and Sal could sympathies with that. He wanted more than anything to hide under a table and wait for it all to blow over.

But he couldn't. The Syndic's probing eye was gathering for another stab at him. He could feel it looming, threatening, building. He concentrated all his strength on maintaining the Cellaton Mandala, the only defense he had against it, and was seeing the spinning circles so clearly that he didn't notice when they arrived at the School building.

Standing still was much harder than going with the flow. They were buffeted by passers-by until Shilly dragged him into a laneway, out of sight. Outside, Josip looked frantically around for Lodo. Thess joined him a second later, shaking her head.

This way, said a voice in Sal's mind. It seemed to come from further down the lane.

"Lodo?" Shilly asked, her fingers digging into Sal's arm.

Don't let Thess and Josip see you go, said the voice. *Their determination to follow will betray us.*

Sal and Shilly slid slowly along the crumbling stone of the laneway wall until the others were out of sight. They dared to pick up speed, heading deeper into shadow. As they passed an open doorway, hands reached out and grabbed Shilly.

She gasped--but let them be dragged through the door when she saw who it was.

"Dad!" Sal clutched at his father and was hugged back just as hard.

"We must be very quiet," Lodo said from deeper in the shadows. "Sproule and his officers will be looking for us soon, if they aren't already. And the others."

Sal's relief was short-lived. "I feel them. It's getting stronger."

"We must move quickly. If I can get you into the workshop, you'll be safe. I'll open another entrance at a safe distance to let you out."

"Can you do that from the inside?" asked Sal.

"No. Only from the outside. If we all went in, we would be trapped. They would find the entrance and starve us out."

"Would they find it?" asked Shilly.

Lodo nodded. "I have little hope that we'll get there unnoticed. Instead I'll concentrate on getting you there *safely*, close the entrance forever, then open another entrance when I'm a good distance away. With luck, they won't realize what we're doing until it's too late."

Sal's father nodded understanding. "You make it sound easy."

"I only hope it will be." The old man studied Sal and his father for a brief moment, then turned to Shilly. "You can go now, if you wish. I don't want you caught up in this against your will."

Shilly looked flabbergasted. "But I don't want to go," she said.

"Are you sure?"

"What's the worst that could happen? If I get dragged off to the Haunted City, at least I'll have company."

"Perhaps no worse than that," said Lodo. "I can guarantee nothing, I'm afraid."

She pulled a face. "Well, whatever. I'll take my chances. There won't be much left for me here if I don't."

Sal could tell that she was putting a brave face on her fear, but he admired her for it all the same. He put his hand on her shoulder, and she reached up to squeeze it tightly.

"Thank you," said Sal's father. "Sal and I owe you both an enormous debt."

"No," said Lodo firmly. "This is a gift, and I offer it freely. You owe me nothing." His gray eyes pierced Sal in the gloom. "You too, Sal. Remember that."

The sound of the crowd had ebbed. They eased out of the doorway, Shilly first, into the lane. Lodo led them away from the weathervane, which pointed due west and seemed to be turning slowly in defiance of the wind. Lodo kept an eye on it, and Sal guessed that it pointed not to the Haunted City but to the Alcaide, the elected head of the Strand. Wherever he was, the vane would reveal him.

It was only useful, however, if it was visible. The moment it was out of sight, Lodo stopped looking for it.

There were still people moving about in the darkness. Every now and then, another globe would blow, prompting a new wave of shouting and running. The group of fugitives moved as quickly as they could among the shadows, stopping whenever they caught a glimpse of blue or black robes among the villagers. Every shout made Sal jump. He felt that his guilt must be visible for all to see, like a bright sign painted on his back: *Here!*

They moved through the inner streets without impedance, and as they reached the edge of the town, the number of people around them thinned even further. It was beginning to feel almost too easy, when, without warning, the probing eye burned into Sal like a brand, and he knew that he had been found.

"I felt that," said Lodo. "Is it...?"

"Yes." Sal could barely talk through teeth clenched in pain. "It's her."

"Sooner than I thought. We must move quickly then." They abandoned stealth and broke into a trot. Almost immediately, someone shouted for them to stop. They ran faster, following Lodo through a series of narrow lanes and over fences. They lost their pursuers briefly in a rundown grain store, and gained a few seconds to recoup.

Lodo pulled Sal's father closer. "The buggy will run--Josip saw to that before it was taken--and it's fully fuelled. Keep that as a last resort."

"Where is it?"

"That I don't know. I'm sorry." The old man shrugged. "But someone must. It'd be hard to keep a secret like that in a small town. It may be stored in a barn belonging to someone friendly to the Sky Wardens. Sproule, for instance, although that might be too obvious."

A clattering of feet near the entrance to the grain store sent them moving again. The relentless pressure of the eye was changing, now that it had found Sal. It battered his mind like the waves on a shore, each wave threatening to overwhelm his will. At the same time it brought pursuers closer to him. He felt as though he was at the center of a giant cyclone, tugged by powerful forces in a thousand directions at once.

More shouts. More people had seen them. This time Sal saw blue robes among their pursuers. The Sky Wardens were moving in as they did in his worst dreams: powerful, unflagging, all-seeing. He ran away from them as fast as he could, but was conscious of Lodo lagging behind. The old man wasn't used to such vigorous physical activity.

"We won't make it!" Sal cried.

"You--go on--ahead," Lodo gasped. "I'll draw them--away."

"No!" Sal's father shook his head as he ran. "We stand together."

"And fall--together!"

"If that's what must happen. We have to try, at least. Maybe we can hold them back long enough to make it to this workshop of yours."

"Sal's talent." Lodo stopped talking to direct them down a street leading to the dunes. They were about halfway. "You could use--Sal's talent."

"Never. The last time I used the Change, I lost Seirian. I swore never to use it again."

"Vows were--made to be--broken." Lodo glanced at Sal. "Will you--give your--father--permission?"

Sal didn't hesitate. "Yes."

"So, Dafis?" Lodo panted, made almost speechless by exhaustion. "Yes--or no?"

The end of the street turned into a track that wound between the dunes down to the beach. Sal strained to maintain his pace in the soft sand. Behind him, the imprints of their footsteps marked their escape route as clearly as flaming torches. They wouldn't last long if they continued this way.

"Yes," said Sal's father.

"Turn here, then," Lodo said, indicating another track leading inland through the dunes on their right. Sal and Shilly helped him stumble forward, onto the second track. "Down there." Lodo pointed off the track, into a valley between dunes. "Shelter."

They did as he told them and a found a small, out of the way space. Lodo collapsed onto the sand, his chest heaving, and waved Sal's father closer to him.

"Illusions," he said. "Make them think--we're going the wrong way."

Sal's father nodded. "I haven't done this for a long time."

"That you do it right now--is all I care about." The old man wiped his forehead. "Give me a minute to recover."

Sal went to his father's side and put his hand on his shoulder. They exchanged a brief look, then Sal felt the familiar hot-cold sensation creeping up his spine.

His father drew a shape in the air with his tattooed left hand. Sal couldn't tell what it was, but he felt its effect on the world around him. It was different from what Lodo had taught him: no more subtle or less powerful, just different. He guessed it was the way Sky Wardens worked.

"I've hidden the turn-off," his father whispered, "and added one further on. It will confuse them, if nothing else. When you're ready--"

"We move now." Lodo leaned on Shilly's shoulder to get back onto his feet. He led them out of the sheltered nook and through the dune valleys. Voices grew nearer, then faded away. It was impossible to tell exactly how close pursuit was getting. It was also impossible to travel in a straight line, prevented as they were from mounting the top of a dune. With every step, their already-sore muscles ached more.

A chorus of shouts rose behind them. Lodo turned at one point and threw a handful of sand over their footprints. The sand sparkled briefly like stars, and the footprints were gone.

"Too late," said Sal's father. "How far to go?"

"Not far." Lodo stopped and scratched lines in the sand. "A new trail will distract them, at least. This way."

A wind sprang up, making progress even more difficult. Clouds gathered above, covering the stars like ink spreading through a pool of water. With them, Sal's unease grew. He still felt the eye bearing down on him. It wasn't confused by the illusions. It knew exactly where he was, and would never let him go.

They reached the end of a valley, and Lodo drew them up short.

"They're ahead," he whispered.

"And behind," said Sal's father.

"What are we going to do?" Shilly's face was pale in the fading starlight.

"The only thing we can do, I guess." Lodo took a deep breath, and pointed up to the top of the dune beside them. "Sal, you go first. They won't harm you, if they see you at all."

Sal didn't like his chances, but knew they didn't have another option. It was either go over and hope the growing darkness would cover them, or stay where they were and be caught like bandicoots in a trap.

He slithered up the side of the dune onto the top and collapsed there, exhausted. Nothing happened. He waited there, trying to keep a low profile against the sky as his father followed, then Shilly. Lodo was making his way up when the sky exploded.

It was as though someone had turned the sun on in the middle of the night--but it wasn't the sun. It was a single bolt of lightning arcing down from the sky. It lasted only an instant, and brought with it a deafening clap of thunder, but it left behind dozens of fizzing, bright spheres that floated in a string between sky and land like pearls in an enormous necklace.

Sal had heard of ball lightning before, but had never seen it. The light the balls cast was pinkish and not as bright as daylight--but sufficient to do the Sky Wardens' work.

The three of them standing on the top of the dune were illuminated perfectly, as were their pursuers. Sal saw two groups of them in deep black below them, not far from where they had climbed. More were scattered across the dunes. Atop a crest four or five dunes away stood two familiar figures, one large and the other small, both dressed in white. Sal shuddered at the sight of them. The light was like a bed sheet pulled back to reveal a nest of spiders.

Sayed! The voice reached into Sal's mind like an octopus's tentacle. *Stop running, Sayed. Your place is with us, now.*

"No!" he screamed, but the wind whipped his words away. He felt his father stand close to him, felt his hand grip his shoulders, followed by the pleasurable sting of the Change thrilling through him.

A gust of wind struck the Alcaide and the Syndic in return, making them stagger to keep their balance. But the Syndic's voice was as strong as ever.

There's no use fighting, Sayed. You cannot escape your destiny.

He felt the eye flexing its power again. Somehow his father resisted it. "I said *no!*"

Join us, Sayed! You cannot run from us forever.

Leave my son alone. Sal's father's voice joined the mental exchange--strong, confident and full of determination.

A wave of anger raged against Sal and his father. *Why should we listen to you--a thief and a liar?*

The only liars here are you. Sal's father resisted the assault, but Sal could see what an effort it took--and could feel the toll it was taking on him, too. He felt as though his head was going to cave in, such was the demand his father was making on his talent.

Unexpectedly, the Syndic laughed. *Do you really believe that? Are you so misguided?*

Her laughter did more damage than any of her mental attacks. *What do you mean?*

You know very well what I mean. Her tone was vicious. *Sayed is not yours. He is Highson's, and he belongs to us.*

That's not true.

It is, and you know it!

But it makes no difference.

It makes every difference! He is ours, *Dafis, not yours. Give him to us!*

No!

Sal felt as though he had been punched in the stomach. *Not yours?* He looked up at his father--at the man he had never questioned was his father--and felt his resolve falter for a second. *He is Highson's.* Everything he had held true in his life was being undermined. He had nothing else *but* his father to hold on to, and if that was swept away from him, he would be lost.

He is ours.

But he also knew that he didn't belong to anyone, least of all the Syndic. Telling the truth or not, she had no right to undermine his relationship with his father. The man beside him, whose arm he was still holding, was the man he would love as a father, no matter whose son he might *actually* be. Her attempts to break that love, to break them apart, were worse than wrong: they were cruel, perhaps even evil.

Sal felt a new form of anger flow through him, then: pure and, in his mind, totally justified. And with it came a hatred that seemed to come from somewhere outside him, as though he was no longer quite himself.

"Leave us *alone!*" he cried, instinctively striking out at the Syndic with everything he could muster. He felt the Change pouring out from within him in a raw, ill-defined way, burning the air and turning the sand to glass where it struck. Its intensity took the Alcaide and the Syndic by surprise, blowing them off their feet. Wardens, Alders and ordinary villagers alike shielded their eyes and dropped face-down onto the dunes. There was a sound like the world tearing in two, as though it were a page in a giant book. It left no echoes, simply ceasing as soon as Sal was spent, and letting the howling of the wind back in.

Sal felt as though he had been bled dry, and almost fell. He was aware of a terrible consternation around him, but couldn't concentrate. His vision was blurry. He saw red in the blur, a long way off, and felt his father's alarm. In a second or two he had recovered enough to see what was going on, but he couldn't believe it at first.

The top of the dune where the Alcaide and the Syndic had stood was now nothing but a smoking crater. The Alcaide had fallen not far away, and was bleeding from a wound that spread from his chin to the top of his head. He was kneeling on the sand, still conscious, blood pouring in a torrent down his white costume. The Syndic lay nearby, and Sal couldn't tell if she was alive or dead.

Then the wind sprang up in a vortex around them. Sal had just enough time to be afraid when the Alcaide raised his voice in an answering torrent of rage and sent a reply toward him that knocked him flat and stopped his father's heart instantly.

Sal landed halfway down the side of the dune. He felt his father dying above him, out of reach--felt his father's mind reach out for him in defiance of the pain and the loss.

Seirian ...

"Dad! No!"

He tried to move, but could barely raise his head. Shilly was beside him, calling his name, but all he could feel were his father's fading thoughts as they sank down into darkness, into the Void Beneath--and disappeared forever.

"No! Lodo, help him!" He heard the despair in his voice but could do nothing to stop it.

The old man appeared on the top of the dune, and his voice spoke into their minds.

You have to run, he said. *They thought your father threw that bolt. That's why they killed him. If they find out it was you, they'll kill you as well.*

Sal struggled to his feet. The night was full of shouting and the ghastly glare of the ball lightning. "But--"

Don't argue! Lodo's voice was terrifyingly urgent. *Shilly, take him away from here! Go with him! I'll hold them off long enough for both of you to get clear.*

"I can't leave you," Shilly protested.

You can and will. You can't help me, anyway. Go now, while you still have the chance!

Shilly moaned and pushed Sal down the dune, away from the old man straightening up above them, his arms opening up as though to embrace the sky. Sal forced himself to follow her, even as he felt a white heat flickering across the dunes, sparking through sand grains and setting the spiky bushes alight. He could hardly see where he was going, and for a moment headed directly for the smoking crater that was all that remained of where the Alcaide and the Syndic had been standing when he lashed out at them. But Shilly's hand firmly tugged him away. Her cheeks were wet with tears that looked like jewels in the ghostly river of light rising in the valleys.

No one stopped them. People were too busy running away from the new phenomenon. Ball lightning and fiery sand were too much for them--and when the earth started trembling, even Sal was afraid.

"Where are we going?" he shouted over the rising rumble from beneath his feet.

"I don't know!" Shilly shouted back. She was weeping so much Sal was amazed she could see at all. "I don't know."

"This way!" A voice called them from a gap in the dunes. "Follow me!"

Sal glimpsed Tom's distinctive silhouette darting away, and followed without thinking. It was his turn to tug Shilly along, stumbling occasionally as the Earth kicked, but always getting back up to follow the small boy as he ran inland.

Behind them, the sky was aflame and the Earth seemed to rise up in defiance. The ground was littered with the bodies of dead seagulls. A tremendous battle of wills between the Alcaide and Lodo was taking place via the elements, and Sal couldn't tell who was winning. He was afraid to look. He concentrated on putting one foot ahead of the other as fast as he could, until he and Shilly finally came abreast of the boy they were following.

"I dreamed this," Tom gasped. "I dreamed the fire in the sand. I dreamed it!"

Sal didn't stop to ask what it meant. He just ran, wherever they were going, and tried not to think of his father.

They came at last to a farmhouse. It was dark and empty. Tom didn't take them to the front door, but led them around the back. There, a barn stood near a chicken coop. The birds were awake and making a fuss. Through the barn door, Sal saw light glinting off the front of the buggy.

"Tait told me about this," Tom said, slowing to a walk and leading them forward. "I'm sorry he gave you away. I'll never talk to him again."

Sal didn't know what to say in return. His mind felt trapped. His father's death had stopped the world for him, and everything that had happened afterward seemed as in a dream. They could take the buggy and run--they might even make it to freedom, if Lodo kept the Sky Wardens at bay long enough--but that would make the dream a reality. There would be no escaping it, then.

"Well, *I'm* sorry, too," said a voice from the darkness inside the barn. Sal felt cold as Kemp stepped out into the light, as pale as a ghost in the darkness. "If you think you're going anywhere in this, you'd better think again."

Sal felt Shilly tense beside him. "You--"

"No." Sal let go of her hand and stepped forward. "I'll talk to him."

"You'll have to do more than that," Kemp sneered. He reached behind him and produced an axe handle.

"Is that your answer to everything, Kemp?" Sal still felt drained by his attack on the Alcaide, but there was a vestige of talent still left in him. He felt light-headed, dangerous, over-confident. He had told Lodo that he didn't want to kill anyone, but he might already have broken that promise once. It would be all too easy to do it again.

"You've done enough already, I think," he said to Kemp. "You stole the necklace and everything else to make us look guilty. You lied to get us into trouble. You kept us here, and we couldn't escape. You," he spat, "killed my father as much as the Alcaide did."

Kemp's eyes glittered in the darkness. He flexed the axe handle, but no longer looked as confident. "Your father's dead?"

"That's right, Kemp, and I'm going to take the buggy. Are you going to kill me to stop me? Are you going to kill Shilly and Tom as well? Are you going to die trying? I thought you *wanted* me to go!" Sal felt a horrible knot curling in his gut. "I swear that if you so much as try to stop us, I'll do everything I can to finish this now rather than later. What's it to be?"

Sal didn't know what was showing on his face, but it made the bully think twice. Kemp swallowed, and lowered the axe handle.

"You're a freak," he said, stepping out of the barn. "We're better off without you."

Shilly moved forward. "You can talk, whitey."

Kemp made to go for her, but Tom stood between them. "Not now," said the boy. "Not now."

Voices carried from the scrub behind them. Sal looked and realized that the light had faded from the sky. He pushed past Kemp and into the darkness of the barn. He knew the buggy well enough to navigate it by feel, but he wasn't used to sitting in the driver's seat. An image of his father sprang to mind--as he had looked when they traveled those thousands of kilometers together, hair trailing in the wind, a satisfied smile on his face, but Sal pushed it down, with the grief. There would be time for that, too, later.

The keys were in the ignition. He turned them, and the engine started first time. He put the buggy into gear and drove it out of the barn. Shilly climbed in awkwardly, but without hesitation.

"Tom?" The sound of the engine almost covered the approaching voices. No doubt their pursuers had heard the engine and would be hurrying to head them off.

The young boy shook his head. "Later."

Sal glanced at Kemp. The big albino was looking uncertainly from them to the front of the property, in the direction of their pursuers. Before Kemp could change his mind about letting them go, Sal put his foot down and let the sudden acceleration press him back into his seat.

EPILOGUE:

GLIMPSES OF THE SKY

TWO days out of Fundelry, Sal dreamed.

First he saw the women on the horizon. He recognized two of them, now. The small one was Shilly, as he had thought before. She was the closest of the three, her arms outstretched as though to embrace him. The second was the Syndic, crouched jealously below her segment of the sky, waiting for her chance to strike again. The third was far away but coming slowly nearer, watching him as closely as the other two. Sal couldn't guess who she might be.

There followed a series of strange, disjointed images: Kemp in a golden tower looking out at a city of glass; a globe of light, burning painfully bright and surrounded by nothing but darkness; another city, this one half-buried in sand and inhabited only by ghosts; Tom's brother, Tait, leading a blue-robed man across a desert; two desiccated bodies hanging on either side of a shadowy tunnel mouth; a woman with features similar to Sal, but much older, talking to what looked like a granite statue twice her size; lastly, a crippled, hollow man who couldn't possibly be--but was--his first teacher: Lodo.

Then the dream settled down again, and he found himself in the end of the Polain story. The world had moved on by the time the butterfly merchant saw trial before a judge, his mind broken and his life in tatters. His beloved city had already forgotten him, finding new heroes to glorify and new villains to condemn.

In the dream, Sal wasn't listening to the story his father never had a chance to finish. He wasn't any of the major characters, either. He was Nemdo's grand-daughter, the girl whose birthday the elderly clerk had missed. Thrust into the spotlight of grief by another man's greed, caught up in tale of obsession, deception and self-destruction, she cared little for butterflies.

All she wanted was her grandfather back.

Sal stirred in his sleep, half-awake, and felt Shilly doing the same. But he didn't move other than to get comfortable. He rolled over to face her and watched the starlight reflecting off her wet cheeks. When sleep finally returned, he didn't dream. By the time the sun rose, they had already resumed their journey.

CPSIA information can be obtained at www.ICGtesting.com
Printed in the USA
LVOW06s1641210713

343857LV00001BB/265/P

9 780759 285170